SUZANNE FORSTER IS . . .

. . . the #1 National Bestselling Author who "has firmly established herself as one of the brightest lights in the romance genre."*

Romantic Times

SHAMELESS IS . . .

. . . her hottest, most suspenseful book, a scorching novel filled with the sizzling sensuality that has made Suzanne Forster a star.

Forced into marriage with Luc Warneke, the man she most fears, Jessie Flood fights desperately to protect herself, her child—and her heart.

Praise for the writing of **Suzanne Forster**, Winner of the *Romantic Times* "Most Sensual Writer" Award

"A stylist who translates sexual tension into sizzle and burn with bold, dangerous heroes you want to lie for, die for, and cry for."
—*Los Angeles Daily News*

" . . . So strongly written the passion will envelop you as these two transform before your eyes. I loved every breathtaking word . . . Her dialogue is as witty as any Hepburn/Tracy movie."
—*Rendezvous*

Shameless

SUZANNE FORSTER

BERKLEY BOOKS, NEW YORK

SHAMELESS

A Berkley Book / published by arrangement with
the author

PRINTING HISTORY
Berkley edition / February 1994

ISBN: 0-425-14095-4

BERKLEY®
Berkley Books are published by The Berkley Publishing Group,
200 Madison Avenue, New York, New York 10016.
BERKLEY and the "B" design
are trademarks belonging to Berkley Publishing Corporation.

PRINTED IN THE UNITED STATES OF AMERICA

10 9 8 7 6 5 4 3 2 1

DEDICATION

Allan, this one's for you. You never doubted, even when I did. You always told me the "crazies" were a sign of creative genius, despite all evidence to the contrary. And you even let me wake you up at all hours of the night to read my work to you. If that's not love . . .

ACKNOWLEDGMENTS

Heartfelt thanks to my editor, Carrie Feron, who saw the spark all those years ago and patiently nurtured it to a candle flame. Next time let's go for a bonfire!

I also owe a great debt of gratitude to Jim Sevrens, general manager of *The San Francisco Examiner*, for so generously sharing his time and expertise with me, and for illuminating the technical and philosophical aspects of the newspaper business in a way that none of the books could.

A very special thanks to my writing buddies, Leslie Knowles, Linda Hartman, Susan Macias and Anna Eberhardt, who read this book in bits and pieces and never once suggested that I get a shredder.

And finally, to Anna and Olivia, my fellow founding members of The Bad Girls Club, hats off for inspiring the scene that was so "bad" it didn't make the cut!

"Nowhere are there more hiding places than in the heart."
—German Proverb

Shameless

CHAPTER
·· ONE ··

SPRING 1994

WHEN THE GOOD citizens of Half Moon Bay, California, whispered of scandals and sex, the name on their lips was Jessie Flood. Perhaps what intrigued them most about the remote and eerily beautiful young woman of twenty-seven was her sudden and precipitous rise to wealthy widowhood.

"Makes no sense," the whispers went. "Not a jot of sense. Everyone knows Jessie Flood is common as dirt, white trash if we're being honest. So how did she end up married to a multimillionaire like Simon Warnecke?"

No one knew the answer to that question, but it didn't stop them from speculating. And some of the gossip was based in fact. Simon Warnecke was rich. And he was dead. Brought down by a lingering, wasting illness and buried only three weeks earlier, the reclusive sixty-five-year-old media baron was widely known as the nastiest son of a bitch in six counties, perhaps in all of northern California. But what intrigued the locals even more than Simon and his money was his young wife's checkered and mysterious past.

Some of the gossip was malicious—"Shameless slut, she blackmailed Warnecke into marrying her. Had something to do with that love child of hers, sure as bad wine turns to vinegar. Anybody's guess who the father is." But most of it was quieter, almost reverent—"She's fearless as the face of death itself. I saw her back down three armed men the day she saved Simon Warnecke's life. Probably hexed 'em with those weird, moon-blue eyes of hers."

The speculation went on and on, the stories becoming more

breathlessly mythic as they were counted and recounted. But as the town's curiosity mounted, so did the odds against it ever being satisfied. Because only Jessie Flood-Warnecke knew how she'd come to be a vastly wealthy widow and the heiress apparent to a media empire . . . and Jessie wasn't talking.

Black was her color. It did little to enhance her fierce, pale countenance or her winter-blue eyes. And it gave the tiny, crescent-shaped scar on her upper lip an unnatural prominence. But it suited her mood perfectly. It didn't matter that no one in the small coastal town bothered with widows' weeds anymore. She wore them with solemn defiance—and without a hint of survivor's guilt. She'd been wearing black ever since her husband passed away, and though it had nothing to do with mourning the loss of a loveless marriage to a man thirty years her senior, she took strange comfort in the color's severity. Yes, black suited her. She might just go on wearing it for the rest of her life.

Jessie Flood-Warnecke rarely consulted mirrors. Unlike her stunning older sister, she had never counted beauty as one of her natural assets. But tonight was different. Tonight the moon was full and frightening, and something restless stirred within her. The unfamiliar turbulence had brought her to stand in front of the long mirror of her Portuguese rosewood armoire. Behind her the terrace doors swung open with a beseeching creak, as if blown by the westerlies. A freshet of rose-scented air teased the loose tendrils on her nape, stirring them into a momentary frenzy.

Unaware of the shadowy figure of a man poised in her doorway, Jessie went about her evening rituals, drawing several antique agate-headed pins from her heavy hair. Her mother had called it lioness hair, not red, not gold, but a coppery mane of such thickness it hid Jessie's face from view when she bent forward.

As she unbuttoned her black cashmere cardigan, she was aware of the fullness of her breasts against the inside of her wrists. For so long she had not thought of her body as anything but an efficient machine, that the contact surprised her. Her flesh was oddly responsive tonight and, as she glanced up, she caught her own reflection in the armoire mirror.

The nakedness of her emotions startled her. Need was swimming in her huge pale eyes, and the crescent scar above her mouth tugged at her upper lip, drawing it back to incredibly sensual effect. Her neglected body seemed as determined to remind her that she was born in sin, a sexual creature, as she was to deny it. She'd been feeling restless for some time now, and she couldn't help but think that it must have been Simon's death, or even the ordeal of the funeral three weeks ago, that had triggered something dormant inside her. And yet she knew it wasn't just the emotional desolation of an arranged marriage that made her look so gaunt and starved for human contact. This was something deep-seated. Female hunger. Female shame.

She shed the sweater, letting it drop in a heap at her feet. The front closure of her black satin bra released with a touch of her fingertips, but instead of removing the lingerie, she let it remain and closed her eyes to a heady rush of freedom. Her flesh tingled. It wasn't a question of control. She could master these impulses as she had everything else in her life. If the flesh was weak, her nerve wasn't. She was a product of the rugged Pacific coast, of the Santa Cruz hills. Jessie Flood had been brought up in squalor and deprivation, tested by life.

No, this wasn't about control, it was a matter of need. Creature need. She craved the comfort of her own flesh, longed for its solace, and with every second that passed, the sensations intensified. A breath quavered in her throat as her cool fingers drifted over warm skin. Her stomach muscles fluttered with another ripple of longing. *God, so sweet, and yet out of her reach. What was it she sought? Not sex, not this. What was it?*

A salty mist from the ocean crept into the room. Ghostings of crushed rose petals swirled around her. Enveloped in perfume, she indulged in the guilty pleasure of her own body for a moment . . . until the rustle of belling curtains drew her attention.

She opened her eyes, sensing that she wasn't alone. To her horror, she realized she was right. There was another image in the armoire mirror. A man's form was discernible through the sheer curtains that billowed at the terrace doors.

She didn't ask who it was. She didn't even pick up her

sweater in an attempt to cover herself. Instinctively, she edged toward the Bombe-style desk next to her bed and pressed a button concealed under the ledge. A drawer slid out soundlessly. It held a nine-millimeter Beretta handgun and an ammunition clip.

She slipped the clip into place with a precision that came with practice. The "very wealthy widow" knew how to handle the weapon. She'd been a security guard in the poverty-stricken days before her marriage to Simon Warnecke.

"Move out from behind the curtain," she said, targeting the silhouetted form as she turned.

The figure remained still, shadow-wrapped.

Jessie felt a flash of both foolishness and relief. For an instant, she wondered if it was nothing more than that, a shadow. She moved closer, guardedly closer.

"*I have a gun,*" she announced.

The shadows swirled and shifted, coming alive.

Her finger tightened against the Beretta's trigger as the barrier of sheer curtains was pushed aside. A man stood in the open doorway, cut in half by light and darkness. His face and upper torso were shrouded, but she could see him from the waist down—the wrinkled silk of his Versace slacks and jacket, a black ribbed T-shirt and a silver mesh belt that glowed like a concealed weapon.

"Step into the light," she ordered.

He moved into the room, throwing off the shadows. The lamplight climbed his body, revealing lean, aggressive hips, a clenched gut and wide shoulders, heavy with muscle. A sensual shadow of a mustache snaked from the curve of his upper lip into the hollows of his cheekbones, then flared with the blunt angles of his jaw. His hair was sable black, a tumult of waves and flames that swept back from a widow's peak on his forehead and spilled to his shoulders. Taken all at once, the dark sensuality of his unshaven features was breathtaking.

Full recognition didn't come instantly. Jessie's senses were too stunned by the sight of him. But within seconds, she had begun to shake so violently she could hardly hold the gun steady. Nerves sparked painfully along the raised tendons of her hand.

"Luc," she breathed. "You bastard."

Her body went taut, her breath short in the chill night air. The town was right about Jessie Flood-Warnecke. She was afraid of nothing . . . except this man.

"Jessie?"

The intruder's gaze flashed from the gun to her partially bared body with a curiosity that verged on insolence. His head lifted and his dark lashes lowered with predatory sexual interest, as if he were so certain of her inability to use the weapon that he was already thinking about taking it away from her, taking it away from her and—

She released the Beretta's safety with a savage click.

Her body began to quake as she realized what she was going to do, what she had to do. She was torn by warring impulses, caught between rising horror and the will to survive, to protect. Her instincts were jumbled, wildly chaotic, and yet at the center of it all, there was a thought. One desperately lucid thought. *No one had to know.*

Luc Warnecke posed a terrible threat—to her and to everything that was precious to her. She could put an end to that threat now, tonight. She could say she hadn't recognized him. She could say she'd taken him for an intruder, that she'd been in fear of her life. No one had to know.

The insolence had vanished from his expression. Now there was wonder in his eyes as he stared at her, wonder and disbelief as he took in the rigid fury that arced from the frozen lift of her head all the way down her arm to the extended gun. She wasn't bluffing. He'd just realized that.

Her hand trembled as she aimed the gun at his chest, at precisely the place where his jacket pocket covered his heart. She knew he had an inhuman capacity for cruelty, but surely he was mortal like the rest of mankind. Surely he had veins and arteries, two painfully pumping chambers, a *heart.*

Do it, she told herself. *Somehow she had to do it.*

Her index finger tightened and froze. With a cry of frustration, she jerked her hand back and took aim again.

"Jessie, no!"

"Welcome home, Luc—" Her voice broke as she squeezed the trigger.

CHAPTER
·· TWO ··

HE WASN'T DEAD and he wasn't dreaming.

Vaguely aware of those two things, Luc Warnecke moaned aloud, struggling toward consciousness like a drowning swimmer. The pain was real, agonizingly real. The lower half of his body felt leaden, paralyzed.

He opened his eyes with effort, grateful for the room's dim light. Even the low glow of a bedside lamp brought him pain. His head ached ferociously as he tried to make sense of where he was and what had happened. He remembered ringing the front door chimes and then, when no one answered, walking around to the back of the house. A light in the east wing bedroom suite had caught his eye and he'd gone to investigate . . .

The rest of it came at him all at once, like a spasm of memory induced by truth serum. In his mind's eye, he could see the Beretta belching fire and he could hear the hollow crack as it discharged. She had shot him in cold blood, and though he remembered her targeting his chest, she'd frozen at the last minute as if she couldn't go through with it, then pulled back frantically and re-sited the gun—at parts other than his heart. The firestorm in his thigh left no doubt as to where he'd been hit.

"*Sweet Christ.*" The words hissed out as he realized what she'd done to him. His wrists were tightly bound, but he had some mobility inside the sheet that covered him. He reached down gingerly, his jaw muscles seizing, his forehead beaded with sweat. Gauze and tape had been hastily applied to what felt like a superficial wound on his left thigh. She'd grazed him, he realized with great relief, taken out a chunk of flesh at worst. "She didn't hit anything vital," he muttered under his breath. *"Thank God for that."*

"It's a little late for prayer, Luc."

He glanced up and saw her coiled in a wingback chair by the room's marble fireplace. She wore a black satin nightshirt, and with her legs drawn up and her heavy copper hair tumbling around her shoulders, she was the picture of privileged womanhood at ease. But the hush in her voice and the lethal weapon pointed in his direction spoke volumes about her state of mind.

Jessie Flood had changed in ways Luc Warnecke could not have begun to imagine. As a child she'd been unflinching in the face of danger and unswerving in her loyalties, even to the point of recklessness. The legacy of her deprived childhood was still evident in her lean, slender body and her freshly scrubbed features, but the tomboyish girl he remembered had matured into a strange, forbidding beauty. Red hair flamed around a pale face dominated by icy, compelling blue eyes.

"I shot you," she informed him as if by any chance he'd missed that fact. "I didn't kill you, but the moon is full and the night is young."

Sweat chilled the back of Luc's neck. The image of a reckless, half-naked female menacing him with a loaded gun was seared into his frontal lobes. It was a vision straight out of an avenging angel fantasy, and though his life was at stake, or maybe because it was, the whole episode seemed insane and electrifying, almost erotic.

"Any chance you're going to tell me why?" He forced the telltale hoarseness from his voice.

"Why I didn't kill you?"

"Why you shot me, for Christ's sake!"

She gazed at him, lips pursed, then shook her head.

"Who carried me in here?" he demanded to know. "Who cleaned and bandaged this gunshot wound? You *did* clean it, didn't you? Or can I count on gangrene to accompany my skull fracture?"

"My caretaker brought you here and dressed the wound. As to whether or not he cleaned it, I really couldn't say."

Heat poured through Luc's nostrils. He'd been looking for a way to excuse her actions, to blame himself for frightening her, but she was starting to piss him off. *Seriously.* He searched her stony features and curled form for any sign of vulnerability.

"You should have killed me, Jessie," he said, his voice soft, menacing. "Even a novice hunter knows it's a mistake to wound your prey. It makes it deadly."

Fear flashed through her composure like faraway lightning. He caught its glitter in her pale eyes and in the whitened scar above her lip. His nerves jumped, urging him to act despite his injury. *Move! Take her now while she's open.* But before the impulse could fire his muscles, her fear had crystallized into icy rage. The lightning had become icicles.

She raised the gun, training the barrel on the space between his dark eyebrows. "Don't even think about it," she warned. Her thumb hovered near the safety as if she were allowing herself to imagine in gruesome detail how he would look with a bullet in his brain. She wet her lips and swallowed.

"Murder One," he cautioned. "You've got the motive, Mrs. Warnecke. They'll say you wanted your dead husband's only son out of the way, that you were eliminating any possibility of a claim on Simon's estate."

The safety clicked as she released it.

"Jesus, not again," he breathed.

She stroked the trigger restlessly, and then her finger contracted and the hammer clicked against an empty chamber.

Luc's heart rate soared, spiked by outrage. The gun wasn't loaded!

"Bang," she said softly.

"What the *fuck* is your problem?" he snarled. His heart was hammering so hard he could barely think. He shared a history with Jessie Flood that went back to their early childhood. It was tangled and tender, as poignantly conflicted a relationship as any two people could hope to have had. She'd been an unswerving ally once, a kindred spirit. *But he hated her at this moment, hated the bitch.*

"You're my problem," she said, mouthing the words as if they were a blood curse. "You."

She was lit with a cold, pale flame, but he knew she was ready to ignite inside that deadly calm. He'd seen the fear, the icy rage. He'd seen them, but he didn't understand them. If anyone had been betrayed in their relationship, it was him.

Ten years ago she had implicated him in the death of Hank Flood, her drunkard stepfather. And last year she'd married Luc's sixty-five-year-old father. It was inconceivable to him that the Jessie Flood who had been his friend could have entangled herself with a monster like Simon Warnecke . . . for any reason.

"What am I supposed to call you these days? *Mom?*"

The contempt in his voice was savage.

Jessie Flood drew into herself even more tightly. She hated this man. She hated him blindly, without thought or reason, the way angels hated mortal sin. But she had also cared for him once, impossible as that now seemed, and it was those two warring emotions that held her paralyzed. She had loved Luc Warnecke the way she'd done everything in her world, unconditionally and without limits. She would have laid down her life for him. She would have done anything. But God, the hurt he'd inflicted. She hadn't seen him in ten years, and yet her memory of the violation she'd suffered at his hands was as raw and real as if it had happened yesterday.

"Even if I tried to explain why I married your father," she said coldly. "You would never understand."

"And you know why! For God's sake, Jessie—you, of all people, should know *why*."

It was true. What he said was true. Jessie did know why. Luc had suffered through a nightmarish childhood, but she hadn't allowed herself to think about him in a sympathetic way in a very long time—and she couldn't relent now. It wasn't just herself she was protecting. She had to guard against Luc Warnecke as if he were her deadly enemy. He *was* her deadly enemy.

"Your timing is perfect," she informed him. "You didn't make Simon's funeral, but you're here in plenty of time for the reading of his will."

"I'm a Warnecke. I'm entitled."

"You're entitled to nothing. Simon disinherited you years ago, and I can assure you, he had no deathbed change of heart. He's left everything to me—the property, the controlling interest in Warnecke Communications, and all his other holdings. He wasn't a man for grand emotional gestures, as you no doubt could vouch, but he vowed to me that you would never get your hands on what's left of his business empire or his personal property."

"His personal property being you?"

Jessie's face heated. He had an amazing gift for making her feel cheap. The Floods had been considered little better than poor white trash in Half Moon Bay, and cheap was a label she'd been stigmatized with since childhood. The disgust in Luc's expression told her what he must be thinking—that she'd married Simon for the money, that she'd turned into as conniving and accomplished a golddigger as her sister, Shelby. But what infuriated her even more than his censure was his gall. Who was Luc Warnecke to take the moral high road? How dare he pass judgment on her, or anyone else?

"I want you out of here," she said.

"You shot me, lady." He kicked off the sheet, exposing the wound on his thigh. "Unless you want to go to jail for assault with a deadly weapon, you're stuck with me."

Jessie's mouth went dry. He'd exposed far more than the injury, and she was sure he'd done it intentionally. The challenge in his eyes was not only insolent, it was becoming more sensual with every heartbeat.

Another woman might have acknowledged the violent clutch of her stomach muscles as something other than pure hostility. She might even have conceded that the sight of a half-naked man in black bikini briefs was disturbingly titillating. It wouldn't have been too farfetched an admission, even for Jessie. Because Luc Warnecke's body was damn near magnificent by almost any estimation. His T-shirt was hiked up just enough to mesmerize even the most reluctant voyeur, and the dark hair that speared down his hard, flat belly mingled erotically with a riot of equally dark curls rising from the depths of his briefs.

But Jessie would sooner have admitted to robbing the blind and the infirm than to any of those prurient thoughts, not even to a simple stirring of female curiosity. If her stomach was clenched, it was with disgust at his blatant attempt to shock her, and if her neck was hot and damp, it was leftover adrenaline. Perhaps she did harbor a mild interest in the drastic physical changes he'd undergone since their childhood years, but that was completely understandable.

He'd been nineteen when he left. He was nearly thirty now, and from every indication, his body had matured in ways she wouldn't have believed possible. He'd been slat-thin as a young boy and he'd walked with a slight limp from a badly set break. But at the moment she couldn't even be sure which of his powerfully muscled legs had been broken.

"Apparently you don't *mind* being stuck with me," he observed.

She dug an ammunition clip from the pocket of her night-shirt and brandished it in the air. "I want you out of here now," she said. "If you can't make it on your own, I'll call Roger."

"Roger?"

"The college student who carried you in here. He lives on the grounds, in the caretaker's cottage."

"You call Roger, and he's a dead college student." Luc grimaced with pain as he heaved himself to a sitting position and settled his feet on the antique Persian rug. "What the hell did you hit me with?"

"I never touched you. You fell backward into the glass door and hit your head. I'm surprised the impact didn't kill you."

"Don't hold your breath." His features contorted as he tried to stand, but couldn't manage it. He struggled with the rope binding his wrists, worked one hand free and fell backward, collapsing onto his elbows. His face was ashen, drained of blood. If he was fighting to stay conscious, he was losing the battle.

"God, my head," he moaned, rolling to his side. He gripped his skull as if it were splitting open and let out a choked sound. A moment later, he shuddered and slumped to the pillow.

Jessie uncoiled slowly, straining to get a better look at him. His shallow respiration was the only indication that he was still breathing. "Luc?"

She rose and approached the bed cautiously. Her training had taught her to be wary of tricks, but the look of him frightened her. His lips were bluish, and his shirt was soaked through with perspiration. He'd hit his head, which meant he could have a concussion. He could even be hemorrhaging internally. Under any other circumstances, she would have called for medical help, but a gunshot wound required a police report and she couldn't risk that.

She had little choice but to call Roger back. There was a telephone on the writing desk, and as she crossed the room she tugged her robe together. She'd made no attempt to explain the situation to the caretaker beyond telling him there'd been an accident. She would have to now.

Setting the gun and clip on the table, she picked up the receiver and quickly tapped out the numbers. *Answer it*, Roger, she thought as the phone began to ring. Suddenly a shadow flared from behind her and a finger stabbed at the disconnect button. The dial tone buzzed in her ear. He'd tricked her!

"Hang it up," he ordered.

Adrenaline surged as Jessie tried to remember her self-defense training. She dropped the receiver and grabbed for the gun, but his hand was there, blocking her. The Beretta and clip went flying off the table. Whirling around, she thrust her shoulder into his chest, butting him with such force they both lost their balance and tumbled over. Luc hit the floor first, cushioning Jessie's fall. The impact should have incapacitated an injured man, but before she could get free, he'd dragged her over his body and pinned her to the floor.

"You were *faking*?" she cried, furious.

Luc's jaw clenched on a groan of agony. "I'm not faking anything," he grated. He grasped her wrists and shifted his weight onto her. "I've got a hole in my leg, thanks to you, and my goddamn head feels like it's coming off. I want to share the grief, that's all. I don't like being miserable alone."

Just the thought of being so close to him was abhorrent to Jessie. Everywhere she looked there was bare skin, dark body hair and heaving muscle. His rough grip bit into the flesh of her wrists, and the heat of his body washed over her in waves. She stiffened under his hot gaze, trying not to let him touch her with any part of his body that hadn't already made contact.

Her heartbeat slowed to hard, painful jerks. "If I scream, the whole house will come running."

He forced her wrists together and clamped a hand over her mouth. "Knock yourself out," he invited.

She burned to assault him with every obscene word in the English language, either that or bite a chunk out of his hand. But instead she went utterly still. Retaliation would have brought her so much brutal satisfaction that it was too dangerous even to contemplate. Even to breathe seemed risky. She was poised on the edge of hysteria, close to flying apart, and she couldn't let that happen. There was too much tangled rage inside her, too much savaged pride. She couldn't reach the gun, and her only other weapon was the truth. But if she assaulted him with that, she destroyed herself as well.

He pushed himself up, anchoring her wrists on either side of her head as he glared down at her. "You've got my attention, Jessie. I hope that's what you wanted, because it's my turn now. Didn't they ever teach you that in school? How to take turns?"

She refused even to look at him.

"Apparently not. I'll bet they didn't teach you not to play with guns either, did they? Or that nice little girls don't shoot at people. You could do with some manners, *little* girl. You need to be taught how to behave in polite company . . ."

His cynical tones penetrated her thoughts like an unwanted touch. Her only defense was icy silence.

He shifted his weight as if he were pushing himself up to take a better look at her. "Are you going to talk to me?" he pressed, his voice roughening. "Or are we going to play Miss Manners right here on the bedroom floor?"

Jessie's pulse quickened, responding to the deepening rasp in his tone, the crude sexual insinuations. She stole a glance at him and saw exactly what she feared. He was taking in her dishevelment as if he'd just noticed that her satin nightshirt was tangled up around her waist and gaping open at the neckline, as if he'd just realized that he had a trapped and vulnerable female beneath him.

She wrenched up with her hips, twisting and turning frantically as she tried to dislodge him, but her writhing only made things worse. His breathing slowed and deepened as he watched her struggle, and to her horror she realized she was arousing more than his interest. He could see her breasts heaving and feel the heat of her lower body grinding against his. With a moan of despair, she rocked up, bucking against him with her pelvis, the only part of her body she could move.

His thighs tightened like a vise as he loomed over her.

"Hold still, for Christ's sake—" His eyes darkened as she wriggled and squirmed beneath him. "Unless you'd rather fuck than talk."

"Bastard," she breathed at him.

"So you *can* talk?" A faint smile touched his lips. "In that case, maybe you'd like to explain this vendetta of yours against me. It's not enough that you implicated me in a murder and drove me out of town. You had to marry Simon, my blood enemy, and then tonight you tried to shoot me on sight right here in this house, *your* house? The house I grew up in?"

She retreated again, seething silently. She would have taken strychnine before she'd have told Luc Warnecke the reasons for any of her actions, including marrying his father. As for why she'd shot him, he could damn well stew. *She* remembered every moment of the night Hank Flood died. At the inquest Luc had testified that he couldn't recall anything about the fight with Hank except that Hank was unconscious but still alive when Luc left the Flood home. It enraged her that he didn't remember, that he had had as convenient an excuse as an alcoholic blackout for blotting out everything about that night.

"Come on, Jessie," he warned, shaking her with a quick jolt of his body weight. "I didn't make this pilgrimage because I was homesick."

The slight shift in their positions gave Jessie an unexpected opening. She arched up and caught him with her knee, smashing it into his groin as hard as she could. The agony that shook through him was raw and guttural, but it didn't rock his brutal grip on her arms. His eyes lit with a savage light as he jerked her off the floor, hauling her toward him until their trembling mouths were just inches apart. His strength was inhuman, his fury insane.

"God*damn* you," he snarled.

Jessie moaned frantically, desperate to stop him. As he bent toward her, she spat at him. He flinched away, hesitating for an instant before he caught her again and shook her so hard she couldn't breathe. The moisture mingled between their lips as his mouth came down on hers. He kissed her roughly, deeply, forcing her head back until she was helpless to do anything but submit to him. There was no passion in it, only punishment. He was subjugating her as if she were his mortal enemy. She should have been horrified. And yet the shock of his body against hers, the forced intimacy of his lips, threw her into chaos, into a wild riot of sensation that left her dizzy and gasping.

The response staggered her. She wanted to believe ·it was fear arousing her, but the painful excitement of her stuttering pulse was beyond her ability to deny, however urgently she might have wanted to. She could feel every nuance of his mouth as it moved over hers, smothering her mute protests. She could feel the hair on his bare legs abrading her skin, and his heartbeat, wild, thundering everywhere, even in his hands. His body trembled with a ferocity more primal than anything she'd ever experienced. It was as if he'd released all the violence, all the anguish in his pent-up soul.

He broke the kiss, holding her back as their eyes locked and held. She was trembling, choked with emotion. He was breathing heavily, undeniably aroused. There was a time when she would have given anything to see that breathtaking flare of sexual desire in his eyes. It was all she'd ever dreamed about as a girl. But now it made her stomach churn with painful, sickening excitement.

"At least I got that much," he said, his voice breaking. "I've been wanting to get my hands on you for a long time now, but never more than when I walked into your bedroom tonight."

A shudder racked her, draining her of whatever strength she had left. "Let me go," she implored. "I won't scream and I won't try to get away."

"You're not going anywhere until you tell me what I want to know."

He released her, letting her drop back to the carpet, but his weight still held her fast and she was too spent to fight. Nothing would have given her more satisfaction than to give him the answers he wanted. It was all she could do not to flay him alive with the truth. She wanted to scream out accusations, to lash out and avenge herself. Instead she said what she knew would enrage him the most.

"You want to know why I married your father? *I loved him.* That's why I married him. Simon and I were in love."

Hatred flared through him, galvanizing him. He reared up, clenching his hand as if he meant to destroy something with his bare fist, and then with one obscene and violent word, he rolled off her, freeing her. "Get out of here," he said. "*Get out.*"

Jessie struggled to gather herself together, to pull herself up. As she hit the floor, she saw that her satin nightshirt had come undone. She glanced at him as she buttoned it hastily, and saw a look of such icy contempt on his face it made her skin crawl. He was looking at her as if he didn't know her, as if Jessie Flood had turned into a woman without a soul. Maybe she had. Maybe that was the Warnecke legacy.

Her throat tightened as she saw his obvious agony. His leg wound had come unbandaged, and it was bleeding heavily. He pulled off his T-shirt to stanch the flow.

Her voice softened oddly as she spoke. "You shouldn't have come back, Luc."

He looked up at her, his dark eyes burning. "And you should have killed me, Jessie. You're going to wish you had before I'm through."

CHAPTER
·· **THREE** ··

THREE WEEKS EARLIER

"YOU NEED A good kick in the head this morning?"

"What's the problem, Slick?" Luc Warnecke turned from the window of his Denver office to face the benevolent wrath of the gravelly voiced staffer he'd recently promoted to an executive vice-presidency. The lean, handsome, prematurely snowy-haired woman was now his chief administrative officer, but as his top aide she'd been wife, mother, in-house spy and all-around hatchet person at Worldcom, Luc's media company. In point of fact, she ran the place no matter what her desk plaque said. Every busy C.E.O. needed a Mary Greenblatt, Luc had decided years ago. The only thing she'd never tackled was his social calendar, and he might have to speak to her about that the way his sex life was going.

"Those rowdy twits you call a task force are waiting for you in the media room," Mary informed him, plunking the morning mail on his desk, a stack of letters which she'd apparently picked up from his secretary. "Can't you hear 'em?"

Luc was absently aware of the din from across the hall as he glanced at his watch and rose to get himself a fresh cup of coffee from the silver urn on the sideboard. He'd assembled some of Worldcom's best and brightest to research the company's expansion possibilities with an eye to taking on CNN, the electronic news giant. After several weeks of intensive research, the "twits" were going to pitch him their ideas this morning.

"What would I do without you, Slick?" he said.

"Go straight to hell in that arrest-me red Ferrari of yours, I suppose," she grumbled. "Speaking of which, where the hell *are* you going?"

Luc brushed past her on his way out of the spacious, glass-walled office. "To the staff meeting, of course."

"No, you're not."

"I'm not?" He turned with a quizzical expression, ready to be set straight. He listened when Mary Greenblatt spoke. He trusted her trenchant instincts about human nature implicitly, and more often than not, he acted accordingly. In turn, she protected him as she would have her own offspring, like a lioness. Luc had never had protective parents. His mother had died when he was six. His father had been a sadistic brute. He needed Mary.

"You've got a telephone call," she informed him. "Your beleaguered secretary practically begged me to tell you. I think she was afraid to do it herself, poor thing."

"Who is it? My Ferrari mechanic?"

"That would be good news. This is Gilbert Stratton, your deceased father's attorney. He's calling about Simon's will."

Luc's mood darkened swiftly. "What about the will?"

"I don't know. I tried to intercept the call for you, but Stratton didn't see fit to discuss it with me. At any rate, I thought you might want to prepare yourself." She headed for the door, although whether it was to give him some privacy or to make a quick getaway, he couldn't tell.

"The twits can wait," she told him. "Take the call."

"*Stratton* can wait," he muttered. As Mary disappeared through the door, Luc hit the button on his intercom. If nothing else, he would let the attorney twist in the wind for a while. "Val," he said, "ask Mr. Stratton to hold on, would you? Tell him I'm busy . . . praying for my father's immortal soul. That should be good for a laugh."

Luc's heart was clubbing the wall of his chest as he took his cup of coffee and walked to the window. Once again, Mary was right on the mark. He did need time to prepare. She'd said Stratton's call was about the will, but it couldn't have anything to do with a bequest. *Simon would sooner have left his worldly goods to the village idiot than to his only son.*

He gripped the coffee cup with both hands, pressing it into the heel of his palm. The news of his father's death had blindsided him. He hadn't even known the reclusive SOB was sick. Still, he had to admit it was an interesting way to end the cutthroat poker game he and Simon had been playing for the last several years. The old man had folded, leaving Luc high and dry with the winning hand. Simon had won by default.

Luc had eclipsed his father's empire in sheer size, but that was never the goal. He'd wanted to take over Warnecke Communications, to absorb it into Worldcom without a trace, yet he'd been blocked at every turn from acquiring even one share of the privately held stock. He'd also been blocked from head-on competition with his father, since both of the Bay area's major newspapers had been in the Warnecke empire for years, protected from antitrust laws through a federal waiver. As a competitor Simon had been unassailable. As a father he'd become something of a cartoon monster in Luc's mind, the bogeyman of a terrorized child's nightmares. But as an adult the rage and shame were still intact. That hadn't changed.

Luc squinted through a blinding shaft of sunlight at the rambling downtown skyline of Denver, Colorado—rugged outpost of the media establishment's bicoastal nerve centers. He'd come here partly because it was starkly different from his hometown, both in geography and climate. Denver had a wide-open-spaces optimism about it, with no moody, creeping fogs and no darkened corners lying in wait. It was also corporate offices for the tiny, struggling newspaper chain Luc had picked up at a bankruptcy sale—with the help of the modest trust fund his mother had left him—and then parlayed into a "growing behemoth," according to *Newsweek*.

Luc had liked the sturdy, midsize city immediately, well enough to have bought a home in the foothills and a condo for skiing in Beaver Creek, though his business travels kept him from spending much time in either. He even liked the local coffee. It was strong, scalding and satisfyingly bitter.

He took a swallow of the caustic brew, aware of the sharp snag in his throat. Time to cut Gil Stratton down? he wondered, glancing at his watch. The attorney's eyes should be bugging out of his head by now.

Setting the cup down, he walked to the phone and hit the button that activated the speaker unit. "Gil?" he said.

"How are you, Luc?"

Stratton's sonorous voice filled the office, but the attorney's booming cordiality was as suspicious to Luc as it was off-putting. "What's this about?" Luc asked, determined to dispense with the formalities.

"You were remembered in your father's will. I just wanted you to know."

"I beg your pardon?"

"Well, it's a small bequest," Stratton explained on a note of apology. "But I'm sure it will mean a great deal—"

"Cut the crap, Gil. What did he leave me, an exploding attaché case, a car with stunt brakes?"

A nervous chuckle. "It's a painting, Luc, some sort of family portrait, I believe. That's all I can tell you, since I haven't actually seen it. We'll ship it to you there in Denver, if you like. Simon requested a formal reading of his will, but there's no need for you to attend. You understand."

A muscle burned in Luc's jaw. A family portrait? Jesus, Simon *was* sick. "Not attend the reading of my own father's will? I wouldn't think of committing such an unforgivable breach."

"What? Luc, really now, there's no point, is there? You'll only upset—"

Luc slowly depressed the disconnect button, strangling off Stratton's voice with nearly as much enjoyment as he would have strangled the man if he could have laid hands on him. He'd never planned to attend the reading. Now he was considering the possibility, if only to watch Gil Stratton squirm.

The mail was stacked on the desk in front of him where Mary had left it. He fanned through the letters absently, more to restore a sense of control than because he was curious. He'd intended to go through the pile after his meeting, when he and Val could take care of any necessary correspondence immediately. But an unopened envelope marked PERSONAL AND CONFIDENTIAL caught his eye. Struck by the way his name and address were printed in an odd, childish scrawl, he decided to let his task force sweat it out a little longer. In this case waiting would only sharpen their killer instincts, he knew. Like hounds held at bay, they would be all the more eager. He'd long ago realized that delaying the moment of satisfaction was sweeter than instant gratification.

Luc ripped open the envelope and scanned the note inside. It was written in the same hand as the address—a childish scrawl clearly meant to disguise the sender's identity. "STAY AWAY FROM HALF MOON BAY," it read. "HANK FLOOD'S DEATH WAS MURDER AND I HAVE NEW EVIDENCE LINKING YOU TO THE CRIME. IF YOU RETURN, I'LL GIVE IT TO THE POLICE."

He studied the four lines with bemused interest. As extortion threats went, this one was amateurish at best, especially since Hank Flood's death had been ruled accidental after a coroner's inquest. Though Luc had been a primary suspect, there hadn't been enough evidence to warrant formal charges or a trial. And besides, the man had been dead ten years.

Still, the stigma lingered and Flood's death remained a mystery, perhaps most of all to Luc. He'd suffered a concussion and some yawning black hole in his mental processes had swallowed up several hours of his life that night. He had his own theories about what had really happened, however, some of which involved Jessie Flood. But he hadn't been in a position to do anything about those theories until recently. He'd simply been biding his time, delaying gratification in favor of letting the moment of satisfaction sweeten.

Perhaps now was that moment, he thought, slipping his hand inside his jacket to tuck the note securely into the deeper of the two silk-lined pockets. Someone was going to trouble to keep him out of Half Moon Bay. And if his intuition was correct, that someone was scared. *All the sweeter.*

CHAPTER
·· FOUR ··

HALF MOON BAY

LUC HAD ALREADY begun to question the rewards of delayed gratification as he kicked the Persian runner aside and rose off the bed, testing the steadiness of his bare feet on the cool, rubbed wood floor. The night's events had left him off balance and he wanted something solid underneath him. He could feel his thigh muscles gripping as he took his first steps. The pain was sharp, but he kept going, intending to get himself over to the telephone and leave a voice-mail message at the office for his second-in-command. It was nearly midnight. Mary wouldn't get the news until morning, but he knew she'd be overjoyed to hear he wasn't coming back any time soon. She loved running the place herself, the old despot. He also wanted her to know he'd be staying at the Warnecke mansion, rather than one of the resort hotels on the coastal highway.

"Hey, Slick," he growled into the phone receiver a moment later, "if I told you I'd just had my butt shot off by a half-naked woman, would you believe me? No, of course not. No one would believe me. So let's just say I've had a little accident and the 'family reunion' is going to be extended indefinitely."

As he went on, bringing Mary up-to-date on the status of several pending acquisitions, Luc felt his bare foot come up against something cold and hard. The Beretta. Jessie had left it behind. He bent from the waist, grimacing as he picked up the weapon. He'd avoided guns most of his life, perhaps because of his father's fixation with them. This one felt unusually heavy in his hand. It also felt damn good to be holding it instead of staring up the barrel.

"I've got the Powerbook with me," he told Mary as he slowly turned the gun in his hand and sighted an imaginary target. "So you can fax anything that's urgent on the Rancom acquisition. You're the clean-up batter while I'm on the bench, Slick. Let's hit a home run on this deal."

He hung up the phone and glanced around the room. He was in the west wing, and though it wasn't the part of the house where the family had resided, he was surrounded by touchstones, nonetheless. The room was furnished with his mother's carefully selected antiques. Her scent, lilies of the valley, still lingered in the heavy fabrics, though she'd been dead a quarter of a century and, sadly, he barely remembered her.

Echos. It was the name his mother had given this house for the eerie reverberations created by the thirty-five foot cathedral ceiling in the front hall. His father had considered the echo chamber a structural defect and had spent a fortune to eliminate the effect. Simon's obsessions had required everything to be perfect, flawless, including his offspring. Or perhaps especially his offspring. Luckily he hadn't been able to "perfect" the echo any more than he had his defective son. But insane bastard that he was, he'd ripped the place apart trying.

Luc left the gun on the desk and began to walk stiffly, exercising his leg. Christ, he could hardly believe he was back after ten years. It was safe to say this wasn't the hero's homecoming he'd imagined. His father wasn't supposed to be dead, Jessie wasn't supposed to be Simon's widow, and the Warnecke empire wasn't supposed to have fallen into enemy hands. What the hell had happened?

As a boy, Luc had believed that human cruelty was innate, that God had failed in his experiment with mankind and should have left the earth barren after he flooded it. It was Jessie Flood who'd made him believe that maybe God hadn't failed. The flinty little redhead who'd invariably had a stray baby animal tucked in her jacket pocket and who worshiped butterflies, had singlehandedly been the instrument of his salvation. She had saved his life when they were kids. She'd been his truest friend, his only friend.

What the hell had happened?

He continued to pace the room, oblivious to the stitching pain. The staggering news of Jessie's marriage to Simon had come through family lawyers. It had felt like the final in a series of betrayals, and the cold fury of his reaction had swept him like an ice storm. But what had surprised him tonight was his explosive jealousy. Imagining her with his father had enraged him, even though he'd never considered Jessie in romantic, possessive terms. He'd never thought of her in explicitly sexual terms . . . until tonight.

Their "reunion" was as blindingly etched in his mind as the negative of a snapshot. He would never forget the sight of her pale, stiff shoulders and the fluid quiver of her breasts as she held him at gunpoint. He would never forget the illicit impulses she'd sparked in his male flesh. Even with everything that had happened between them, he'd always believed some bond of friendship might remain. But she had ceased being Jessie, friend of his youth, tonight. She had become a female— a bewildering, fascinating, outrageous she-devil of a woman. And he had wanted her.

His blood ran faster, spurred by his thoughts, and the heat that flowed into his muscles eased the strain of his movements. He began to walk more naturally, favoring his injured leg less. After a few more moments he searched out his clothing, finding his jacket, slacks and shoes in a cherrywood armoire.

He quickly dug into the inner pocket of his jacket, and was relieved to find what he was looking for. She hadn't gone through his clothing, then, or if she had, she'd wisely left things where she found them. There would be plenty of time for the little surprise he had planned, he reasoned, returning his jacket to the hanger. First he wanted to get the feel of things around here, find out who was really running the show in Simon's place. He'd never liked guessing who his adversaries were. He wanted to remained fixated on Jessie as he dressed, and on the sexual heat she'd generated in him. Even the erotic way she'd undressed had mesmerized and confused him. If her older sister, Shelby, had staged a personal striptease, it wouldn't have surprised him. But not Jessie, never Jessie. She was the only decent thing about the notorious Flood family.

By the time he finished dressing, the sharp pain in his thigh had become a dull, drawing ache. The throbbing at the base of his skull had also eased, and the snarling beasts from his childhood had been driven back into their cages. He hadn't returned to Half Moon Bay to get bogged down in the emotional wasteland of his youth. He had plans for Simon Warnecke's empire which required him to be more ruthlessly cold-blooded than Simon himself had ever been.

Looking around, he spotted the Beretta's ammunition clip on the floor next to the mahogany Chippendale dresser. He picked it up and dropped it into his shirt pocket, a trick he'd learned from her tonight. He didn't want to be at a disadvantage the next time he dealt with his father's widow.

Sleep was impossible, a luxury she couldn't indulge herself in. Not tonight. Not with him in the house. Even though he was in a separate wing with a nasty injury, her daughter Mel was far away from him, and Jessie had locked herself in her bedroom suite, she was not reassured. Fortunately Roger Metcalf was just moments away, in the caretaker's cottage on the grounds, and a phone call would bring him running. That would have to suffice, because she couldn't call the police. They would almost certainly ask questions.

She had already thought through the steps she would take to deal with Luc Warnecke. Tomorrow morning her first phone call would be to Matthew Sandusky, the CEO of Warnecke Communications and publisher of *The San Francisco Globe* and *The Bay Cities Review*. Matt had always been more a son to Simon than an employee, and in the last year, as Simon's illness had progressed, he'd become a friend and ally to Jessie as well. He was tough-minded and pragmatic, and yet sensitive. Matt would know what to do about Luc Warnecke.

Now, as she sat at her dressing table, pondering the display of ceramic butterflies she'd been collecting since childhood, the delicate figurines seemed to come to life for a moment, fluttering before her eyes. Her breath caught dizzily, quavering in her throat as if something sharp were lodged there. She was still painfully on edge in a way that no amount of contingency planning could forestall. *She was frightened, dammit.*

It didn't seem to matter that she'd thought through everything so carefully . . .

She began to sort through her collection, arranging the figurines into clusters of crystal and ceramic, wood and metal. She'd read somewhere that people fell into two categories, splitters and lumpers, with the former focusing on the distinctions between things and the latter on the similarities. With her eye for likenesses, Jessie was clearly the latter. She'd been compelled to find the unifying patterns in things for as long as she could remember, much the way other people cleaned and reorganized their closets or color-coded their socks in periods of uncontrollable anxiety. It was her way of imposing order on a disorderly world.

She had also cloaked herself in a hooded robe of black terrycloth. Even as a child she'd had a propensity for dark colors, as if their very boldness could throw up a protective barrier. She'd always suspected it had something to do with her mother's fragility. A timid beauty given to sheer fabrics and pastel hues, Lynette Flood had needed protection.

Unfortunately neither of Jessie's calming devices were working tonight. She was freezing inside the heavy robe, and even reorganizing figurines required more focus than she could give it. She needed something to relax her. Rising from the dressing table, she glanced at the terrace doors, wondering if she should chance a swim in the pool. Few in the household ever used it, including her small staff, so there was little chance she'd be noticed, and yet—

A splotch of darkness on the antique Hamandan carpet caught her eye, and even before full recognition hit her, she shuddered inwardly. She had shot a man in cold blood tonight. That hardly seemed possible now, but at the time the decision had felt like an ordination from some dark god of justice, her only plausible choice.

An unfamiliar scent assailed her as she hugged the robe around her. The woodsy fragrance held traces of the exotic, hints of sandlewood and smoke. If it were his cologne, she hadn't noticed it before, but that was understandable. Their bodies had not only come into contact; they'd been fighting like combatants.

Flashes of his cold face and hot eyes came back to her unbidden. She could feel the dominating power of his hands, the muscled strength of his arms. The cologne permeated her senses as she remembered the heat and the sweat and the scathing kiss. It *was* his scent, she was sure of it. She felt as if she'd been marked, as if the irrefutable evidence of his manhandling were all over her body.

She unzipped the robe and stepped out of it, letting it lie in a heap on the floor as she headed for the bathroom. A moment later, drenched in the hot, pulsating jet spray, she reiterated her plans for calling Matt Sandusky first thing in the morning, and then she ducked her head under the water, willing herself to relax under the pommeling pressure.

As the needle-like spray hit her, she became aware of a fine-tuned trembling that seemed to come from deep under the surface of her muscles. The woman who had never allowed herself to succumb to fear was panic-stricken, she realized. She soaped herself vigorously, scrubbing until her skin stung and the color rose to a bright pink hue, and then she consciously willed herself to relax, letting the water wash and bubble over her as she imagined the unsteadiness in her limbs being rinsed down the drain.

The huge bathroom was thick with steam as she stepped out of the shower and took a towel from the heated brass bar. She bent forward and dried her naturally wavy hair first, then stood and threw her head back, flinging its damp weight off her face. As she tossed the towel on the hamper and went to get a fresh one, she noticed a dark form through the steam.

The sight stopped her in mid-stride. The tile floor was slick with condensation, and yet she was aware of the terrible effort it took to draw back her foot and to straighten her spine from a reflexive crouch. This time there was no moment of uncertainty; she knew who it had to be—and the trembling inside her intensified.

Luc was standing at the entrance to the bathroom, watching her as if he'd been there for some time. The animal curiosity in his gaze was charged with heat and rampant insolence as he slowly took in her nakedness, letting his eyes slide from the water droplets clinging to her breasts to the blazing thatch of curls at the juncture of her thighs. Jessie caught a flash of the erotic hunger in his eyes that she remembered from the past. It had never been directed at her, however. His eyes used to flare like that when he looked at Shelby, her older sister.

She rushed for the cabinet, opened it and pulled out a towel, but by the time she'd covered herself, he'd already entered the room. She would have killed him if she could. But this time he had the gun.

CHAPTER
··FIVE··

"YOU FORGOT THIS," Luc said, indicating the Beretta. He flipped the gun into the palm of his hand and held it up.

Jessie clutched the towel around her, instinctively taking his measure as she gauged her chances of escape. It was the second time in one night he'd violated her privacy this way.

"Is this how you get your kicks?" Her voice was faint, but discernible. "Watching unsuspecting women? Stalking them like some kind of pervert?"

He leaned up against the door frame, casually indolent as he surveyed the water droplets glistening on her shoulders. His gaze traced the slow stream of a bead that purled along the ridge of her collarbone, hesitated and then sluiced, trembling, into the valley of her breasts. "You didn't qualify that enough. It's not just unsuspecting women that bring out my voyeuristic tendencies. I like my victims to be naked, and whenever possible, wet."

"Leave the gun on the nightstand on your way out," she told him. "And since you've clearly recovered enough to walk, don't stop once you've left the room. Keep going, Luc. I want you *out* of this house."

"It's dangerous to leave guns lying around."

He spoke softly, gazing at the gun for a moment before raising his dark eyes to hers. He was playing with the weapon, playing with her.

She watched him, oddly fascinated. It began to dawn on Jessie that she was dealing with someone very unpredictable, a dangerous man. She had never seen Luc like this before. She did not even know who he was.

"People get hurt," he said.

"Then give the gun to me." She held out her hand.

It was a mistake. Perhaps the mistake he'd been waiting for. This was going to be payback, she realized, for what she'd done to him. An eyebrow lifted, and at one corner of his lips, a faint smile moved. The effect was to cast shadows across the planes of his face and to sensualize his mouth with brooding nuances . . . with breathtaking hints of his capacity for cruelty. It hit her then as it hadn't before that he was not the abused boy she'd once loved or even the nineteen-year-old who'd shattered her bright dreams. He was an adult male, a virtual stranger in those terms. And he was armed.

Her first instinct was to back away as he neared. When she didn't give in to the impulse, her body went crazy. Her breath began to tremble and her thigh muscles surged, as if urging her to run.

He was at least six feet tall and he seemed immeasurably larger, as if some aggressive force had expanded the space he occupied. She'd been pinned by his superior strength in the fight they'd had, but it was his expression that held her now, his eyes. She'd never seen such cold, black intensity, and yet she couldn't wrench herself away from the hypnotic horror of the moment.

"Don't," she pleaded, though he hadn't done anything yet.

He took in her erotic distress with all the slow, practiced arrogance of the voyeur he claimed to be, but he didn't say a word. Instead, he brought up the gun and nudged the barrel into the knot of her terry cloth towel. The act in itself was implicitly sexual. With a slow turn of the gun's handle, he undid the knot and the towel fell away, exposing her.

The room was steamy, but the air that hit Jessie's bare flesh was cool. Her delayed reaction was a sharp, dizzy little cry of alarm.

A flicker of hunger lit his eyes, and his lips parted expectantly, as though he'd just drawn in a deep breath. His gaze drifted over her stiff nipples and down her body, and Jessie went rigid, trembling with outrage.

"Kill me first," she whispered.

He loomed closer, silent, breathing. Cold metal flashed.

She flinched as he reached out, unable to bear the thought of his skin on hers. He captured a skein of her damp hair, feeding it through his fingers, and then she made the mistake of looking up at him. Their eyes locked.

She wanted to back away from him, to break the painful current, but just as before she couldn't get her body to respond. His dark gaze told her he had every intention of taking advantage of the predicament. As if daring her to resist him, he released her hair and trailed his fingers up and down her arm, brushing the side of her breast with a feather stroke.

"Who the hell are you?" he breathed.

She stared into his eyes, defiant. But her flesh leapt as he touched her again. "Your *father's wife*." Jessie barely got the words out. She was dizzy with the shock of his heat against her body, reeling from the sudden intimacy. His scent enveloped her in woodsmoke and intoxicating drafts of sandlewood, and her nerves reacted wildly, inexplicably, as though she were a woman responding to a man she wanted, as though she were excited instead of repelled. His fingers caressed on her swelling flesh, bringing her a deep sexual shudder. She moaned from somewhere outside of her body, part startled pleasure, part disbelief.

Every movement he made was agonizingly slow, and yet she was swimming in confusion. She felt paralyzed with sensation, while her mind raced madly. Her flesh was weak and yet powerful at the same time. Her body had turned into a tyrant that wouldn't allow her to resist him. She ought to be fighting instead of submitting. She had controlled her life up to now with an iron-fisted will, so why couldn't she control this craziness? Why didn't she stop him? *And why was she responding?*

"You can't," she said, her breath catching on a sob.

"I know." He reached down with a caressing gesture and opened her legs. "I know," he murmured again, but he didn't stop. A moment later he was stroking her inner thighs. His breath bathed her in steamy warmth. "I can't . . . shoot . . . my father's wife."

The smooth glide of steel exerted a magnetic pull on Jessie's senses. She was mesmerized, paralyzed. The barrel felt like satin against her skin. Deadly satin. The weapon dipped and purled like a cool breeze, caressing her exquisitely.

A throb built in the moist heat between her legs, and when the steel's coolness touched her there, a terrible pleasure flared through her. She whimpered helplessly, sagging toward the floor as her legs threatened to give way.

The gun clattered against the wet tiles, and Luc caught her by the arms. "*Jesus,*" he whispered. The profanity seemed to break from some warring place inside him, as if he were suddenly caught up in it too, as if he were a victim of the same chaotic confusion she was.

She let herself be tugged into his arms, let herself be smothered in the angry heat of his embrace. And then, still bewildered, she realized he was trembling too. He tipped up her head and bent toward her, his mouth soft and searingly hot as it touched hers. The kiss triggered a strange, steamy longing within her. It forced a moan through her lips.

Suddenly she was aware of the nakedness of her own body and the fever heat of his. The fires inside him seemed to burn through his clothing and penetrate her flesh. He felt hard and beautiful, hard and overpowering. Yearnings flared through her like spring lightning.

She wanted it, this wild sweetness.

She wanted it. With him.

Her mind shouted at her to stop, and she tried to obey it, tried desperately. She told herself to push him away, to strike out at him, but her fingers dug into his flesh, betraying another emotion. The sound that strangled in her throat was a whimper of need.

"Jessie—"

His mouth turned hungry and hot, so unbearably sweet on hers. She could feel him everywhere, all over her, stimulating her senses into a frenzy. His fingers caressed the taut resistance of her buttocks. And then his palm rode the crest of her hip and curved itself to the fiery red curls between her legs, creating an ache so deep, she nearly convulsed. *No, please! No!!*

Jessie wrenched away from him, staggering backward. "Get away from me!"

His eyes were black, incendiary as he glared at her. His rapid-fire breathing harshened to words. "What's wrong? You can't handle me? Maybe I'm not gentle enough? Or sensitive? *Like Simon?*"

She was more stunned than insulted. Her body was alive, clamoring for him. She could feel the pressure of his hand between her legs as vividly as if it were still there. But outrage was flooding her too—at what he'd done to her, at what she'd let him do. Long overdue, it made her shake with the insanity of the situation.

Her hands trembled uncontrollably as she crouched down to pick up the towel. Somehow she managed to get the terry cloth wrapped and knotted around her, and as she rose to face him, she called on the anger, the cleansing fury, that had killed her love for him ten years ago. Remember that night, she told herself. *Remember what he did, and hating will come easy.*

She spotted the gun on the floor by the cabinet. Her mind seized the opportunity, calculating her chances of getting to it.

With a knowing glance he bent down and scooped it up. "You don't mind, do you?" he said, tucking the weapon into the waistband of his slacks. "I've grown attached to it."

"Get out of here or I'll call the police!"

"That would be a mistake," he warned. "I don't think you want that kind of headline hitting the tabloids, do you? BLACK WIDOW TRIES TO KILL RENEGADE STEPSON."

"I don't give a damn about headlines. I just want you out of here."

"Then give me some answers." Waves of sable-black hair had fallen onto his forehead. He forced the tumult back, revealing the widow's peak as he raked his fingers through it. "You've come a long way, baby. I want to know how you did it. How did Jessie Flood, the kid from Trash Alley, end up inheriting a fortune? How about letting me in on that little secret, Jessie? And why are you scared of me? I'm curious about that too."

"Frightened of you?" she sneered. "Not a chance."

"Then why am I sporting a gunshot wound? And why are you so damn anxious to get me out of this house?"

"Because I don't *like* you, Luc."

"Really?" He glanced at her breasts, leaving no doubt as to the direction of his thoughts. "I wonder how you get it on with guys you do like?"

"*Get out.*"

"You know where to find me," he informed her. "If you should want me for something, *anything,* I'll be in the guest wing."

"You can't stay in this house."

"Watch me." Smiling darkly, he turned and left.

Jessie dropped into a crouch and huddled there on the floor, her shaking fingers pressed to her face. She prayed he wouldn't come back and find her this way, but it was several seconds before she could marshal the strength to do what she knew had to be done. At last, on wobbly legs, she got herself into the bedroom and picked up the telephone. She took another moment to calm herself before she punched out the numbers. The phone on the other end rang twice, and a recorded voice came on the line. She left a three-word message. "Luc is back."

CHAPTER
·· SIX ··

"GENTLEMEN." MATT SANDUSKY rose in a futile attempt to bring some order to the chaotic all-night skull session of his newspaper executives. *The San Francisco Globe*'s circulation and ad revenues had taken a nosedive in the last year and his loyal lieutenants couldn't agree on how to bring the paper out of its death spiral. Hell, the contentious SOBs couldn't even agree on the price of a cup of coffee these days.

Murray Pratt, the *Globe*'s general manager, pretended to be hurt as he pursued a point with Pete Fischer, the paper's brilliant and irascible managing editor. "Insensitive? What's that supposed to mean, Fischer? I brake for full-frontal nudity, don't I? And anyway, what's wrong with a Sunday bondage and discipline update? I'd read it."

"Hell, you'd write it!" Fischer slapped his forehead with groaning disbelief. "Did I say insensitive? Forgive me, Murray. I meant crass and venal. You'd sell your arthritic mother for ten new subscribers."

Murray snorted. *"My* mother? I'd sell her for one."

Matt cracked the conference table with his palm, drawing startled glances from around the room. "I think we're past the point of effectiveness here, don't you?" He gave himself points for diplomacy as he swept the exhausted group with his gaze. "Let's call it a morning, shall we, gentlemen?"

Fischer yanked at his tie in apparent bewilderment. "Did he call us gentlemen, Murray? I think we've been insulted."

"Get out of here, you Philistines!" Matt roared, stabbing his hand toward the conference-room door. "The party's over."

Seeming pleased to have gotten a rise out of his normally decorous boss, Pete Fischer stood, saluted and left, looking every bit as fresh as when they'd started the session the night before. Not only was the managing editor a smart-ass, Matt decided, he also had the shiny little eyes of a rodent, a species of animal Matt particularly abhorred.

Matt grabbed a glass of melted ice water and held its coolness to his aching forehead while the rest of the half dozen managers straggled out. As the new president of Warnecke Communications and publisher of the *Globe*, he was caught in the cross fire between the business and editorial sides of the paper. Unfortunately the two warring factions appeared to be locked in mortal combat.

Moments later he was in his executive bathroom, wincing at the sight of his own bloodshot eyes in the mirror. The dark circles, deep grooves of fatigue and beard stubble were frightening. "Call 911," he muttered. "I'm going to die of grunge if I don't get a shower, a shave and a change of clothes."

No one would have believed it to look at him now, but earlier this year, he'd turned up on a "ten most eligible bachelors" list. It was an annual ranking by *San Francisco*, a slick Bay Area magazine. The magazine's staff had praised him for his sartorial elegance and his Ken-doll haircut, making an especially big fuss about his clean fingernails.

It had been much simpler to cultivate a Savile Row look when Simon had been running the show, he mused. As he wearily bent to splash some water on his face, Matt heard the intercom buzz in his office. His secretary's concerned voice carried to the bathroom.

"Mr. Sandusky? I picked up the messages from your home machine as you asked. There's one from Mrs. Warnecke and it's very odd—just three words—'Luc is back.'"

Ten minutes later Matt had pulled his silver BMW 750iL out of the Warnecke parking lot and into the morning traffic on Mission Street. He hadn't even taken time to run a comb through his hair, much less shave or shower. Luc Warnecke's return to Half Moon Bay could spell disaster—especially for his own ambitions. Warnecke Communications was already unstable, and the media were constantly speculating about the *Globe*'s financial problems and the company's leadership crisis. And it was no secret to the business pages that Luc had been searching for a vulnerability in the company for years.

Matt's thought processes went into high gear as he headed for the isolated Warnecke estate south of Half Moon Bay. He had not gone so far as to keep Simon's son under surveillance in recent months, but he'd kept tabs through reliable contacts, and he was aware that Luc had made several unsuccessful attempts to buy into Warnecke Communications.

Simon had kept the majority of the company's stock specifically to guard against the possibility of a takeover by his competitors, or in later years, by his renegade son. Luc had been blocked so far, but it would be a grievous mistake to underestimate him. He'd matured into an adversary as tough as he was smart. Matt had never seen a more spectacular rise to success. It generally took a deal with the Devil to amass the fortune Luc had in just under a decade. Though he'd folded two of the newspapers in his chain in recent months, that hadn't put a dent in his momentum. In the last few years he'd branched out into radio, cable and the "niche" magazine market with enormous success. His tabloid paper, *The Zodiac*, had grown at an unprecedented rate, despite a sluggish economy.

None of that seemed to have satisfied the young Turk, however. Luc undoubtedly coveted the respect and stature an eminent newspaper like *The Globe*, with its caseful of Pulitzers and press club awards, could give him. In short, he lusted after the Warnecke birthright. The question was what else did he lust after? And how did he plan to get it?

By the time Matt arrived at Echos, he had formulated a preliminary plan of attack. The only thing that remained was to convince Jessie he was right, which would be no easy task. She could be implacable when the mood struck her. Somehow she had to be persuaded that she was no match for Luc Warnecke.

The housekeeper let him in and sent him to Jessie's bedroom suite in the mansion's east wing. He found her standing at the windows that looked out on the gardens, stiff and pale as she gazed at the bright haze that hid the dawning sun. The rich, dusty scent of roses laced with cloves and orange peel emanated from the baskets of potpourri she had stashed around the room, giving the place the ambience of a Victorian parlor. She hadn't slept. That much was obvious from the loosely wrapped black silk kimono she wore and the bluish bruises under her eyes. Several cloisonné combs were buried in her vibrant red-gold hair, as if in an attempt to lift and dignify its wildness. But the lush waves spilled from the delicate buttresses like a fountain, lending her a sensuality that was breathtaking.

Matt's gut clenched. He'd never seen her look so oddly vulnerable or in need of creature care. "Are you all right?" he asked, his voice straining.

She glanced around as if coming out of a trance and saw him standing across the room from her. Blinking slowly, she surveyed his chestnut hair, loosely knotted tie and generally unkempt appearance as if it were unfamiliar, which was no great surprise since she knew him to be meticulous. What did surprise him was the fragile crystal object she was holding in her hand.

Her collection of butterfly figurines took up much of the surface space of the dressing table, supplanting the array of cosmetics most women would have had. She wore very little makeup, though Matt had often thought some color in her cheeks would have offset her strange blue eyes, which could quickly become piercing. But what arrested him now was the way she was absently stroking the crystal wings of the butterfly she held, as if it were a worry stone. Things were worse than he'd thought. It wasn't like her to be so distracted.

"He's been here, hasn't he?"

She dipped her head, still holding the butterfly. "He's here now . . . in the guest wing."

"He's staying at Echos? God! Simon must be turning over in his grave."

"Luc is dangerous, Matt. I want him out of here."

Apparently he didn't have to convince her of that. Something already had. Matt loomed protectively as she stroked the butterfly, her eyes glittery with emotions too entangled and complex to read. Fear, though. He thought he saw fear. He wanted to take her into his arms and comfort her and the impulse surprised him. He'd never thought of her as needing comfort. She'd always been totally self-contained.

"I'll deal with him, Jessie. I'll get rid of him if I have to throw him out myself."

"No!" She looked up in alarm, then flushed deeply. "We have to convince him to leave. Otherwise there might be trouble."

"Trouble? What happened? Did he hurt you?"

"No, not in the sense that you mean. He—" She walked to the dressing table and set the butterfly down, her fingertips whitening against the crystal. "He didn't hurt me," she repeated.

Matt was left to stare at her, bewildered. He knew the history of the Warnecke-Flood debacle as well as anyone. Better, actually—Simon had enlisted Matt's help over the years, including having him track down a top criminal attorney to keep Luc's neck out of the noose during the inquest into Hank Flood's death—all on the condition that Luc leave town and never return. Hank's death was finally ruled an accident, but nobody really believed that. It was Jessie's testimony that had implicated Luc in the first place. Under cross-examination, she'd contradicted her own sister Shelby's eyewitness account of the "accident" by volunteering that Luc and Hank had been in a fistfight the night Hank died. Jessie's remarks had been damaging, especially in light of the fact that she and Luc had once been friends, but if she was motivated by anything other than the truth, she hadn't revealed it. Matt was beginning to wonder what else she hadn't revealed.

She was taking exaggerated care with the butterfly, he realized, apparently intent on returning it to the exact spot she'd taken it from.

"What if Luc decides to contest the will?" she asked.

Was *that* what had her worried? "There'd be damn little point," he assured her. "He was written out years ago."

"But couldn't he say Simon was incompetent, or—"

"Jessie, you've been watching too much television. The will is ironclad, believe me. His attorneys have assured me of that."

"There won't be any surprises? I can count on that?"

She glanced at him in the dressing table mirror, as if she didn't want to look at him directly. He'd never seen her this way. Insecure, jumpy. It wasn't anything as base as greed driving her, he was sure of that. She'd never expressed any unusual interest in the Warnecke money, except perhaps in the security it provided for her daughter. If anything, she'd seemed somewhat daunted by the size of her imminent inheritance.

"Why did Luc show up here?" he asked, gazing into the mirror in order to continue the uncanny conversation he was having with her reflection. "What does he want?"

"I don't know. Maybe he knows how irrational Simon was toward the end, maybe he knows about Mel."

"What about Mel?"

"That I have a daughter, that she's illegitimate."

The gossipy, small-town speculation about Jessie's daughter had been fueled by the fact that Jessie disappeared shortly after the inquest, the summer of her sixteenth year, and returned that winter with a redheaded infant in her arms. It might have been the typical unwanted teen pregnancy story, except that nothing about Jessie was typical. There were even rumors that Mel was not Jessie's biological child at all, but Shelby's. Matt had his own theory about Mel's parentage, as did practically everyone else, he imagined. But he'd never raised the subject with Jessie. He wouldn't have dared.

Jessie had begun to stare at herself in the mirror again, but this time it was with a slowly-dawning awareness, as if she were noticing her state of dishabille for the first time. She drew her kimono together and secured the tie, her movements slow but very deliberate. And then, with a surety Matt hadn't seen since he arrived, she scooped up her hair and rearranged the combs, levering them into the coppery wealth until it was all piled on top of her head, crownlike, except for a few wispy tendrils.

Within that period of suspended seconds, the soft glitter of fear in her eyes had been replaced by something harder. And when she looked at Matt again, the cool self-sufficiency she was known for had returned full measure. "I don't care how you do it, but I want Luc Warnecke out of my house. Today."

He nodded, the gallant knight, obedient to his queen's every whim. "Consider it done."

Luc awoke at ten to blinding brightness. Sunlight burst through the mullioned panes of the bedroom windows and shattered into a thousand dancing hot spots, at least one of which was burning a hole through the goose-down comforter and into the flesh of his ankle. He moved his leg, felt the refreshing coolness of untouched satin against his skin and smiled. He'd survived the night. No one had crept into the room and shot him in his sleep. And the superficial graze on his thigh was only a dull ache.

He checked to see that the gun was where he'd stashed it behind the armoire, then showered quickly and dressed, leaving his hair damp and the dark stubble on his jaw unshaven. He'd already sensed that Jessie had blossomed into a flaming neat freak. The bedroom's antique knicknacks were grouped according to type—enamel boxes here, wood carvings there—and even the dainty guest soaps in the bathroom had been sorted into schools of fish and piles of seashells. Thus it gave him perverse pleasure that he had nothing to wear but last night's darkly wrinkled, bloodstained slacks. His fresh clothes were still packed in the trunk of his rented car.

As he came down to breakfast, it seemed the entire household had gathered in his honor. The spacious dining room gleamed with family silver and warm, polished woods, its myriad surfaces reflecting the sunlight that poured from the garden room beyond. Lustrous candelabras decorated the mahogany sideboards, and a Georgian tea service presided over a fruitwood stand.

Jessie had posted herself in front of the crystal cabinet, and she was flanked by a tall, lean man with dark blond hair, whom Luc recognized as Matt Sandusky. The other two people were unknown to him, although he guessed the husky, wary-eyed young man on Jessie's other side to be Roger, the college student. And the dark-haired twentyish woman with the French braid looked like an assistant of some kind, or perhaps a maid.

They made an interesting picture, all four of them lined up and watching him as he entered. With some irony he realized how much they reminded him of a ready audience. Fortunately he had something planned to entertain the troops this morning. And with a rapt audience like this, it was going to be hard holding off.

"Good morning," he said, not entirely successful at hiding his amusement.

Jessie's response was a barely perceptible nod.

Her hostility might have been off-putting to most men, but he found it strangely attractive. She seemed willing to go to almost any lengths to protect herself and to achieve her ends. He understood that kind of tenacity, even admired it.

"You remember Matt Sandusky," Jessie said.

Would that he could forget. Sandusky was what he, Luc Warnecke, son of Simon, was supposed to have been—a man in control of his destiny from the moment they taught him how to tie his own shoelaces. Having started as Simon's protégé, Sandusky had made the transition to surrogate son in record time. Luc's place at the dinner table had barely been cold.

"Drop by for breakfast, Matthew?"

"Breakfast was at nine." Jessie's voice had an edge sharp enough to cut paper.

The man in control of his destiny broke in quickly, amiably. "How have you been, Luc?" Matt inquired. "It's been a long time."

So we're going to be civil, Luc thought. *Terribly* civil. "Too long, Matt. I'll have to make it a point to visit the old homestead more often. Will you be here?"

"What brings you back?" Matt asked, pointedly ignoring Luc's question.

"Why, the reading of the will, of course. Should be a party, huh? Wouldn't miss it."

The response was thunderous silence. Matt cleared his throat, and Jessie looked as if her breakfast hadn't agreed with her.

"Apparently I've missed the food," Luc said, feigning regret. "Any chance I could get a cup of coffee? And if it isn't asking too much, I'd like to get these clothes laundered." He drew the fabric of his pant leg taut. "These slacks in particular. I suppose there's nothing that can be done about the bullet hole, but I hope the blood will come out."

Sandusky looked incredulous, then faintly irritated. "How the hell did you get a bullet hole in your pants?"

"It wasn't easy," Luc assured him, glancing at Jessie.

"Gina," Jessie said quickly. "Will you please get Mr. Warnecke some coffee? And Roger, why don't you see if there's any apple cake left? Warm it up, would you?"

Luc had the satisfaction of watching people leap to serve his every need. Within seconds, the dining room had cleared except for Jessie, who was eyeing Luc uneasily, and Sandusky, who was eyeing both of them suspiciously. Apparently Jessie hadn't told Sandusky that she'd nearly shot his privates off. Luc would have liked to spill the beans, but he didn't want to give up his psychological armlock on Jessie so easily. The longer she squirmed, the better he'd like it. Sometimes justice claimed its pound of flesh in wafer-thin portions, he decided, balancing the scales one slice at a time.

"We were thinking—well, it might be best if you didn't stay here," Sandusky said.

"We?"

"Yes, Jessie and I. There's the country club. Jessie read somewhere that you play tennis. Or what about the Gull House by the shore? That's so beautiful this time of year."

He wondered where Jessie had read about him—the *Time* magazine article about his precipitous rise to fame and fortune? It pleased him that she had. He liked the thought that he was preoccupying her mind. And right now he liked the way that sexy little scar was tugging at her lip. Why the hell was he so attracted to her? It felt adolescent and hormonally induced, but he knew it was nothing so innocent.

"So where would you like to stay, my man?" Matt said, attempting joviality. "I'll be happy to drive you."

"No need. I rented a car. Besides, I'm not going anywhere."

"You can't stay here."

Jessie stepped forward, almost frightening in her quick, cold fury. God, she was glacial. But the nastier she got, the more it spurred Luc to find out what was provoking her. He was increasingly curious about how the coppery-headed urchin he remembered had metamorphosed into a well-heeled gunslinger. She'd been tough before, always that, but never ruthless.

"I doubt if I'll be playing much tennis with this flesh wound," he said. "And a hotel room, well, that's no place to recuperate. I think it's best to be with family, don't you?" He lifted an eyebrow and affected a faint smile.

He pressed on in the face of their mute outrage, making no attempt to hide his noticeable limp as he walked toward them.

"And since we *are* all part of the Warnecke family, in a manner of speaking, this seems a good time to raise a concern that's been weighing heavily on my mind."

"What the hell are you up to, Warnecke?" Matt snapped.

"This," Luc said, producing a folded note from the inside pocket of his jacket, "is what I'm up to."

He handed the note to Matt, who read the four lines silently, sucked in a breath and handed the paper to Jessie. Her reaction was far more interesting. She glanced over the message, blanched and then crushed it reflexively in her hand.

Was she alarmed? Luc wondered. *Or guilty?*

" 'Stay away from Half Moon Bay,' " Luc said, reciting the first line of the message aloud in case either of them had missed something. Hesitating, to be sure he had their undivided attention, he recited the rest of it. " 'Hank Flood's death was murder, and I have new evidence linking you to the crime. If you return, I'll give it to the police.' "

"Apparently you have a secret pal, Warnecke," Sandusky observed. "Any idea who sent it?"

"I was hoping you'd know." He glanced from Sandusky to Jessie. "Do you?"

"Do I what?" she asked defiantly.

"What are you suggesting?" Sandusky cut in. "Why in hell would Jessie send you a message like that?"

"I didn't say *she* sent it." Luc corrected him calmly. "I said she might know who did."

Luc walked over and took the crumpled note from Jessie's hand. As their fingers brushed, he felt her tremble. She was drawn tight as violin strings, he realized. If tension had been a sound, her body would have been thrumming. He wondered whether her reaction had been triggered by him or by the note. As he glanced from her white-lipped agitation to Matt Sandusky's flushed anger, Luc had the distinct feeling that his "secret pal" was right here in this room.

"I'll be fine, Matt. Really."

Jessie's hushed reassurances echoed in the marble foyer, as she walked Matt to the front door. She'd made it crystal clear that she wanted him to leave, but he didn't understand how and when the tables had been turned. He'd thought the object was to get Luc Warnecke out of the house.

"Jessie, be reasonable," he whispered, staying her hand as she reached for the door handle. "Luc's been getting threatening notes. Somebody took a shot at him! You could be in danger having him here. You're probably in danger *from* him."

"I'm the one who took a shot at him, Matt."

"You? What the hell for?" Matt's astonished words rang eerily off the walls, mingling with Jessie's efforts to shush him. "Why hasn't someone had that damn echo effect fixed?" he whispered.

She opened the door, an unmistakable invitation to leave.

"Jessie, I want to help," he said, making no attempt to hide his frustration. "But I have to know what's going on. What happened between you and Luc last night?"

"Just go, Matt, please."

"Jessie, for God's sake! Assault with a deadly weapon is a felony! What did the man do that you had to shoot him?"

She hesitated. "I was alone, it was late, and I was frightened. I thought he was an intruder— Don't push me to say anything more."

He was damned tempted to push her. His lack of sleep combined with the worries of the company had him on edge. Now he sensed that she, the lynchpin of Warnecke, would split wide open with a little pressure. It struck him as odd that she'd always epitomized grace under pressure to him. As Simon's brain tumor had made him increasingly paranoid, Jessie had become stronger, saner, counterbalancing him. It was a quality Matt greatly admired, but he actually preferred her this way. Vulnerable. However, only if he could make her vulnerable to him. Not to Luc Warnecke.

"I'll go," he said. "But only if you promise to call me if things get out of hand."

"I'll call if I need you, okay?"

It was a promise that lacked conviction, but it was all he was going to get. Angered, he went through the door she held open and jogged down the steps toward his car. He'd parked along the semicircular drive that fronted the house, and as he approached the gleaming silver BMW, he nodded to Roger Metcalf, Jessie's new caretaker.

Matt glanced over his shoulder to make sure Jessie had gone back inside before he approached the young man. Roger, working shirtless in the warming, misty spring weather, was trimming the privet hedges. "What the hell happened here last night?" Matt asked under his breath.

A meadowlark called hauntingly from the towering eucalyptus trees that lined the drive.

"I don't know." Roger wiped his brow with the back of his hand. "I got a call from the big house around eleven, and it was her. She was strange, cool, you know, like always, but I could hear something weird in her voice. She said someone had been hurt and she needed my help. When I got there, this guy was out cold on the floor. He'd been shot in the thigh, grazed a few inches below his hipbone." The kid met Matt's eyes. "Made me wonder if she was aiming for another part of his anatomy."

"Jesus—"

"Yeah, no kidding. She had me carry him to a bedroom and clean the wound, and then she swore me to secrecy."

"You didn't hear the gunshot?"

"I heard something, like a car backfiring."

"Why didn't you call me?"

Roger shrugged uneasily. "She made me promise not to tell anyone."

"Roger, for Christ's sake, why do you think I got you this job?" Matt waved off the caretaker's attempt to apologize. "Are you sure it was Jessie who shot him?"

"I didn't see her with a gun in her hand, but it had to be her. There was no one else around."

Matt exhaled and rubbed his jaw, aware of his beard stubble. He wanted badly to get back to his Telegraph Hill condo and take a shower, but he wasn't convinced Roger could handle the situation. He'd hired the college student to do some handiwork for him and then realized it might not be a bad idea to have a contact in the Warnecke household as well. He'd never counted on Roger having to do surveillance work.

"I think Jessie could be in danger," Matt said, glancing up at the house. "I'm counting on you to keep an eye on things, Roger. A sharp eye, do you understand? Don't screw up again."

CHAPTER
·· SEVEN ··

IF HALF MOON BAY had been a woman, it would have been a sea witch, haunting and seductive, a mysterious female not unlike Jessie Flood. That was how Luc had always thought of his hometown, and his impression wasn't changed in any way by his drive into town on the coastal highway that morning.

A low mist hung over the ocean, thickening into occasional patches of fluffy white fog. "Islands on a dark blue sea," Shelley had called clouds. The poet might have been describing the puffs of cotton that floated on the sea breezes today. Luc could remember crouching on the bluffs at Echos as a child and staring out to sea for hours, entranced by the mirages the fog created. Layered in misty tiers, the reflecting qualities of the fog could make ships appear several times larger than they actually were. His dream had been to stow away on one of those giant phantom vessels and slip through the mists into other worlds, sailing on endless blue oceans of sea and sky, a wind gypsy.

Unfortunately his mission today was far less quixotic. Someone was desperate to keep him out of Half Moon Bay, and he intended to find out who it was. Years ago he'd hired a private detective to investigate Hank Flood's death, as much to confirm his belief that Hank had not died accidentally as to prove that he, Luc, had not been the one who killed him.

The detective hadn't been successful in absolving Luc, but he had uncovered some information that triggered Luc's suspicions about who might have wanted Hank Flood dead and why. It had come out at the inquest that Flood had his share of enemies, as well as some highly questionable friends, but the list had been incomplete. Some very interesting names had been left off, and Luc thought he knew why. He hadn't been in a position to do anything about the information then. He was now.

The cutoff to town came up so quickly Luc almost missed it. His first stop was the library, a two-story, no-frills stone structure, as unchanging and enduring as the small town itself. Surprised by the nostalgia that swept him as he let himself out of the car, he took a moment to reacquaint himself with the rustic romance of the seaside community.

Crazy-quilt architecture abounded in the half dozen streets that comprised the town center. Zabala House, a turn-of-the-century bed and breakfast was juxtaposed with the staid towers of Our Lady of the Pillar Catholic Church and by Cunha's Country Store, a huge salmon-pink structure overlooking Kelly and Main, which had once housed the infamous Index Saloon. The bustling charm of Main Street, with its art and antiques emporiums, reminded Luc of a picturesque postcard holding back time and tide.

Even the woman who sat at the library's information desk hadn't changed. Luc couldn't recall her name, but he wasn't likely to forget her brusque manner, short-cropped gray hair and lopsided glasses. Weighed down at the bridge by black electrician's tape, they hung on the end of her nose and, fortunately for him, left her blind as a bat. He didn't want to be recognized just yet.

"Where would I find the newspapers?" he asked, reluctant to interrupt her furious attempt to focus on the computer monitor in front of her.

"Current editions are in the reading section." She waved him toward a small lounge area furnished with couches and magazine racks. "If you need something earlier, we have editions going back to the forties on microfilm."

"And where would those be?"

She pointed a weathered finger toward the back wall of the building. He needn't have worried about her recognizing him. She hadn't glanced his way once. He found the microfilm on his own, but it took some reconnaissance. He'd been an avid reader as a kid, but he'd spent very little time in this library. His health problems had kept him confined to Echos, and his father's obsession with making a Warnecke out of him had turned the estate into a prison yard.

Luc's only refuge had been the library at Echos. He'd often crept there in the middle of the night to lose himself in Arthurian legends, Homer's *Odyssey* or anything else that was magical and heroic enough to transport him out of the hell of his daily existence. His mother's death had left him nowhere to turn for nurturing, but fortunately she'd passed on her love of books to him. That legacy and the memory of her caring must have been what kept him from going insane. Or had he gone insane?

"Mister? You gonna use that machine, or what?"

Luc glanced down at a wiry-haired, freckle-faced imp of a kid who was glaring up at him as if prepared to fight for the use of the viewer. Luc had never been very comfortable around kids, but this one was so painfully homely he was cute.

"Yeah, 'fraid so," Luc said, greatly tempted to turn the machine over to the boy.

"Know what, mister?" the kid informed him, glowering at him fiercely. "You look mean as rattlesnake piss, but that don't scare me."

As the kid stalked off, Luc realized he'd been threatened, shot and, now, insulted. *Welcome home, Warnecke,* he thought ironically. *Great to have you back.* If his reception so far were any kind of an omen, he was in big trouble.

Staring at the cassette in his hand, Luc seated himself in front of the coldly impersonal machine, shoved the tape into the holder and pressed a button that whirred time backward. His stomach knotted as the first headline came up. INQUEST TO PROBE DEATH, PUBLISHER'S SON PRIME SUSPECT.

He was reading *The San Francisco Globe,* his father's own flagship newspaper. Simon had been criticized at the time for capitalizing on a family crisis, but Luc had never questioned his father's real motive. It was Simon's way of openly washing his hands of his inept son. His one last fatherly act had been to hire a top-gun attorney to advise Luc and make sure he escaped the inquest's probe unscathed. The price Luc had paid for freedom was disinheritance and banishment. It was the last time he'd ever seen his father.

Though Luc had long ago blocked the nightmare of the inquest from his mind, it was almost impossible not to relive it as he skimmed over quotes from the actual transcript. It was Jessie's sworn statements that had implicated him. If it hadn't been for her testimony, no one would have known he was at the Flood place that night, and yet she admitted to the police that she hadn't been there when the actual fight took place. In fact, the authorities hadn't been able to locate her for questioning until the next morning. Where the hell had Jessie been that night?

Shelby's testimony was troubling too. She'd changed her story after the police questioned Jessie, corroborating her sister's version of the incident. Fortunately Shelby had stuck with her statement that Hank died when he hit his head against the cast-iron stove rather than from Luc's blow. Since she was the only eyewitness, her testimony had pushed the decision toward accidental death.

Luc sat back, staring at the screen. But why had Shelby changed her original story so radically? There'd always been bad blood between the Flood sisters, which made it all the more suspicious that, where this situation was concerned, they'd found some common purpose. Frustrated, he continued his search and came across a reference to Matthew Sandusky's being questioned by the police about the incident. *Bingo,* Luc thought. This was the connection he'd been looking for. Or a part of it anyway. Sandusky had never been called to testify at the inquest, but the police must have sought him out for a reason. They'd been following up on some kind of lead, perhaps the same one Luc was.

Luc was still pondering the implications of Matt's involvement when a finger tapped his shoulder. He came out of the chair instinctively, whirling around. The nearsighted librarian gasped in horror and tried to jump back, but she couldn't. Luc had gripped her wrist.

"I'm sorry!" she cried. "Someone else wants to use the machine."

The scowling boy peeked around from behind the woman's skirt, his eyes narrowed with fearful expectations. "See! Didn't I tell you he was psycho?"

It took Luc a moment to realize what he'd done. He was at a loss to explain, so he apologized to the woman and released her, resisting the impulse to straighten her sweater and push her glasses back up on her nose. He even nodded reassuringly to the watchful kid, who immediately flipped him the bird.

"Don't I know you from somewhere?" The librarian stepped back and peered at Luc. She pulled the enfant terrible close, as if to protect the boy with her voluminous skirts.

"No, I don't think—"

"Wait a minute," she said, her eyes widening with startled recognition. "Aren't you? Oh, my, Lord, you're that Warnecke boy, aren't you? The one they said killed—"

"*Killed?*" the kid blurted. "Holy moly! Who'd he kill?"

"You could be next," Luc warned, silencing the little fiend with a dark look. Heads had begun to turn their way, and the hushed room had begun to buzz.

"Whatever brought you here?" the woman asked.

"To Half Moon Bay?"

"To the library." The emphasis she put on the last word made it sound as if she meant *her* library and that he might even be violating the sanctity of such a place.

"Nostalgia," Luc admitted, smiling darkly. "I'm planning a little family reunion." He indicated the microfilm machine, determined to bring the awkward conversation to a quick close. "I'm done with it, thanks."

"A family reunion?" She jabbed her glasses up on her nose, scrutinizing both him and the scanner. "This is an odd place to be planning something like that. Did you find what you were looking for?"

"I did," Luc assured her. "And then some."

"No fair, Gina! You said any story I wanted! I asked for the one about the girl who prayed for breasts."

"*Ma che, bambina! Impossible?*" Gina Morelli, the nanny who'd been hired during Simon's illness to help out with Jessie's nine-year-old daughter, rolled her eyes at her convalescing charge, giving Melissa Warnecke the Italian version of "No way, José." "So what's wrong with *Little Red Riding Hood?*"

"What's wrong? It stinks, that's what's wrong." Mel seemed barely able to contain her monumental disdain as she flopped backward into the mound of pillows on the window seat where she'd been resting.

"*Black Beauty*?" Gina suggested, grasping at straws.

"A deal's a deal," Mel came back, her voice still soft and raspy with the residue of last night's asthma attack.

Gina felt as if she'd just made a bargain with one of the Devil's budding handmaidens. She had strict orders from Jessie to keep Mel occupied in her room today, but the child had spent so much time confined because of her chronic asthma that it was increasingly difficult to find things for her to do. Mel had been wheedling and coaxing all morning to go outside. In desperation Gina had finally promised to entertain her with any story she wanted. She should have known the cheeky little bugger would pick something X-rated.

"You know the story," Mel prompted. "The one where the Italian girl takes off her clothes, goes out on the roof and talks to the moon."

Gina nodded wearily. "I know the story." She'd told Mel the fable in a moment of weakness. Impetuous as always, Mel had decided one day that she wanted to learn Italian, and she'd coaxed Gina into telling her about Napoli, Gina's hometown in southern Italy. Homesick, Gina had regaled her with her mama's favorite folktales, and somehow that one slipped out.

Mel rolled to her side and propped a fist under her chin, her stunning turquoise eyes wide and guilelessly fixed on Gina. "What was it the girl said to the moon? I forgot."

Gina sighed in defeat and rose from the table where she'd been working on a jigsaw puzzle of a sun-drenched Italian vineyard. She walked to the window seat and hugged her young charge, saddened that Mel had to lead so restricted a life. She sympathized wholeheartedly with the child's longing to go outside. Like most nine-year-old girls, Mel was a tomboy at heart, with the pluck of a pint-size adventuress, which made it especially hard for Gina to watch her languish. Gina had often secretly thought that Jessie was overprotective—*ansiosa,* a worrier, like Gina's own mother—though she'd kept that thought to herself.

"All right, Mel," she said, settling back into the opposite corner of the window seat. "I'll tell you the story. But only if you promise not to rat on me, okay? This is just between us, *capisce*?"

Mel's eyes sparkled like gems. "*Sì, sì, capisce.*"

"Okay," Gina said, gazing out the window at the budding rose gardens, Mel's mother's pride and joy. "There was a young girl from Naples named Sophia, and she was madly in love with a beautiful young boy named Enrico, also from Naples. But he thought of her as a child, and she was desperate to show him she was a woman. So she took off all her clothes one night and went out onto the balcony of her parent's apartment. There, standing naked in the moonlight, she held her arms up to the full moon."

"And said . . . ," Mel prompted.

" '*Santa Luna, Santa Stella, fammi crescere questa mammella.*' "

"Right," Mel whispered reverently. "*Santa Luna, Santa Stella,* holy moon, holy star—What's the rest?"

"Holy moon, holy star, make this breast grow for me."

"Ah, *splendido,*" Mel said enthusiastically. "But that wasn't all, right? She had to touch her breast and say it eight more times, right?"

"Yes, nine times in all, without a single mistake. And she was so nervous about getting caught that it took her all night to get the prayer right—and her father, well, he found her. He made her confess—first to him and then to the priest—and they never let her see Enrico again."

"*Che tristezza!*" Mel sighed. "That's so sad. But she grew breasts, right? Bazooms as big as the moon?"

"Well, I don't know how big they were—"

Mel began to tug at her sweater sleeve.

"What are you doing?" Gina asked.

"Getting undressed."

"*E pazzola?* Are you crazy? Why?"

"So I can pray to the moon, silly. How am I ever going to get any breasts if I don't get naked and say the prayer?"

Gina tapped the windowpane with her knuckles, pointing out the obvious. "It's still morning, Mel. The moon won't be out for hours. Besides, you'll get breasts when you get them, *bambina.* No matter what you do."

Mel glanced out at the drizzly sky and sagged back to the pillows, looking so disconsolate that Gina felt the need to cheer her up. "You tell me a story now, okay?" Gina coaxed, tucking a plaid flannel throw around Mel's legs and feet. "The one about the half moon?"

" 'The Legend of the Half Moon'?" Mel whispered, her eyes widening. "You know I can't tell that story, Gina! Mom wouldn't like it."

"But your mom, she isn't here." Gina's voice was low and conspiratorial. "And we've already got one secret."

"Gee, I don't know . . ."

As Mel continued voicing her reluctance, Gina noticed Luc Warnecke's rental Alpha Romeo pulling into a driveway alongside the house. Though she was intensely curious about the forbidden legend, her attention was drawn away from Mel's story as she watched Luc let himself out of the chrome-red sports car. He arose from the low-slung chassis and made his way toward the house, a compelling figure with his dark hair spilling onto his forehead and his slate-gray trench coat belling behind him. The coat had a caped collar, which gave it the look of a flowing cloak.

She'd been aware of something both alluring and sinister about Luc the first time she met him. His darkly lashed eyes and moody, kissable mouth had forced her mind immediately to thoughts of sex. Dark and groping backseat-of-the-car sex, if she was being truthful. He was the kind of man her Italian mama had warned her about, a man women instinctively feared, yet were drawn to. But today there was something else about him that compelled her, a stormy intensity that signaled he had some mission in mind.

She attributed the catch in his gait to the gunshot wound, but she remembered hearing that he'd had a mysterious accident in childhood. Luc Warnecke was something of a legend around Echos and perhaps even in Half Moon Bay. Jessie had never spoken of him, and neither had Simon, the Warnecke patriarch, but Sarah, an aging housekeeper who'd worked at Echos up until a few months ago, when her health failed, had known Luc before he was exiled and had whispered of him in guarded terms.

Gina had only picked up bits and pieces of the family's tangled history, but she'd heard enough to intrigue her. Plus she'd been given explicit orders by Jessie to keep Mel out of sight until Luc was off the premises. Jessie hadn't explained her reasons, but Gina had formed her own conclusions, and she was more than curious to know if she was right.

She heard the front door slam, then listened quietly for a moment as the sound of Luc's footsteps grew louder, almost as if he'd entered the children's wing and were coming down the hallway toward Mel's room. *Gràzie a dìo!*

"Mel, you stay here," Gina said, springing up from the window seat. "I have to go out for a moment."

"What's wrong?" Mel asked.

"I think someone's coming." Gina rushed toward the door, hesitating just long enough for a quick look in Mel's vanity mirror. She smoothed back her dark hair, tucking stray wisps into her thick braid, then thrust the tail of her soft apricot polo shirt back into her jeans. "I have to go see."

"Ah, shit—I mean spit," Mel groused. "Just when I was getting to the good part."

"Mel! Where do you hear such language?"

Mel grinned, delighted. "How do you say 'shit' in Italian? Wouldn't that be great? I could swear, and no one would know it."

"Me, I'd know it." Gina arched a stern eyebrow. "Stay here," she warned. "Right here, *capisce?*"

Gina let herself out of the door and hurried down the hall. A gasp slipped out of her as she rounded the corner and saw Luc heading straight for her. She stopped short, her body vibrating with checked momentum. *What had brought him to this part of the house?* she wondered.

"Are you looking for someone?" she asked.

"You'll do."

"I will?" She was reluctantly aware of the sensuality simmering in his expression. *Insolènte,* they called it in her country, a trait guaranteed to excite feminine curiosity. She found herself wondering what it would be like to be the woman his dark gaze brushed over appraisingly, the woman who provoked his slow, moody smile. And what was worse, she could quite easily imagine him turning all that sensuality on her—pressing her to the wall and sliding his hands up her skirt—if she'd been wearing a skirt, which she wasn't, *thank God.*

"What is it you do here?" he asked.

Her heart was pounding as if he'd suggested something unspeakable. "I . . . help Jessie."

"Help her with what?"

"Whatever she needs, errands, phone calls, correspondence." None of it was true. Gina's duties consisted of some light housekeeping and tending to Mel.

"How about this correspondence?" He drew a folded note from inside his trench coat and handed it to her. "Ever seen it?"

Gina read the threat with growing alarm. The Hank Flood incident had occurred well before her time with the Warneckes, but she'd heard the gossip. "I've never seen it" was all she could manage as she handed the note back to him.

"You're sure?"

His searching gaze seemed to imply that she was holding something back. Did he think Jessie had sent him the note? And that she, Gina, was somehow involved?

A faint, staccato noise came from down the hall behind them. Gina froze, recognizing it as a series of sneezes.

"What was that?" he asked.

"Nothing," she insisted quickly. "I must have left the television on."

"Are there any children in this house?"

A pink flush of heat had been steadily creeping up her throat. Now it deepened to scarlet. "Why do you ask?"

"Why don't you answer?" He plucked the note from her fingers and thrust it back into his coat pocket. The darkness that flared through his features made her fear that he might decide to investigate the sounds he'd heard.

"Where's Jessie?" he asked.

"She's gone out." That wasn't quite true either, but Gina said no more. Jessie had gone out for a walk after breakfast, but Gina was sure she hadn't left the grounds. She was also virtually certain she couldn't pull off a more elaborate lie with Luc Warnecke. His eyes seemed to bore right through her. In the five years since she'd come to this country first as an exchange student, then as an au pair, she'd found American men to be charming, and for the most part, more deferential to women than their European counterparts. But this one was a demon.

Luc glanced down the hallway past Gina, staring at the corridor that led to Mel's room. Gina tried desperately to think of a way to distract him. What if Mel should wander out? How would she ever explain that?

To Gina's great relief, his gaze flicked back to her.

"Tell Jessie I'm looking for her," he said. With a barely perceptible nod, he turned and disappeared down the hall, leaving her to stare after him. The drag in his stride was barely noticeable.

As she returned to Mel's room, Gina felt as if she'd had a brush with certain disaster. Relief had just begun to ease the tension in her breathing when she opened the door. But she knew the moment she entered that something was wrong. The window seat was empty. "Mel?" A quick visual search of the room told her the child was gone.

CHAPTER
·· EIGHT ··

IT WAS THE first moment of serenity she'd had since Luc arrived. Surrounded by roses and lilacs, by frilly yellow daffodils and pale wisteria drooping from the arbors, Jessie felt soothed as if by a gentle, unseen hand. This was her sunken garden, her secret garden. Her hands gloveless, she worked carefully, plucking a curled leaf here, a wilted bloom there, from the delicate butter-cream lace petals of the new tea roses she'd planted that winter. Moistened by cool sea breezes, the budding flowers virtually dripped with intoxicating sweetness.

Her stolen freedom was far from perfect. She was worried about her daughter, though she had seemed fine that morning. Mel was hypersensitive to her surroundings, a small antenna for trouble. Jessie was afraid Mel would notice her mother's agitation and that the child's asthma attacks would be triggered.

There were other obligations Jessie had been neglecting too. Certain duties came with being the widow of a very rich man, the most pressing of which was Simon's company, Warnecke Communications. Simon had wanted her to be involved, and she had shared his belief that newspapers could be an important force for change in a community. His will would almost certainly assure her of controlling interest in the company and a directorship on the board. She needed to prepare herself for that responsibility, to formalize her ideas on how the newspapers could be revitalized. Even though Matt would be running the company with her blessings, she wanted to have a voice.

A sound caught her attention as she knelt and picked up her clippers. The faint, bleating cry rose from the depths of the ravine. Instantly her serenity vanished. The clippers slipped from her hand and clattered noisily against a metal pail filled with gardening tools. At the same time that her mind told her it was a child's voice, she knew it was Mel. And then another sound, an animal's snarl, pierced her as sharply as the thorns of the roses she was pruning.

Frozen in a crouch, she was unable to move for an instant. Since the day she first found her daughter on the floor, unconscious from lack of oxygen she had realized that asthma could be fatal. The experience had left her with a fear of losing Mel so great it had temporarily paralyzed her. It still did today.

Another snarl galvanized her. This wasn't an asthma attack. Somehow Mel must have crossed paths with a wild dog or a coyote. Maybe more than one. Gut instinct brought Jessie to her feet. Simon had a caseful of guns in his study, but there wasn't time. She picked up the garden shears and ran.

Please, God, don't let anything happen to her.

The ravine was beyond the gardens, less than three hundred feet away, but the panic surging in Jessie's heart told her she would never get there, never be able to save Mel from this unseen threat, whatever it was. Her feet hit the ground thuddingly hard, each impact rattling her senses.

As she neared the edge of the gorge and scanned the area, she realized the frantic cries were coming from the bottom of Devil's Drop, a clifflike precipice a hundred feet south of where she stood. Had Mel fallen? Jessie stumbled down the side, seizing onto scrub brush to keep from falling herself. The shear's handles struck her thigh as she lurched from one foothold to another in the loose rocks and shale. Pungent smells of damp earth and rotting leaves rose from the ground that gave way under her feet. She couldn't see Mel, but she'd already envisioned her child surrounded by snarling coyotes.

No, please. Don't take her from me.

"Mel! Where are you?"

There was no answer, but the strange, gasping cries grew louder as Jessie neared the bottom. They seemed to be coming from beyond a rocky abutment where the ravine jackknifed toward the ocean. It took Jessie several moments to slog her way down, and when she finally reached level ground, her calf muscles were trembling so violently she had to hesitate.

She called out Mel's name and got a raspy, indistinguishable reply this time. The sound struck at her heart and sent her stumbling toward the abutment. When she rounded the buff, she saw the little girl crouched down.

"Mel? Are you all right?" She rushed to the child, thinking she must be trapped in some way.

"The coyote, it's hurt," Mel cried in despair. Her hands and face filthy, she flung herself at Jessie. Jessie saw immediately why the child was so distraught. Her relief at finding Mel safe was torn away by a sharp gasp. A full-grown coyote was pinned to the ground beneath the mountain of earth. Coyote packs were not uncommon in the foothills, but it was usually hunger that brought them this close to civilization.

"Can we save it?" Mel asked.

Jessie hugged the child close, sick with dread. It was more than the animal's fate that frightened her. The anguish in Mel's voice told her that her daughter had picked up Jessie's own fatal compassion for anything wounded. "Of course we're going to save it," Jessie promised.

The coyote's whine was piercingly sharp. The animal scraped wildly at the ground with its front paws, snarling and trying to escape as Jessie approached. It was clearly terrified, but its fight to get free quickly proved exhausting, and it dropped to the ground, panting and wild-eyed. She edged forward cautiously, trying not to excite the animal any further. By the time she was close enough to move the debris, the coyote barely had enough strength left to whimper.

Please let me be able to save it, she thought, beseeching any benevolent higher force that might be listening. Let me do this one thing, if only for Mel's sake. Even if I'm not worthy, surely the animal is, surely the child is.

"Stay back," she said, waving Mel away as she noticed the child creeping closer. The clippers became a digging tool as she worked at the rock and shale, flinging clumps away. The granite cut at her hands, but she kept at it, shoveling until she saw several larger rocks were pinning the animal down. She would have to roll them away. She knelt down and positioned her shoulder against the largest boulder, levering one foot against a shelf of hard-packed clay behind her.

"Why can't I help?" Mel asked.

The child's voice implored her, but Jessie was concentrating hard as she struggled to dislodge the rock. It was much heavier than she'd expected, but it was tilted at a sharp angle. If she could budge it even an inch, she might be able to use the rock's own inertia to roll it off.

She dug in deeper, heaving herself against the boulder repeatedly, her knee grinding against the sharp stones embedded in the ground. The battering her shoulder took was excruciating. Every muscle felt bruised, but finally, seemingly under the force of her will, the rock began to give.

She heaved again, gasping triumphantly as the boulder rolled free. It took her a moment to gather her forces and stagger to her feet. She was shaking with fatigue and relief, her eyes welling with tears. But as she looked down at the coyote, she felt the blood drain from her face.

"Stay back, Mel!" she cried, moving to block the child's view. She didn't want her to see the animal's condition. Jessie could hardly bear to look at it herself. The hindquarters were hopelessly crushed, beyond anything that surgery could ever repair. It was a miracle the coyote had survived this long. Numb with despair, Jessie tried to think what could be done, but even as her mind was racing over options, she knew there was only one. "Go home, Mel."

"What?"

"Go back to the house." Jessie's voice was raw with regret and resignation as she turned to Mel. Her promise to the child could not be kept, and there were no words to soothe away the fear and confusion she saw etched in Mel's upturned face.

Mel lifted her hand as if she could somehow forestall her mother's will. "But why?" she asked urgently. "The coyote isn't free yet. If you're tired, I'll help you."

"Mel—"

Her turquoise eyes sparkled with tears. "No, Mom, please."

Jessie's arm sliced through the air as she pointed up the ravine in the direction of the house. Somehow she found the strength to glare fiercely at her daughter. "Do as I say, dammit! Go!"

Mel turned slowly, her face crumbling with childish grief. Jessie's heart broke as she watched her daughter leave. If only she could tell her why she was sending her away. It seemed cruel not to, but the animal's plight was desperate, and explaining what had to be done would have robbed Jessie of whatever scarce reserves of courage she had left. If Mel had broken down, Jessie might have broken down too, and that would have drained her of purpose. She had to act now, quickly, or she wouldn't be able to act at all.

Her only thought was to put the animal out of its misery, but when she turned back to look at it, her whole body began to quake. The coyote stared up at her, a soft whine in its breathing.

The suffering in its eyes made her think of another time, another injury that had taken place in this ravine. It made her think of a helpless young boy and the suffering in his eyes. Her heart had split wide open that day. She'd been transfigured with love, with compassion. Her instincts had been to preserve life, to save another human being at any cost.

How could she possibly destroy this animal?

She glanced at the clippers and shuddered. No, that was unthinkable. There must be a humane way . . . As the animal gazed up at her, so beautiful and so still, she breathed in sharply.

"You know that I'm trying to help don't you—"

Her voice broke, but in that split-second where life meets death, where hope and despair are indistinguishable, she felt the ancient bond she had with this animal and with all living things. She felt the animal's helplessness, its dumb trust and resignation. And she felt her heart open up with the sweetest, saddest love of all. An act of mercy was a strange and agonizing thing, she realized. It poured fire on the wound in order to cleanse it. It transfigured whoever it touched. Once that act had demanded that she save a life; now it demanded that she take one.

Please, God, she thought, help me.

She looked around for a heavy rock or other potential weapon, but the thought was unbearable. When she turned back to the coyote, she saw its eyes were closed. She stumbled over scrub brush to get to the animal. As she knelt to touch the silk of its muzzle, she crumpled to the ground, her head bent. Her prayer had been answered. The coyote was gone.

A light mist hung in the air, giving the estate grounds the dewy ambience of a secluded garden as Luc walked through them. The sweetness of wild lilacs and climbing roses about to burst into bloom was almost overpowering. His destination was the ravine, and he'd expected to be besieged by demons when he revisited that part of his past. But somehow the flowers and fragrant mists seemed to soften the harsh memories, overlaying them with the bittersweet patina of a dream.

He had heard the snarls of an animal earlier and wondered if there was a pack of wild dogs in the area. Now, as he approached the silent canyon, he picked up a raspy noise. The faint, silvery rhythm made him think of eucalyptus leaves scraping against each other in the wind. But there was an urgency in the sound that spurred him to walk faster, and when he reached the edge of the gorge, he saw a child collapsed on the incline below him. She was doubled over and gasping for breath, as if she'd been trying to climb the side and couldn't make it.

"Hang on," he called to her, starting down the slope.

She looked up as he reached her, her thin, dirt-smeared cheeks sucked in with the effort to breathe. Her turquoise eyes, so startlingly bright, were reminiscent of another woman's. But he barely had time to register that fact as he scooped her up in his arms and started up the face of the hill. The muscles of his injured leg strained painfully under the added weight. The grade was steep, but his only thought was to get her to level ground where she could feel stable and safe. He'd had his own bouts with respiratory problems as a child, and he knew firsthand the suffocating panic of not being able to breathe. Dealing with the fear was half the battle.

She was a frail little thing, mostly knees and elbows inside the blue jeans and gray sweatshirt she wore, but she had a grip of steel. Her hands were entangled in the denim fabric of his jacket, clinging frantically. He talked to her gently and hugged her close to the warmth of his body as he climbed. Her choked gasps had eased a little by the time he reached the top, indicating that the worst of the crisis had passed. He'd intended to leave her settled on the ground until she'd stabilized completely, but the grass was still damp, so he continued walking toward the house, cradling her in his arms.

It occurred to him that for a man who had very little use for children, he'd spent a great deal of his day in perilous contact with them. Actually, it wasn't so much children that disturbed him as the helplessness of childhood. Kids were hearts waiting to be broken, he'd decided a long time ago. All that hope in their eyes, all those bright, naked yearnings. It was all there in their faces, as ungovernable as sunlight. They couldn't hide it. And he couldn't see it without thinking about the pain they were going to go through when some trusted adult shattered their hopes.

He felt another tug at his sleeve and realized his trembling cargo was trying to tell him something.

"S-she . . . let it . . . die."

"Let what?" He lifted her closer and was surprised to see that her smudged face was wet with tears. He hadn't realized she'd been crying until now. "What happened?" he asked.

She struggled to tell him, but he couldn't catch much of what she said except that an animal had been badly hurt, and someone else had been involved. She was clearly distraught. A faint blue vein pulsed in her temple, and the tremors that racked her thin frame were as much emotional as they were physical. Another wounded heart, he realized, saddened.

She shook with what must have been a sob and curled into him. Aware of the rising ache in his throat, he absorbed her shudders until she quieted. "It hurts," he said, perhaps as much to himself to her. "I know it hurts."

He gathered her up, holding her even more tightly as a strange, impassioned impulse overtook him. He knew there was no way to protect her from the pain that life had in store for her. If she were lucky, she would be stronger for what she had to go through, but if there had been some way to safeguard her, any way at all, he would have done it.

"I'm going to take you inside," he told her, indicating the big house with a nod of his head. "When you're feeling better, we'll find out where you live and contact your parents."

"I live here," she said.

"Here? At Echos?" He gazed at her searchingly. "What's your name?"

"*Melissa!*"

It wasn't the child who'd spoken. Someone had screamed the name from behind them. Luc turned and saw Jessie plunging up the side of the ravine. She had a pair of garden shears clutched in her hand, and her eyes burned with a wildness that was pure animal fear as she sprinted toward them.

"What are you doing with her?" she cried.

Luc steeled himself as if to ward off a demon. The child in his arms emitted a plaintive sound and burrowed her face into the denim material of his jacket. He understood her reaction completely. Jessie looked like a crazy woman, her red hair flying.

"Put her *down*," Jessie insisted, her breath coming in quick, harsh pants as she reached them. She glared at him with a ferocity he knew could be deadly, especially since she had a sharp object in her hand.

The child clung to Luc as if she were afraid he might actually abandon her to this harridan. Luc sheltered her protectively, although he knew she wasn't in any danger. Jessie was furious with him, not the child. That much was clear. Intuition told him that he'd stepped into the middle of a family crisis. He was the interloper, and if the circumstances had been different, he might have gracefully bowed out.

"*I want you to put her down.*"

"She's having trouble breathing," he pointed out evenly. "I found her trying to get up the side of the ravine, and I'm taking her to the house."

Jessie thrust out her arms. "I'll take her."

Luc was about to reject that option when he felt the little girl tugging on his jacket sleeve. "She's my m-mother," Melissa said, stumbling over the words. The tip of her nose was red, and her chin trembled, collapsing as she fought back tears.

Jessie's child? Luc felt his chest tighten oddly, but he couldn't have defined what he was feeling at that moment any more than to say it was profound surprise. "Well then," he said, "if she's your mother, I guess you ought to go with her."

She ducked her head into his shoulder, muffling a sob. "No! I hate her. *She* let the coyote die."

"Mel, there was nothing I could do," Jessie started. Her voice broke, and her eyes swam with anguish as she stared at the child's huddled form. "The animal was badly hurt," she tried to explain. "It couldn't be saved. Please, Mel—"

Luc had begun to understand what must have happened and why they were both so shaken. The snarls he'd heard earlier had been from an injured animal. Jessie's obvious torment stirred his sympathy. She seemed to be suffering as much as the child, and yet when she glanced up and saw Luc studying her, the pain vanished from her expression, swiftly replaced by hostility. Clearly she didn't want anything from him, even sympathy.

"Give her to me," she said stiffly.

Luc was reluctant. He had no right to deny a mother her child, but he felt as if he were abandoning Mel in some way. Still, he had very little choice. He was about to hand her over when the nanny burst out of the house and ran toward them.

"Melissa!" she cried. "I've been searching for you everywhere!" Gina rushed up to them, her arms outstretched.

Luc now had two women ready—no, demanding—to unburden him. But Mel was still clutching at his sleeve, and he realized with some surprise that he wasn't anxious to give her up to either one of them. He rather liked the feel of this clinging little thing snuggled into the contours of his arms. She elicited a protective response he'd felt so rarely in his life it seemed like an entirely new feeling to him. The sad quiver of her lashes over her serious gaze and the red tomboy curls tucked into her cap spoke to his silent heart in a way that nothing else had in a very long time.

But Gina wasn't to be denied. When Luc didn't offer the child, the nanny came forward and scooped Mel out of his clutches with motherly deliberation.

"*Gràzie a dìo,*" Gina said, clucking over her young charge. "Thank God you're all right, Mel. You should not have snuck away like that."

"Take her into the house, Gina." Jessie's tone was stern and emphatic.

Gina flushed, immediately apologetic. "I was only gone from her room a moment."

"We'll talk about it later." Jessie gave her a dismissive nod, in no way mollified, it seemed. "For now would you please see that she gets a warm bath, some clean clothes, and make her a cup of savory tea."

"Savory?" Mel roused herself a little, just enough to voice a complaint. "That stuff is disgusting. It tastes like dirty socks."

"It's good for you," Jessie insisted as Gina swung around and carted the unhappy child off. "Drink every drop!"

Jessie continued to stare at the house even after Gina and Mel had gone inside, giving Luc the distinct feeling she was refusing to look at him. The silence that fell between them was charged with his unvoiced questions and her rigid profile.

"Whose child is she?" he asked after a space of moments.

"Mine," Jessie said emphatically.

"Yours? How interesting . . . An immaculate conception?"

Jessie shrugged. "If you like."

"I don't. Who's the father?"

"Simon," she said swiftly, defiantly. "Mel is my daughter by Simon."

Luc found that prospect ludicrous. "How old is the child? Six? Seven? You and my father weren't even married two years."

"Children *are* conceived out of wedlock."

Luc plowed a hand through his dark hair, holding its weight off his forehead as he stared at her. "Let me get this straight. You had an affair with Simon, bore his child and then married him several years later? Sorry, it doesn't wash."

"Think what you like." Jessie flared at him. "Melissa is the reason I married your father. Who else's child could she be?"

The scar that pulled at her upper lip was white against the pale heat of her skin. It was a flaw that kept her from being beautiful, perhaps even from being pretty. But at the same time, it was sensual and fabulous. It set her apart in a way that even her flaming red hair couldn't. Mel shared some of Jessie's more spectacular traits, the red hair being one. But at the same time the child brought to mind another likeness that was even more striking.

Who else's child could she be?

"Mine . . ." Luc was thinking aloud, remembering the turquoise eyes, the sharp cheekbones and the angular face. "Mine and Shelby's. Your sister thought she was pregnant when I left."

Jessie flinched as if he'd struck her. She knew he'd wanted to marry Shelby, but Shelby had rejected his proposal when she learned he'd been disinherited and banished from Half Moon Bay by his father. She'd refused even to see Luc.

"Shelby had an abortion," she told him coldly.

Watching his head come up, Jessie had a moment of fleeting triumph. She had struck back, but her satisfaction at having hurt him didn't compare with the sudden torment of wondering if he were still in love with her older sister.

"Where is she now?" he asked.

She assumed he meant Shelby. *Of course he meant Shelby.* "We don't keep in touch," Jessie retorted acidly. "The last I knew she was in New York, trying to break into the fashion industry. Knowing my sister, she's probably running a modeling agency by now. Either that or she's found herself a benefactor, someone wealthy enough to finance her dreams of glory."

"I guess you'd know about that, wouldn't you? Benefactors? Which dream of yours is Simon's money going to finance? As I remember you wanted to be an intrepid explorer, didn't you, the female Sir Richard Burton? You wanted to travel the globe and maybe open an animal preserve somewhere?"

Jessie was stung. Those were silly, secret wishes she'd confided when they were children. It shouldn't have disturbed her so much that he'd thrown them in her face, but it did. She felt foolish and exposed, as if he'd broken faith in some unforgivable way. That part of their past was still precious to her in a way that he'd just proved he could never understand. She'd kept it separate and inviolate by not allowing him into any part of those memories. This man wasn't the young boy she'd befriended. *He was not that sad, wild, frightened boy.* Her mind had blocked that possibility.

"You'll never guess where I spent the morning." His significant pause goaded her into a response.

"Where?"

"The library, going over old newspaper accounts of the inquest. Interesting reading. If it hadn't been for your testimony, I might never have been dragged into it. But I guess you already know that, don't you, Jessie? Shelby claimed Hank came home from a barroom scuffle in an alcoholic stupor that night, that he tripped and hit his head on the Ben Franklin stove. Everyone knew Hank was a drunk, and they seemed more than ready to believe her until you told the police I was there, that Hank and I fought."

"Shelby was willing to lie to protect you." Jessie spoke quickly but firmly. "I wasn't."

"Ah . . . so it was the truth you were after. Always the noble quest where our Jessie's concerned. Did it occur to you in your zeal that I could have ended up behind bars for a very long time? Shelby too, for that matter?"

Wind sifted in the trees that bordered the ravine. The sun broke through the haze briefly, sending a shaft of light into the gardens where they stood. Pale and golden, it struck the metal blades of the shears. As she glanced down her heart began to pound. *You should have killed me, Jessie. You're going to wish you had before I'm through.* His words, his very words. Their stark promise of disaster was even more real to her now than on the night he'd said them.

"Shelby disappeared after the inquest," Luc went on, seemingly unaware of Jessie's preoccupation. "And then Simon had me run out of town on a rail. I never got a chance to talk to your sister about that night and I never really knew if she was pregnant. I always wanted to get her version."

"*Don't,*" Jessie said. If she had ever doubted—or wanted to doubt—that this man was her enemy, she couldn't any longer. He'd already begun an investigation, and he was going to probe and prod until he'd uncovered everything—all of it, the snake pit of secrets that one violent, endless night had spawned. "Leave it alone," she warned harshly. "You have no idea what you're getting into, Luc. If you persist in this, you'll only hurt us all."

"Hurt us *all*? What do you mean?"

She had said too much. With a furious turn away, she walked to the house.

Luc watched her, fascinated as she strode off. If Jessie Flood still harbored any jealousy toward her older sister, she needn't have. Shelby, with her turquoise eyes and her seductive smiles, had been plenty of challenge for him as a teenager, but this woman . . .

She was a warrior who would do almost anything to safe-guard her own. He'd never run into such raw, nerveless courage. It almost made him forgive her for shooting him. She was also clearly desperate to protect something, and he intended to find out what. He was going to pry open the locked door on Jessie Flood's secret life, whatever the hell it was. He'd already started by reopening the Hank Flood situation to his own personal investigation. It was all part of a piece, he realized, a Gordian knot waiting for him to find the right string to pull.

He felt the stirrings of sexual heat as he watched her walk to the house, as coldly ferocious as any jealous goddess, a thunderbolt in her grasp. He'd been obsessed with regaining possession of his father's holdings, the empire that should have been his birthright, for most of his adult life. But he was starting to wonder if there wasn't something he wanted even more.

CHAPTER
·· NINE ··

NEW YORK

THE MANHATTAN RESTAURANT'S lighting was low, indirect and suggestive of furtive romantic liaisons in shadowed corners. The menu was continental and the decor arty, yet severe. The furnishings and china were black on black, the linens creamy white and the cutlery burnished gold. An elegant, single-stalked white lily graced each table, but the room's other accents, though sparingly placed, set the tone. They were antique brass and speakeasy red with 1920s sex and swank evident in every art deco lithograph and Tiffany lampshade.

A sleek brunette sat alone at a table in a narrow alcove off the main dining room. She was playing with a crystal flute of foaming champagne, fingering the glassware's smooth phallic lines as if it were an adult toy, and generally looking as if she might want to have unlawful carnal knowledge of it if something better didn't come along.

She could have been a high-fashion model in her spiky black heels, miniskirt and men's tuxedo jacket. Three strands of choker pearls that looked real adorned her slender neck, and a red rosebud was pinned to her lapel. She was a nineties Jezebel with a touch of class and just enough chilly disdain to make men salivate. And no one knew that better than she did. Show her the man alive who didn't love a sassy, sexy bitch of a woman, and she would show you a man whose testosterone wasn't pumping any better than a west Texas oil well.

She glanced up every now and again, eyeing the fiftyish gentleman seated at a table facing her from the opposite side of the alcove. At the moment he was preoccupied with loading caviar onto a toast point, an activity which called *his* hormone count into question, especially since she'd been intent on making eye contact with him since he'd arrived. She'd flirted openly whenever he'd looked her way, but he'd barely seemed to notice her slow, tantalizing smiles, bouncing foot and stroking fingers. Some men didn't respond to subtlety, she reminded herself. Apparently it was time to rock his world.

At the far end of the alcove a young couple sat at a corner table, completely engrossed in each other. They were the only other diners in the area. The brunette considered her options. Dropping a hanky was too dainty, and though she would have loved the sheer outrageousness of it, flashing him was too risky in such a public place. She needed a showstopper, but she didn't intend to get tossed out of the restaurant for indecent exposure, not after all the planning that had gone into this scheme to further her languishing career.

It hit her then, the perfect ploy. Was there a man alive who could resist a woman on her knees?

Tugging on her dangly jet earring, the brunette picked up her purse and rose as if to go to the ladies' room. As she strolled past the oblivious gentleman, she gave her shoulder-length hair a quick toss and her earring dropped to the floor next to the white-fringed cloth that covered his table. Without a word, she knelt to fetch it, glanced around to see if anyone was watching and then slipped underneath the floor-length tablecloth.

With a silent giggle of delight, she positioned herself in the V of his legs and drew a seamstresses's gadget from her jacket pocket. His wide-braced thighs and expensively tailored slacks all but whispered "Come to Daddy, baby."

Douglas Asterbaum, president and CEO of one of Wall Street's largest brokerage houses, had just dribbled a golden spoonful of glistening black Beluga onto a wafer-thin triangle of toast. He was about to top the caviar with a dab of sour cream, some minced onion, and then pop the luscious morsel neatly into his open mouth, when he realized something was amiss. His jaw went slack.

Fish eggs hung in the air as his attention was swept to another part of his anatomy. The silk of his trousers rustled against his legs as if a breeze had crept under the table and were swirling about down there. It was quite a remarkable sensation, almost as if something were slithering up the inside of his slacks and inching straight toward his—

A startled look crossed his long, craggy, patrician face, and in the next flurry of seconds his eyes grew wider, taking on a glazed wonder as the rustling became more and more pronounced. He could easily have convinced himself he was imagining the cool, breezy sensations, if they hadn't been so persistent. But something was stroking him like silken feathers, caressing him in the most perverse yet pleasurable way. He wasn't a man given to indulging the senses, except where food was concerned, but he'd never felt anything quite so riveting. As the feather crept upward, his nerves tingled hotly, his buttocks tautened, and his thoughts leapt in anticipation of what was to come. Finally a moan slipped from his throat at the same moment that the toast point slipped from his fingers.

When he could gather the presence of mind, he lifted the tablecloth and peered into the void. A seductive smile greeted him as the beautiful creature poised in the space between his thighs stopped whatever fabulous thing it was that she was doing to his nether regions.

"Hello," she said brightly. "I'm Shelby Flood, the image consultant who's been trying to get an appointment with you since last Christmas, remember? If you've got a minute, I'll finish measuring your inseam." She stretched her hot pink measuring tape from his quivering thigh to his groin. "Ummmm, yes, a little more room in the crotch, I think."

Asterbaum stared at her in mute amazement. Oddly the question that took preeminence in his mind was whether or not he remembered her. He took pride in his ability to storehouse names and faces, a feat that was amazing in itself, considering the number of people who vied for his attention on a daily basis. But this wasn't a fair test by any standards. She was totally out of context. If she'd come by his office or dropped by his table at Le Cirque, the way most of those who curried favor did, he would have had a familiar reference point and any number of visual clues. As it was, gazing down at her between his open legs, with her lovely face so near his . . .

She trailed her fingers slowly up his fly and toyed with the zipper tab, pursing her lips as she began to draw it down. Her fingers stroked over him, making him throb and bulge with pleasure. "Goodness," she murmured, "aren't you adorable. I'm afraid we're going to need a great deal more room."

Her lips were pouty and moist, her turquoise eyes vibrant. And her long, red fingernails were not, well . . . totally unfamiliar. "Shelby Flood, wasn't it?" he said huskily. "Of course, I remember you."

"I thought you might." With a dazzling smile she returned her attention to the more immediate problem of his too-tight crotch. After a moment Asterbaum let the tablecloth drop. Toast points and caviar were completely forgotten as he gazed at the far wall with a look of rapt, unfocused pleasure.

Shelby Flood loved to watch fabulously successful men sleep. Their vulnerability made her feel powerful, and Shelby fed on power—her own and others. She knew from experience that most successful men—the self-made ones in particular—had steel traps for brains. They were always on guard, always vigilant, careful to cover their own asses while they did reconnaissance on their enemies. Paranoia ran rampant in the corridors of power, and the mighty defended their positions jealously. But when the mighty slept, they were as vulnerable as babies, as naked as the next guy. Unconsciousness, she had decided, was the great equalizer. It was the only time such men were truly unguarded. And it was the only time she halfway liked them.

In more whimsical moments, she even imagined herself as a princess of darkness, one of the winged succubi who attacked and seduced men while they slept, sucking them dry of all vital fluids. She liked to think of herself in that way, a sexual sorceress. She liked to think that she had sucked Douglas Asterbaum dry.

Now, curled up in an overstuffed chair, opposite the pedestal waterbed on which Asterbaum slept, she watched his nostrils flare rhythmically. The warrior's rest, she mused sardonically. She would allow him a bit more recuperative time before they did battle again. It was the least she could do, considering what he was going to do for her.

Beyond the glittering window walls of the penthouse bedroom, slashes of magenta and purple flared across the skyline. Dawn was breaking over the city. The sun was rising like a whip, streaking the retreating flanks of night with its rich, bleeding light. She loved Manhattan in the morning, especially from thirty stories above the streets. She'd insisted they stay at the Manhattan Towers even over Asterbaum's objections. Although she didn't tell him, she'd once had a premonition that this hotel was going to be lucky for her. Perhaps this would be the day she struck it rich.

The city skyline was growing more breathtaking every minute, its monolithic towers sharpened to silver blades by the brightening blue sky. When she finally looked back at her latest conquest, he was stretching and smiling at her. She kicked up one leg, pointed her toe at the ceiling and then delicately rested her bare foot on the edge of the bed.

"Morning, tiger lover," she purred. "How do you like my outfit?" With a coquettish arch of her back, she opened her arms, giving him an unfettered view of her nudity, including the heart-shaped mole that graced her collarbone. She wore only one article of clothing, a man's silk tie perfectly knotted at her creamy throat.

His gaze drifted up the length of her bare leg to the soft sable nest between her thighs. She opened herself just a little, obliging his hungry stare, knowing what it would do to him, especially since she didn't intend to give him anything more than the view. She wanted as much bargaining power as possible with this man. It would suit her purposes perfectly to have him as horny as a mountain goat while she pitched her plan to him.

"Gosh, I'm starving, aren't you?" she asked slyly. "Why don't we have some breakfast sent up?"

He drew down the bed's leopard-print sheets to show her exactly how hungry he was.

"Hold that thought," she murmured.

A short time later they were on the terrace, having breakfast served. As the waiters set down fluffy golden omelettes and baskets of buttery brioche and poured rich black coffee, Shelby continued to tempt her prey. She had carelessly tied the hotel's terry robe so that the lapel gaped whenever she bent forward, allowing for alluring glimpses of her breasts. But it wasn't her body she was selling. That was merely the bait. The concealed hook was her vision of the new Douglas

Asterbaum. She had her sights set on future glory, and that very much involved Asterbaum's present.

Her leather tote bag sat next to her chair. From it she drew fabric swatches and a portfolio that contained photos of her fabulously groomed clientele. None of them was nearly so eminent as her companion, but then that was why she was here, to snag a big fish.

"I've *un*dressed you, Doug," she said, bending over to touch his knee beneath the table. "Now let me dress you. Let me show you how good that can be. I know what women respond to—money, power, a touch of arrogance."

He dismissed her grand vision with a patronizing glance and less than ten seconds of contemplation. "No one calls me Doug," he said, picking up that morning's edition of *The Wall Street Journal*. The pages snapped crisply as he leafed through to the stock report.

"But surely after . . ." It was Shelby's first falter, and she hated sounding uncertain. She could feel fear curling around the edges of her heart, and her reaction was frustration, heat, even anger. But more than anything, she hated being ignored. Each snap of the paper provoked her to greater irritation. She wanted to slap the damn thing out of his hands.

"Of course, then . . . Douglas, *Mr*. Asterbaum." With a silvery sound that was a little too sharp-edged to qualify as laughter, she slipped her fingers under his robe, inching toward the part of him that had responded so faithfully to her ministrations. "I can make you irresistible, Douglas—a god."

"I own Wall Street," he informed her, crunching the paper down to peer at her over his Ben Franklin reading glasses. "I already *am* a god."

Stung by the casual rebuff, she withdrew her hand. Douglas Asterbaum was a born-again dickhead, she decided, letting her smoldering temper flare. He'd used her! He'd never had any intention of giving her his business. He hadn't even allowed her to tell him how she planned to revitalize his image, the asshole. Crème de la scum! She liked him much better unconscious.

Shelby's sulk deepened as she glared at the newspaper, which very effectively blocked her access to the man who owned Wall Street. But as the minutes ticked by, and her lurid fantasies of castration became boring, she gradually came to terms with the practical realities of the situation. So this fish had wriggled away. It was a big ocean, and she had bait to spare. As her mind began to whir again, already on to the next adventure, the focus of her turquoise eyes shortened until she realized she was staring at a fascinating headline: MEDIA TYCOON'S ESTATE WORTH MILLIONS.

She skimmed the article's opening paragraph. "Simon Warnecke dead?" she murmured. Her pursed lips slowly curved into a contemplative, Madonna-like smile. Maybe it was time for Shelby Flood to pay a visit home.

CHAPTER
·· TEN ··

THE LAW OFFICES of Stratton, Stratton, Steiner and Pierce occupied the entire fifteenth floor of the Bank of America building in the financial section of downtown San Francisco. The old and prestigious firm had been handling the legal affairs of the Warnecke family for nearly four generations. When the venerable Gilbert Stratton III, suffered a lung aneurysm in his sixty-fourth year and retired to the family compound in Marin County, his son, successor and namesake, Gilbert IV, took up the reins with barely a ripple in the calm feeder stream of succession. Like the Warneckes, the Strattons were a dynastic family in the time-honored tradition, passing the torch from father to son, ensuring the continuity of bloodlines, the rightful line of descent and, especially, the legitimate accession to power.

But if the rumors were true, all that was about to change. Today was the reading of Simon Warnecke's last will and testament, and for the first time in over one hundred years, the family empire was about to be handed down to an outsider, a woman, who though she bore the Warnecke name, had not a drop of Warnecke blood.

All of those considerations were very much on Luc Warnecke's mind as he entered the musty, mahogany-paneled offices of Gilbert Stratton IV and took a chair on the opposite side of the hallowed chambers from his stepmother and Matt Sandusky.

His stepmother. Luc had drawn in a breath the moment he'd caught sight of Jessie. Forbiddingly pale and wintry, she hadn't even bothered to glance his way when he'd entered. But that hadn't stopped him from taking in every detail of her appearance. Devoid of makeup and with her lioness hair drawn back into a punishing knot, she resembled a Christian martyr during the reconversion of the Huns.

The black suit she wore was far too severe for her fair coloring, but somehow she managed to look ravishingly sexy anyway. At least to his mind. He could hardly keep his eyes off the long, slender, silk-stockinged legs that tapered from her narrow skirt. Tantalizing, those legs. Rigidly drawn together, they forced thoughts of the very thing they seemed expressly to be militating against—sex.

It would not have pleased her to know she was virtually ensuring that his thoughts would escalate to male fantasies and that those fantasies would be darkly erotic. The very rigidity with which she held herself only challenged and excited him more. He could barely reconcile the glacial creature she'd become with the teenage tomboy he remembered, but that didn't keep him from craving an explosive confrontation with her. Maybe it was what incited him most.

" 'I, Simon Warnecke, being of sound and disposing mind and memory, do hereby declare this to be my last will . . .' "

Gil Stratton had begun reading the document. Luc let his attention be drawn to the proceedings, and as he silently listened to his late, great father's words, he was pleased at his own dispassion. He felt very little of anything hearing Simon's final wishes being recited aloud, except maybe contempt for the man's twisted obsessions. But even that emotion was muted today.

Perhaps dispassion from his son was a fitting fate for Simon Warnecke. It stripped him of his power. Revenge had been Luc's raison d'être for as long as he could remember, and yet now he felt oddly empty, as if some mysterious catharsis had taken place in the last few days. What had happened to the black wrath he'd reserved especially for his father? Had vengeance lost its unique appeal? Or had he simply transferred his hostility to Jessie?

" 'I do hereby give, bequeath and devise to Jessie Flood-Warnecke . . .' "

Luc glanced up, not surprised to find that Jessie hadn't wavered from her mannequinlike calm. So total was her apparent self-containment, she didn't even seem to be breathing as

Stratton read Simon's first bequest.

" ' . . . to my wife and trusted companion, who once risked her life for no other purpose or earthly gain than to save mine, and who proved herself in a multitude of ways as a woman of great courage and even greater moral character, and who devoted herself throughout the months of our marriage to the guardianship of my physical health and well being . . .' "

From the strange quiet inside him, Luc listened as Jessie was bequeathed everything that should rightfully have gone to him. She was not only named executrix, she was left all the real property—Echos, a beach house in Malibu and a Victorian townhouse in Pacific Heights—as well as the bulk of Simon's personal property and business holdings, including the jewel in the crown—controlling interest in Warnecke Communications. She was given virtually everything but the pot of gold at the end of the rainbow.

Luc couldn't seem to manage a complete breath as Stratton finished the bequest. The pressure in his chest muscles made even the thought of respiration an effort. But it wasn't anger he felt. It wasn't even envy. It was curiosity—avid, nearly uncontrollable curiosity. *How* had she done it? How had she gained the love and trust of a man who wasn't capable of love and trusted no one? It was a paradox, and to him, a consuming mystery.

The remaining bequests included the establishment of a substantial trust fund for Melissa, to be awarded on her twenty-fifth birthday, and a sizable chunk of Warnecke stock to Matt Sandusky, Simon's "most valued friend, confidant and eminently capable chief executive."

Luc settled back in the chair, his arms folded, his jaw hot with the sudden tension of maintaining control. The envy that was missing at Jessie's windfall stirred inside him now toward the man who had displaced him in his father's estimation. It was nothing personal. Luc didn't dislike Matt Sandusky; he just wanted him blown off the face of the earth for no other reason than that he existed.

Sandusky, himself, seemed more than pleased with Simon's generosity and reached over to clasp Jessie's hand. Luc didn't miss the gesture or the proprietary way that Sandusky hovered. There was more than business involved in his intentions, or even friendship. The man was laying the groundwork. Luc had always believed that males were biologically wired to catch the implicit mating signals of rivals. How else had the species survived? Sandusky was staking a claim. And why not? He stood to gain far more than a wife. He stood to gain an empire.

Resting a scuffed Topsider on his knee, Luc decided to get himself good and drunk when he left this museum. Mary Greenblatt had been firing off faxes to his notebook computer all morning concerning the Rancom deal. Through the miracle of modern technology, he and his second-in-command were never more than a fax away, but even Mary, who waited for no one, would have to wait for Luc Warnecke today. He hadn't tied one on since the night of Hank Flood's death, but this fiasco seemed as good a reason as any.

" 'And finally, to Lucas Simon Warnecke,' " Stratton intoned.

Luc glanced at the attorney, instantly wary. He hadn't expected Gil to actually read the bequest, especially since he'd tried to convince Luc not to attend.

" ' . . . my only son and sole surviving blood relative, whom I disavowed and disinherited over ten years ago, and who surely must have believed it was his sworn purpose in life to defy and disappoint me. To Lucas, I leave nothing but my profound regret that he and I were so fundamentally opposed, and the watercolor portrait of his mother, Frances Seaton Warnecke, which once hung over the mantel in the family living room at Echos. She was able to tolerate his physical and moral failings, whereas I could not.' "

The pain that raked Luc was so poisoned with fury, he could hardly tell one emotion from the other. Moral failings? That was rich coming from a man who'd had Frances Warnecke's portrait taken from the mantel, over twenty years ago, because she'd had the bad taste to die in a messy way. Luc had often wondered how his mother had come to be so confused that she'd fatally mixed prescription drugs.

Disgusted with Simon's proclamations from the grave, Luc rose from his chair. Everyone in the room turned to look at him. Jessie jerked to life, fixing him with an alarmed stare, and Sandusky sat forward as if prepared to spring up. Even Stratton came out of his trance long enough to stop droning. Clearly they all thought he was going to blow the lid off the place, perhaps even threaten to contest the will. Luc had something far more interesting than that in mind, but this wasn't the time or the place to announce his plans.

"Spend it foolishly," he said, returning Jessie's watchful gaze. "As for me, I'm going to head for the closest bar and ruminate on my moral failings."

A whiff of lemony astringent stung Jessie's eyes as she swept a dampened cotton ball in upward strokes over her cheekbones. The best antidote to a complicated situation was a mindless task, she'd long ago realized. But, apparently, meticulously cleansing the morning's residue from her face wasn't mindless enough. Her skin was shiny clean and she'd accumulated a small mountain of moist cotton, but her thoughts were anything but serene. She was still tormented by what had happened at Gil Stratton's office that morning.

She'd prepared herself for an ugly scene the moment she saw Luc enter the room. However, instead of creating an explosive confrontation, he'd been broodingly quiet and watchful through it all, as if biding his time. The bitterly cruel reference to Luc's mother had caught them all off guard, including Luc himself. Jessie was not forgiving by nature. She couldn't afford to be, but the stab of pain in his eyes had saddened her. She'd actually wanted to console him in some way, but there'd been no opportunity. He'd stalked out of the room so abruptly it had left her breathless.

She picked up the crystal butterfly on her dressing table and stroked its wings pensively. She couldn't afford to feel sympathy for Luc Warnecke, not even for one careless second. Still, she knew how it felt to lose a loved one at a young age, and in her case, it had been her mother too. Lynette Flood had run away, abandoning her husband and two daughters, when Jessie was eight.

Jessie remembered her mother mostly as a quiet, rather timid woman who tried mightily to please and pacify her demanding and sometimes belligerent husband. She rarely succeeded. Hank Flood never abused her physically, but the emotional torture of his constant tirades turned her into a bewildered, haunted shell. Jessie had often thought that was exactly what Hank wanted, to rob his young wife of her wistful beauty and keep her too psychologically beaten down to leave him.

Lynette had surprised him. She had surprised them all. One afternoon she'd left to do the grocery shopping and never returned. Both Jessie and Shelby had found notes hidden under their pillows. Full of sadness and shame, Jessie's note had begged her to understand. "Please believe that I am doing this to save my life," her mother had written. "Hank will never let me go, but he's a good man at heart and you're better off with him than on the lam with me."

On the lam. Jessie would have loved nothing more than to have gone on the lam with her sad, beautiful mother. Lynette had signed the note "Lost Butterfly."

Jessie hadn't understood any of it at the time. She'd felt frightened and desperately alone. She'd hated her mother for leaving her. But in time she'd come to understand that the desperate things people did were often acts of great courage or dark despair. Her mother's act must have been both.

The butterfly's crystalline coolness burned Jessie's cheek as she held the figurine to her face for a moment before returning it to the dressing table. Her mother's disappearance had left a void she would never be able to fill, but somewhere in her heart she knew she must have forgiven the lost butterfly. Lynette Flood couldn't possibly have known what a nightmare she'd wished upon her two young daughters by abandoning them to the care of their stepfather. Other than the fact that he drank too much, no one really knew what breed of monster Hank Flood was incubating in the dark heart of his lanky, six-feet-four-inch frame—or the violent way he would meet his end on a freezing November night. Shelby least of all, undoubtedly to her everlasting regret.

Jessie rose from the vanity and crossed the dressing room to the rosewood armoire for a pair of jeans and a sweater, her gardening clothes. The house had begun to feel close and confining, and she longed to be outside in the fresh air. As she untied her kimono, a rasping noise caught her attention. It sounded as if someone had opened and shut a chest drawer in the other room.

"Gina?" Jessie pulled her kimono together and looped the ties. The soles of her bare feet were icy cold against the warm nap of the carpet. It wasn't the nanny, she realized. Gina wouldn't have entered her room without knocking unless it was an emergency, in which case she would have answered by now.

Jessie rounded the corner that opened onto the bedroom itself and came to a swaying halt, her toes digging into the carpet as if to anchor her in place. She saw his shoes first, a pair of scuffed Topsiders resting on her antique tortoiseshell chest. Her first reaction was a flustered rush of recognition. Her second was annoyance at having been caught off guard. She should have known it was him the instant she realized someone was in her room. Who else in the house would so determinedly violate her privacy this way?

Luc was lounging on the couch near the bedroom's fireplace, studying a silver-framed photograph he held in his hand. With one leg drawn up as a prop for his forearm and the raglan sleeves of his black sweater pushed up to his elbows, he looked as rakishly handsome as a model for a casual men's wear ad. His expression held a mix of skepticism and disdain, but it wasn't his looks that concerned Jessie at the moment. It was the picture. She recognized it immediately as a wedding portrait of her and Simon that she'd put away long ago. Luc must have gone through the drawers of her Sheraton secretary to find it.

"I like bigger ceremonies myself," he said, looking up as if he'd known she was there all along. His darkly lashed eyes took in her presence slowly, as he sized up her hastily tied kimono and her unpinned tresses. "And I would have wanted my bride to blush."

Through some alchemy of self-control and divine grace, Jessie found the composure to shrug off his inspection. She lifted her shoulders with an air of supreme nonchalance, as if the whole incident were terribly boring to her, as if Luc were some sort of incorrigible teenager who had nothing better to do than annoy the authority figures in his life. "What are you doing here?" she asked. "In *my* room?"

He continued to examine the photograph with perverse interest. "Where did the holy event take place? It looks like the gazebo right here in the garden."

She remained silent, refusing to be baited into an explanation of her quick and inauspicious wedding to his father.

It *had* taken place in Echos' gardens, and there'd only been two witnesses, Matt Sandusky and Roger Metcalf, the college student Matt had recommended to help out around the house and grounds.

Luc flipped the picture around so that Jessie could see herself. "You don't look very excited, Mrs. Warnecke," he observed quietly. "Isn't a girl's wedding supposed to be the most exciting day of her life?"

"This *is* the nineties." She refused to look at the photograph. She knew well enough what Luc was implying. The exquisitely framed picture had documented the grimness of the affair rather than camouflaged it. "And I was hardly a girl."

Her hands had curled into fists. She slipped them into her kimono pockets, determined to smother within the cool timbre of her voice any hint of the violation she felt. "I'd like you to leave," she said.

"I'm sure you would. It must have been quite a strain inheriting the Warnecke millions this morning. You probably need your rest."

"I'll survive, thank you."

"I have no doubt." The photograph ended up facedown on the love seat next to Luc. Settling back, he draped an arm across the back of the love seat and crossed his legs on the table as if he'd just declared himself lord of the bedroom and all he surveyed, including her. Especially her. The tilt of his head was casual enough, but the darkening menace in his eyes sent another message. Hot with male curiosity, it exuded a warning that was pulsatingly sexual. It told her he didn't much give a damn what she wanted, because he wasn't going to give it to her anyway. It also told her that he wasn't there to discuss the relative merits of wedding photography.

The scent of rose petals and oranges swirled from the potpourri baskets, and for a moment, the light from the terrace doors brightened blindingly. Jessie's senses sharpened, trying to take in the disparate elements. Instinctively she glanced around at the intercom on the far wall.

"It's too far away," Luc said, as if reading her thoughts. "You'll never make it."

She turned to him, wary.

"Maybe you'd better sit down, Jessie."

"Why?"

He shrugged, apparently taking a certain cruel satisfaction in the fact that he'd rattled her, even if only for a second. Luc Warnecke had a sadistic streak, she realized. If she hadn't understood that before, she did now. There was nothing casual about him. He was watching her with the cold, probing intensity of a swaying cobra. His dark eyes sought out every flaw, every weakness, any quiver of vulnerability no matter how slight. He took pleasure in her pain and confusion.

In the rising panic of her thoughts, Jessie had a chilling flash of insight and knew this was the riskiest situation she'd ever been in with him. There were no guns and no imminent violence, but on an intuitive level, she realized that he intended to win this mysterious war he was waging at any cost. He meant to bring Jessie Flood-Warnecke to her knees before he was through with her.

"Why sit down?" Luc nodded to the chair nearest her. "Because I'm about to make you an offer you can't refuse, that's why."

"What does that mean? Cut the crap, dammit. I don't like games."

"Oh, but I do. I like games, especially these games." His voice turned cold. "Sit down, Jessie."

"What are you talking about?" she demanded, hating herself for giving in to the burgeoning panic she felt, hating him for triggering it. "What offer?"

He glanced at the chair again, his meaning clear.

"Go to hell," she said, drawing a clenched hand from her pocket.

He almost smiled, and in some remote, still-sane corner of her mind, Jessie knew this was exactly what he wanted from her. Defiance. She was rigid with anger, easily toppled. To win against him, she had to be fluid, to play along with him. But she couldn't do it. Nothing short of brute force could have induced her to sit down at that moment. She had to defy him and he knew it.

"What do you want?" she asked. *You sadistic son of a bitch.*

"God, what don't I want?" He laughed softly, apparently willing to concede round one to her. If she wanted to die on her feet, more power to her. "For starters, I still want to know how you did it, Jessie. You'll forgive my interest as the black sheep son, but how did you get Simon to leave the whole goddamned empire to you?"

"I didn't get him to do anything." Her denial was quick and vehement. "Simon and I shared a common vision for the company. He wanted to breathe new life into the newspapers without sacrificing the quality or the integrity. He hated tabloid journalism."

She'd said it intentionally, well aware that at least one of the newspapers in Luc's chain was considered a tabloid. It was slur directed at content, not the size the name actually derived from. "I plan to carry out Simon's wishes, that's all."

A muscle moved in Luc's throat, the only evidence that she might have struck a nerve.

"So you're going to be involved in running the company?" he said. "How does Sandusky feel about that?"

"Matt and I have discussed Warnecke's future, and I'm sure he'll be totally supportive of any role I want to play."

"And have you discussed *your* future—yours and Matt's? Did you know he plans to take Simon's place in the bedroom as well as the boardroom?"

"What?"

"Apparently you didn't. Lucky me, getting to break the news. Your CEO has matrimony in mind, Jessie. He's going to wait the appropriate period of time, of course. But he'll pop the question soon."

"You're wrong! Matt has never said anything about marriage, and even if he had, it wouldn't be any of your business. This is totally inappropriate, dammit. I want you to leave."

"*Appropriate?*" He raked a hand through his hair, holding its darkness off his forehead as if he were both amused and perplexed. "What would you know about that? Was it appropriate to shoot me in cold blood? Was it appropriate for you to marry a sick old man thirty years your senior and pawn your kid off as his?"

She inched backward, holding the lapel of her robe together. The intercom was on the wall behind her. If she could get closer to it without signalling her intentions—

"Don't be stupid, Jessie."

"I asked you to leave." As her heel came up against the baseboard, she found the intercom button with her fingers. "If you don't, I'll call Roger."

"Roger?" He snickered, a dark sound. "What's the point? *You* could put up a better fight than Roger."

Her hand hovered near the button, then dropped away. The fire that razed her throat was as much frustration as anger. There was no way to fight him now. He had just stripped her of her last weapon. He wouldn't have cared if she had called the Marines. He would have welcomed a free-for-all.

"How did you do it, Jessie?" he pressed. "I can think of a couple obvious ways a woman could manipulate a ruthless SOB like Simon. One is sex. The other is blackmail. But let's face it, you couldn't have been a very good lay. You're too uptight."

A gasp burned in her throat.

Luc rose from the love seat to the sound of shattering glass. The wedding portrait had dropped to the floor.

"Get out of here," she said.

He swept back his dark hair with a deep stroke of his hand, revealing the widow's peak. "You can't say you weren't warned, Jessie. I told you that night . . . you should have killed me."

Her lips could barely manage the words. "What do you mean?"

"I hold the whip hand now. I've already begun to investigate Hank Flood's death, and I've got a damn good idea who did it. Unless you agree to the terms of my offer, I'll blow things wide open. I'll hire private detectives and do whatever it takes to find out what happened."

"And what if the evidence proves *you* killed Hank?"

"That's a risk I'll have to take." He went silent, watching her with narrowed eyes, as if struck by the terrible tension running through her.

"What is this thing you're offering?" she bit out. "What terms are you talking about?"

"You're not marrying Matt Sandusky."

"I never intended to—"

"You're marrying me."

"Marrying? You?" There was an energy flickering in the depths of his eyes that might have been a smile. "Are you insane?" *Was* he insane? There was a thin line separating obsessional thinking from madness. Was this another legacy passed down from Simon? "Why would you want that? And what makes you think I'd do it?"

"Because you have no choice. It's the only way to stop me from reopening this investigation. I'm betting you've got something to hide, Mrs. Warnecke—how interesting that you won't even have to change your name—and I'm also betting you're the one who sent me that threatening note. You didn't want me anywhere near Half Moon Bay, because I didn't kill Hank Flood. And you know who did. Well, buckle your seat belt, Jessie, because I think we *both* know who did it. And I intend to have a hell of a good time proving it."

Jessie was desperate now. She prayed he was bluffing, but she didn't dare call him on it. She mustered all her strength into her voice. "Why marriage? You could simply force me to sell you my shares. You could take over Warnecke Communications. That's always been your objective."

"Why settle for the company, when I can have the empire— the holdings, the houses . . . the widow?"

"Marrying me won't give you any power! The shares are mine. I control them."

"And I control you, so to speak."

"*Blackmail?*"

"Exactly."

"I'll never submit to that!"

"I'm afraid you will. Because if I should find out in the course of the investigation that Mel is my child, I promise you there will be a custody battle to end all custody battles. It'll be smeared all over the rags—those 'tabloids' Simon hated so much. And I think you'll lose."

He was threatening to take Mel, her daught—The thought snapped off like an icicle, frozen mid-word. In her heart Jessie knew he would do it. Since he'd arrived, it had been the driving fear of her waking life. Secretly she had always believed that Luc was driven to possess, and perhaps to destroy, everything that was Simon's. She'd sensed his capacity for both vengeance and self-destruction, and he'd just confirmed it. He didn't care if he took them all down with him, even a child. He didn't care who he hurt—

"Mom!"

The cry came from outside in the hallway. Someone was pounding on her bedroom door! Before Jessie could think how to respond, the door flew open and Mel burst in. The little girl's voice was raspy with excitement. She could hardly catch her breath. "Mom, look! Look who's here!"

As Mel ran to Jessie, someone else appeared in the doorway, a stunningly seductive ghost from the past.

"My, my," Shelby Flood said, smiling at the scene before her. "What a quaint photo opportunity this is." Her vibrant turquoise eyes swept from Jessie's gaping robe and stricken expression to Luc's dark surprise, and finally to the shattered picture on the floor.

Jessie's sense of disbelief was so great she was unable to move. She stared at the three of them in mute horror. She felt as if she were surrounded by the enemy, intimately and inescapably linked to them by bonds and blood. This wasn't an act of God or destiny. It couldn't be. No higher power would be so intentionally cruel as to bring them all together like this.

Only Jessie knew the truth of what happened on that one night of explosive violence and pent-up passions. She knew it all, everything, and she'd spent a decade building what she thought was a fortress to wall off the snake pit of betrayals, lies and deceit. Her only goal had been safety, containment. But now the fortress was crumbling around her. How could she possibly keep the past buried now?

How had it come to this?

CHAPTER
··ELEVEN··

HALF MOON BAY

IT CREPT DOWN Main Street like an alien spaceship coming in for a landing. Sleek and white, rolling low to the rain-washed pavement and glowing lambently in the sunlight, the limousine barely made a sound. It moved as if carried by air currents, a hovercraft of immense and almost sinister proportions. Its hood ornament, a horse, with wings spread, encompassed by a silver circle, appeared to be flying out in front of it.

Street traffic slowed to a halt as the gleaming apparition rippled through its midst. Bill Weaver, clerk at the feed and fuel company, nearly dropped the twenty-five-pound bag of dog kibble he was carrying as he lurched backward in the crosswalk, stumbling to get out of the way. He hadn't seen or heard the thing coming. Neither had the other surprised onlookers who stopped in their tracks to watch.

Only twelve-year-old Jessie Flood had noticed the object materializing out of the mists on the Pilarcitos Creek Bridge. She'd tracked its approach toward the town center with avid interest, certain it was an unearthly manifestation of some kind. And now, as the rest of the town stood and gawked, she began to move along with the car's momentum, her heart surging with painful excitement. She had been waiting for most of her twelve years, hoping something wonderful would happen—knowing it would!—and here it was.

The limo's opaque windows concealed any sign of its occupants, but Jessie searched the silvery mirrors anyway, glimpsing her own blue-eyed reflection as she hurried along the sidewalk, parallel to the limo's path.

"Who is it?" someone whispered as she passed. "Some damned movie star?"

"Hell, no!" someone else answered. "It's Simon Warnecke, the newspaper magnate. Who else around here could afford a tour bus like that?"

Jessie's thoughts leapt with anticipation. The Warneckes were the object of considerable gossip in Half Moon Bay. Not only were they rich, they were reclusive and, as far as she could tell by the whispers, haunted by family secrets and tragedy. Jessie's own stepfather, Hank Flood, had worked for Simon Warnecke once as a handyman, but that was years ago, before Jessie and her mother and sister had moved to Half Moon Bay.

The limo pulled up in front of the bank, and Jessie came to a halt some fifty feet away, breathing fast as the driver let himself out, strode around to the last door and opened it. A tall, broad-shouldered man emerged, his hair slicked back, his posture militarily erect as he tweaked the lapel of his suit jacket, correcting the hang. Jessie watched him walk into the bank and felt a shiver of both fascination and foreboding.

The second figure to appear was a dark wraith of a boy with hair the color of foothills at dusk. When he looked her way, Jessie found herself staring into the darkest, most beautiful gaze she'd ever seen. He lifted his head proudly, defiantly, and his eyes shone out of his pale, gaunt face like deep black pools. They glittered like the eyes of the madman she'd seen in a movie once. But they were also sad like the new young priest's at the mission near Pescadero. And yet most of all, his eyes were wild like the animals that roamed the ravine behind her house, the creatures she loved so much.

It was all Jessie could do to breathe in the presence of that arresting gaze. She felt as if she were staring into the soul of someone outside God's province, a holy man or a devil. She watched in mute wonder as he walked past her and into the bank, her mind formulating a host of questions. What had happened to make him look so defiant and sad? And why was he so thin? The ill-fitting blazer and gray slacks he wore hung on him like hand-me-downs. His posture was rebelliously slouched, his dark hair in need of cutting.

"Who is he?" someone behind her asked.

Jessie had already asked and answered that question in her mind. He was Simon Warnecke's son, Luc. The one they said wasn't "right."

A small crowd had gathered in Jessie's wake, and now the talk began to swirl rapidly, encompassing her in its seductive energy as the locals speculated on one of their favorite topics of conversation—the sins and transgressions of the Warneckes.

"I heard the kid inherited some fatal family disease," a woman offered. "The same thing that killed his mother."

Another scoffed coldly. "It wasn't a disease killed Frances Warnecke, it was suicide. She took sleeping pills after Simon 'Legree' caught her having an affair."

"How d'you know that?"

"I waited on her over at the coffee shop once. She ordered a Tin Can Sundae—I swear, hot fudge and a sprinkle of chopped peanuts. Most beautiful woman I've ever seen."

"Who'd she have an affair with . . . ?"

But Jessie had already stopped listening to the gossip. She had heard it all before—rumors about the mother's mysterious death, rumors that the boy was slow or maybe even dangerous and couldn't be let off the Warnecke property, not even to attend school. She had heard the talk, and if it had held any interest for her once, it didn't anymore.

Nothing could have convinced her that Luc Warnecke was backward now that she had seen him. She had looked into eyes that were haunted by unspeakable secrets. He wasn't slow. He was wise beyond his years. For an instant his gaze had seemed to hold all of life's sweetness, all of its suffering, in its dark grip. And Jessie knew she would never forget it.

Jessie had never been able to resist a mystery. She'd been warned about staying off the Warnecke property, but she had to take the chance, even if it meant getting cuffed around by her stepfather. She'd spent so many sleepless nights puzzling over the riddles that shrouded the Warnecke family, she'd begun to think she might never be able to rest again if she didn't find some way to lift the veil and discover the truth. Nothing had ever consumed her more, even the mystery of her own mother's disappearance. She needed to get another look at Luc Warnecke to convince herself she hadn't imagined him. But most of all, she needed to know what went on behind the stone walls of the Warnecke's cliffside compound.

Hank Flood's dire warnings about trespassing were very much on Jessie's mind this icy February morning as she made her way through the ravine to the chain-link fence that separated the Flood's small plot of land from the acreage of their wealthy neighbors. Glancing around, she ducked through the rusted-out links. She'd chosen this route because it seemed the best way to get onto the property without being discovered. As far as she knew, no one ever came to the ravine but her.

Morning mists rose from the thawing earth as she moved deeper onto Warnecke land. Bushy-tailed gray squirrels scurried up maple trees to safety, and her own frosted breath hung in the air. Pulling her hands from the cozy pouch of her hooded sweatshirt, she began to climb the side of the hill to check out the area and get her bearings. She was halfway up when a flash of white caught her eye, drawing her attention to Devil's Drop, the highest precipice in the ravine.

Startled, she spotted a figure trying to negotiate a spindly tree trunk that lay across the deep gorge. She couldn't see his face, but his whipcord frame and dark hair confirmed her growing sense of dread. It was Luc Warnecke. But what was he doing? Jessie scrambled up the side, horrified as she realized the flimsy bridge couldn't possibly hold him. He must be crazy to try and cross it. The trunk was going to snap any second, and he would fall!

"Stop!" she cried. "Go back!"

By the time she reached the top of the chasm, he was halfway across and already in grave danger. He'd slowed up, and the hesitation had caused him to lose his balance. His arms were flailing wildly, his body swaying, and the tree was buckling under his weight.

"What are you doing?" she cried. "Go back!"

He began to move again, and for an instant Jessie allowed herself to believe he might make it. "Please," she said, whispering a shorthand prayer. But she'd barely got the word out before he stopped. She watched in astonishment as he doubled over, clutching his stomach as if he were in pain.

"No!" she screamed as he toppled off the log.

She ducked her head, shielding her eyes. Nausea roiled up into her throat, scalding her mouth with the bitter taste of stomach acid and fear. Her brain flashed a torturous image of him hurtling through space and the terrible impact when his thin body hit the ground.

The jagged rocks cut into her hands and ripped at her clothing as she stumbled and nearly fell down the side of the ravine in her rush to reach him. The ground was hard and slick, making it impossible to get a foothold. The scrub brush was stripped bare of leaves, its branches sharp as needles.

She found him almost immediately, and the reality was as awful as she'd feared. Crumpled in a heap near the dry creek bed, with one leg bent in a strange direction, he looked like a cartoon stick figure, an unstrung puppet.

Trembling with the need to help him, she bent over his still body. He didn't seem to be breathing, but there was a gash on his forehead, and as she reached with the sleeve of her sweatshirt to touch the cut, his lids fluttered open. The shock of his wild-eyed stare startled a scream out of her.

"Don't touch me," he gasped. "Get away from here."

She dropped back, confused. "I'm only trying to help you," she told him. "I'll go get someone."

"No! Don't do that!" His breath spewed into the crystal-clear air.

"But why not?" She'd seen a mansion through the trees. It was huge, with several wings, an enormous swimming pool and acres of gardens with rose-laden trellises. It looked like a fairy-tale castle where royalty might have lived.

"Don't go near that place," he snarled, grasping her arm. His grip was amazingly strong.

"Okay, I won't," she assured him, beginning to realize that fear was making him wild. He was like a trapped animal, bearing fangs. "Can you get up?" she asked.

Her heart went out to him as he began to struggle, fighting to push himself up and refusing her help when she offered it. Pride, she realized sadly. Even injured, he was desperate to salvage some dignity. He finally managed a sitting position and dragged himself around so that he could rest his back against a shelf of rocks. But that was as far as he got, and

Jessie had noticed something during his efforts that made her heart tighten with horror. His cotton T-shirt was ripped open in the back, revealing furious red welts. He'd been whipped, and this wasn't the first time. Beneath the fresh wounds there was a web work of older scars, white and spidery.

"I think my leg is broken," he said. His face, contorted with pain, made her think of churches and stained glass windows and holy, tortured things.

"Let me get help," she pleaded.

"No! You don't understand. *They did this.*" He was looking up toward the big house.

"Who? Your father? But he didn't make you fall."

He didn't answer, but she knew from her experiences with Hank that adults could be capable of great cruelty toward the children in their care. "But your leg," she argued, wanting more than anything to find a way to help. Though he was older, he seemed urgently in need of a protector at the moment, and in her mind Jessie had already taken on that role. She was constitutionally unable to abandon the frail and the wounded to their fate. She had to help.

"He'll want you to see a doctor, won't he?" she pressed. "You'll have to get your leg set."

He shook his head. "Doctors are vultures who prey on the sick and the weak. Only cowards need doctors." The boy was clearly repeating someone else's words. More tentatively he said, "He'll kill me if he finds me like this. He'll have me destroyed like a lame horse." His voice was dead and faraway as he spoke, but there was a quiver of rage in his eyes.

Jessie sat back on her haunches, stunned. She didn't believe him. She couldn't let herself believe that anyone's flesh and blood could behave so monstrously. That was too painful to absorb. She'd kept herself sane by believing just the opposite. Your parents—your *real* parents—would never hurt you. She'd always told herself that if her mother hadn't gone away, if Lynette Flood had been there to protect her two daughters from Hank, no one would have been hurt the way they had, not even Shelby.

Jessie turned slightly, alerted by the crackle of breaking twigs and leaves. It sounded as if someone were coming through the underbrush toward them.

The boy waved her away. "Go!" he whispered. "It's dangerous. Our caretaker shoots trespassers on sight."

Now Jessie knew he was exaggerating. He had to be. But the horror churning inside her wouldn't ease. She felt as if she were going to be sick to her stomach. She'd seen Luc Warnecke's scars with her own eyes. Someone had beaten him. That couldn't be exaggerated. If this was the caretaker coming, what would happen to him? She couldn't stand the thought of him being hurt any more.

"I can't leave," she whispered. "I *can't*. Whoever's coming, I'll talk to him. He won't do anything as long as I'm here—"

"He'll kill you!"

He hissed so fiercely, Jessie jumped back. His face was etched with raw, desperate fury. She thought she saw tears in his eyes.

"Get out of here!" he demanded savagely. "It'll go worse for me if you don't."

She backed off slowly, sick at heart. "I'll come back," she promised, her voice breaking. "I'll help you get away from them!" She didn't want to leave him. She'd never felt braver or stronger in her life. She was sure she could face down his enemy, any enemy. She wanted to stay. She wanted to fight, but she could see his terrible anguish. No matter what he said, or how angry he was, she knew he wasn't trying to protect himself. He was trying to protect her.

Please, she thought, speaking to a God who seemed to have forgotten kids like her and Luc Warnecke. *Don't let them hurt him anymore. Keep him safe. Keep him alive.*

Fixing Luc's beautiful dark eyes in her mind, she turned and started toward home at a run. She wanted to remember him. She had to remember him, for she had a terrible feeling it might be the last time she would ever see him.

Jessie came back to that place every day for weeks, but she never saw another sign of Luc. At first she prayed he'd escaped, but as the days wore on, she began to fear they truly might have done something terrible to him. Still, she returned each day after school, holding vigil by the ravine and watching the house from the cover of foliage. Sometimes she saw a bearded man she assumed was the caretaker doing chores around the grounds. Other times she saw Simon Warnecke himself taking solitary walks through the gardens. But no one else. Not Luc. Never Luc.

She wanted to tell someone or call the police, but she knew no one would believe her. And if the law found out she'd been trespassing, they would probably throw her in jail. So there was nothing she could do but wait and watch and hope. And then one day everything changed.

She was paying what was meant to be her final visit to the ravine when she saw a figure sitting on the ledge of Devil's Drop. His legs dangled over the side of the precipice as he faced the ocean beyond it. He was wearing baggy denim jeans and a sweater that was too big, but from where she stood, he looked for all the world like any other teenage boy taking some time to contemplate life. But it wasn't any other teenage boy. It was Luc.

She came up behind him quietly, not sure how to let him know she was there. "Can I sit down?" she asked. Her heart was a drumbeat, thundering so insistently she was sure he must have been able to hear its pulse in her voice.

When he didn't answer, she moved around so that she could see his face. His expression was pensive, his features lean and chiseled with thought. As before, she found herself totally absorbed with the feral presence he exuded, but there was something else, something different about him today. It was compelling, almost frightening if she were being truthful. No clothing, however normal, could hide the survival instincts that were crystallized in his dark gaze. He lived on his wits, like a wild creature. *What had they done to him?*

He hadn't answered her question, but he also hadn't made any attempt to rebuff her, so she decided to take that as a yes. She sat down next to him, positioning herself so that her legs were hanging over the side too.

"I haven't seen you. I thought maybe you got away." *I prayed that you got away, that you weren't suffering.*

Still no response. After several moments of silence she ventured another question. "How's your leg? Was it broken?"

He nodded.

"Is it still hurting you?"

"Jed Dawson, the caretaker, set it," he said, as if that answered her question. His voice had the remote, faraway quality she'd noticed the day she found him. It was as if he were talking about someone other than himself, another boy who lived Luc Warnecke's life for him and took the whippings.

"They didn't take you to the clinic?" she asked.

"My father didn't want a doctor involved."

No doctor? A caretaker had set his leg? What sort of insanity was that? It wasn't Luc who was dangerous, she realized. It was his father! At least Luc was alive, she told herself.

She began to talk quietly about herself then, keeping her secrets, allowing him his. She described how she lived with her sister and stepfather in an old clapboard house overlooking the gorge, how her mother had run away when she and Shelby were younger, and how Hank had gotten drunk that night and broken up the place—and many nights since. "I hate him," she said finally, softly.

For the first time Luc looked her way, his expression as haunted as she remembered ever seeing it. "I wonder what's worse," he said quietly, "hating your father, or having him hate you?"

Jessie touched his hand.

His eyes glittered and he turned away, but he made no attempt to brush away the tear that rolled down his cheek. It was as if he were too shell-shocked by the nightmare in his mind. He simply accepted the offer of her hand and continued to stare at the jagged rocks of the ravine as if he were remembering something even more horrible than the fall from this precipice.

There was something agonized in his slow, silent tears that Jessie dared not probe into. She ached for him, but at the same time she knew that some things were too terrible to talk about. She would have taken his pain gladly if there were a way it could have been transferred to her. But he couldn't even speak of it, so there was nothing for her to do but ache and wait and hope that he could feel the tenderness flowering in her heart like the spring bounty that blossomed here every year.

She'd felt an affinity for Luc from the moment she set eyes on him. Perhaps at first she'd pitied him as she might have any victim of cruel circumstances, but then she'd come to realize that wasn't the nature of the bond between them. They were alike, she and Luc. He was an outcast, just as she had been most of her life, the object of both pity and scorn for her family's "trashy, no-account ways."

People thought Luc was different too, a freak. They couldn't see past his silent eyes to the pain. Or else they hadn't bothered to look. But Jessie could feel the pain flowing from the connection their hands had made. Something had happened between them today, and nothing would ever be the same from this moment on. She knew that. Her life was to be entwined with Luc Warnecke's in every possible way, in the most profound and unimaginable ways.

"You pregnant or something?" Shelby inquired as she wandered into the kitchen after school one afternoon. "Where are you going with all that food, punk?"

"Shit," Jessie muttered under her breath. She'd wanted to get out of the house before her sister showed up. "Pregnant?" she fired back, stuffing the unwashed fruit and vegetables she'd purloined from the crisper bin into the largest pocket of her knapsack. "I'm not the one letting strange boys fondle my breasts *in* the gymnasium *under* the bleachers *by* the water fountain *after* the Stupid Cupid St. Valentine's Day Dance!"

"You haven't got any breasts." Shelby came around the other side of the table, her vivid eyes narrowed with sisterly suspicion. "What's going on, punk? Where do you disappear to every afternoon? I've been getting stuck with dinner around here, and you know what a rotten cook I am. It's a wonder we're not all dead of ptomaine."

To Shelby, "punk" was an affectionate term, but Jessie knew her days were numbered. Shelby wasn't blessed with a generous nature. Her sister would not continue to cover for her much longer. Nevertheless Jessie tossed the pack over her shoulder and headed for the door. "Just one more night, okay, Shel, okay? There's some ground chuck in the frig. Mix it with the Tuna Surprise from last night. Hank'll be drunk again probably. He'll never know the difference."

"Tuna Surprise? Yuuuuuck!"

Shelby's wail of disgust followed Jessie out the door.

Jessie's heart was pumping as fast as her legs by the time she reached the place where she and Luc had been meeting for several months now. It was alongside the ravine, under an arbor of big-leaf maples, which provided just enough cover to closet the two of them away from the rest of the world and make them feel as if nothing could touch them.

But something was different today, Jessie realized immediately. Luc wasn't there when she arrived. A whispering of dread welled inside her, but she forced the sensation away and began to empty her knapsack in anticipation of his arrival. She'd arranged the feast on the smooth surface of a broken tree stump when she felt something brush the back of her neck.

She nearly leapt out of her skin. Whirling up, she twisted around, but saw nothing. "Luc?" she whispered. The dread she'd been fighting welled again. Lately she couldn't shake the feeling that something bad was going to happen, that they were going to be discovered and separated. Her fears bled into the happiness she felt when she was with him and tinged it with sadness. Sometimes she was afraid to see him again because of the heartache that was building up inside her.

As she crouched by the stump, she felt the tickling sensation again. A hiss of laughter made her look up into the flowering trees. Luc was perched on the branch just above her, clutching a leafy bough in his hand. He looked like a jungle cat about to pounce.

"Look out!" he warned. He swung over the branch and dangled from it like a gymnast, then dropped to the ground, landing on his good leg. "Mmm, pears," he said approvingly, looking over the smorgasbord she'd laid out. He smiled at her with his great, dark animal eyes and began to eat.

Jessie watched silently as he wolfed down the raw fruits and vegetables. Months ago, as a punishment, his father had banished him from the dinner table. When she'd first started bringing food to this place, he hadn't been able to eat much of it. But in the last few months he'd begun to thrive, feasting on the bounty she provided. He was getting better before her eyes. Stronger, bigger and more beautiful. If he looked less like a sleek wild animal to her, that was all right too. Wild animals often died young and tragically, and she wanted Luc Warnecke to live.

"I've got an idea," she said when he'd finished eating. "Let's meet outside the fence tonight after everyone's in bed, okay? We'll go on an odyssey, like Homer, that Greek guy you told me about."

An odd look crossed Luc's face, and Jessie realized he was apprehensive. As far as she knew he'd never been off Warnecke property except with his father. "Will you come?" she pressed. "There's something I want to show you. It's beautiful, Luc, a special place."

There was a vibrance in her voice that hadn't been there before. He heard it too, and his eyes changed as he looked at her. Something moved in their depths, a quality of interest she'd never noticed before. A brand new awareness was taking shape, growing between them, Jessie realized. Not yet thirteen, she was a little frightened by it.

The moon stretched itself across the surface of the bay like a carpet of opalescent white, rippling as if it were waiting impatiently for someone to step aboard and be carried away to magical, faraway places.

"Isn't it beautiful?" Jessie glanced at Luc and saw by his expression that he was captivated. His eyes glowed with silvery light, with moonfire. She'd wanted to bring him here ever since he'd told her about the legend of the half moon. He'd insisted the story was part of the town's folklore, but she felt sure he'd made up the sad and lovely tale about a young Indian boy who was afraid of the dawn. She was also sure the legend had some special meaning for his life.

"Let's dive into the moon," she said suddenly, breathlessly. "Want to?" She pulled off her cardigan sweater and shivered.

"Go swimming? It's freezing."

Luc looked dubious, but Jessie wouldn't be talked out of it. She was trembling with excitement. "We have to, Luc," she said imploringly. "That's why we're here tonight, don't you see? The moonlight will be our protection, our good luck. It will cling to us like fairy dust and ward off anything evil."

She grabbed him by the hand and pulled him toward the water, kicking off her shoes as she ran. "Come on," she cried, unbuttoning her jeans and shimmying out of them. "The

moon moves across the sky, just like the sun. It won't be here
forever."

He stepped away from her, staring at her with both wonder
and apprehension as she stripped off her clothes in front of
him. When she was down to the skin, she glanced at herself
and saw what he was gaping at. Her naked body was caught
somewhere between childhood and womanhood, with breasts
just beginning to blossom.

She wanted to cover herself up. Instead she made a dash
for the water and dove into the moonlight. "It's freezing!" she
screamed as she burst up through the surface.

"I told you." Luc laughed nervously.

"*Come in*," she coaxed, treading water as much to get her
blood circulating as to keep herself afloat. "Please, Luc! You
have to. Something bad will happen if you don't."

He began to take off his clothes then, stepping out of his
loosely tied tennis shoes and shucking his jeans with a quick,
tight sigh. When at last he peeled off his jockey shorts, she
saw the part of him that had dominated her secret thoughts for
some time. He was nearly a year older now, and his body had
grown and strengthened, including a full and undisputed claim
on sexual manhood. She probably would have blushed if she
hadn't been so frozen. He was beautiful.

She watched with building excitement as he walked to the
shoreline. His gait was awkward because of the badly set leg,
but she knew he would be graceful in the water in a way that
he couldn't be on land.

He splashed in and dove, sinking into the murky black-
ness like an enchanted sea creature and disappearing without a ripple to reveal his path. She was beginning to wonder whether he'd struck out for the ocean when he burst
up beside her. Laughing and gasping for air, he dragged her
close and then swam with her to shore, where they could
stand.

"Where did you learn to swim like that?" she asked a
moment later, as she rose out of the bay with him. They
stood facing each other, water streaming down their bodies.

"In the pool at Echos."

"You're wonderful."

He flushed with pleasure. "Thanks . . . you too."

In the silence that followed Jessie was aware of her own breathy, shivering anticipation. Her breasts were rosy pink and throbbing from the coldness. Her nipples were as stony as the pebbles beneath their feet, but they tingled in a way that stones never could.

She and Luc had built a cocoon of friendship and trust over the months, sharing their war stories and their loneliness. They were misfits who'd taken comfort in the knowledge that they weren't totally alone in their strangeness, or their pain. Only now that trust was gone. Suddenly they had nothing to say to each other. Not a word.

They were on the brink of some breathless new discovery, approaching a bold and unmapped terrain that nothing in their experience, not even Homer and his epic odyssey, had prepared them for. They were on their own now, forced to find their way through this new and frightening maze of feelings, their hearts soaring wildly, their minds gripped with sweet yet violent and bewildering sensations.

Jessie turned away from Luc's gaze in confusion. "We have to get dressed," she said, suddenly quaking with cold. "If the moonlight dries while we're standing here, the charm's no good."

"Are you making that up?" Luc asked.

"Yes," she admitted.

Again their eyes met, and in some way they both understood that if they acted on this thing that was happening between them, it could change everything and their relationship might never be the same again.

"Can we come back?" Luc asked. "Tomorrow night?"

They returned to the bay every night for the next two weeks, and it was the most blissful time of Jessie's life. Some nights they simply sat on the shore, gazed at the glittery reflection of the moon on the water and talked about their dreams. Other nights they swam in the almost ritualistic way that had become their good luck ceremony, always stopping to stand opposite each other for a few moments in water up to their waists, before they rushed to the shore to dress.

One night they stood much longer, stared much harder. And when at last the water had stopped streaming down their naked bodies, they were still deeply lost in each other's gaze.

"We can't let the moonlight dry," Jessie reminded him, her voice softly imploring. "The charm won't work."

Luc touched her damp hair with the hesitation of someone whose curiosity had not quite overcome his fear. She couldn't breathe until he finally touched her face, and then she released all the pressure from her chest in a warm rush and tilted her head back so that he could see the eagerness that was flooding her eyes. She felt like the moonfire on the bay, all silvery and bright, cool and hot.

He bent to kiss her, his fingers lingering near her mouth. As their lips met, his hand played there, at the periphery of her lips, then drifted down her arm, grazing her breast, and she wished desperately that she had something more for him to touch—large, soft breasts and womanly curves like Shelby's. She and Luc had shared dreams of escaping the misery of their home lives, dreams of seeking fame and fortune in the real world. She wanted to travel, to be a modern-day adventuress. But she had never told him that this was her sweetest dream— kissing him. It had consumed her thoughts above all other things, to the point where she'd come to believe she couldn't die a complete woman unless Luc Warnecke had kissed her in the moonlight that danced off the waters of the bay—

"So this is where you've been sneaking off to!"

The harsh words were punctuated by the crunch of gravel on the shore.

"Goddamned kid!" a man's voice snarled.

Luc and Jessie froze in the act of reaching for each other. Blinded by an explosion of light, they crouched in the waist-deep water, recoiling from the punishing beam of a searchlight. The water lapped like ice against their skin.

Jessie grabbed Luc's hand and held tight. She firmly believed he didn't know how to defend himself. He hadn't had to fight off siblings or the bullies that preyed on the weak at school, and therefore it had become her solemn duty to protect him, despite the fact that he was much bigger than she was.

"Get the hell out of that water, Luc! I'll teach you to sneak off at night with tramps."

Jessie's heart sank. The man who'd spoken had to be Luc's father. His voice was terrifyingly deep, full of authority and cold contempt. They would have been better off if the police had caught them.

"At least it's a girl and not a boy," a second man said.

"Find out who the little whore is and get her out of here," the first man ordered. "I'll take care of my son."

"Don't let go of me," Jessie whispered to Luc as the two men waded into the water toward them, their flashlights careening in the darkness.

Jessie felt someone grasp her arm. "Hang on!" she cried, pulling back. She jerked Luc's hand to warn him.

"Let go of her!" Luc shouted. He tried to rise, but there was a terrible sound, a sickening crack of bone against bone, and then Jessie felt him go limp, his hand slipping from hers.

"No!" she cried, groping for him in the watery darkness. She began to fight like an enraged animal, but she couldn't see her captor. As she whirled around, a fist closed in the thickness of her hair, nearly jerking a handful of it out of her scalp, and then another hand clamped over her mouth, strangling off her voice.

She was hoisted up like a rag doll, and then her head hit something solid and the searchlights snapped off. The world went white and silent as she spiraled into a gaping void, sinking like a stone to the bottom of a moonlit bay.

CHAPTER
·· TWELVE ··

"COME ONNNNNN, BIRTHDAY girl. Shake your sweet sixteen-year-old butt or we're going to miss the movie!"

"Jusssst a minute!" Jessie grimaced in despair as she peered into the dizzying distortions of the cheap bathroom mirror. She'd smeared Cover Girl cherrybomb lip gloss up to her nose! If Shelby would stop screeching and let her finish getting ready, they could get out of here already. It wasn't easy trying to look decent when you had Shelby as your standard of beauty. Jessie still felt like a biology class experiment next to her drop-dead sexy sister.

The bathroom lights began to flash on and off.

Jessie swore under her breath, threw the lipstick tube into her embarrassing lunch box of a purse and took a swipe at the disembodied hand that had snaked around the door frame to the light switch. "All right, all right, I'm ready. You can quit being such a jerk, Shelby."

"My god, the J word? Such language from my saintly little sister?" Shelby's turquoise eyes were wide with injured innocence as she peered into the room. "Why so touchy? Are we riding the cotton bicycle this week?"

Shelby stepped full into the doorway. Her glossy dark hair swung around her face in a pageboy that matched the current top New York model's do, and her outfit was a copy of a jumpsuit found in a recent issue of *Glamour* magazine. Shelby had designed and sewn it herself, undoubtedly because she knew it was the only way she would ever come close to a trendy look on the money she made at the Pik 'N' Save where she clerked.

Privately Jessie thought Shelby was prettier than the top

models she tried to copy. Jessie would never admit it, though, not even under threat of torture. Shelby was too full of herself as it was. "What are we seeing?" Jessie asked.

"A double feature—*Attack of the Giant Leeches* and *A Bucket of Blood.*"

"Eeyuuuuu, Shelby! I hate horror movies."

"Tough beans, I'm paying."

"But it's *my* birthday!"

Shelby mouthed the letters BFD and grinned. "Let's go, birthday girl. I've seen both movies three times. I don't want to miss the part where the leeches attack a herd of cows and suck out their brains."

Both girls screamed in mock terror and began a pushing and shoving stampede to the front door.

Jessie wasn't much in the mood for a drippy, catsup-soaked hamburger after the gore-filled movie, but it was part of Shelby's birthday treat and therefore obligatory. Her big sister's generous moods were very unpredictable, and Jessie knew better than to appear ungrateful.

The coffee shop had an authentic, dinerlike atmosphere with red leather booths, chrome-trimmed dinettes and little jukeboxes on the tables that actually worked. Naturally Shelby had picked a booth where she had a clear view of the front door.

"Anybody of interest?" Jessie inquired, picking at her fries. Shelby had casually slipped her cowl-necked sweater off one shoulder, and whenever Shelby started baring skin, it was a sure sign the troops had landed.

"Just some kids from school." Shelby sighed dramatically, pulled the straw from her cherry coke and languidly caught the rolling drops of sticky sweetness with her tongue. Heavy-lidded boredom was Shelby's M.O. these days. Each little sigh and arching nuance indicated that she was about to lapse into a coma from want of excitement. Her sister was the reigning queen of listlessness, Jessie had decided. And since Shelby was graduating this year, the high school crowd had fallen even beneath Elvis sightings on her Crashing Bores Scale.

"Why don't we go?" Jessie suggested, looking for an excuse to abandon her nearly full plate.

"Just a minute," Shelby said, honing in on some new target with the singular focus of a laser beam.

"Who is it?" Jessie's interest was piqued.

"I don't know, but he's . . . *incroyable*. That's French for incredible. Don't look!" she whispered as Jessie started to turn around. "He's coming this way."

Jessie picked up a French fry and made a large J in the pool of catsup on her plate. She and Shelby rarely agreed on men, so it was probably no great loss that she wasn't going to get to check out this one.

Jessie was blotting out her initials in favor of a dirty word when Shelby leaned over and whispered, "Look—quick—now!"

Jessie glanced up as the young man walked by, and her first reaction was surprise. She didn't know what she'd expected, but it wasn't a military-type uniform. She couldn't see his face clearly as he passed, but she caught a glimpse of his profile, and Shelby was right the first time. He was incredible—tall and racehorse fit, broad across the shoulders, narrow at the hips, muscular as hell.

But there was something else that held her attention, something that absolutely wouldn't let her look away. She followed him intently with her gaze aware of his odd gait, as he walked down the narrow aisle, but she still wasn't quite sure what it was about him that held her—until he turned.

"Jess? What's wrong?" Shelby asked. "You've gone white as my napkin."

The French fry slipped from Jessie's fingers. She felt paralyzed, as inert as a statue, her hand suspended in the air. Her face and hands were suddenly icy, as if all the blood in her body had pooled in her feet. "It's him," she breathed.

"Who?" Shelby glanced around to see where Jessie was looking. "The incredible guy? You know him?"

"It's . . . Luc . . . Warnecke." The words came like a programmed computer message. Jessie was still too stunned to know exactly what she was saying. It had been four years since she'd seen Luc, though she had returned to the ravine to look for him many times.

"Luc Warnecke? That weird rich kid who got sent away to military school?"

Jessie nodded. "I thought they killed him," she admitted, her voice going hoarse.

"They don't kill them in military school, Jess."

"Yes, they do." She and Shelby were having two different conversations. Jessie knew that, but she could hardly keep track of her own train of thought, much less her sister's. She hadn't seen Luc since the night they were caught by his father, and she'd heard the blow that had knocked him unconscious, a sickening sound her mind had registered as a death knell.

Afterward the news around town was that he'd been shipped off to a military school, but Jessie didn't believe it. And even if it were true, she knew his father would have chosen a brutal, sadistic place. Luc couldn't have survived that kind of environment with his physical problems. It would have destroyed him. No, he had gone on to something better. She had tortured herself for months, struggling to find some sense of inner peace about his fate.

"Jess? Hey, punk! Are you crying?"

Jessie shook her head, but there was no way to deny the lonely tear that rolled toward her quivering chin. Her heart was breaking. The pain she'd been through, the nights she'd wept over him. Luc Warnecke was gone. Her mind couldn't accept anything else. Her heart wasn't ready to see him alive, grown into a man. The boy she knew had died, a boy she loved . . .

"Jessie? Snap out of it!" Shelby reached over and shook Jessie's frozen hand until Jessie looked at her. "You're like obsessing on this guy. What's the deal?"

"I have to go—" Jessie slid out of the booth, her eyes still on Luc. She was terrified he would see her. She didn't want that. She couldn't deal with that. She had no idea who he was, this riveting dark-eyed stranger in a uniform.

"Good *grief*," Shelby said, groaning.

The last thing Jessie heard as she swept out the door of the diner was Shelby shouting at her to stop.

The sun had just risen, its pale beams slanting into the ravine through every available nook and cranny afforded by the huddled maples. High in the treetops, sharper rays pierced the early gloom like daylight through the dark eaves of an attic roof. The area was quiet, worshipful, as if Mother Nature herself were holding a morning service to usher in the day.

Jessie's mood was equally hushed as she approached the place where she and Luc used to meet. She'd never expected to be here again. Once she'd accepted the loss, she'd promised herself there would be no more self-inflicted memories, no more worrying the wound. It was a promise made to be broken.

He was there when she stepped inside the bower of trees that had been their secret place. He stood facing away from her, gazing toward the ravine as she'd often seen him do. It was as if he'd known she was going to be there, as if this meeting had been planned like all the others when they were younger. Children, she thought. We were children, so hungry and trusting, like broken parts coming together, trying to make a whole.

Her awareness of him in this poignantly familiar setting—especially of his dramatically different height and size—forced her to acknowledge how drastically things had changed in four years, and how much she had wanted them to stay the same. The image of him she held in her mind—the thin body, the dark angel's face—had taken on the reverence of a shrine. But this man was no martyred saint. He was flesh and blood, very much alive, and in some ways he seemed more a stranger to her than if they'd never met. Who was Luc Warnecke now? she wondered.

Leaves rustled in the trees above them, whispering of her arrival. A bird called out in startled flight, and a twig snapped under her foot as she moved toward him.

He turned to her, and she was struck by so many confounding differences, she couldn't comprehend them all. She wanted to run. It was terribly threatening seeing him now, this way. Here. Her mouth had gone dry, and her body felt light and dizzy, as if she were about to fly off into space. But she couldn't. She was unbearably earthbound as she registered this stranger who was part of her past, part of her soul. She was unable to measure the differences in any terms but the terribly intimate details of their past.

"Jessie?" he said, his gaze narrowing on her features.

His voice had deepened, and his gaunt beauty had matured into masculine angles and planes. He was raw, strong, magnificent. His dark hair and eyes still harbored the wildness she remembered, a quality that fought the uniform he wore, giving him a feeling of raw energy almost too tightly contained. The quick, uncomfortable surge of her heart told her that her feelings for him had not changed. She was still profoundly attracted to him, but there was a whole new aspect to it now.

"God," he said, his voice catching. "It's good to see you."

She ducked her head, feeling foolish. "You look great, Luc. Was it military school? Is that where you've been?"

"Yes."

"You could have written." The bitterness in her voice surprised her. She hadn't wanted to reveal that much.

"I did write. Every day."

He'd written. Of course he had.

They both knew what must have happened. The letters had been intercepted, probably before they ever left the school. It gave Jessie a moment's satisfaction to realize he'd tried to contact her, but it wasn't nearly enough.

She turned away as the pain of her thoughts penetrated her anger. She was hurt, terribly hurt. And terribly, terribly in love.

"Jessie . . . it's been a long time. I don't know what to say. I thought about you, I wanted to let you know I was okay, but—"

She could feel the guardedness between them, but was it coming from him or from her? Who was putting up the barriers? There was conflict in his eyes when she turned back. He was trying to reforge a connection, but he didn't know how. He had learned to protect himself while he was gone, developed the survival instincts of a combatant. Perhaps that was good, she told herself. But one thing was very clear. He didn't need her anymore. He could take care of himself.

"You look nice, Jessie. I like your dress."

"Oh, me?" She shrugged off the compliment. Her faded print sundress was ghastly. "This is nothing," she insisted. "You must have grown a foot. What was it like, where you went?"

"Hell," he said flatly. "But it was better than Echos."

He had said a great deal, perhaps without even realizing it. Despite their closeness, he'd never told her the details. She should have known that any environment away from his father would be an improvement, even if it meant that he couldn't see her.

"There was a doctor at the academy," he told her. "He diagnosed my condition as congenital, but it turned out to be manageable with diet and enzymes. As long as I watch what I eat, I'm fine."

That must have been why he'd been so thin when she met him. "I'm glad," she said, meaning it sincerely.

They fell silent, staring at each other, as if dazed by memories and floundering for the right thing to say. Jessie didn't know quite what to think about the way Luc was studying her, but it made her stomach feel odd and empty. Some part of her didn't want these new feelings. She wanted the old bond, the fierce friendship, the jealous guardianship of each other's safety. She felt awkward and overwhelmed. Once, she'd confessed the deepest secrets of her soul to Luc Warnecke, and now she couldn't have a simple conversation with him.

"I have to go," she said.

"Why? Is something wrong?" At the quick, negative shake of her head, he added, "Jessie, I didn't forget you. I thought about you all the time, about the bay, the moonlight."

The catch in his voice told her that was true. He had thought about her, but not in the same way she'd thought about him. His dark gaze moved over her face and body, touching her with an urgency that was almost tender.

"I have to go!" she whispered, stepping back from him.

He called her house the next week. Shelby answered the phone and handed it to Jessie with an exaggerated wink that glued her Revlon Lashful eye shut.

"I thought maybe we could do something tonight," Luc said when Jessie answered.

"Okay . . . Like what?" She stuck a finger in her ear to block out Shelby's disgusting wet kiss noises.

"A movie?"

"No . . . I'd rather go to the bay." She didn't know why she'd said it or what she was trying to accomplish by it. But she knew it would be dark and the moon would be full.

It was the longest day of Jessie's life. She arrived at the cove a few moments after sundown. Luc was already there.

"Race you to the water," he said, pulling his cable-knit sweater off over his head.

Jessie stared at him in surprise. The moonlight bouncing off the bay was dazzling in its brightness. It bathed his bare shoulders and chest in iridescence, washing out details. But it wasn't bright enough to obscure the carved definition of his biceps or the fountain of dark hair that swept his pectoral muscles.

"It's freezing," she protested, her voice faint.

"Of course, that's the point. Remember?"

"I didn't bring a suit."

"But I thought that's why you wanted to come here." Obviously confused, he let the sweater drop to the ground. "To dive into the moonlight the way we used to do. Remember you said it was good luck, that nothing bad could happen to us."

"We were kids."

"Yes, we were kids. And now we're not. Jessie?" He touched her elbow. "Is something wrong?"

She nodded. It was as close as she could come to expressing her feelings at that moment. She didn't understand what was happening between them now. It frightened her. She wanted what they'd had, the vulnerability of his needing her. She'd felt safe with him then. She'd been the worldly and experienced one. Now she felt like the child to his adult, and it made her wonder what besides survival instincts he'd learned while he was gone. Had he been with women? Had he already had sex? She'd talked about it, with Shelby mostly, but that was all she'd done.

"I don't know who you are anymore, Luc," she confessed. "I don't know what you want." She looked down, saddened. "And I miss what we were."

"What were we?"

She caught back the huskiness in her voice and went on. "Two lost kids, orphans in a storm."

"*Ah, Jessie.*"

He touched her hair with such tenderness she couldn't bring herself to look at him. She wanted so badly to tell him what was in her heart, but she didn't trust herself to speak. She was bursting with feeling. There was so much of it, she could hardly stop it from it bubbling up into her throat and trying to escape through her shaking fingers as she hid them in the material of her dress. When at last she was able, she unclenched her hands and took a deep breath.

"I'm all right now," she told him.

She tilted up her head, and he bent his. But before their lips touched, he emitted a sound that cut through her heart. It was frightened and sweet; it was lonely. The moonlight bathed them both in its grace as he kissed her, and for a moment they were orphans again.

"I love you," she whispered.

"Jessie, Jessie—you're so sweet."

He caught her hand and drew her closer with an urgency that was heart-melting. Tender words murmured through his lips as if he couldn't control them. As their mouths touched and clung, Jessie felt the thrill of it, of this, their second kiss, running through her like a river of sparkling effervescence. Because of his height, her head was bent back deeply and she was forced to cling to his bare shoulders to anchor herself, but she loved the feeling of falling through space with him as her only mooring.

He stroked her face gently and slipped his hand under her pullover sweater, riveting her senses as cool air mingled with the heat of his skin. She'd wished for Shelby's womanly curves the last time he'd touched her. Tonight her breasts felt full and heavy. Her sixteen-year-old flesh was straining and tingling with a vibrancy that made her moan.

He shuddered and went fierce at the sound, his hand closing possessively on the softness it touched. Suddenly the sweetness was gone, replaced by impulses she didn't understand. His mouth was hard and hungry, wanting more than it gave. The boy of four years ago would never have been so physical or so aggressive, she realized. This was a man. A man who knew exactly what he wanted and how to go about getting it.

"Luc," she gasped. "I can't."

"It's okay," he said, drawing back slightly to look at her. "I thought that's what you wanted."

She shook her head, tears glittering in her eyes.

He pulled her into his arms and held her, but Jessie was afraid. Their relationship was taking a bewildering turn, and she wasn't quite sure what that meant, but she knew something precious was at stake. It would never again be as simple as two lonely kids sharing their pain, huddled together against the storm.

As the cool spring rains gave way to summer's mellow warmth, Jessie tried to reclaim the childhood closeness she'd shared with Luc. She still wanted the bond they'd had, and there were times when it seemed as if they were becoming kindred spirits again. He'd begun to open up more, sharing a gift for painting word pictures that she'd only glimpsed when they were younger. He could describe the sunset over the bay so vividly she would see it with her eyes closed. Meadows of wildflowers were so lovingly detailed, she could smell the perfume. Luc had poetry in his soul, she realized, but he refused to put even a word of it down on paper.

Living at home with Simon seemed to bring out the worst in him. The elder Warnecke wanted his son to work his way up through the ranks of Warnecke Communications, but Jessie could see that Luc hated the idea. He'd learned to bottle up his feelings in military school, and at times she'd find him so taut, he seemed about to explode. There was a ticking-bomb quality about him that made her afraid of what he might do.

Still, they spent a great deal of time together, swimming in the bay, going to movies and debating what they might do with their lives. He'd put no further pressure on her for sex, and she wondered if he were biding his time. She was holding off because she knew restraint was her last refuge. She would surrender everything when he finally made love to her. She would be naked in his arms, naked in every way.

Secretly she obsessed about being with him, imagining the moment in great and excruciating detail. If he had pressed, she would have tumbled in a heartbeat. She loved him for being patient, because he must have known she was a sure thing where he was concerned. But perhaps what she loved best about him was his ability to make her feel that she was bright and pretty and could handle anything life served up. No one else had ever made her feel that way.

He even invited her to Echos for brunch, where she was properly introduced to the fearful Simon Warnecke one fragrant summer morning in the rose garden. She'd expected one of Satan's disciples at the very least. Instead she met a man who drank tea from a bone china cup, ate unbuttered rye toast, and was oddly smooth-skinned and soft-spoken. The elder Warnecke was nothing like the terrifying voice in the darkness who'd branded her a "little whore." Jessie didn't know what to make of Luc's father, even though Luc had warned her he had a politician's beguiling charm.

The time was coming when Jessie would have to invite Luc to her home, but she dreaded it. Shelby could be counted on to live up to her reputation for being outrageous, and Hank, if he was around, would be drunk or on his way. Still, Jessie knew it was inevitable . . . What she didn't know was just how inevitable. Or that the fated occasion would come sooner than she'd planned.

"Oh, Jessseeee!" Shelby trilled one balmy summer evening. "You have company, dear heart."

When Jessie didn't respond, Shelby reverted to type. "Get your skinny butt in here, Jess. It's the rich kid!"

Jessie froze in front of the kitchen sink, up to her elbows in Ivory soap and dinner dishes. Luc, here? Now? She grabbed for a towel, dried her arms and blotted her dripping brow. She was a wreck! An unsalvageable shipwreck! As she rushed into the living room, straightening her damp cotton blouse and cutoff jeans, she felt like Cinderella receiving the prince.

Only this was no fairy tale, she saw instantly. This was the end of the world. Luc looked irresistible in a denim jacket and jeans worn to holes at the knees. Shelby had on a black halter top and shorts that flashed enough creamy white skin to snowblind a ski patrol. Worse, she'd planted herself in front of Luc, her shoulders exposed in their totality, and she was making good use of both of them.

"Hi," Luc said, tilting around Shelby to smile at Jessie. "Hope you don't mind that I stopped by."

"No, that's fine." Jessie smiled wanly.

"What's wrong with you, Jess?" Shelby chided, motioning for Luc to take his choice of one of the living room's two peeling Naugahyde chairs or the matching sofa. "Get your friend a drink."

"Coke?" Jessie asked.

"Don't be silly." Shelby flashed Jessie a reproving glance. "Get him some of Hank's Scotch."

"Sure," Luc said, arranging himself in one of the wobbly, too-small chairs. "Scotch works."

As the evening progressed, Jessie consoled herself that Shelby was only playing femme fatale. Her sister loved to get men hot and bothered, but as far as Jessie knew, Shelby rarely if ever "put out." She needed the attention, the symbolic victory of knowing a man wanted her over any other woman. Once she had that, she lost interest. Besides, Jessie reasoned, Luc was younger than Shelby. And Shelby, by her own admission, was bored silly with younger men these days.

Luc seemed more embarrassed than flattered by Shelby's blatant flirting, which confirmed Jessie's belief, which she urgently needed to maintain, that he could never be susceptible to someone like her sister. Jessie's own mute anxiety seemed to draw him like a magnet, and he would glance her way at odd moments, as if to reassure her he would rather be anywhere with her than trapped in Shelby's web.

By the end of the evening, Jessie was glowing with quiet triumph. Hank's friends and the boys from town might sniff around Shelby like so many tomcats in back-alley trash. But they were mostly barflies and immature high school kids, Jessie reminded herself. Luc was different from them, from everyone. He was different like her.

Hank broke up the party early when he rolled in around ten P.M. Surprisingly sober, he glared disapprovingly at Shelby's sexy outfit and took Luc's measure as if Luc were a rival, trying to muscle in on his territory. "You the Warnecke kid?" he asked, none too pleasantly. "Long way from home, aren't you?"

Jessie and Luc escaped like bandits to the soft summer night. Stars twinkled brightly above them and the crickets beguiled them with a sweet, maddening serenade as Jessie walked with Luc part of the way home. She was aware of the intoxicating perfume of wild bramble roses and an odd excitement stirring in her throat that made it hard for her to swallow.

"Will I see you tomorrow?" she asked.

"Sure," Luc said, kicking at rocks. He seemed tense, pre-occupied.

Suddenly, with no warning at all except a funny sound, he caught hold of her and pulled her to him. He kissed her quick and hard, nearly cutting off her wind. "You're nothing like her, Jessie," he said almost angrily. "You're sweet and brave and beautiful. You're *nothing* like Shelby, do you hear me?"

His reaction baffled Jessie, but he took off without giving her time to find out what was wrong. As she watched him sprint down the road and disappear into the darkness, she touched her lips and smiled.

Luc was hers. If nothing else had convinced Jessie of that fact in the coming weeks, the tension that built between Luc and Shelby would have. Their dislike of each other was palpable. It soared to a fever pitch almost on sight and stayed that way until Jessie became forced to referee their heated arguments. They fought about everything from the Bay Area weather to the dilemma of police brutality to the tragedy of world hunger.

"Let's not meet here anymore," Jessie suggested one evening as she and Luc were saying good-bye on the porch.

"Why?" he asked. "Are you tired of dodging bullets?"

She laughed with him and smiled into his dark eyes. Her tender feelings for him rose so quickly they nearly choked her. Neither mentioned Shelby for the rest of the evening.

That night Jessie lay awake in her bed, quaking with the certain knowledge that she wanted Luc Warnecke to make love to her. Her body was a fount of energy, turned in on itself. Her mind had been taken hostage by its own ardent fantasies. There was sweetness and need swirling around inside her, so much of it she could hardly breathe. She couldn't wait any longer to know the magic of physical love with Luc. Not a moment longer. She was ready to risk everything to be closer to him, as close as heaven and earth would allow.

Through her bedroom window she could see a matte velvet sky thick with the diamond dust of beckoning stars. It was after midnight, Shelby was out somewhere, and Hank had long ago passed out in front of the TV. There would be other opportunities to do this thing that her mind and body and the universe itself seemed to be demanding of her, but if she waited, she might lose her nerve.

The moon was high that night. It sent her shadow rocketing out in front of her as she walked around the back of the house, toward the ravine. In her imagination she was already over at Echos, throwing pebbles at Luc's window to wake him. But as she neared the ramshackle garage, which her stepfather was halfheartedly attempting to convert into a rental apartment, a glint of reflected moonlight caught her eye. An empty bottle of Scotch had been dropped in front of the garage door.

Curious, she walked over, and as she knelt to pick it up, she heard the noises. They were coming from inside—the creak and groan of rusty bedsprings, the slap of wet, turgid flesh. Impulsively, she pushed the door open, letting moonlight flood into the room.

Her sharp gasp went unnoticed by the writhing couple inside. The man was shirtless with his pants down around his knees, and the woman beneath him was digging her fingernails into his back, her legs waving in the air. Jessie knew it was Shelby by her bright red fingernails, but the man was shadowed. She might never have realized who he was if the moonlight hadn't illuminated his bare back so brightly. Only one man that she knew had such horrifying white scars on his body—Luc Warnecke.

CHAPTER
·· THIRTEEN ··

HALF MOON BAY 1994

JESSIE NEEDED A drink, preferably a strong one. She entered the library at Echos with no other thought than to gird herself like Joan of Arc for the evening ahead. The prospect of facing both Shelby and Luc at dinner was more than she could deal with unfortified.

Laughter quavered in her throat, cold and faintly hysterical. Her ravishing older sister and her childhood sweetheart were guests for dinner? *What a charming party that was going to be! The three of them would have no end of things to reminisce about.* She'd anticipated the possibility of Luc's return, but not Shelby's, and certainly not both of them at once. But perhaps it was inevitable that they would both show up now, lured like vultures by Simon's death. Apparently they hadn't destroyed her life thoroughly enough with their raging secret love, and now they were back to finish the job.

Jessie dipped her hand into the lead crystal bucket and scooped out a handful of ice. She didn't feel steady enough to handle tongs. She'd invited Matt Sandusky intentionally, hoping his presence would have a civilizing effect. Although the thought of Shelby around Matt, an unconquered male, made Jessie uneasy.

She took a swig of the liquor and grimaced. She detested the taste, but the flush that swept up her throat and the fumes that seared her nostrils made her feel formidable, a dragon. Matt Sandusky was a powerful man, she reminded herself. He might even provide Shelby with a challenge, although Jessie doubted there was a man alive and compos mentis who could resist Shelby once she'd made up her mind to have him. Maybe she would take another whack at Luc, Jessie thought, splashing more lemon Absolut vodka over the ice. That should be good for an evening's entertainment.

She had finished half the drink and was feeling formidable indeed when she turned and saw Luc entering the library. He was wearing faded denim jeans and a loose white cashmere V-neck sweater with the sleeves pushed up, clearly not dinner attire. It was a flagrant breach, and if anyone knew the dinner etiquette at Echos, Luc did. His jaw was unshaven. Even his shoulder-length hair fell in dark rebellion around his face, as if he'd combed it with his hands. With great reluctance she admitted that the contrast of his sable-black hair and eyes against the white sweater was simply riveting.

He was beautiful. He was perverse.

Jessie decided not to notice.

"The lady in black," Luc said as he approached, indicating the rather severe silk wraparound dress she was wearing. "Are we still mourning Simon? Or is this a fashion statement?"

"It suits my mood."

"No shit," he agreed softly.

When she didn't move from in front of the tray of drinks and made no effort to offer him one, he said, "Is this your own personal bar or can anyone get a drink?"

She smiled icily and stepped away. "It's my personal bar, and only I know which of the decanters contains strychnine, but help yourself."

He glanced at her drink. "The vodka looks safe."

"Don't be so sure."

Luc helped himself to a vodka, not bothering with the ice, took a swallow and hissed as the liquor went down. "Just what the doctor ordered, right?" He glanced again at her drink, as if to signal that he knew what she was doing—imbibing her courage.

She swung away from him, stray locks of red-gold hair exploding from her heavy chignon as she snapped her head and walked directly to the fireplace. The flames from the hearth licked up hypnotically, and a cedary smell wafted toward her that might have been soothing under other circumstances. She barely noticed it as she nursed her drink.

"I came down here to talk to you," he said, coming up behind her.

"I'm not in the mood to talk."

"*Get* in the mood."

Her shoulders stiffened. "What is it?" She turned to him.

"I made you a proposal of marriage. I'd like an answer."

"*Never.*"

"Never what, Jess? What is it I'm *never* going to get? An answer? Or you?"

"I'll never marry you, of course. The idea is ludicrous."

"No more ludicrous than you with my father."

She ducked around him and walked to the side bar to freshen her drink. "Why do you persist in this?" she asked him, sluicing more vodka into her glass. This time she didn't bother with the ice. She took a sip, shuddered and turned around. Her stomach was roiling. Please, God, don't let me be sick, she thought. Don't let me be weak in front of this devil, this childhood friend who's turned into a fiend.

"You know nothing about me and Simon," she informed him.

"I know he's a monster and that you inherited all his money . . . So what does that make you, Jessie?"

A monster, she thought defiantly, sadly. Like him, like you, like everyone. We do what we have to do, and sometimes it's monstrous. "If I thought for one moment that you were serious about the proposal, that you were doing anything besides tormenting me, I'd be—"

He walked toward her, the firelight at his back, Satan stepping out of the flames. "You'd be what?"

"Terrified," she admitted. "Being your wife would be terrifying."

He set his drink on the tray and gazed at her for a very long time. "Be terrified then. Because you have no other choice, Jessie. I own you. I have the very thing—the *only* thing—you want and need."

The only thing she needed?

She hadn't voiced the words, but he smiled as if she had.

"Yes, Jessie, I've got it," he said. "Ask me what it is, go ahead. Haven't you ever read the Bible? Ask and ye shall receive . . ."

The tremor was making her hand shake. She set her drink down with exaggerated care, holding onto the glass until her fingers felt steadier. "What is it I need?" she asked him at last.

His smile was so darkly knowing it brought one word to her mind. Diabolical. He was amusing himself again at her expense, playing with her, just as he'd done with the gun and with the wedding picture. She could only imagine what he had in mind, but she knew it must either be humiliating or lewd. She turned away from him, disgusted with herself for taking the bait.

"There's nothing I want from you except your death by the goriest circumstances possible," she said. "Could you arrange that, please? Do us all a favor and step in front of a truck, Luc."

He snorted. "She's asking nicely? Good manners in a violence-prone woman, I like that."

"You have no idea how violent." She had clasped one hand over the other, the web of her thumb stretching white across her knuckles. "Don't forget, I come from the hills, from trash."

"How could I forget? Who else but crazy white trash would have had the guts to try and save a nut case like fourteen-year-old Luc Warnecke. The whole town thought I was crazy, Jessie, a dangerous lunatic, but that didn't stop you, did it?" His voice dropped to something low and husky, almost reverent. "Who else but you?"

She saw him in her mind the way he'd looked that day at the bank—a sad, defiant kid with wounded eyes. *Stop it*, she thought. *Don't try to rattle me with references to the past. I won't be dragged back there at your whim. You can't get to me that way!* But her eyes burned unexpectedly, and the moisture she blinked away was as acid-sweet as the fire in her throat. He'd triggered pain, that old tormenting pain, but it was as fresh and hot as a puncture wound.

She spun around and glared at him. But it was a foolish thing to do. *Terribly foolish.* The vodka had given her courage, but it had also weakened her defenses. There were times, like now, when he looked so much like her memories that it stole her breath away. She blinked slowly, registering how beautiful he was by painful degrees, as if her mind wouldn't allow her to see it all at once, even numbed as it was by alcohol.

"I have what you need, Jess." He was walking toward her.

"No, you have misery, that's all. Misery and the need to destroy everything you touch. Stay away from me, Luc. No! Don't come any nearer!"

He stopped where he was. "You're wrong. What I have for you is the opposite of misery, the opposite of destruction—"

"What do you mean?"

"Peace of mind, Jessie. Couldn't you use a little peace of mind right about now? If you agree to the marriage, I'll stop investigating Hank Flood's death immediately. Tonight. And Mel too. I'll accept whatever you tell me about her parentage, including your story about Simon being her father."

"And if I don't agree?"

"Then I'll blow the lid off. I'll stop at nothing until I get the answers I want. And I'll start with Shelby."

"Did I hear someone call my name?"

Shelby stood in the doorway to the library, her gleaming brunette hair pinned up in a sexy tumble, her slip-dress stoplight red and thigh-high. She was breathtaking as always. She would be thirty-one this year, and she was clearly just entering her prime.

The Flood sisters, Jessie thought. What an act. Shelby has the looks, the charisma, the sex appeal. But I've got the money. Funny how life has a way of balancing the scales.

"No, Shelby," Jessie informed her. "You didn't hear anyone calling you. What you heard was Luc asking me to marry him."

"Really?" Shelby's voice went faint with surprise.

"And I said yes." Jessie picked up her glass and held it high, experiencing a flash of triumph at the surprise in Luc's expression. And the utter shock in Shelby's.

Matt Sandusky pulled his BMW into the crescent drive of the Warnecke mansion and, as he cut the engine, made a mental note to have the car's sound system checked. There was a slight fuzziness in the speakers, just enough to set his teeth on edge. He didn't consider himself any more exacting than the next person, but when it came to fine cars, he expected to get what he'd paid for. Precision. Expensive equipment ought to work, dammit. Why was that so seldom the case?

The caretaker was nowhere in sight as Matt let himself out of the car, another minor irritant in a day of major disasters at work and niggling details at Echos. Roger should have been available to brief him on Shelby Flood's surprise arrival. Matt had no idea how Shelby figured into things, other than that she and Jessie were estranged and it was Luc who'd come between them years ago. The elder Warnecke had taken Matt into his confidence many times over the years, even revealing the rather bizarre circumstances of his marriage to Jessie, but he'd never discussed his son's entanglement with the two Flood sisters.

Sighing heavily, Matt ran his fingertips along the lapel of his jacket to be sure it was smooth. Whatever the reasons for Shelby's reappearance, the "ill wind" had blown home. His role was to see how much containment might be necessary.

The library was vibrating when Matt entered, but it wasn't the tension of an impending explosion. This was the aftermath. Apparently he'd missed the temblor, but the aftershocks were still registering on the Richter scale. The dark-haired vixen in the red dress who was pouring a stiff drink had to be Shelby herself. Luc Warnecke stood by the fireplace, imposing in his silence and looking more the rightful lord of the manor than the interloper. Only Jessie seemed happy to see Matt. Or was it relieved?

"Matt! I'm so glad you could make it," she cried, walking toward him. "You remember Shelby, of course?"

Matt nodded, but the beauteous Shelby didn't bother to glance his way. She had changed considerably from his point of view. The small-town vampiness that had made her Half Moon's reigning heartbreaker had matured into full-blown womanhood. Her don't-give-a-damn attitude was polished to a high gloss, and apparently New York had given her enough sophistication to carry it off.

"Let's have dinner," Jessie suggested as she hooked her arm in his and turned to the others. Her manner was oddly triumphant, especially since Matt also detected a razor-thin edge of hysteria in her voice.

Dinner was interesting in the way that car accidents were interesting. You couldn't not look. Margie, Jessie's part-time housekeeper, served a veal pâté that was redolent with garlic and herbs. She followed it with platters of moist, spit-roasted chicken, braised broccoli and crusty oven-baked potatoes. The food was marvelous, the table conversation edgily polite, but the tension was as hot and thick as Margie's famous espresso. And Matt was especially incredulous when Gina brought Melissa in to say good night to the dinner guests.

Dressed up in a long, white nightshirt with her auburn curls poking out of a matching stocking cap, she seemed delighted to have so many "relatives" around.

Shelby grinned quickly and beckoned for Mel to come to her. "Come here, Rip Van Winkle. Come give your Auntie Shel a good-night hug."

Mel beamed and tumbled into her aunt's arms. Shelby whispered something in Mel's ear, and the two of them began to roughhouse gently as Shelby tickled the child. Mel squealed with laughter, trying to get away.

"Are you a model from New York?" Mel demanded breathlessly. "And do you get to wear beautiful, sexy clothes and get your breasts taped up like Cindy Crawford?"

"Mel," Gina cautioned.

"Gina thinks I have a breast fixation," Mel confided to her aunt. "How long are you going to stay?"

Shelby laughed. "If there were more like you around here, Mel, I might just move back permanently."

The sound of an upset glass put an end to the good-natured fun. "Oh, I'm sorry!" Jessie sprang to her feet. "It was my wine."

"Let's go to bed," Gina said, herding Mel out of the room.

When the meal resumed, Matt took over the conversation, bringing up the weather, sports and whatever else he could think of. Aware that his dinner companions had lapsed into stony silence, he decided boredom was preferable to open warfare and went right on talking, holding forth on the pros and cons of a local development project that would encompass a golf course and a residential tract.

"You used to live here, Luc," he said. "What do you think? Would you like to see the coastal bluffs turned into a country club?"

"I think you're getting on my nerves." Luc raised his wineglass in a mock toast before he drained it.

"Here, here," Shelby chimed in, picking up her glass. "Surely we can come up with a sexier topic of conversation than golf balls. Oh, I know!" She glanced at her little sister and arched one dark eyebrow dramatically. "Jessie, what about your good news? Have you told Matt yet?"

"Shelby, for God's sake," Jessie said under her breath. "When I'm ready to make an announcement, you'll be the first to know."

"Announcement?" Matt was immediately intrigued.

Luc settled back in his chair with a mysterious smile on his face. He looked as if he were ringside at a boxing match with a big bet on the favorite. Already Matt didn't like the odds, especially since he didn't know who the contenders were or what the fight was about.

"How long *are* you staying, Shelby?" Jessie asked sharply.

"I hadn't thought about it, actually." Shelby settled back too, casually trailing vermillion fingernails across the heart-shaped mole on her collarbone. "My visit isn't presenting a problem, is it?"

"When did you ever present anything else?"

Interesting little family reunion, Matt decided. He might have found the situation amusing if he hadn't been so curious about what was going on. There didn't seem to be any harm in watching the fireworks for a while, as long as things didn't get too out of hand.

Matt wasn't a Half Moon Bay native. He'd grown up farther north, in Moss Beach, a decidedly middle-class kid from a decidedly middle-class family. He wasn't modest about his talents, but it was mostly through an accident of timing and luck that he'd risen like cream at Warnecke Communications—Matt's timing and Simon's incredibly bad luck. But despite his success, Matt had retained many of his middle-class sensibilities. His grandmother had always held that if the very rich and the very poor were strange it was because of too much isolation and inbreeding at both extremes. If tonight's dinner were any example, Matt was beginning to believe her.

He was particularly curious about the relationship between Luc and Shelby. Simon had told him that Luc had fallen madly and obsessively in love with Shelby when they were kids, only to be rejected by her after Simon disinherited him. But tonight Luc seemed far more interested in Jessie than Shelby, which made Matt profoundly uneasy.

"How old is Mel?" Shelby was asking Jessie.

"She's . . . nine."

"And when's her birthday?"

Jessie's fork clinked against her bone-china dessert plate. She'd barely taken a bite of the lemon torte. "Why the sudden interest in my daughter, Shelby? You've been gone a long time. I don't remember Melissa getting even so much as a Christmas card from you."

Shelby's sigh was laden with regret. "That's true, but it's never too late, is it? She has my eyes, did you notice?"

Jessie rose abruptly. "Perhaps the three of you would like your after-dinner drinks served in the library? I'm afraid I'm going to have to excuse myself. Something doesn't seem to have agreed with me tonight." She glanced at Matt, which he took as his signal to act.

"Thanks, but I should be going," he said, standing. "Big day tomorrow."

"I'll bet." Luc made the sardonic remark as he pushed back from the table and stood. "I'm going to pass on the drinks too. I've got some business to take care of."

Shelby's eyes flashed dangerously. "Business? At this time of night? Such dedication, Luc. I'm impressed. Unless it's personal business, of course."

"All of my business is personal, Shelby."

"Really? And is that what accounts for your phenomenal success?"

"If I'm successful, it's because when I go after something, I'm relentless. I stalk my prey until it drops. Isn't that right, Mrs. Warnecke?" He turned to Jessie, gazing at her despite her unwillingness to acknowledge him. "Look who I had for a role model. What do you think, Jessie? Am I as nasty an SOB as my father? Did I make the grade?"

Jessie went pale and Matt could hardly blame her. Luc was being unnecessarily cruel. Matt had sensed the explosive tension from the moment he entered the room. Now he was convinced there was a conspiracy of silence here and he was the odd man out.

Where the hell was Roger? he wondered again. He would put the caretaker on this one immediately. Matt was more than curious now, he was deeply concerned. Shelby had a wicked tongue, but he didn't see her as posing any serious threat to Jessie or the family business. Luc was another matter entirely. He wanted a way into the big shiny red apple that was Warnecke Communications, and Jessie was the wormhole, so to speak. Matt had never thought of himself as an alarmist, but his intuition told him Luc posed the gravest of threats. If Jessie had shot him, it was only out of some need to protect herself.

Of the two, Luc Warnecke was the one with killer instincts.

CHAPTER
·· **FOURTEEN** ··

SOMEONE WAS SWIMMING in the pool.

Jessie thought she was dreaming of tidal water luxuriously lapping against some distant pebbled shore. Drowsily she clung to sun-drenched images of golden sand and azure seas, only reluctantly giving up her idyll as she recognized the seductive sound drifting through the open window for what it was—the slow liquid ripple of a body moving through water. A strong swimmer, she could tell, by the steady, almost leisurely pace of the strokes and the absence of splashing.

Dozing fitfully against a heap of rose-scented, silk pillows, she reached over and switched on the small Tiffany lamp next to the bed, then rubbed her burning eyes until they watered. It was one A.M. Apparently someone else hadn't been able to sleep. She tried to imagine who it might be as she rose from the bed and pulled on her kimono. Roger often did laps, and Shelby had once been a strong swimmer. Her sister had tried out for an intercity swim team when they were kids. She'd even swum in a few meets, before the tedium of daily practice began to bore her.

Wishful thinking, Jessie realized as she peered through the triptych of bay windows facing the pool and gardens. It wasn't Roger or Shelby. The swimmer's gleaming dark hair shone in the moonlight. Muscled and sleek, he glided back and forth across the length of the Olympic-size pool with a grace that only the buoyancy of water could lend him. He would always walk with a limp, but he could swim. God, he could swim.

Jessie was absently aware that she was twining the strap of her crepe-de-chine chemise around her fingers and that her kimono had slipped off her shoulder. Her hand was ice cold against the heat of her skin. She had spent the last several hours before dozing off rehearsing her lines for the inevitable confrontation with Luc, and she would undoubtedly be awake the rest of the night if she had to wait until morning. Now was as good a time as any, she decided. She who hesitates—

But she was nervous, almost unbearably so. The terra-cotta bricks felt cool and coarse against her bare feet as she stepped out onto the terrace. Moths flitted and swarmed around the patio lights, and the night smelled of beach fires and mossy mists. Beyond the patio dining area a short flight of steps took her to the recessed pool and cabanas. "Luc?" she called out softly, hoping to get his attention without waking up the whole house.

He glanced up, but continued to swim. She wasn't sure he'd seen her, and she was prepared to give him the benefit of the doubt until she realized he was looking directly at her as his head came up with each stroke. She moved to the side of the pool, but instead of acknowledging her presence, he rolled onto his back and began a leisurely backstroke.

There was only one way to get a jackass's attention, if memory served her. Since the pool area was short on brickbats, she picked up one of the life preservers, took aim and snapped it like a Frisbee, hoping to clunk him in the head. It zinged right past him and landed several feet away in the water, but it got his attention.

He managed a rude gesture without missing a stroke.

She was waiting for him at the ladder when he pulled himself up. "I'd like to speak to you," she informed him tersely. "There are some things we have to get straight."

She broke off as he planted his feet firmly on the tile and rose to his full height. The water sluicing down his torso drew her eye to his body like a magnet. Though it was the last thing she wanted, or intended, she found it impossible not to follow the path of the waterfall that flattened his silky chest hair, snaked toward his belly and streamed down his thighs. Every muscular ripple and ridge was accentuated, every sable hair gleamed against his toned and hardened flesh.

He was rivetingly virile.

Some women would have been intimidated.

Jessie was instantly wary. She'd given very little thought to the fact that he would be wet and nearly naked. If there'd been a robe anywhere within reach, she would have handed it to him in a flash. But there was no robe, and his bathing suit, while not a bikini cut, wasn't a great deal more substantial. Carbon black against his drenched body, it became the next magnet.

Oddly, what flashed into her mind at that moment was their very first encounter with each other's nakedness. She'd been shivering in the bay, watching with a young girl's fascination and a virgin's startlement while he stripped off his clothes in the moonlight. He'd been fourteen then and fully matured, or so she'd thought.

But she'd been wrong. Now his hipbones arced into powerful pelvic muscles that were clenched against the chilly night air. And those same muscles seemed to cup and thrust his sex against the clinging material of the suit. He was enormous, she realized, her senses galvanizing with alarm. Not aroused. Just big. Built that way. An adhesive bandage was taped to the inside of his thigh, but she barely noticed.

He hadn't said a word, she realized suddenly.

Her head snapped up, and she met his probing gaze. His mouth curved into a smile, and one eyebrow flattened sardonically. *Take a good look,* he seemed to be saying.

"You had something on your mind?" he inquired.

"I have plenty on my mind—" She flushed at the unfortunate choice of words and at his droll reaction. "These are my terms," she bit out. "The marriage will be in name only. There will be *no* physical intimacy. None whatsoever. We'll have separate bedrooms, separate lives. We'll wait a decent interval, of course—"

She broke off as he stepped toward her.

"Do you understand me?" she asked, edging back as he kept coming. "Those are my terms!"

He was pushing her, pressing her, *crowding* her.

"What are you doing?" she demanded, although it was painfully obvious what he was doing. He was backing her down. Reaching behind her to make sure there was nothing there, she crept backward, trying to maintain the distance between them.

"Stop," she whispered finally.

But he didn't stop. He kept coming until she was flush up against the terrace wall. And then he moved in even closer, forcing her to press herself to the cold, gritty stonework and clutch her kimono together. "What is this? Some pathetic attempt to frighten me?"

Luc braced his hands on either side of her head and trapped her against the wall, dripping chlorinated pool water all over her satin robe. "You're in no position to be setting terms," he told her. "Ours will be a union in every sense of that word. And as for decent intervals, I have some business that will take me away for exactly two weeks. When I get back, we're getting married."

Jessie glared at him in silence, caught in the furious pounding of her own heart. She resisted the impulses firing inside her, resisted calling him names or striking out at him, though her hand ached from clenching. "We'll see about that," she said, her voice shaking with suppressed anger.

He bent his head as if to kiss her, and against every rational impulse she possessed, she let him.

As his lips touched hers, she slumped against the wall, her hands falling away from her kimono. Everything seemed to flow out of her in the breathtaking intimacy of that connection. It was like a tremor from the center of her being, from the center of the earth, a powerful negative charge. The air gushed from her lungs, and the strength drained from her body, sapping her of purpose and will. Her legs bowed inward, and she could feel herself sliding down the wall. She had no traction. It was only her hands, her fingers curling desperately into the niches of the stone wall behind her that kept her on her feet.

Luc's body remained arched over hers, his arms locked on either side of her head. He would have let her fall, she realized absently. He would have liked her to fall. He wanted her weak and ineffectual, a stunned and helpless female. He wanted to control her with nothing more than the touch of his mouth, the sting of his teeth and tongue.

And strangely she didn't seem to care at that moment that he was the enemy, or that his goal was her naked, shuddering defeat. Her head was tilted back, and she was totally absorbed in the kiss, in its pull on her innermost self, her vital parts. She was trembling like a baby. She'd never tasted anything as delicious as his lips as they moved and hissed over hers, sweetly bleeding her of every last spark of energy.

He drew back, breathing deeply. "These are *my* terms, Jessie. I am going to marry you. And I am going to fuck you. But not necessarily in that order."

"No!" Her backbone arched painfully against the rocks. The sensations that swept her were fraught with revulsion and with such hammering excitement she couldn't breathe. She couldn't wrench herself away from him. God help her, there was something dark inside him—and something just as dark inside her that responded to what he was saying, what he was doing.

He bent and kissed her again, hotly this time, nipping at her lips with his teeth, stinging her like a swarm of bees on wild clover. His breath burned into the aching warmth of her throat, and his words seared her dazed thoughts like lasers. If only he'd give her a moment to breathe.

But he wouldn't give her that much, not even a moment. He gathered up a handful of her hair, locking her head in the position she'd thrown it, with her chin thrust high and her throat arched dramatically.

"Can you feel me?" he asked, gazing down at her as he slipped the strap of her chemise off her shoulder and cupped her bare breast. His voice was dark with passion, with an electrifying quiver of sexual hunger. "I want to peel off your clothes and pin you up against this wall, Jessie. I want to kiss your breasts and taste you between your legs—"

"No!"

He bent to kiss her, and as the heat of his mouth moved over hers, she bit down viciously, drawing blood. He released her with a soft hiss and touched the cut on his lower lip, staring with disbelief at his fingers.

"Can you feel *me*, Luc?" she whispered, fury in her slow, shaking words. Before he could respond, she pushed past him and escaped.

Roger Metcalf moved back into the shadows of the shrubbery, watching avidly as Jessie yanked up the strap of her nightgown, flashed across the terrace in a vapor trail of black satin and disappeared into her room. The French doors closed with a whoosh and a sharp crack, followed by the thud of a dead-bolt lock.

Great tits, Roger thought, filing that piece of information away in his own personal data bank rather than for Matt Sandusky's benefit.

Roger continued to hover, waiting to see what Luc would do.

A terry bath sheet hung over the back of a pool chair. Staring at Jessie's locked door, Luc used a corner of the towel to blot his bleeding lip. He looked as if he couldn't decide whether to take her dead-bolted door on for size or call it a night and go to bed. Roger chuckled silently. Luc and Jessie Warnecke were going to make one interesting couple.

Roger could hardly wait to tell Sandusky what Warnecke had in mind. It was a brilliant ploy actually. Instead of raiding the company, Luc was marrying it. However, given what had been happening since Luc showed up, Roger had to wonder about the odds of the newlyweds making it through their honeymoon alive.

Luc draped the towel around his neck and departed the terrace. As Roger was about to leave himself, he realized that someone else had been spying on the festivities. Standing in an open second-story bedroom window above the terrace, a woman appeared to be gazing down at the pool area. The drape of ruffled curtains concealed her face from Roger's view, but something about the curve of her exposed body signaled that she was more fascinated than shocked by what she'd seen.

She was wearing a silvery nightgown, but it was her pose that held his attention. She had one hand splayed on her thigh, and she was tilted forward just enough to draw attention to her indrawn shoulders and jutting breasts. Mmmm, Roger thought, smiling lazily, I wouldn't mind coming up on that from behind. The woman's sleek, catlike body was less full-breasted than Jessie's, but no less sensual. She had to be either Shelby or Gina, the au pair.

Roger was betting on Shelby. He slipped a hand into the pocket of his sweatpants, aware of his own growing excitement and feeling the pleasure of skintight nerves and muscles.

• • •

Shelby reached up and pushed open the sheer curtains, letting the perfumed breezes waft into her room. The midnight fragrances of lilacs and wisteria felt cool against her hot skin. Her nerves were sparking and vibrating, her flesh was tingling, but she wasn't thinking about sex. At least not about having sex. She was thinking about that other thing that made her blood heat and rush, the most powerful aphrodesiac there was—money.

Things had changed markedly in Half Moon Bay since she'd left. Luc Warnecke was all grown up, for one. All grown up, studly as hell and hot on her little sister's tail. That might have bothered Shelby more if she hadn't understood so implicitly what was motivating him. Jessie had the Warnecke money, and Luc wanted it back. Life was incredibly simple when you didn't complicate it with wishful thinking.

No one knew better than Shelby that material wealth was the great motivator, the American Dream and Manifest Destiny all rolled up into one big fat cigar. Once you had it, you could afford to be altruistic and help your fellow man. Money wasn't the root of all evil. That, she had long ago decided, was a patently absurd notion. Money made a person generous and benevolent and fair. Only the poor suckers who didn't have any, and were scrambling to figure out how to get some, were reduced to evil. Sometimes Shelby wondered if she were the only one on the planet who understood that.

She turned away from the window, contemplating the luxurious room with more irony than envy. Speaking of *mucho dinero,* her little sister was rolling in it. How had Jessie done it? Shelby wondered with grudging pride. How had her strange, fierce sibling accomplished what she, Shelby, had been trying her whole life to do: jump up in the air and land in a pile of money.

Shelby sank down on the bed, stretching herself out diagonally across the plush satin spread, until her toes touched the brass bedpost at the bottom and her fingers touched the one at the top. She smiled secretly, congratulating herself on her timing. Things certainly *had* changed in Half Moon Bay. The lowly Floods had shot up the social scale as if they'd been launched from a cannon, and Shelby had every intention of cashing in on the situation.

CHAPTER
·· FIFTEEN ··

JESSIE'S FINGERS HESITATED on the keyboard of her word processor. Her senses jumped, alert to the slightest vibration. The noise she'd just heard sounded like her office door creaking open. Her mind leapt automatically to the only person she could imagine who was warped enough to sneak up behind her.

"Get the *hell* out of my office!" she said, whirling and rising out of her typist's chair.

Shelby jumped back a foot. "For God's sake, Jessie!"

"*Shelby*—" Jessie let out a taut, recriminating sigh. "You nearly scared me to death."

"Hey, it's mutual." Shelby shook her dark pageboy smooth, like a glossy black cat whose coat had been ruffled. With a practiced flick of her wrist, she adjusted the voluminously padded shoulders of the dusty rose sweater she wore over matching leggings. "A little tense this morning, are we?"

Jessie sank back down, the wheels of her typist chair screeching across their plastic platform. "Was there something you wanted, Shelby? I've got a deadline on this piece for the Op-Ed page. Matt's going to stop by to pick it up."

"Pretend I'm not here." Her sister glanced around the room as if she were already thinking about redecorating.

"No, Shelby," Jessie explained patiently. "This is work. I need to think, to compose."

"Sure, go ahead." Shelby had already begun to browse. Trailing the pungent scent of Red, her favorite perfume, behind her, she inspected the books on Jessie's shelves, which consisted of fact and fiction about the newspaper business and reference books on every possible topic from Amazonian herbal medicine to female sexual perversions. "Compose away," she murmured. "You won't bother me."

Jessie swung back to her word processor, determined to ignore her sister if such a thing were possible. After a sleepless night she had decided the only way to get her mind off the impending disaster with Luc was to immerse herself in a less personal sort of disaster. The local business community was currently trying to shut down a topless barbershop on a zoning technicality. The problem interested Jessie because of its First Amendment implications. She tended to write most of the editorials concerning Bill of Rights issues. But she had yet to come up with a workable angle, and the deadline for the morning edition was that afternoon.

"What are you? A reporter or something?" Shelby wandered over to peer at Jessie's monitor. "WHEN IS NUDE LEWD?" she said, reading the headline aloud.

"I write an occasional editorial for *The Half Moon Bay Monitor*." Jessie refrained from reminding Shelby that she had just inherited a small media empire, which included the local paper. She'd also done local-interest feature articles as specials to *The Monitor*, but at the moment she didn't have the time or inclination to do anything other than distract herself with impassioned editorials. Where Warnecke Communications was concerned, she was more than grateful to have Matt at the helm until she could take a more active role.

"The *occasional* editorial. Is that right?" Shelby's voice rose unpleasantly. "The widow Warnecke, journalist, woman of letters, champion of nude barbers and undoubtedly the homeless too? The Jessie Flood I remember was more concerned with not *being* homeless."

"Things change."

"Tell me about it. When's the wedding?"

"I don't know. Maybe there won't be a wedding."

"Oh? Trouble in paradise?" Shelby had discovered a freestanding world globe in her travels around the spacious, wood-paneled office and library. She gave it a spin and then continued exploring as if she were conducting some kind of mental inventory.

Jessie gave up the diversionary tactics at that point. Shelby had all the finesse of a battering ram. There was no way to dodge her when she was coming at you head-on. "Thanks for your interest," she said, "but Luc and I haven't firmed up our plans yet. Maybe we'll elope."

"And deprive this berg of the juiciest ceremony since Liz married Larry?" Shelby winked as if they were sharing a great inside joke. "I can see the invitations now—'We request the honor of your presence at the marriage of Mrs. Simon Warnecke to her own stepson.' Gosh, won't that be fun for the ladies' auxiliary? Besides, I was hoping to be your maid of honor. Mel could be the flower girl. Hmmmm, let's see. What shall we do about the best man? Does Luc actually have any friends?"

Jessie swung around in her chair and faced her sister squarely. "I doubt you'll be here long enough to worry about the ceremony. When *are* you leaving, Shelby? You never did answer my question last night."

Shelby ran her forefinger along the tip of one perfectly tapered dusty-rose nail. "Well, now that you mention it, there is this business trip I've been thinking about taking. Nothing firm yet, but if things were to work out the way I hope, I might have to leave very soon. Of course, I'd hate to miss my little sister's big day, but—"

"If *what* things work out?"

"Oh, didn't I tell you? I'm looking for investors. I've made a few phone calls and come up with zip so far. However, if some visionary venture capitalist should decide to bankroll my image consulting agency, I'd be forced to start coordinating things immediately, wouldn't I? I couldn't do it from here, of course. I'd need a larger, cosmopolitan city as a base of operations—San Francisco, for example. *If* I had the backing . . ."

Jessie was beginning to wonder if she had the word "sucker" writ large across her forehead. If this wasn't outright blackmail, it was close enough. Nothing would have given her greater pleasure than to kick Shelby out on her dusty-rose butt, but she couldn't afford to antagonize her. There was precious little sisterly love lost between them, but there were ties, blood ties, and a deeper, even more insidious kind of bond. She and Shelby shared an unspoken pact and had since earliest childhood. They were keepers of the secrets.

"May you get hit by the gravy train," Jessie said gamely,

turning back to the editorial. She was beginning to understand the local business community's frustration. A weed was growing in their rose garden, but they weren't allowed to pull it up because the weed had as much right to its share of community soil as the roses, or so the argument went. The problem seemed insoluble.

"I considered giving you a shot," Shelby said, coming around to the window Jessie faced so she could reclaim her sister's attention. "I might be persuaded to part with a piece of the action for a member of the 'family'—a silent partnership, something like that."

"Let me get back to you on that, okay?"

Sharp nails clicked loudly against the windowpane, a sure signal that Shelby was warming up the battering ram. "I know why Luc's marrying you," she said. "What I don't understand is why you're marrying him. What could you possibly have to gain?"

"None of your business, Shelby."

"Do you love him?"

"What do you think?"

"I think you've gone crazy."

"That makes two of us."

The statement came from behind Jessie, but she immediately recognized the voice as Matt Sandusky's. She sighed and hit the Save function on her keyboard, then turned the computer off. Damn! She hadn't wanted Matt to find out this way.

"I'm sorry, Matt," she said, rising and turning to face him. Her heart sank when she saw how distraught he looked. His eyes were bloodshot, his suit wrinkled. She'd never seen him with a hair out of place until recently. "I was going to tell you."

"Really? When?"

"Soon . . . as soon as I could. How much did you hear?"

"Enough to know that you're considering marrying Luc. Jessie, we have to talk."

"I think that's my cue to exit." Shelby flashed Matt a dazzling smile and shook her black-cat hair into place. "What a *pleasure* to see you again, Mr. Sandusky. We had so little time together at dinner, I didn't have an opportunity to tell you what I do." She whisked her gaze over his dishabille as if she could steam-press him with her turquoise blue eyes. "I dress men, important men like yourself. I'm an executive image consultant, and my clients are some of the most powerful investment brokers on Wall Street. You've heard of Douglas Asterbaum?"

As if by sorcery, she conjured a business card from the dusty-rose cloud of her sweater and slipped it into the wrinkled breast pocket of Matt's suit as she brushed by him. "I'm available for private consultations," she murmured.

Matt flushed hotly and brushed at his jacket.

Jessie glanced away, giving him time to recover and Shelby time to make her exit. It wasn't his fault. Most men needed CPR to recover from Shelby. When Jessie was sure her sister was gone, she walked over and shut the office door. As she turned back, Matt grasped her by the arm.

"Jessie, I'm not going to let you do this."

His forcefulness alarmed her. "How could you possibly stop me?"

"By talking to you, of course, by bringing you to your senses. I can't imagine why you'd even consider marrying Luc. What could he have said or done to convince you to do something so crazy? Can't you see what a risk you're taking? This is dangerous!"

"Dangerous? In what way?"

"In *every* way. To you personally, to the business. Luc wants Simon's empire, and you've got it. He'll do anything to get it back."

"Even marry me," Jessie offered sardonically. "Poor bastard must be desperate, right?"

"I didn't mean it that way. You're a beautiful, desirable woman, but that isn't what Luc's after. You were right about one thing. He is desperate, desperately sick as far as I'm concerned."

She shook her head. "Angry, yes, but not—"

"Sick! He's obsessed, and obsession is a sickness. Don't marry him, Jessie. Not unless you've got a death wish."

She grew quiet, and finally she turned away from him and gazed out the window at the rose gardens. The muted cry of a meadowlark carried across the grounds from one of the cypress trees, and the haunting sound seemed to accentuate Matt's warning.

"You're not going to do it, are you?" he asked.

"I have to."

"Why? For God's sake, *why*?"

"I can't explain that now, but you'll simply have to trust me. Some things in life are nonnegotiable. This is one of those things."

"Nonnegotiable? What does that mean? Is he forcing you? Blackmailing you? Jessie, if there's something you need to tell me. I can help—"

"No . . . you can't help. Not this time. What I need now is your trust and support." She turned back to him imploringly. "I need your friendship more than I ever have, even more than when Simon was sick."

"Damn." His voice shook as he collapsed on the nearest chair. After a moment he seemed to gather himself together, and when he looked up, his eyes had a strange, almost piercing focus. "You're going to force me to say this, aren't you? Whatever Luc's told you, whatever threats or promises he's made, you have to understand that it's a smoke screen. He's only interested in taking control of the company, and once he marries you, he'll have everything to gain by edging you out. It wouldn't be difficult to arrange, Jessie. It could be as simple as an accident."

Jessie might have laughed if she hadn't been so astonished. "Matt, really—an *accident*? Now you are being an alarmist." Her voice took on a soothing quality. He was trying to frighten her, and the only way she knew how to deal with him was to acknowledge both their fears. "You must believe me, Matt, I'm not doing this impulsively. I do understand about Luc's obsessions, and I have no intention of letting him take control of either me or the company."

"How do you plan to stop him?"

That will all depend on Luc, she thought. As always, she would do whatever she had to to see that she and her daughter survived. That was the one constant of her life, it seemed. "For one thing, I want to learn the ropes, Matt, everything there is to know about Warnecke Communications. Luc will be gone for two weeks. That should give us time for a crash course. As for the rest of it, you'll just have to trust me. I'm doing the right thing. It's the only thing I can do."

"It's not you I don't trust, it's him." He fought open the top button of his shirt and yanked his tie loose. "I think you're making a fatal mistake, but if I can't persuade you of that, then at least let me set up a meeting with Gil Stratton. If you're still determined to do this after you've talked with him, we'll get you an ironclad prenuptial and whatever other legal armor we need to protect you."

She turned to him. "No prenups, Matt. Luc would never agree—"

"Jessie—you can't marry him without one, for Christ's sake. It's suicidal! Surely he, himself, will insist on some kind of written agreement. He has as much to lose as you do."

Jessie nodded, more to end the conversation than because she agreed. Poor Matt, he didn't understand that Luc's hold on her couldn't be shaken by legal contracts. It was too insidious for that. "All right then, have something drawn up, but keep it simple. At least we can take steps to protect Mel if something unforeseen should happen."

"Unforeseen?" Matt muttered. "That's a charming way of putting it. We'll also want to lock in a predetermined division of the existing property and anything acquired in the course of the marriage."

"Of course, do whatever you have to in the event that the marriage doesn't survive—"

"I don't give a fuck whether or not the marriage survives." Matt's face was as bloodless as the white shirt he wore. "It's you I'm worried about, Jessie. What if you don't survive?"

"My, my, what do we have here? Is the groom running out on the bride?"

Luc glanced up from the bag he was packing to see the woman responsible for ninety percent of his wet dreams in adolescence.

"What? And make Jessie's day?" He tossed the shaving kit he was holding into the bag.

"Need some help packing?" Shelby Flood inquired.

He was about to tell her he was done, but not surprisingly she didn't wait for him to respond. She strolled past him, flopped down on the bed and draped herself invitingly over the bedspread. With a slow smile and a quick tap of her gold-sandeled foot, she dropped the lid of his suitcase.

"Thanks," he said, his voice heavy with irony.

"Anytime."

Luc felt a sexual call to arms, the same mindless reflex that had sent the overactive glands of a sixteen-year-old kid into hormonal floodtide.

He'd learned a lot about human nature from Jessie's big sister. She was the kind of female who offered it with one hand and took it back with the other. She'd taught him that a man could be in love sexually—to the point of *insanity*— but not emotionally. She'd also taught him about the power of secret ambitions and dreams. Everyone had them. Few admitted to them. Shelby not only admitted to hers, she acted on them. That set her apart. It gave her an in-your-face honesty he couldn't help but admire.

"How have you been, Luc?" she asked.

There was a husky intimacy in her voice that called to mind every explosive coupling they'd had as teenagers. One day he'd been crazy in love with her, ready to marry her, and the next, a bomb had detonated in his face. His father threatened to disinherit him, Shelby threatened an abortion, and the local police threatened to fry him for the murder of Hank Flood. *Just one of those days.*

"I'm getting by," he answered, meeting her startlingly blue eyes. His breath snagged on something sharp, and there was a moment of fusion, a swift, intense connection between them that told him he was not completely immune to her. Not immune, but smarter.

"You're doing better than that," she said, looking him over as if she approved of everything about him. "Image is my business. And by the way, I like your outfit."

"What? This?" He'd thrown on jeans with the knees out and a white linen dress shirt, open at the neck, to travel in.

She nodded appraisingly. "It works. There's just one accessory you might consider adding."

"Such as?"

Her lips curved into a sexy, mischievous smile, and she rolled up onto all fours like a cat. She crept toward the end of the bed—toward him—on her hands and knees, her hips swaying, her limpid gaze drifting up and down his body.

Jesus, he thought. What a piece she was. In his mind she was naked, her breasts swinging, inviting him to take a look . . . and take it from there.

When she reached him, her face was even with his belt line.

"The button fly's always a good touch," she said, looking up at him.

He had the damndest hunch that she was going to put her mouth to his crotch and take a bite out of him. There was just that kind of glint in her eyes. When she didn't, when she sat back on her haunches instead, he almost breathed a sigh of relief. "I think Levi gets credit for the fly," he said.

"But you get credit for what's inside it," she murmured, laughing as if she might want to take some credit for that too.

"I'd love to get my hands on you," she said, laughing. "To dress you, Luc, to try some wild new things on you. The RUB look maybe? Rich Urban Biker?"

"I don't think so, thanks. I'm more an 'unlook' kind of guy."

"I could work with that." She wet her lips contemplatively, studying his outfit. "An unlook. I like it. But you're not there yet. I'd undo more buttons and flip up your collar, then I'd add a tie, loosely knotted. I love ties . . . and anything else that hangs long on a man."

He groaned softly. "Don't you ever quit, Shelby?"

"Where would that get me? As a matter of fact, I've got a proposition for you," she said, rising up on her haunches to reinvent him in her image, buttons undone.

"That's what I was afraid of."

A sound in the hallway drew Luc's attention, but Shelby didn't seem to notice. She was in the process of flipping up his shirt collar when Jessie entered the doorway.

He didn't have time to explain—and probably couldn't have found the words anyway. The astonishment in Jessie's eyes, the wincing stab of pain, left him speechless.

"Oh, shit," Shelby whispered.

"Jessie," he started. "I—"

Jessie wheeled around and left without a word, but not before the confusion in her expression had flickered like a smoldering fire and then flared into something else, something quick and savage. It was hot enough to be jealousy and wild enough to be homicide. Jessie had already proven that she harbored a violent streak, but that wasn't what had rendered Luc mute. It was the pain in her eyes. God, it had pierced him through the throat like an arrow.

When Shelby returned to her room Jessie was already there, standing by the fireplace. Shelby was apprehensive—if not frightened, then at least wary of her little sister. Jessie's expression was neither angry nor accusing. It was piercingly focused, and very, very deliberate.

"I know how it must have looked," Shelby said.

"It looked like what it was. You were coming onto him."

"No, not in that way. We were kidding, it was fun."

Suddenly Jessie flared, coming at her. "You are such an incredible bitch, Shelby." Her voice dropped to a whisper. "This is my home. How could you be so disgustingly obvious?"

"Jessie, I—"

"Don't do it again. Don't cross me, Shelby. Because it's going to get nasty if you do."

Shelby bristled. "I'd be very careful about making threats if I were you."

Jessie hesitated in front of her, indignation written into her posture. "But you're not me, thank God. I'm almost glad you hit me up for a loan, because it gives me the great pleasure of telling you to go straight to hell. Not only won't I finance your ridiculous business venture, but if I hear of you approaching anyone else in this town, I'll expose you for the scam artist you are."

She strode past Shelby and out the door before turning back. "Consider yourself warned," she said softly. "I want you out of my house, and I'm going to get you out, one way or the other. In the meantime, don't make the mistake of getting in my way."

Shelby had a smart-ass retort on the tip of her tongue, but she wisely checked it, letting her sister think she'd won the battle. Unlike Jessie, Shelby had no interest in symbolic victories. She wanted to win the war.

CHAPTER
·· SIXTEEN ··

"TO HELL WITH ad revenues!" Pete Fischer growled. "What are we, pimps peddling this newspaper to the highest bidder? I don't care how much money Xavier Sandler's department stores represent, our advertisers don't dictate editorial policy! I'm not killing the story."

The executive offices of *The San Francisco Globe* and *The Bay Cities Review* were in an uproar. Pete Fischer, managing editor of both newspapers, had called a Sunday morning meeting, and he and Carter Dunlop, Warnecke's chief financial and legal officer, had been at each other's throats all morning.

Jessie watched the fireworks with growing unease. For the past couple of weeks she'd been involved in what Matt liked to call "executive boot camp." He'd been tutoring, mentoring and generally cracking the whip over her in preparation for a directorship on the Warnecke board, as well as for her upcoming marriage. Matt had readily agreed that the more she knew, the less likely Luc was to persuade her to use her influence and voting power against the best interests of Warnecke Communications. She was determined to deal with Luc from a position of knowledge.

"No one suggested you kill the story, Pete," Dunlop reasoned. "But what's the point of antagonizing a powerful man like Sandler with a page-one headline?"

"Maybe we could bury the story in Classified?" Fischer's tone was nasty. "Would that make your pal Xavier happy?"

"What are you suggesting?" Dunlop asked.

"That your country-club golfing buddy doesn't have the right to barter his friendship with you for special consideration."

Dunlop sprang from his chair. "My personal life has nothing to do with this, you son of a bitch. What are we, reckless whistle-blowers or responsible journalists? No formal charges have been brought against the chain. All we have are allegations, for God's sake! We could lose more than Sandler's advertising by running the story. We could lose our shirts if he decides to sue us for damaging his business."

Fischer rose too. "Charges *were* filed. Two months ago a woman on the housecleaning crew was tied up and forced to fellate her attacker."

"Those charges were dropped," Dunlop argued.

"Right, because the plaintiff refused to identify the man who did it. Somebody got to her, Carter, and we've been sitting on this story ever since. My best reporter's been following up on the latest allegations all week. She's documented peepholes in the dressing rooms, and she's got three more women who claim to have been sexually assaulted, a cleaning woman and two sales clerks. They didn't report it to the cops because the store manager implied their jobs would be at stake if they did."

Dunlop shook his head regretfully. "It's their word against the manager's, Pete. We need more. It's too risky."

The air that jetted from Pete Fischer's nostrils could have been fire. "It's a cover-up, dammit, and that's news! Some creep is stalking women in one of the swankiest department stores in town. If we don't break the story, the Oakland or San Jose papers *will*."

As the confrontation became more explosive, Jessie, who had done nothing more than observe so far, glanced at Matt, who was seated across the gleaming mahogany conference table from her. She didn't understand why he hadn't intervened. He'd made no attempt to referee the free-for-all, but he had looked her way occasionally as if to see how she was dealing with the byzantine inner workings of the *Globe* newsroom.

"It's a page-one story," Fischer was insisting loudly.

"Even if Sandler doesn't sue, he'll almost certainly yank his advertising," Dunlop warned. "Operating expenses are up, circulation is down. We can't afford another setback, dammit."

"I say let him yank. If Sandler can buy us off, anyone can." Fischer turned to Matt. "Where do you stand on this?"

Matt propped his elbow on the table and splayed his hand across his chin thoughtfully. "Sorry, Pete," he said finally. "I'm with Carter. I think we should err on the side of caution. Our numbers are down. The paper's in trouble. There's the bottom line to consider here."

Fischer slammed his palm down on the table. "Then find yourself a bottom-line manager! I've had it. I'm turning in my badge."

Fischer's threat plunged the room into shock. The silence contrasted eerily with the invectives that had been flying all morning. The managing editor swept the entire group with a scowl that accused each one of them of a personal betrayal. Shaking his head wearily, he stalked toward the door.

Jessie glanced at Matt, waiting for him to act. The paper couldn't afford to lose Pete Fischer any more than it could afford to lose the Sandler chain's advertising. Surely Matt saw that something had to be done. Jessie had sensed for some time that a confrontation between the editorial and business side of the paper was coming to a head. *The Globe* was a house divided against itself. As President and CEO, Matt was the one who had to take control and bring the warring factions together. *Why wasn't he doing something?*

"Christ, Pete," Matt said, rising, "this isn't like you, man. You're no quitter."

"I'm not quitting!" Pete snapped. "I'm being undermined. I'm being forced out. If our advertisers are running this paper, why do you need me?"

"Wait a minute, Pete!" Jessie sprang up. "I think there might be something we're overlooking." As she turned from Pete's glowering skepticism to the group of newspaper executives, she felt the stigma of her own background rise up sharply. She was a kid from the wrong side of town without even a high school diploma to her credit. She'd passed her GEDs with flying colors, but she doubted that would carry much weight with this group of distinguished, college-educated overachievers. She was totally out of her depth, but she couldn't stay silent any longer. For all their sophistication, these men were too entrenched.

"With all due respect, gentlemen, the way I see it, the problem runs deeper than ad revenues and circulation. Forgive my bluntness, but the problem starts here, with *you*."

A restless shuffling moved through the room, but Jessie plunged on. If she stopped, she might not find the courage to start again. "You're all so busy protecting your own turf you've overlooked the real bottom line," she told them. "Warnecke is made up of factions, yes, but those parts equal a whole entity. When you form armed camps and try to destroy each other, you destroy yourselves. If the paper dies, you die."

She was well aware of the narrowing eyes and stiffening shoulders. They didn't like her lecture on team spirit one bit, and she could hardly blame them. Still, she went on. "You've been arguing journalistic integrity versus profit margins all morning. And both are critically important to the paper's welfare, but aren't there some other issues here too? Don't we have some responsibility to our readers? We're a public trust. Doesn't that give us a First Amendment mandate to report the news to our subscribers?"

She looked at each one of them in turn, just as Pete Fischer had done. "This is Sunday, isn't it? Where are your wives and children today? Shopping? How would you feel if some twisted Peeping Tom were watching your daughter undress at this very moment, possibly even assaulting her?"

It was a personal appeal that flew in the face of professional objectivity, but she strongly believed that the newspaper, and perhaps the entire industry, was languishing precisely because it had *stopped* being personal and involved. She was already beginning to sense that there might be a niche for her to fill at this newspaper after all. She wasn't a reporter and she wasn't a bean counter, but as the voice of the community's concerns and needs, she could offer a fresh perspective that might help balance the two. Ad revenues and ace reporting were givens. No one questioned their essential role, but a newspaper needed a conscience too.

"I'm with Pete," she said, softening her tone. "I think the story belongs on page one, but I want it fair and balanced, and I want Sandler to have an opportunity to respond. Perhaps we could assure him that once the problem is resolved and the safety of the customers is assured, we'll run follow-up stories. It could even net him some free advertising."

A quick glance at the beleaguered managing editor told Jessie she had his support. Pete Fischer smiled and gave her a thumbs up. Carter Dunlop was regarding her with wary interest, and Matt Sandusky looked like a startled teacher whose least likely student had just passed a tough exam.

The twilight sun was a snifter of rich, aged brandy, pouring molten amber over the foothills of the Santa Cruz Mountains as Jessie pulled her black Jaguar XJS into the driveway of Echos. The car was a gift from Simon, a very expensive show of his gratitude. She had taken a real risk saving his life. She still carried the scar on her lip. She'd refused his gift at first and then discovered after they were married that he'd simply parked the beautiful beast away in his stable of cars, as if letting it lie there in wait until she was ready.

Now she cut the engine, sank back in the deep bucket seat and closed her eyes. Her exhaustion was so profound she could hardly breathe. It had been a frustrating, challenging and thought-provoking two weeks, but she had loved every minute of it. The apprenticeship had affirmed her decision to be actively involved with running the company and not just a figurehead on the board. Matt's support had pleased her greatly too. If only her life could continue as it had these past days.

On that hopeful thought, she let herself out of the car.

Puccini's soaring major chords greeted her as she opened the door. Jessie winced and touched her forehead. Apparently Gina was introducing Mel to Italian opera, or vice versa. The music was lovely and poignant, if a tad loud.

"*Mama! Buona séra!*" Mel cried the moment Jessie entered the living room. "Come see what Shelby and I did today. You're going to love this."

The last person Jessie wanted to deal with that evening was Shelby, but she didn't have the strength to resist as Mel dragged her through the atrium, across the terrace and out to the rose garden. She'd never seen her daughter so animated. Mel's asthma seemed to have miraculously disappeared since Shelby arrived. She wasn't even breathing heavily.

"What's all this?" Jessie asked. The garden was festooned with crepe-paper flowers and garlands in gaudy pinks and yellows. Shelby was waiting for them by the gazebo, which had been lavishly decorated with balloons, more garlands and a rainbow array of oriental lanterns. Backlit by the falling sun, it bore a frightening resemblance to a vintage Fellini movie. Jessie wanted to wince all over again, but she couldn't. Her daughter was waiting with bated breath for her reaction.

"It's for the wedding," Mel explained. "I wanted it to look nice when you got married tomorrow. Aunt Shelby helped me."

Jessie glanced accusingly at Shelby, who should have known better. Tomorrow's ceremony was in no way intended to be a celebration. Jessie would have preferred a quick civil ceremony at the courthouse, except that in a small town anything so public was guaranteed to generate all kinds of gossip and speculation.

Shelby took a prolonged swallow from the wineglass she was holding. "Mel's excited," she said with a little shrug. "Besides, I didn't think a few balloons could hurt."

A bottle of blush Zinfandel was chilling in a bucket of ice on one of the garden's white wrought-iron tables. "How about some wine?" Shelby asked as she refilled her own glass. "You look as if you could use a drink."

"Come on, Mom," Mel coaxed. "Have some vino. Gina's Italian mama told her wine is good for anything, even *fifa matrimonio*. That's bridal jitters."

"I'll try to survive," Jessie said dryly. She was beginning to understand what was going on. Mel had undoubtedly picked up on the tension between her and Shelby and was anxious for them to patch things up. She couldn't have missed the pressure building up between her mother and the "relatives" who'd moved in on them. With some irony Jessie recalled her pep talk to the newspaper executives about team spirit. If theirs was a house divided against itself, then what about this place, Echos? Talk about an armed camp.

Jessie had done her best to avoid Shelby since Luc left. The scene she'd come upon in his room had been a devastating reminder, like having the past flung in her face. Shelby had been on her good behavior ever since, to the extent that Shelby understood the concept. But Jessie knew better than to trust in miracle conversions where her sister was concerned.

"Mom?" Mel prompted. "Are you okay?"

"That's highly debatable." Jessie kicked off her Ferragamo pumps and dropped into one of the wrought-iron chairs, drawing Mel alongside her. "I'll have that wine, Shelby. Thanks."

"Do you like the decorations?" Mel asked, snuggling into the chair next to her mother.

"I love them, hon. They're . . . festive."

"What are you going to wear tomorrow?" Mel glanced up at her, blue-eyed and curious.

"What *are* you going to wear?" Shelby seconded. She brought Jessie her wine, then pushed a chair away from the table and sprawled in it, kicking up her jean-clad legs.

Jessie hadn't allowed herself to think about details like her dress. She'd barely begun to accept that the wedding was going to happen. "My Alexander Julian has an ankle-length skirt."

"Don't tell me," Shelby cut in dryly. "It's black, right?"

"Mom, not black!" Mel groaned and flopped forward like an unstrung puppet, her head on Jessie's knee.

"It is a spring wedding," Shelby suggested.

Jessie realized with some horror that she was going to have to give up her protective coloration. The thought made her unaccountably nervous, as if some psychic shield were being stripped away. If it were possible to absorb strength from a color, she had. "The Alexander Julian will be fine," she insisted. "It's just going to be us, family."

"Yuck," Mel said softly, glancing at Shelby. "Why did we even bother to decorate?"

"We'll wear pink polka-dots and purple flounces," Shelby assured Mel. "We'll be so obnoxiously bright, the minister will have to wear sunglasses."

Mel seemed to think that was hilarious. She collapsed in giggles, and Jessie was consumed with envy at Shelby's ability to make her laugh. The child had taken to her sister's irreverent, carefree style so readily that Jessie realized how starved Mel must have been for some fun to offset the somberness of her life at Echos. Jessie knew she'd been overprotective because of Mel's health, but there had been other threats too, other dangers.

Gina appeared to announce that dinner was cannelloni, an Italian favorite of Mel's. Shelby passed on the spicy dish.

Jessie was simply too tired to eat and begged off too, but sent Mel with her blessings. "Take it easy on the cheese," she called after the bouncing nine-year-old. "And no vino!"

Shelby sighed. "Ever the mother."

Tucking her legs underneath her, Jessie nursed her wine and watched the last glorious flashes of amber light as the sun descended into the Pacific. The briny smell of the outgoing tide overwhelmed even the rich florals that emanated from the rose garden. Jessie felt enveloped by the powerful mix of perfumes and by the sky's radiant pink and golden hues. The effect was wondrously soothing to the spirit, but it couldn't quite offset the strained silence between her and Shelby.

"What have you told Luc about Mel?" Shelby asked.

The inevitable question. Jessie had seen it coming for some time. She set down her wine. "I told him that Mel was Simon's child—mine and Simon's."

"Did he believe you?"

"No, but he's willing to accept it."

"Interesting." Shelby rested her head against the back of the chair as if she were contemplating that idea. "Be a hell of note if he ever found out the truth, wouldn't it?"

"What does that mean?" Jessie was instantly on guard. Shelby was more than capable of blackmail. She'd already proven that.

"It doesn't mean anything. I was just wondering if you'd thought about telling him what really happened. It doesn't seem like a great way to start a marriage, does it? Basing your entire relationship on a lie?"

Jessie rose from the chair and walked away from the table. After a few steps she turned back, her voice low and vibrant. "When did you ever worry about lying your way into or out of a relationship, Shelby?"

Shelby's gaze was focused deeply on the wine she was swirling in her glass. "Apparently I struck a nerve," she said. "Forget I brought it up."

Jessie couldn't dismiss it that easily. She knew Shelby too well. Her sister *had* struck a nerve, and she would keep right on applying the prod until she got the response she wanted. "Don't make the mistake of trying to manipulate me, Shelby. I'm not one of the legions of slavering men in your life. Your act may have worked on Luc. It may even have worked on Hank all those years ago, but it won't work on me."

"Hank?" Shelby looked startled, then indignant.

"You aren't going to pretend that nothing happened between you and our stepfather?"

"Hell, yes, something happened. But God, Jessie, I was barely fifteen. What happened was child abuse." Shelby's drink hit the tabletop as her legs came off it. She sat forward, as if poised to spring up.

Jessie returned her sister's accusatory glare. "I didn't say it wasn't, Shelby. But that didn't seem to stop you from making the most of it, did it? Was it child abuse the times you seduced him? Or only the times he seduced you?"

Jessie felt her stomach roll as she asked the questions. The situation still filled her with queasy revulsion. She'd never questioned Hank's guilt. He was the adult, and that made him the responsible party. No matter how much Shelby had teased and taunted, he should have kept his hands off her. But it disturbed her that Shelby had turned into a teenage nymphet whenever she'd wanted something.

Jessie had tried desperately to make sense of it, to understand what drove Shelby. She'd always been beautiful, even as a child she'd favored Lynette, their mother. But in every other way, she'd been Lynette's alter ego. Shelby had once vowed to Jessie that she would never be a victim like Lynette, allowing a man to humiliate and abuse her. She would use rather than be used. Even then she seemed to have a sixth sense for the moral failings of the opposite sex and an instinctive knack for turning their weaknesses against them. Perhaps it was her way of protecting herself. Once Jessie might have been able to understand and to forgive that protective impulse, but she'd lost the ability to empathize with her sister long ago, when Shelby turned her seductive wiles on Luc.

Shelby was out of the chair and pacing, seemingly distraught. "Did it ever occur to you— No, what am I thinking about? Of course it didn't. It couldn't possibly have entered your mind that I *might* have been trying to protect my little sister. What do you think Hank would have done if I hadn't been there, Jessie? He would have gone after you, dammit. *He would have gone after you.*"

The tip of Shelby's nose was red, and her eyes appeared to be welling. Jessie saw the sparkle of tears, she heard the throatiness in Shelby's voice, and a part of her wished she could believe it was genuine. After all these years she still wanted to give her sister the benefit of the doubt, but it was impossible. There had been too many betrayals. "If Hank had so much as looked at me that way, I would have killed him."

"Oh, don't be so goddamn righteous, Jessie. Haven't you ever done anything you shouldn't have?"

Jessie glanced up and met Shelby's eyes for a brief, jagged moment, but she didn't answer.

"Sure, maybe I did manipulate Hank," Shelby continued furiously. "So what? He didn't hesitate to take advantage. He got what he wanted too."

"Hank is dead," Jessie pointed out. "I doubt he wanted that."

"Maybe not, but he deserved it," Shelby flared. "The man was a bastard! He deserved to have his head bashed in. And we both know who did it, don't we?"

The moon was a jewel-like crescent, rising through the blue cypress trees of the ravine. Nearly half-full, it made Jessie think of the legend Luc had told her when they were children, a beautiful yet ominous story of a boy whose life was forever altered by one impulsive, desperate act. Darkness was descending over the gardens. A coyote howled somewhere in the distance, and Jessie absorbed its forlorn sound with an inner shudder. She didn't answer Shelby's question. There was no safe answer, only the harrowing truth.

CHAPTER
·· SEVENTEEN ··

THE PREVAILING WESTERLIES were blowing up a storm. Warm spring winds whipped the crepe-paper garlands adorning the gazebo, and a phalanx of dark clouds brooded on the horizon. As wedding days went, this one was shaping up to be less than perfect. But perhaps it was exactly the right day for *this* wedding, Shelby thought as she observed the groom through the glass walls of the atrium where she'd paused to size up the situation. Luc Warnecke was standing at the entrance of the gazebo, as if waiting for his bride to appear.

He commanded attention, not so much because of the stone-colored wool crepe suit he wore or the way his lush dark hair was brushed back off his forehead, Italian gangster–style. It was the single-minded focus in his expression that drew the eye. He had the intent gaze of a man who'd just cornered the market on some vital commodity and was waiting to see if his investment would pay off.

Dolled up in hot-pink satin, Shelby let herself out a side door of the atrium and took a roundabout path through the rose garden as she studied her future brother-in-law, who was the only one besides her who'd shown up for the blessed event so far. She would have dressed him differently—in a navy blazer with the Warnecke crest on the breast pocket, gray slacks and a snowy white formal shirt—an eminently civilized look to offset the gangsterlike intensity. Yes, she would have tamed him just a little for this occasion, knowing full well the fun of undressing—and unleashing—him later. The truth was Luc Warnecke stimulated her fashion imagination. If she'd had the money she needed to launch her agency—and if he'd been a starving young male model—she would have snatched him up in a minute for her ad campaign. And for a few other things as well.

"Aunt Shel!" Mel came tumbling down the terrace steps, resplendent in bouffant red taffeta. The ruffled dress looked as if it had been intended for Christmas or Valentine's Day. Shelby laughed and curtsied, presenting her own creation. She'd tacked a vibrant purple crepe-paper garland to the hemline of her hot pink sheath.

"Don't we look *great*?" Mel said.

"We're blinding," Shelby agreed wryly, tweaking the crimson bow that tied back Mel's auburn hair.

"The minister won't be able to see the bride and groom without squinting," Mel crowed. She looked around, squinting herself. "Where is the minister? I hope he didn't get lost."

"He's in the library talking with your mother."

Gina appeared behind Mel, holding out a cardigan sweater. "Here, put this on, *bambina*. That looks like a terrible storm brewing, doesn't it?" She tisked as if stormy wedding days were a bad omen.

Shelby had been thinking that very same thing.

"Oh, there she is!" Mel's voice dropped to a hush as Jessie walked out onto the terrace. She was flanked by Matt Sandusky, who also seemed concerned about the weather, and by another man, who could only have been the minister. A short, solemn gentleman with white hair, he was wearing a dark suit rather than a clerical collar.

We're off to the races, Shelby thought. She'd never been worried about the minister showing up, but she wouldn't have bet on Jessie. If Luc looked proud of having brokered a fabulous deal, Jessie looked grimly determined to recoup her losses in whatever way she could.

"Isn't she beautiful?" Mel whispered.

"*Bella*," Gina agreed.

Beautiful? Shelby would never have described her little sister that way. Jessie's face was translucently pale except for slashes of pink beneath her cheekbones that were as hot as Shelby's dress. Her red hair looked as if it had been dragged kicking and screaming into a chignon, with defiant curls flying every which way in the wind. And her eyes flashed the cool

blue fire of an acetylene torch. Jessie was formidable certainly—a slender young lioness protecting her lair—but not beautiful. That implied a certain breathless feminine vulnerability
that even Shelby herself didn't pretend to possess.

Shelby glanced at Luc and saw that he was riveted by
Jessie. His admiration was evident, but there was something
else shimmering in his eyes, something even beyond the sexual anticipation a man might normally have for a woman he
was about to bed. Shelby felt a surprisingly sharp twinge of
jealousy. She'd thought she was beyond such things, but the
feeling persisted, a piercing sensation just beneath her breast-
bone. *Surely Luc didn't love Jessie?*

Hardly able to breathe, Shelby glanced at Jessie again, at
the way the wind was stinging her lips and upthrust chin, and
wondered what it was that Luc saw in her.

Luc's gaze never wavered from the sight of his future
bride. More than anything at that moment, he was struck
by how bewitchingly imperious she looked. Flanked by her
two nervous white knights, she could have been an iron-willed
princess being forced into an arranged marriage for the sake
of crown and country. She carried no flowers, and her sheer
dress flowed down around her ankles and dipped low in the
neckline, revealing breasts so full and pale they looked like
moonglow against the dark night of her bodice. She'd chosen
an interesting color for the occasion. The dress was stunningly
cut. And it was black. Was she mourning Simon's death or her
imminent marriage?

He clocked every stride of her approach to the gazebo,
noting each defiant flash of her bearing and carriage. She
avoided looking at him so there was no chance of eye contact,
but he wondered what would have happened if she had looked
up, if their eyes had met. Would the heavens have broken
open? Would the gazebo have been struck by lightning?

Jessie had only one mission in mind—to get the ritual over
with and then pretend, to whatever extent she could, that it
had never happened. She didn't expect the marriage to last
six months, especially when her new "husband" learned that
she had given Matt temporary power of attorney as well as her
proxy to vote the controlling interest in the company Simon
had left her. Once Luc realized he wasn't going to get what he

wanted, which was access to her voting shares, she was sure he would eventually tire of his game of revenge upon Simon's memory and leave. Playing one-upmanship with a dead man couldn't be very satisfying to someone as restless for challenge as Luc seemed to be. She was counting on that.

She brushed past Luc and entered the gazebo without looking at him. She'd felt nothing up until that moment, other than a sense of going through the motions, blessedly devoid of any emotion, including the icy anger that had sustained her. It wasn't until she'd taken her place inside the enclosure that she experienced the tiniest frisson of panic. It was barely discernible, like a high-pitched whistle that registers on the nervous system rather than the ears.

The gazebo's walls seemed to press in on her with the inevitability of what was about to happen. She didn't even have to look around to know that she was trapped. She could feel it. The only sounds that came to her were the eerie rustle of crepe paper in the wind and the sudden jerk of her heart as the minister walked around her and took his place. A moment later she felt Luc move alongside her. And suddenly Matt Sandusky and Shelby were there too, as witnesses.

The minister attempted to break the ice with some conversation, but Luc discouraged him in polite tones, suggesting that they start the ceremony immediately if everyone were agreeable. His voice sounded unbearably calm.

"Yes, please, let's get on with it," she agreed. Jessie had requested the shortest possible ceremony, hoping for the Las Vegas version, where they cut immediately to the I do's and the pronouncement. But even a short ceremony was going to be interminable, she could tell. Her marriage to Simon had been pleasant compared to this.

The sound of a light rain against the roof of the gazebo drew her attention as the minister began. The storm had started, but its gentle pattering was oddly soothing, as was the scent it coaxed from the velvety red roses climbing the walls of the gazebo. She had always loved the orgy of sweetness that came with the first flowerings in spring, and a soft rain seemed to intensify the fragrances, releasing them into the air. Some of her fondest childhood memories were of the bramble roses climbing wild and free up the side of the ravine behind their house. They were a haven for bumblebees and darting butterflies.

"We are gathered here in the sight of God," the minister informed them in sonorous tones.

Jessie breathed in deeply, concentrating on sense memories, on flowers and the building intensity of the rain. She tried to block out the minister's words, but they penetrated her thoughts like the persistent tick of a clock's second hand. Worse, their solemn meanings and the reverence with which he recited them made her all the more aware of the hypocrisy of her marriage to Luc, especially since she'd dreamed of exactly this sort of ceremony as a child, in this gazebo, *to this very man.*

A piercing pain nearly cut off her breathing.

"Do you, Jessie Flood-Warnecke, take this man . . . ?" the minister was saying.

"Yes." The word rushed out too abruptly, more in an effort to stop him than anything else.

The minister hesitated. Clearly it wasn't what she was supposed to have said, but he seemed reluctant to correct her.

A moment later he was pronouncing them husband and wife.

"You may kiss the bride," he told Luc, eyeing Jessie warily as he made the suggestion. "If you wish," he added.

"It is my fondest wish," Luc said, his voice edged with masculine irony.

It may be your *last,* Jessie wanted to fire at him. But Luc's hand had closed over hers, and he was gently tugging her around to face him. She resisted him with clenched fingers, then moved stiffly with his lead, not wishing to cause a scene in front of her child, the minister, or even Matt.

Luc's eyes darkened irresistibly as she glanced up at him. He placed his hands on her upper arms, and she averted her gaze, shrinking into herself and trying to lessen the contact as much as possible. But she couldn't avoid him when he finally curved a hand to her face. With one deft and surprisingly gentle move, he tilted her head up for the traditional kiss.

Someone coughed in the small wedding party.

A bird screeched in the trees above them, echoing the tension that was building inside Jessie. She told herself that it was just a kiss, empty symbolism. It meant no more to her than the ritual of the marriage itself. She had agreed to marry him, and now she had no choice but to get this sham of a ceremony over with as quickly as possible, sparing everyone more awkwardness.

She told herself all of that as he bent toward her, seemingly in slow motion, but even a chorus of saints and angels from on high probably couldn't have stopped the desperate impulse that flared through her as he drew near. Galvanized, she bobbed up on her tiptoes and quickly brushed her lips over his cheek, barely touching the edge of his mouth.

"*In name only*," she whispered.

Startled, he let her back away, as if he wasn't at all sure what to do with her. And then his eyes caught fire and his hands gripped her arms. "Not a chance," he said, lifting her up until her feet were barely touching the floor. "*You're mine now*," he said under his breath. "You're Mrs. *Luc* Warnecke and everything that implies."

He hesitated a breath away from her taut, trembling lips, prolonging the anticipation and Jessie's anguish. There was something powerful and controlling in the way he held her, as if he intended to keep her suspended until every last ounce of fight had drained out of her, until she was too weak to do anything but submit. His face was angled so closely that his dark eyelashes brushed her cheekbone, but still his lips hadn't touched hers.

"Do it," she said through clenched teeth.

"Do what?" he asked, dragging it out of her.

"*Kiss me.*"

There was a sob in her voice, but it wasn't pain, it was sheer, unmitigated fury. She wished the gazebo would be hit by a blazing comet, and she wouldn't have cared if the entire Bay Area had been wiped out in the collision.

Tension hissed between them as he moved his mouth over hers caressingly, barely touching her lips and yet electrifying her at the same time. Her body went taut and then wild. Her heart shuddered with despair. *If you let him do this to you*, she told herself. *If you let this bastard arouse you again, you're more debased than he is!* But she couldn't stop her responses any more than she could stop the storm that was rising around them. Luc Warnecke was as electric as the storm—a powerful, irresistible negative charge. And she was a lightning rod.

She bit down in frustration, catching the edge of his lip.

He jerked back furiously. "If you draw blood this time," he warned, "I'll take my conjugal rights here on the floor of this gazebo."

Jessie heard a gasp and knew the others must have caught his whispered threat. She went still, praying Mel hadn't heard. For some mysterious reason, the child seemed happy about this marriage, and she didn't want to frighten or disillusion her. Fortunately, Gina and Mel were outside the gazebo, looking on, probably too far away to pick up anything.

A crack of thunder split the clouds above them, and the wind whistled through the latticed walls of the gazebo, whipping Jessie's dress. "Get in the house!" someone shouted as the sky went black and the rain began to batter at their shelter like hailstones.

Jessie turned to see where Mel was and saw Gina rushing with the drenched child toward the house.

"Here," Luc said, pulling off his jacket. He threw it over Jessie's shoulders, but she pushed it off and twisted away from him, nearly ripping the heel from her shoe as she lurched down the gazebo steps. The storm had given her a reason to escape him, but she didn't even have time to be grateful. She was too concerned about Mel. She was already envisioning a trip to the emergency room—a horrible way to spend her wedding night, but better than the alternative, she decided.

When she reached her daughter's room, she saw that Gina already had Mel's wet clothes off and was drying her hair with a towel. Mel, in fact, was grinning like a Cheshire cat and loving every second of the drama.

"Wasn't that great, Mom?" she said. "I'll bet no one's ever had a wedding like that before!"

"I'll bet no one has," Jessie agreed with a bleak smile.

The antique carriage clock ticked loudly on the fireplace mantel. Gleaming softly in its brass scrollwork case, it accentuated the bedroom's silence as it cast a golden glow over the room. Jessie was only absently aware of the passage of time the clock marked as she sat huddled amid the black satin pillows on her bed, staring at the sodden shambles of her wedding dress on the floor.

The door handle turned with a click. Springing alert, she drew up her legs and tucked her terry robe around her. It was inevitable that Luc would show up. This was her wedding night. He was her husband.

He hesitated on the threshold as the door swung open. He'd changed out of his wet clothes, into gray workout sweats, and his hooded jacket hung unzipped, revealing shadowy suggestions of the torso she remembered too well from their swimming pool encounter. Ripples of muscle definition were evident even under the dusting of black body hair that streaked up from the drawstring waistband. He'd obviously worked out to achieve that build. She found herself wondering if it was strictly a male thing, or if he was unconsciously compensating for the bad leg.

"I thought you might like something to take the chill off," he said. He had a brandy snifter in each hand.

"No, thanks."

"Is Mel okay?"

"She's never been better."

"How about you?"

"I've never been worse."

He drew in a breath, and Jessie braced herself for the counterattack. But when he spoke, his voice held a note of husky contrition. "You probably won't believe this," he said, "but I didn't intend for it to turn out this way. I thought we might be able to—"

"To what?" she cut back, unable to imagine what two people so fundamentally opposed "might" be able to do.

He entered the room and set the snifters on the mantel, next to the clock. "I don't know . . . to talk, to find some common ground. We had some once. We were close as kids."

"That was another lifetime." She felt annoyed when he brought up their childhood, as if he were playing unfairly. "As for common ground, I'd say we have plenty of that, wouldn't you? Plenty of dirty, mucky common ground. We're standing on a sinkhole full of it!"

"My father, for example?"

"My *sister*, for example."

"I didn't get involved with Shelby to hurt you. I was young and embarrassingly naive. Besides, it wasn't that way with you and me, Jessie. We were buddies more than anything else, right? *Compadres?* I thought you felt the same way about me as I did about you."

"Pity? Is that what you felt for me? Because that's about as deep as my feelings went for you, Luc. That crippled kid routine always works on suckers like me. And of course we know what attracted Shelby, don't we?"

She curled into herself, pulling the robe around her and staring at the huge knot she'd made of her terry-cloth tie. *Was he cut up yet?* Jessie wondered. *Was he bleeding?* Because if words were knives, he should have been hemorrhaging.

His shadow flickered in the firelight. Her throat was so tight it hurt. That was the effect he had on her. He turned her into a hurtful, eviscerating shrew. When she looked up, he was still there, gazing at her, puzzling her out as though he didn't understand why she was so determined to fight with him. He could afford to be calm and magnanimous, she reminded herself. He had what he wanted—the keys to his father's kingdom.

He walked over and handed her the brandy. She took it reluctantly, shivering as she did so. She was freezing. Even the fire couldn't warm her.

"We're married," he reminded her. "We took vows. We should at least talk about what that means."

I took one vow, she thought. *In name only.* "What do you want it to mean? You forced me into this sham."

"I don't want there to be this hostility."

"Then you're living in a dreamworld. When was the last time you were forced into something against your will? It makes a person hostile." For a moment she almost allowed herself to hope that he might understand how impossible this was for her. People couldn't be blackmailed into having a relationship.

"Do you remember what happened in the gazebo?" he asked.

"There was a wedding, if I recall."

"One hell of a wedding, if I recall. You didn't want to be anywhere near me. You wouldn't even look at me, and then the skies opened up when I kissed you. You can tell me that

I forced you, but you can't tell me you didn't respond. You shook in my hands, Jessie. You came apart when our lips touched, not from fear, from excitement."

Something quivered and pulled tight, reverberating deep inside her. Panic? Excitement? She couldn't tell one from the other anymore, and no matter what he believed, that frightened her terribly. She was as taut as a hairspring, coiled like the inner workings of the antique clock ticking on the mantel.

"I want you to leave," she said, remembering the words he'd whispered and the note of obsession in his voice. *You're mine now*, he'd vowed. If he truly believed that she'd responded to him out of desire—and if he'd forced her to kiss him believing that—*what was next?*

His shadow enveloped her as he moved from the firelight.

She crept to the far side of the bed, her senses quickening. "Get out of here, Luc," she warned him softly. "Because if you don't, if you lay a hand on me, or even look as if you're going to, I'll have you charged with rape."

His laughter sounded darkly. "That should make the tabloids jump for joy. Black Widow Claims Bridegroom Raped Her. What a feeding frenzy that would be."

Jessie tipped up the brandy snifter and drank deeply. The liquor seared its way down her throat, filling her with fire as she turned to the windows that faced the ocean. Absently aware of the turbulence outside, she wondered what it would be like to get good and drunk and raise some hell in the family tradition of the Floods. She could remember the knock-down-drag-outs when Hank had been drinking Black Velvet all night long. Shelby was often drawn into those free-for-alls, though Jessie didn't understand why at the time. Now she assumed it was because of Hank's secret interest in his stepdaughter.

As a toddler Jessie would hide in the crawl space by the furnace when the brawling got violent. As she grew older, she took on the job of referee, trying to make sure no one was badly hurt. More often than not, someone was—her. She got her lip split and suffered more than one sprain and dislocation for her efforts. But they also taught her how to deal with volatile situations and helped prepare her for some of the more dangerous aspects of security work.

"If you were girding your loins to fight off a rapist," Luc said, breaking the silence, "this visit is going to be a disappointment. I came here for another reason."

She stared into the fiery glow of her brandy, slow to respond. "What reason is that?"

"I have to go away again, and I want you to come with me. It's business, but I was hoping we could make a pleasure trip out of it too, though that seems pretty unlikely under the circumstances."

"Unlikely? Try when Hell freezes over."

Have it your way, his shrug seemed to say. But it also implied that she was making a huge mistake. "This is a trip you might want to make, Jessie," he said mysteriously. "I've got something in mind, and it involves Warnecke Communications."

"How interesting, especially since you don't own a share of stock and never will." *At least not while I'm alive*, she thought. "In what way could you possibly hope to be involved?"

"Somebody had better get involved before the company's profit margin flatlines," he warned. "The newspapers' circulation are down, the radio stations' ratings are the lowest they've ever been. You should be thinking about modernizing, bringing Warnecke Communications into the Information Age."

"And how would we do that?"

His snifter sat on the mantel. He reached for it, cupping the bowl with his long fingers in a way that was rivetingly sensual without meaning to be. "By selling shares and expanding." He swirled the brandy until it glowed like molten lava in the snifter.

Jessie couldn't catch her breath. Surely he didn't mean—

"By going public," he said. With mounting dread she listened to his rationale.

"My father was buried in bedrock," he assured her. "He believed in preserving the grand tradition of print journalism and to hell with progress. With typical Warnecke arrogance, he acted as if the revolution in electronic media didn't exist. Do you have any idea what's going on out there, Jessie? Within the next decade there's going to be an explosion. Cable channels will mushroom from fifty to five hundred, and they're developing the technology to bring video feed to personal computers. The possibilities are *unlimited*."

"Some traditions should be preserved," she said stiffly. It was an argument she'd first heard Simon make, and she believed in it fervently. "This may be the Information Age, but the media has an obligation to do more than just 'inform' people. Newspapers can and should make their readers think, arouse them and get them to participate in the events that shape their lives."

He clearly wasn't swayed by her argument, but the glint of interest in his eyes told her he was impressed by the fact that she'd made it. "That's all very passionate," he said, "but not very practical. I believe in tradition too, but not at the expense of circulation and sales."

"And I believe in sales, but I'd never sink to publishing glitzy half-truths to get them." There. She'd done it. She'd thrown down the gauntlet. His eyes flashed with anger, though he would probably deny it. Had she impugned his integrity? The thought made her want to laugh out loud.

"Aren't we righteous." He snorted softly. "You could publish the Ten Commandments on stone tablets, and it wouldn't change anything." He moved closer, as if he what he wanted were to strip her bare of the plush terry robe she wore and everything else—the mansion, the expensive trappings. "Success may be for sale, Jessie, but class runs in the blood. You don't get it by publishing a prestigious paper."

"In other words, you publish trash and I come from trash. Is that what you're saying?"

"I'm saying marrying a Warnecke doesn't make you one."

"What does marrying *two* of them make me?"

"A mouthy bitch?"

She sprang from the bed, furious. "No! You alone get the credit for that, Luc. Whether you believe it or not, your father was incredibly kind to me."

He drained his brandy in one toss and strode to the door. "I'm making this trip with or without you," he told her. "And when I get back, I'm going to make a presentation to Warnecke's board of directors. Somebody has to yank the company out of the dark ages."

So that was how he planned to do it, she realized, astonished. He wasn't after her voting shares, he was going to launch a frontal attack! "That will *never* happen, Luc. The board was handpicked by Simon. They're his people, all of them." Her voice had risen in pitch, but she didn't care. Let the whole house hear her. "If they won't sell to you, do you think they'll listen to you tell them how the company should be run?"

"They'll listen—not because I'm a Warnecke, but because I'm a hell of a lot more successful than Simon. And a lot shrewder than Matt. They'll listen because it means dividends, Jessie. *Money*."

With that he walked out. The clock on the mantel seemed to have caught Jessie's racing urgency, ticking in time to her jumbled thoughts, her heartbeat. She didn't doubt that Luc might be right about the effect he would have on the board, and that only left her one option. She picked up the phone to call Matt Sandusky.

CHAPTER
·· EIGHTEEN ··

"HAVE YOU EVER seen anything like her?"

"They call her the cool gray lady."

"She's a beauty, isn't she? Look at the voluptuous curves on her—"

"My God, the size of her peaks."

"The swell of her bays—"

The hushed voices were raised in tribute to one of the finest examples of Queen Anne architecture in all of the foggy city. It was the third Tuesday of the month, and the San Francisco Historical Society had paused in their walking tour of Pacific Heights to admire a magnificent three-story Victorian that was fabled for its cool, slate-gray elegance. Gathered in the shade of a leafy Texas yew and rapt in their appreciation of the rounded bay windows, ornamental gables and grand observation tower, the small tour group barely noticed when the Victorian's garage doors whooshed open and a sleek midnight-blue Mercedes purred past them.

As Luc ferried into the narrow two-car garage the roomy sedan he'd rented for the trip, Jessie studied the crowd that had collected in front of Simon Warnecke's San Francisco residence. They were admiring a piece of California history that now belonged to her, she realized. At times like this, she became aware of, and awed by, her incredible good fortune. Her life had been transformed so drastically she could hardly assimilate the changes. One of the ways she coped was by going about her daily business, doing whatever had to be done, and trying not to notice too closely that she'd come into an immense fortune. But it was going to be very difficult to do that any longer, she admitted, glancing at Luc. He would be a constant reminder that her life had now taken another sharp detour into the uncharted future.

Again she wondered if she'd made the right choice by coming with him on this trip. Her first hurdle had been convincing Matt that she was in a perfect position to find out exactly what Luc intended to present to the board. She'd argued that unless they knew what Luc had planned in the way of modernization and expansion, they couldn't prepare an effective counter-argument.

Matt had seen the wisdom of her position immediately, but he was worried about her. "Never forget that you have something Luc wants," he warned. "Marrying you brings him one giant step closer, but it also puts you directly in his way. Don't underestimate him, Jessie. He's capable of anything."

She doubted it was possible for her to underestimate Luc. He posed threats Matt wasn't even aware of. But at the moment her chief concern was with Luc's plans for the evening ahead of them. He'd been surprisingly civil on the forty-five-minute drive, even solicitous compared to his usual behavior. But he'd refused to tell her anything about the itinerary for their stay, saying only that he didn't want to "ruin the surprise."

"Why don't you open up the house?" he suggested now as he cut the car's engine. "I'll get the luggage."

The first floor seemed forbiddingly empty as Jessie entered from the garage stairway. She had dismissed the permanent household staff when Simon was no longer able to travel. Now she wished she hadn't. The agency that handled the cleaning, maintenance and gardening was marvelously efficient, but that wasn't the same as having someone in the house. At the very least another person would have been a buffer between her and Luc.

Still, the place looked wonderful. She'd only notified the agency of their trip that morning, but the cleaning crew had already turned on the heat, opened the drapes and given the house an airing. There were freshly cut flowers in the formal parlor, and the brass andirons in the fireplace were piled high with logs.

"I'll take these up to your room," Luc said, carrying in her suitcases. He'd draped her garment bag over his shoulder. "I thought you might like to freshen up. I ordered dinner in from a favorite restaurant of mine. They won't be delivering it for another hour, so take your time."

"All right . . . fine," Jessie said, watching as he started up the golden oak staircase to the bedrooms on the second floor. It was interesting that he'd taken on the role of host when the house was, in fact, hers. She was also at a loss to explain his sudden display of good manners. He'd been civil to the point of friendliness since the wedding, which she found both disarming and highly suspicious. In her family an unexpected attack of niceness had meant someone wanted something.

What did Luc Warnecke want in return for his goodwill? she wondered as he turned on the landing and disappeared up the second flight of steps. As long as he was going to be pleasant, she might as well enjoy the novelty. It probably wouldn't last long.

He'd taken her things to the master bedroom, a large, airy chamber with a southern exposure, beautifully draped bay windows and a Victorian four-poster bed. He was hanging her garment bag in the closet as she entered the room. Was he going to draw her a bath next? she wondered with some amusement.

"Will you be ready to eat in an hour?" he asked, walking past her to the door.

She touched her fingers to her forehead. "I'm really very tired. I thought I might just take a bath, do some reading and go to bed."

He turned back at the doorway and regarded her with a look of dispassionate interest. "In that case, sleep well. If you need anything, use the intercom. I'll probably be downstairs for some time."

Sleep well? Jessie's eyebrows shot toward the ceiling as he gave her a neighborly nod and shut the door behind him. What was he up to? She stared at the door intently, then glanced at her garment bag, wondering what a bride should wear to a honeymoon dinner when she had no intention of consummating the marriage. Her lips pursed with a secret smile. Black, of course.

An hour later, as twilight was drenching the interior of the house in a peachy-gold ambience, she descended the stairs in a pair of satin lounging pajamas and matching high-heel slippers. The outfit was a totally self-indulgent impulse ordered from a lingerie catalog years ago, while she was laboring as a security guard at the bank and probably feeling terribly unfeminine. She'd never worn it before.

She entered the parlor to the glow of a small, cozy fire crackling in the hearth and Mozart's "A Little Night Music" playing low on the stereo. The bay windows had been thrown open to the deepening sky and the cooling breezes, and an iced bucket of champagne waited on a Louis XVI table near the fireplace.

Edwardian sofas in red plush faced each other on either side of the antique table. Luc set down his flute of champagne and rose from the far sofa as Jessie approached. "I'm glad you decided to come down." His dark gaze brushed over her pajamas appreciatively, letting her know he liked what he saw, and then he pointed to the candlelit table he'd set up by the bay windows. "I hope you're hungry."

She was, ravenous.

The champagne was vintage French, a premier grand cru and perhaps the driest, most effervescent brut Jessie had ever tasted. She drank two entire glasses of it while they nibbled at enormous iced rock shrimp dipped in a sinfully rich and tangy red ginger sauce. The second course was bouillabaisse, a spicy broth full of clams and mussels in the shell, which Luc ladled fragrant and steaming from an electric crock.

Jessie had no room left by the time Luc served the main course, a succulent scallops and shataki mushroom cassoulet. Luc was more adventurous, and while he sampled the rich shellfish baked in buttery garlic and bubbling cheeses, Jessie savored another glass of champagne and gazed out at the deep purple evening, watching the trolley cars clang back and forth at the intersection atop the hill and the street lamps sprinkle the glistening tracks with quicksilver.

The night seemed magical in some way she couldn't explain. It was like a scene from a children's movie where teakettles could dance and sing or trollies could soar off steep hills into flight with their tracks trailing behind them like silver ribbons.

She had drunk too much, she realized, setting down her champagne glass. She felt flushed and dizzy. And she was fantasizing, something she hadn't done since childhood. Worst of all, she was enjoying Luc's company.

"What made you decide to come down?" he asked later, as they sat across from each other on the sofas.

He lifted the dripping bottle of champagne from the ice bucket and refilled Jessie's glass, though she knew she ought to have some coffee instead. The room seemed to be aglow, mellowed by the flames from the fire, and her head was still spinning pleasantly. She couldn't remember the last time she'd felt so relaxed, certainly not around him. It was enough to make her wish she could let down her guard and really talk to him, even if only for a moment or two. She hadn't realized how weary she was of being constantly on the defensive.

"I came down out of curiosity," she admitted. "And hunger."

"Did you satisfy either?"

"The hunger, yes. I'm working on the curiosity."

He settled back and stretched an arm along the back of the sofa, seemingly charmed by her candor. A faint smile softened his mouth. She'd rarely seen him smile without some malice darkening his expression. It was an absorbing sight. His black hair caught the firelight, and a small golden flame burned in each of his irises, as if there were a low blaze kindling inside him.

"Go ahead," he told her, "ask me anything. I'm yours to interrogate."

He was wearing doeskin moccasins, and he'd rested one of them on the knee of his draped linen slacks. But perhaps what fascinated her most was the way the mock turtleneck of his tweedy sweater brushed against the underside of his chin when he tilted his head down to look at her. Was his skin smooth there, she wondered, as soft as his doeskin moccasins? Or was it roughened with the five o'clock shadow that was already beginning to deepen the contours of his jaw?

Something quickened inside her, filling her with the crazy desire to ask him just that question. Instead she laughed at her own impetuousness and took one last sip of champagne. Clearly she'd had more than enough to drink. *Next she would be asking him why he fell in love with Shelby instead of her.*

She clutched the elegant crystal flute as a soft pain blurred her senses, fuzzing the outlines of the glass in her hand. It was a ghost, that pain, an echo of the heartbreak that had engulfed her so many years ago. It had been her enemy once. She'd denied and suppressed the grief; she'd fought against feeling anything. But now, muted by time and the magic of a firelit evening, the piercingly tender sensation compelled her. It was tinged with sweetness. It stirred yearnings that reminded her of everything she'd longed for and lost. Luc had been her one shining chance at happiness in a life that promised to be as lonely as it was sordid. As young girls will do, she had pinned all her hopes and dreams on him.

Jessie closed her eyes, suddenly dizzy. It was the champagne making her feel this way, she told herself. It had magnified and distorted her emotions, making them seem more significant than they were. She was intoxicated, that was all.

But try as she might, she couldn't stem the flow of remembered pain. Or the insistent clutch of longing. It was evident in the awkwardness with which she set the champagne glass down and drew her hand back, burying it in the folds of her lounging pajamas. It was sighing in the air that escaped with her breathing. And it was there in her eyes as she looked up at him . . .

Could he see the memories in her gaze?

Was he remembering, too?

One of Chopin's nocturnes was playing softly in the background. Against the hush of Jessie's heartbeat, the music spun an enchanting web of melancholy and sweetness, building to a gentle crescendo and breaking into a run of shivering beauty. Jessie had rarely experienced such poignance. Every chord, every grace note tugged at her heart.

Luc sat forward, looking at her as if he meant to say something but couldn't find the words. He seemed on the verge of rising and coming to her. Jessie had the terrible feeling he'd seen everything, read every naked, foolish thought in her mind. She ducked her head, breaking the vital connection between them.

"Jessie?"

"Too much champagne," she said, closing her eyes to a sea of swirling darkness. "I feel woozy."

"I'll open the terrace doors. The fresh air will help."

A cool breeze bathed her, and she lifted her face to it, acutely aware of the tidal heat rushing up her throat and the stinging warmth of her skin. When she opened her eyes, he was crouching next to her, concerned.

"Let's go outside," he said. "It will clear your head." He took the hand that was clenched in her lap and began to work some circulation back into it, cradling it in both of his. Jessie was surprised by the gesture, then riveted by it. Her throat felt full and tight. She'd had no intention of going out to the terrace with him, but there was a quality of gentleness, a sensitivity, informing his dark gaze that reminded her of another time, another person.

"Come on," he said, helping her to her feet.

"I'm drunk," she admitted, terribly embarrassed as she tilted against him.

"No big deal," he assured her. "It happens to the best of us." Supporting her, he got her clear of the table, and they started toward the terrace.

"Can you tell?" she asked, gazing up at him.

"Tell?"

"That I'm drunk? Is it like . . . obvious?" Before he could answer, she'd tripped over the oriental carpet that lay in front of the terrace doors. The rug balled up in a clump as she attempted to get clear of it. With a soft squeak of alarm, she pitched forward, clutching at Luc as one of her slippers became hopelessly entangled in carpet fringe.

They both lost their balance, but somehow Luc managed to stay on his feet. He checked Jessie's fall, bracing himself against the door frame, and then he hooked a hand under her knees and lifted her into his arms. He was amazingly graceful, considering his bad leg. The only thing missing as he carried her out to the garden was one of her black satin slippers.

Jessie felt as light as dandelion fluff in his arms, and the sensation made her pleasantly giddy. "The rug attacked me," she informed him. "You saw it, didn't you? You were a witness."

"Want me to call the rug police?" With a slow, inquisitive grin, Luc blew a scatter of red curls out of her eyes and set her on her feet.

"I'm not actually drunk," she explained, kicking off her other slipper to avoid standing at a dizzying angle. "I mean, not falling-down drunk or anything."

"Of course not," he agreed. "Anyone can get tangled up in carpet fringe. I do it all the time."

"You do?" She turned in his arms to face him. "You too?"

He smoothed back the curls that kept tumbling onto her forehead and nodded solemnly. "Me too. Never could walk straight," he admitted ruefully.

Was he referring to the leg that had been broken when he was a child? Jessie was terribly touched. She wanted to comfort him, but his smile was tinged with self-deprecating irony.

"Let's start a self-help support group," he suggested. "What do you say?"

"For the balance-impaired?"

"Why not? We'll have an 800 number. Chevy Chase will be our spokesperson. Jerry Lewis could run a telethon. Gerald Ford could—"

She began to laugh, charmed by his willingness to have fun at his own expense. She stopped just as suddenly. "Why are you doing this?" she asked.

"Doing what?"

"Being nice to me."

"It's easy to be nice to you when you're this way."

"What way? Drunk?"

"No, nice."

"Oh . . . then you're being nice because *I'm* being nice? Not because you want something?"

Jessie might have asked the question even if she hadn't been tipsy. She'd probably always been too straightforward for her own good, but by the swift darkening of his expression, she could see she'd made a mistake. She'd triggered something instinctively touchy in him, and it was changing the mood of their encounter, turning it toward intimacy.

"What kind of fool would I be if I didn't want something, Jessie? You're beautiful . . . You're my wife."

Dizziness swept her again. She tried not to lean into him, but it was almost impossible for her to keep her balance. Some sort of gravity that had nothing to do with physics seemed to be pressing in all around her. She was already in his arms, already as close as she could be without actually brushing up against him.

"I think I can stand on my own now," she told him.

He made no move to release her, and her reaction was to glance up at him, her heart crowded with questions.

"To tell you the truth," he said. "I do want something."

"I was afraid of that."

He laughed and straightened the collar of her pajamas, freeing a burnished tendril of hair that had attached itself to her damp, flushed throat. "Why?" he asked. "Do you know what I want?"

"My kingdom, my castle—and my rose garden, I suppose?"

"Your rose garden is safe," he assured her, continuing to stroke her throat in a way that made her fingertips want to curl. "All I want is a little more of this, Jessie, what I'm feeling right now. This tender thing that's burning between us. Is that possible?"

His voice was earnest, irresistibly husky.

Jessie's heart caught painfully. *Don't trust this,* some guiding instinct warned her. *Don't trust him.* There were so many reasons not to, and the most urgent among them was the grief he'd already caused her. And yet something was haunting her, an impulse that was stronger than her doubts and more insistent than her heartache. *Nostalgia,* she told herself. *It had to be that.* She was caught up in an uncontrollable desire to regain what they once had. She drew in a breath, refusing to acknowledge the other possibility that came crashing into her mind. *No, it couldn't be that.* This tender, piercing sensation she felt was not love.

"You didn't answer," he said.

His hand moved to the curve of her back, startling her, and as she arched against its warmth, their bodies touched accidentally. Their thighs brushed first, a fleeting stroke, but the contact left Jessie both energized and wildly weak.

"Anything is possible . . ." She wondered at the words even as they spilled from her throat. She didn't dare look at him. But she could feel the pressure of his touch. Male and insistent.

He was everywhere, closing in around her, his scent enveloping her in sandlewood and smoke. His fingers purled up her spine, and she bumped into him again, her belly grazing his hip, her breasts flirting with his rib cage and lightly kissing his taut bicep. The sensations were riveting. Wherever they touched, no matter how briefly, it felt as if some gentle, vibrant current were arcing between them, running from his body into hers and teasing her startled senses into a sweet frenzy. Like the caress of a masterful, sweetly dominating lover, it left her languid and feverishly weak.

"I can't do this," she said breathlessly.

"You can't dance with me?"

"Dance?" The classical album seemed to have run its course. Now a slow, poignantly romantic ballad was playing. It was a Jeffrey Osborne song called "Just Once" that Jessie particularly loved. She searched Luc's face, momentarily lost in the lonely beauty of his dark eyes. Did he like the song too?

The singer was asking if there was a way to finally make things right . . .

Luc drew her hands up around his neck and clasped them there. "Just once," he said, sliding his palms down the length of her arms. "Dance with me . . . just this once."

As his hands continued to drift down her body, a moan quavered in Jessie's throat. His thumbs grazed the sides of her breasts, stimulating her so vibrantly that she shuddered and nearly melted inside. "On your honor?" she whispered, fighting the desire to cling to him as they began to sway to the music.

"On my honor . . ."

The bittersweet song swirled around them, weaving a magical spell that spun them back in time. Within a few short stanzas Jessie had given in to her need to be pressed up against him. With a sigh, she dropped her cheek into the curve of his shoulder and curled her fingertips into his nape. Suddenly they were sweethearts at a high school dance, Luc nuzzling into her curly red hair like an overeager teenage boy, aching with the need to go all the way, and Jessie clinging to him as if she were his best girl, hopelessly in love and dreamily anticipating the moment when they would finally be alone and he would thrill her with his ardent kisses.

He brushed his lips over her temple, humming softly along with the music, and she realized that this was her adolescent fantasy. It was everything she'd dreamed about—dancing with him, being his girl, even doing "it" with him on some deep, dark night when they'd been swimming in the bay. *Ah, Luc,* she thought, sighing. *I've waited so long for this dance. And wanted it so desperately. You'll never know how much.*

As the music faded to a close, he slowed with her still wrapped tightly in his arms. They gradually came to a stop, eyes shut, hearts beating in synchronous rhythm. He drew back and touched her face, and Jessie knew he was going to kiss her. But she knew something else as well. It wouldn't stop with a kiss. *He* wouldn't stop. He was aroused. She could feel the heat of him wedged tightly between the groove of her thigh and her pelvic bone. The realization spurred excitement so intense, she experienced a sharp, fleeting regret that she had vowed not to consummate their marriage.

He smoothed her hair with the back of his hand, feathering the fluid curve of her cheek, the silk of her earlobe. She looked up, drawn by the brightness flaring in his dark eyes. She'd expected to see desire and it was there in all its male glory. But she hadn't expected to see the other qualities, surprise and wonder, a sparkle of tenderness and something even sweeter, need. His thumbs curved into the softness of her cheeks. His breath was oddly shallow. He was shaken, she realized.

It was hard for her to imagine that he might be feeling the same things she was—the longing to be close, the vulnerability that came with wanting someone so badly you forgot to be cautious. But as that possibility took hold of her thoughts, panic set in. If he actually was feeling those things—any of them!—then she had to stop him. Whatever he had in mind, she couldn't let him do it. She could have mustered the strength to resist a sexual overture, even a forceful one. She had before, several times. But an emotional appeal from Luc Warnecke? She would never be able to withstand that. She was falling apart at the thought. If he were to tell her what she'd always wanted to hear—that he cared—she would be irretrievably lost. That was all he needed to say to render her defenseless, she realized. *The only thing he had to do was care.*

"God," he said softly, still gazing at her. "Are you feeling the way I am?"

"Giddy?" She nodded, her heart pounding wildly. "Maybe we both had too much to drink," she suggested.

"I'm high all right, but it isn't the wine. It isn't even the music or this place, Jessie. It's this rush of feeling. It's incredible." He shook his head, laughing huskily as if he didn't quite know what to make of the situation.

"Luc, don't laugh like that," she implored, velvet-voiced and breathy.

"I beg your pardon?"

"I just wish you wouldn't laugh like that, and maybe you shouldn't look at me that way either—"

"Not look at you? Jessie, I—"

"You *promised*," she reminded him quickly, extricating herself from his arms.

"I promised not to look at you?"

"No, you promised it would be one dance. Nothing more."

"True, but who knew this was going to happen, who knew we were going to feel like this." He drew in a deep breath as if he were about to declare himself in some way. "There's something I've been wanting to tell you," he said. "Something besides the fact that you look irresistible tonight. Jessie, I—"

"No!"

He seemed stunned as she stepped away from him. Red slashes of confusion ruddied his face, and his hand dropped as if by instinct in front of him. She had embarrassed him and the realization tore at her. She didn't want to leave him this way, but she had to. There would be no hope for her otherwise. She had to move quickly, take advantage of his surprise.

She didn't dare stop or look back as she fled up the stairs, even when he called out her name.

Luc shook his head, laughing in bewilderment, just the way she'd told him not to. But this time a shudder touched him. Heat radiated from his aroused body in waves, forming a buffer against the cool night air. He had no idea what had frightened Jessie off, and even if she'd bothered to tell him, it wouldn't have helped much with the jackhammer that was raging in his chest. What the hell was going on with that woman? He'd had better luck with her when he was rough and graphic about his intentions. At least she'd responded then. Show her a little tenderness, and she took off like a frightened rabbit.

He heard her bedroom door shut, followed by the click of a metal latch sliding into its groove. She also had a penchant for barricading herself in bedrooms. Apparently she hadn't yet figured out that a locked door wouldn't protect her . . . not if he wanted to get to her. And God, he did want that, to get to her. He ached with it, ached everywhere, even in the angry jerk of his heartbeat.

This was going to be one long, *hard* night.

He'd already made up his mind not to go after her. There was nothing he could do to bring back the magic and nothing he could say that would make him feel any less an idiot for having succumbed to it, even momentarily. He'd been caught up in the naked yearnings that suffused her misty blue eyes. Whether she'd meant to or not, she'd drawn crazy, tender things out of him. She'd made him want to kiss the tiny, blushing scar above her lip and bring the tipsy, half-serious smile back to her face. And then she'd made him feel like a fool for wanting those things.

Still, he would like to have known what set her off. When a woman was all over a man one minute and running for cover the next, there were a limited number of conclusions that man could jump to. He'd already narrowed them down to two in her case. Either she was deep in the throes of denial or she was an amazingly talented tease.

Denial, he decided, staring up the empty stairway. Jessie Flood was many things, but she wasn't a seductress. That was her sister, Shelby's territory. The insight soothed his male pride a little, but it didn't solve a more immediate problem. He loathed cold showers and the thought of taking things in hand on the first night of his honeymoon held very little appeal. But he *was* aroused. Sweat filmed the back of his neck and crept down the path of his spine.

Swearing softly, he sought refuge in the liquor cabinet.

Moments later, having cracked a fifth of Scotch that was older than he was, he turned to the stairway again and found himself imagining her there, her pajama top falling open, her head bowed in self-conscious invitation, her eyes just meeting his. The flush of desire that swept through him was hot as a blown fuse. A sigh of disgust welled inside him. God, but he felt like an idiot. What the hell was wrong with him, standing here all alone in the dark like a pathetic teenage kid, dreaming about a beautiful, unapproachable girl?

Jessie leaned against the locked door, her head thrown back, her eyes shut. How could she have done such a thing? What had possessed her to run away just as he was about to say something that promised to be wonderful! The moment was lost and she couldn't imagine that there would be a chance to recapture it, not after the way she'd rebuffed him.

The moan on her lips was rife with self-reproach. *She would never know what he was going to say.* But what else could she have done? She'd felt so exposed and vulnerable. A gentle word would have been her undoing.

And yet how she'd longed to hear that gentle word.

Regret burned in her heart, searing its way to her throat as she took a deep breath. She'd waited so long to be treated like that, catered to like that, *courted* like that . . . by him. You've blown it, Jessie girl, she thought. You didn't miss the moment, you dug a hole and buried it. And undoubtedly made your unpredictable bridegroom furious in the bargain.

Her eyes came open.

A surprised smile made her lower lip unmanageable until she caught it between her teeth. *Her* unpredictable bridegroom? When had she started thinking of him in those terms? Dread knifed through her excitement as she realized that her relationship with Luc Warnecke was rapidly approaching another turning point. She'd loved him and hated him. She'd even tried to kill him, but this was entirely different.

This was almost too threatening to contemplate.

Was she starting to like him a little?

CHAPTER
··NINETEEN··

IT WAS A perfectly glorious morning for atonement. Silvery sunlight spilled into the master bedroom through deeply curved bay windows with a radiance that rivaled the heavenly gates. The large, airy room enjoyed a southern exposure, and the windows' creamy sheers seemed to have magically collected and pooled every drop of light the sky had to offer that day. Birds chirped among the lacy white blossoms of the fruit trees outside, and from the near distance came the melodious clang of the trollies, already about their business on this busy weekday morning.

Jessie hoped all the lively activity was a good sign as she sighed and stretched herself awake, reluctant to rouse from the satin depths of the canopy bed. The European featherbed mattress hugged her shoulders and hips like bouyant, sun-warmed clouds, encouraging her premonition that the timing was right for making amends. With both Heaven and the weather on her side, she might have a chance at brightening Luc's mood this morning.

She couldn't imagine he'd be very cheerful after last night. She'd heard him leave the house shortly after she'd gone to bed. He'd returned hours later, apparently the worse for his escape into the night. He'd stumbled, muttered and slammed doors, a dangerous thing to do in a structure that was nearly one hundred years old.

She threw off the covers and slid out of bed, shivering at the abrupt change in temperature. Despite the lavish light, the air held a slight chill that probably wouldn't burn off until afternoon, and then only if the warmth didn't condense into a creeping fog.

Jessie, there's something I've been wanting to tell you—

Her thoughts buzzed with Luc's husky overture throughout the entire time it took her to shower and dress. He'd already complimented her on her looks. Was it wishful thinking to wonder if he was going to say something else, perhaps even to declare his feelings? Was he going to tell her he loved her?

The sweater she was holding slipped from her fingers. In the time it took her to crouch and pick it up, she'd already dismissed the idea as ludicrous. Luc had made it clear on many occasions that he didn't feel that way about her and probably never had, except maybe as a buddy sort of thing when they were kids. He'd been caught up in the mood of the moment. He'd been carried away by wine and soft music, just as she had.

If only she'd handled things better.

One last sideways glance in the cheval glass confirmed that her indigo pullover sweater was deeply cut in front, revealing sea-swells of cool bosom and at the same time promising to drift off one shoulder. On an impulse, she had looped her hair into a Grecian knot, from which spilled a curly fall of red-gold firelight. She was rarely so calculating about her appearance, but the task ahead of her seemed to call for a bit of feminine strategy, unfair or otherwise. Still, it struck her as rather bizarre that she was primping for Luc. Her obsession with his romantic inclinations was even more curious, considering that a month ago she'd almost put him in his grave.

She found him in the breakfast room, though it was so dark she might not have noticed him sitting at the end of the table if he hadn't muttered something unintelligible when she walked in. The cozy, plant-filled corner room looked out over both the back and the southern gardens—or it would have if he hadn't had the window shutters tightly closed.

"Good morning," she ventured, throwing open the shutters on the less sunny eastern window first. The back garden was small, no larger than the house's front parlor, but it was chaotically abloom with spring flowers. Glowing daffodils and pale pink narcissi sprang from terra-cotta pots, and sprays of mauve wisteria hung from a wooden arbor painted moss green. It was Jessie's favorite spot this time of year. She'd only stayed at the house a few times in the two years she'd been married to Simon, but she'd already chosen her favorite rooms. In the winter she loved the family parlor with its red Mahal carpet, golden oak paneling and roaring fireplace.

Luc winced and ducked his head at the light, clutching his coffee mug with both hands. A thermal carafe of the pungent brew sat on the table in front of him like plasma. The only thing he lacked was an intravenous feed.

He was clearly hung over, so Jessie proceeded carefully.

"Can I join you?" she asked him, opening the china cabinet on an eighteenth-century Minton breakfast set and helping herself to a coffee cup hand-painted with a delicate seashell motif.

"If you must," he said. "But close those damn shutters."

She rattled the knobs a bit as if to close the shutters, then left them exactly the way they were. He would have to get used to the daylight eventually; there was going to be ten or twelve more hours of it.

"I'm sorry about last night." She took a chair opposite him, enduring his skeptical glare as she poured herself some coffee. "No, I really *am* sorry," she insisted. "I shouldn't have run off like that."

"Then why the hell did you do it?"

She took a sip from her cup and swallowed it with great difficulty. The coffee was bitterly strong. "I'm not sure," she admitted. "I suppose I was confused by what was happening, maybe even frightened by it."

He looked up at her, braving the light. "Jessie Flood, the fearless wonder. Frightened?"

Worse, she thought. Panic-stricken. She brought the coffee cup to her lips, resisting the impulse to confess her fears in more detail. For some reason the desire to confide in him was unaccountably strong. Perhaps it was his obvious discomfort that made him seem sympathetic. Or maybe it was because they were alone here in the house, and she desperately wanted an ally instead of an enemy. But to unburden herself fully meant going into their past, and she couldn't do that without endangering others. The chain of circumstances was as hopelessly entangled as a web work of nerves. One couldn't be cut free from the others without damaging them all.

She wanted to look away, to inspect the maple tabletop for water rings or to search the depths of her coffee cup for a sign of the future. Instead she forced herself to meet his probing gaze, aware that she wasn't going to allow him in any further than she already had.

"Do I frighten you now?" he asked.

"In your weakened condition? Hardly."

"Touché." He bent his head and rubbed his neck, grimacing.

If only he weren't so mussed up this morning and wary about the eyes, she thought. His hair drooped onto his forehead in dark waves that were almost curls and zigzagged over his ears, spilling haphazardly onto the nape of his neck. He had not totally lost the boy's vulnerability. Last night had proved that. But he was a man, very much so, with a man's need to dominate his world. Her other experience with him had proved that. The dichotomy of child and adult in him filled her with bittersweet remembrances, and at the same time it set her senses on edge, sharpening their acuity with an excitement edged by fear.

"Maybe we could stop frightening each other for a while?" he suggested.

"And do what instead?"

"Something less taxing, like talking?"

She startled herself by how rapidly she took him up on the idea. "It's a glorious day. Everything's in bloom. We could go for a walk."

He released his grip on the coffee mug long enough to shield his eyes. "It's a little bright out there for me, and anyway, I'm not a great walker."

Not a great walker. Because he didn't enjoy walking, or because of his childhood limp? Whatever he'd meant, it was an interesting admission.

"How about something to eat?" he suggested. "Ever been to the Cliff House?"

She smiled. "No, but I've heard it's nice and dark inside." The restaurant was a famous landmark near the Presidio that had been destroyed by fire and rebuilt four different times. She'd always wanted to go there, partly out of curiosity, but also because such dogged perseverance in the face of disaster was inspiring to someone who'd dealt with as much adversity as she had.

"Let's go," he said.

"Okay, but what will we talk about?"

He shrugged. "Politics? Religion? Sex? We could even discuss business. Or maybe something neutral like when, how and where we're going to consummate this marriage. Take your pick."

"How about the weather?" she suggested.

Jessie's first impression of the restaurant's interior was one of dark rich woods and sky-high windows, shimmering with hazy light reflected from the Pacific. The view of Seal Rocks, two rugged outcroppings rising whale-like out of the choppy gray water, was magnificent, but Luc wasn't of a mind to sightsee. He picked a table in the darkest corner of the restaurant and immediately ordered a Bloody Mary. Hair of the beast, Jessie assumed.

His mood was reflective as he nursed his drink. She needn't have worried about their breakfast conversation, because it was some time before he said anything at all, though he appeared to have a great deal on his mind. "I can't forget the way you looked last night," he told her.

Jessie glanced up at him as she cut a wedge from what was left of her Eggs Benedict. She had an enormous appetite and had tucked into her breakfast the minute it was set in front of her, polishing off half of it while Luc sat and drank, watching her. He'd eaten nothing. "That sounds like a pickup line," she said.

His laughter had a surprised quality. "If I were trying to pick you up, I'd never resort to lines. I'd probably plan an abduction on the scale of the Lindbergh kidnapping."

She didn't know whether to be flattered or alarmed. "That's a little extreme, isn't it?"

"Don't be modest, Jessie. Given our recent history, I'd be crazy to leave anything to chance."

He settled back in his chair, all very casual, but she was intrigued by the roguish twinkle in his eyes and the sexy burr that rustled his voice like nap velvet. "And just how would you plan to go about this abduction?" she asked.

He gave her a careless once-over, glancing at her hair and eyes and lips as if her looks weighed heavily in his answer.

She wondered ironically if she were pretty enough to warrant kidnapping, but didn't ask. His gaze drew up a physical rush of sensation, sending all other thoughts from her head. It was quick, arrogant, male. It made her feel as if he'd taken advantage in some way that he shouldn't have, as if he'd pulled her into one of the restaurant's dark alcoves and furtively slipped his hands beneath her sweater to fondle her.

"I'd do this," he said, continuing to study her intently.

"What?"

"This. Watch you."

Perspiration dampened her upper lip. She was aware that her indigo pullover had shifted forward on her shoulders, revealing a wealth of creamy cleavage, and the sleeve of her sweater had kept its promise and parted company with her shoulder. His eyes seemed to be following the path of the sensual shadow that played in the slope of her collarbone before it dipped into the cleft between her breasts. She drew up the drifting sleeve.

"If I were a kidnapper," he informed her quietly, "I'd stalk you for days before I made my move."

"Really?" Her heart began to rush.

"I'd watch you from the shadows, taking note of your comings and goings, tracking your every move. You would sense me there, watching you, lying in wait, but you would never see me."

"Never?"

"No. But I'd be there. Always. Everywhere. You would feel me all around you, an invisible presence, the caress of unseen hands. You would feel me every time you undressed and every time you touched yourself, like tonight when you draw the sweater over your head and unhook your bra and pull down your panties. Tonight your hands will be my hands. Tonight you'll feel me there—and tomorrow. And the next day."

She set down her fork, food forgotten.

"I'd be a constant presence," he went on, his voice low. "And before I was done, I'd know you better than you know yourself. I'd know what you were going to do before you did it. That's how I'd catch you off guard. By knowing when you were going to blink, and striking then, in that split-second while your eyes were closed and you were blind. A preemptive strike, they call it."

She shuddered visibly.

"I could go on," he assured her.

"Don't."

He smiled darkly, evidently enjoying himself. "By the way, when I told you I couldn't forget how you looked, I meant a fantasy image that came to me after you left last night. I imagined you standing on the stairway, your pajama top undone, your head bowed as if you couldn't bring yourself to look at me."

Her fingertips curled toward the emptiness of her palms. "Couldn't look at you?"

"No, not at first. You reminded me of a young girl who wanted something urgently, but couldn't bring herself to ask, a young girl ashamed of her own desires. I was fascinated by which impulse would win—desire or shame."

"And which did?"

"Desire, I think. It took my breath away when you finally glanced up at me. I've never seen such turmoil before. It was haunting, beautiful."

"But it wasn't really me," she hastened to remind him.

"Wasn't it?"

"No, of course not. I was in my room—"

He seemed not to have heard her. "You kept me up all night, Jessie. No matter how much I drank, I couldn't erase the image of that blushing, stricken girl on the stairway. I don't think anything will ever erase it."

Another shudder touched her. She held indelible images of him in her mind, too. Some of them as heartrending as a broken body lying at the bottom of a ravine. Others as full of tender surprise as the look in his eyes when they stopped dancing last night. Now she searched his features openly, wondering if it would ever be possible to connect with him again, the person who had been the center, the heart of her life. His shadowed, watchful expression was an enigma. It seemed as if he were three separate men—the boy, the military school cadet, and now this powerful, incomprehensible man.

He was her adversary, she told herself. She didn't want it to be true, but it was. She could never surrender, never trust him, never confess. And yet she wanted to, even knowing the danger. Some deep longing clutched at her, begging her to end the battle and give in to whatever destiny had planned for her and Luc Warnecke. Surrender, even to him, would bring the sweetness of closure, a little death. There would be such peace in abandoning her burdens, whereas now she had no peace at all. It was a crazy thought, but she couldn't resist it. If only she had the courage to give in completely and have it over with, to let him either cherish her tenderly or destroy her at will, whichever he wanted. Anything he wanted.

You will feel me every time you touch yourself. Your hands will be my hands.

"Your eyes are dense with blue," he observed. "The pupils have all but disappeared, even in this light. I wonder what you're thinking now? What you're feeling?"

"My abductor would know," she said softly.

He moved back in the chair, shifting into shadows that nearly concealed his smile. His voice was slowed, thick. "You want it, don't you? You want to be stalked. You want to be watched from the shadows and taken captive . . ."

She flushed . . . and felt the first sweet thrill of letting go.

CHAPTER
·· TWENTY ··

SHELBY WAS RESTLESS. Weddings always had that effect on her. While most young girls were dreaming of seed pearls and veils, Shelby had been studying the fine art of filching cosmetics from Burrell's Drugstore on the corner of Miramontes and Main. Now, conspicuously single at thirty-one, she still couldn't relate to the wedding fever that struck most women like a swine flu epidemic. Virginal white had never flattered her tawny complexion, except perhaps in the form of peekaboo lace lingerie.

And yet as she gazed out at the sweeping view from the second-story guest bedroom, she knew her inner turbulence had more to do with dissatisfaction than disdain. Jessie's wedding was a milestone that had forced her to take stock of her life, and lately she wasn't thrilled with the inventory she'd compiled. She'd always believed men tended to clump women into one of two general categories—madonna or whore—and since it was still a man's world by any intelligent analysis, the smart woman played her chosen role to the hilt.

Jessie was a born madonna. Saintly and self-sacrificing, she'd always seemed perfectly willing to settle for noble poverty if that's what life handed her. She'd taken the high road, whereas Shelby had been traveling the low road with apologies to no one. What confounded Shelby was the result. Jessie had all but proven Shelby's theory. She was a damn good madonna, and she had a mountain of money to show for it. But so was Shelby a damn good hooker. She should have been wildly successful at something by now—or at the very least a lavishly kept woman.

As she turned away from the rugged splendor of the coastline, her rising frustration was edged with despair. Her mood wasn't helped by the fact that she was staying in Echos, the real estate she'd always coveted. Even the brilliantly sunny weather depressed her. Why wasn't she lying under a coconut palm on a tropical beach somewhere in Cabo or the south of France? At what point had her life turned down a dead-end road? God, but it pained her to contemplate the possibility that Shelby Flood wasn't even a very good tramp. Now, there was failure for you.

She was planning a suicidal shopping spree a short time later when the sound of laughter filtered through her open balcony doors. Only mildly curious, she walked out on the small veranda and saw Mel splashing at the shallow end of the pool. Gina, who was much too ingratiatingly efficient for Shelby's taste, was seated in a lounge chair, reading.

"*Ciao*, Aunt Shel!" Mel called out, spotting Shelby immediately. "Want to watch the *bambina* swim?" Standing in hip-deep water, the child plunged in headfirst, flailing with great determination but very little forward motion. *Takes after her mother,* Shelby thought, arching an eyebrow.

"Fabulous, Mel," she called out, dreading the thought of a prolonged exhibition. She liked her little niece well enough, but children were a sometime thing for Shelby, and she was hardly in the mood today. She waved as Mel resurfaced, then turned back into the bedroom. Maybe she could get that studly young handyman—Roger or whatever his name was—to drive her into San Francisco and wait while she shopped.

A piercing scream whirled her around. Mel was thrashing wildly in the water, and Gina had leapt from the chair. She was bent over the side of the pool, trying to reach Mel. The child had swum out over her head and couldn't get back.

"Jump in," Shelby shouted to Gina, knowing there wasn't enough time for her to get downstairs. "Pull her out."

"I can't swim!" Gina cried.

Shelby grasped the railing. As she stared with frozen horror at the struggling child, she realized Mel was only a short distance from where she'd started her swimming demonstration. "It's not over your head at that depth," she called to the au pair. "You can walk out to her!"

Gina jumped in feet-first and reached Mel within seconds.

As she tugged the gasping but very much alive child into the shallows, Shelby realized what good 'ol Aunt Shel was going to be doing with the rest of her day. *Oh, joy,* she thought.

Teaching the *bambina* to swim was not as tedious as Shelby had thought it was going to be. By noon she had Mel dog-paddling well enough to get herself from the middle of the pool to the side, and when they resumed the lessons in the afternoon, Mel insisted on learning to swim underwater.

"Mom's never wanted me to learn to swim because of my asthma," Mel confided.

Shelby had pretty much forgotten about Mel's condition, especially since the child hadn't so much as sniffled. She was sure Jessie wouldn't like what she'd done, but then, her little sister never liked anything she did, and Jessie wasn't around, so to hell with her. "You're going to be a regular dolphin before I'm through with you," Shelby boasted.

Mel wrinkled her nose. "Isn't that a football team?"

"So you'll grow dorsal fins, swim with whales *and* run for touchdowns."

"Sharks have dorsals."

"Well, whatever dolphins have, okay, smart ass?"

"Just call me Flipper." Mel grinned, and Shelby clamped her hand to the child's head and dunked her. Before the afternoon session was over, Mel was wriggling along the bottom of the pool like a porpoise. As many children will do, she'd taken naturally to swimming underwater. Shelby was proud of the nine-year-old's progress. The kid was a trooper, a real spark plug. And she was having fun, Shelby realized, oddly gratified.

Shelby was having fun too. She'd forgotten how luxuriantly sensual swimming underwater could be. Maybe the next time she was in Cabo, she'd try snorkling. Or better yet, maybe she'd talk Roger into joining her for a midnight skinny-dip. That should improve her mood.

The moment dinner was over that evening, Mel begged to go back to the pool. Gina vetoed the idea, pointing out Mel's already puckered body parts and the possibility of cramps. Shelby agreed they were both waterlogged, but somehow the two of them ended up out by the pool anyway, sitting on the side and dangling their feet in the water instead of swimming.

By way of conversation Shelby suggested that Mel might try out for the swim team once she'd built up a bit more stamina. Mel seemed thrilled at the idea, but Shelby knew the real obstacle was Jessie. Privately she'd already made up her mind to speak to her sister. Mel had taken to swimming with a zeal that was almost desperate. The kid needed to test herself, to prove her mettle at something. Shelby understood that kind of desperation.

"Look!"

Mel's hushed excitement broke the companionable silence that had fallen between them. She was pointing to something at the deep end of the pool, but Shelby couldn't see what it was. Shelby watched in confusion as Mel scrambled to her feet and went around to that end. Kneeling at the side, she pulled off her baseball cap and dipped it into the water as if there were something floating there.

"What are you doing?" Shelby asked.

"I'm trying to scoop it up with my hat, of course."

"Scoop what up?"

"Can't you see it?" Mel pointed to the moon's rippling reflection on the water. The silvery-white half disk shimmered large on the pool's surface. "You know about the legend of the half moon, don't you?"

" 'Fraid not, sport. What is it?"

Mel shook her head, suddenly grave. "If you don't know, I can't tell you, but the half moon has incredible power if you can capture its light. It could probably cure my asthma, help me grow huge breasts and make me into an Olympic swimmer."

"No shit," Shelby said, winking at the child. "Then go for it, *bambina,* by all means. And by the way, if you loved your ol' Aunt Shelby, you'd give some thought to sharing. I could use some cosmic power these days."

"No problem," Mel said, deep in concentration as she dipped her hat again. "I'm sure I can spare a moonbeam or two."

Shelby smiled to herself as Mel's cap seemed to fill up with glowing luminescence only to have the light vanish the moment she pulled it out of the water. The child tried several more times, then rocked back on her haunches in exasperation.

"Anyway, it's just a stupid legend," Mel grumbled as she came back around to sit with Shelby. "Probably not a word of truth to it."

"Yeah, right up there with the Tooth Fairy," Shelby agreed. "She never left me a damn thing when I was a kid."

"I wish Mom had never told me the *damn* legend," Mel said, copying Shelby's world-weary tone almost exactly. "It made her cry, and she's never wanted to talk about it since. Why doesn't she like Luc?" Mel asked out of the blue. "She married him. Don't you always love the person you marry?"

"Not necessarily. Sometimes people marry for companionship or convenience. For example, did your mom love Simon?" As long as the child was in an exploratory mood, Shelby decided she might as well satisfy her own curiosity.

"Yeah, sure. I think so anyway. Simon was sick. But Mom seems to hate Luc—" Mel broke off, glancing at Shelby as if for confirmation.

"True." Shelby shrugged. She wasn't one for protecting kids from the truth. She'd always believed they already knew the bottom line intuitively and were waiting to catch adults in the "noble" lie. *Of course there's a Santa Claus, darling.* And then there was the biggest lie of all—*It's okay for Daddy to touch you this way. You're his special girl.*

Shelby swallowed back the queasiness that gripped her stomach. She forced a smile, ruffling Mel's tousled auburn curls. "Honey, if you want to know why your mom married Luc, you'll have to ask her. I don't have a clue."

"Jessie Warnecke marries her own *stepson*, and you didn't feel the need to mention it?" Pete Fischer fired the question at Matt Sandusky as Matt approached Fischer's booth in the small Italian trattoria. *The Globe*'s managing editor didn't even give Matt a chance to sit down and order a drink before he dropped the bombshell.

And Matt needed a drink at that moment—a straight shot of something—though he rarely indulged in anything stronger than beer or wine at lunch. "How did you find out?" he asked, glancing from Fischer's lean, aggressive features to Murray Pratt's pudgier, deceptively placid presence. Pratt ran the business side of both Bay Area papers and had been considered indispensable by Simon because of his managerial finesse and his crucial connections.

The Warnecke board only had eight members in total, including Matt and Jessie. Simon had hoarded the company's stock, bestowing shares in Pete and Murray's case only because he'd been in danger of losing the brilliant managers to his competition. The other four board members, all close friends and business acquaintances of Simon's, had been given an opportunity to buy in years earlier, when Simon needed the cash to purchase a second major newspaper. None were actively involved in the company's operation, except to the extent that they were interested in protecting their dividends.

"I got a call, Matt," Pete was saying. "And even if I hadn't, I run a couple of newspapers—or have you forgotten? How long did you think you could keep that sort of news quiet? Marriage is a matter of public record."

"Who called you?" Matt asked.

"No idea. It was an anonymous tip."

Matt had a damn good idea. He was virtually certain that Luc or someone in his organization had leaked the information with the intention of frightening the board members about the company's stability. Matt was somewhat surprised Luc hadn't sent a press release. Anything Luc could do to weaken the board's solidarity at this point would be to his advantage if his intention was to divide and conquer. It was a cheap shot, but this was a high-stakes game and lofty ethical concerns were an indulgence only those with uncontested power could afford. Luc was playing to win. Simon would have been proud of his son, Matt thought with bleak irony.

"The wedding was a small private, *family* affair," Matt advised both men. "Jessie didn't feel the need to ask the board's permission—"

Pete's disdainful snort cut him off. "I should think it was private. Christ, marrying her own stepson? That's scandal-rag gossip, Matt. Wait until it hits the streets."

"Should be good for circulation," Murray deadpanned.

"Yeah, but where do we run it?" Pete rolled his eyes. "The society page? Hot business tips?"

"How about sports?" Murray suggested. "WARNECKE WIDOW GOES TWO FOR TWO."

"We don't run it," Matt snapped. "Not even a paragraph in nuptials. It's no one's business who Jessie Warnecke marries. Our readers aren't entitled to that information for the price of their subscription, nor are they interested, I would guess."

He was bullshitting, of course. Everyone was interested in a juicy scandal. It was heroin for the masses, a quick fix of excitement in an otherwise tedious existence. Matt spent the rest of the luncheon recovering lost ground. He stopped short of confiding he had Jessie's power of attorney, but he emphatically assured his two right-hand men that the company was stable at the uppermost level despite Simon's death and Jessie's marriage, and that he, Matt Sandusky, was still very much in charge.

As he excused himself without eating, he had no idea whether or not he had reclaimed their allegiance. His mind was already on to other, more serious concerns as he walked out of the restaurant into the bright afternoon sunlight. Jerking his lapel, he drew his trench coat up on his shoulders and smoothed the collar to ensure that the material hung straight. The meeting had impressed upon him the need to deal swiftly and decisively with this matter. Luc Warnecke could not be dealt with in any conventional way. It was time to beat the devil at his own game.

CHAPTER
·· TWENTY-ONE ··

"WHO'S THERE?" JESSIE sat up in bed, stirred awake by an unfamiliar noise. It was four A.M. The pendulum clock's haunting chimes had just sounded, and in the deep silence that followed she'd heard something, a creak of turning hinges, the sigh of old, breathing wood.

"Is someone there?" she asked again. Her voice thinned as the possibility of some unseen danger took hold. She glanced around the darkened room but saw nothing that could explain what she'd heard. Moonlight filtered through the window sheers, illuminating the southern corner of the room. The bays were closed and locked, as was the door.

Turning back to the darkness, she saw him standing in the alcove near her writing desk. A man hovered in the shadows, watching her, lying in wait. Fear slammed through her heart, crowding up into her throat with such force she couldn't speak. Her fingers gripped the satin quilt, frozen. Her heels dug deep into the mattress, seeking purchase. She couldn't see the details of his features, but there was something terrifyingly familiar about him.

The clock ticked out a frantic sound.

Shadows rustled and flared. Jessie reared back, stopped by the bed's headboard. He was moving, coming toward her! She tried to scream for help, but it was hissing fear that burned through her throat, not words. She could feel something pressing in on her, enveloping her—icy air and hot hands, the gleaming eyes of a deadly presence.

"Luc?" His name slipped out involuntarily.

She groped her way to the far side of the bed, and then just as suddenly as he'd appeared, he was gone. Vanished from the room. Had she closed her eyes? Was she dreaming? He'd disappeared somehow, slipped through a locked door or evanesced into thin air. The only thing that lingered was his scent, a haunting blend of sandlewood and burning incense.

Jessie rearranged the fresh flowers she'd cut in the garden earlier that morning, mixing several graceful stalks of deep purple iris in with the pale, blushing tulips and lacy yellow daffodils. She was hoping to brighten up the front parlor's pervasive gloom, and the arranging calmed her, giving her something to do while she waited for Luc to return. He'd already left on some unspecified business when she awoke that morning.

The nervous flutter in her stomach was a strange mix of dread and disappointment. She'd spent last night convincing herself that she'd dreamed the intruder in her room, but this morning the feeling of being watched had returned. Though Luc was gone, the sense that she wasn't alone wouldn't go away. And neither would his words—*You want to be stalked. You want to be watched from the shadows and taken captive.*

Hazy light glimmered, aura-like, in the front parlor window. Jessie drew back the lace curtains, watching long, low fingers of fog creep down the street. The weather had changed drastically since her breakfast with Luc at the Cliff House yesterday, but that was typical of the Bay Area. It was their encounter that haunted her thoughts.

They'd left the restaurant in a state of hushed expectation and walked to the Mercedes without a word. The minute she'd entered the car, Jessie had felt entrapped by something inevitable. It was a strange, yet deliciously vulnerable feeling, and she'd wondered where Luc was taking her. To her surprise and bewilderment, they'd ended up in Chinatown, wandering seemingly without destination among the bustling, saffron-scented streets, surrounded by blue-tile pagodas and scarlet street lanterns.

A dark, narrow shop resembling a converted opium den had beckoned. When Jessie hesitated at the doorway, Luc coaxed her inside. The gloom was alleviated by glowing candles and a golden haze of incense. A fascinating hodgepodge of porcelain and cloisonné cluttered the shop's shelves, but Jessie was

drawn by a display of intricate jade and ivory carvings. With
her eye for details, she immediately discerned similarities that
made her wonder if they'd all been carved by the same artist.
However, one stood out as distinct from the rest.

Luc hovered behind her as she picked up a small ivory
likeness of a reclining nude woman. The figurine was sensual
to the eye and smooth to the touch. It shone with a paleness
that was as cool and luminescent as moonlight.

"Can you guess what it's for?" Luc asked.

"An executive paperweight?" Jessie ventured, half-serious.

"It's for the modest Chinese woman."

Jessie didn't understand.

"When she's ill," Luc explained. "She takes the doll with
her to the doctor's office and points out the afflicted areas."

"Without having to disrobe?"

"Exactly . . . She shows him where it hurts."

Luc's voice had a hushed, slowed quality that compelled
Jessie to imagine the scene between this modest Chinese woman and her doctor, a god-like physician watching with silent
male authority while the blushing patient was forced to point
to vulnerable body parts on a naked doll. It seemed a situation rife with sexual innuendo, far more erotic than actually
undressing.

Jessie was also unavoidably aware of Luc behind her.

She returned the figure to the shelf. She wanted to suggest
that they leave, but she sensed that Luc had been to this place
before and that he might have brought her here for some
reason he hadn't yet revealed. The scent of sandlewood and
exotic herbs permeated the shop as she glanced around. Not
unlike Luc's cologne, the smoky bouquet seemed to be coming
from a doorway curtained by glittering jet beads at the back of
the room.

As she turned her attention to a small, exquisite cloisonné
butterfly, which would have been a perfect addition to her
collection, Jessie heard the beads jingle and clink against one
another. Luc called her name. He was standing by the back
doorway, and he'd drawn open the beaded curtain as if he
meant for her to enter. The long, caped trench coat he wore
flared to black in the swirl of candle fire and incense, and
Jessie was struck by how the flickering light played over his

features, shadowing his cheekbones and sensualizing his mouth
with the mesmerizing sensitivity she'd seen once before . . .
and the cruelty.

"Come have a look," he said.

She entered a vault-like room of brass-handled drawers. One
entire wall was studded with the small, dark wooden com-
partments, bizarre storage space. The opposite wall was lined
with shelves of tattered books, alchemist's paraphernalia and
glass beakers filled with mysterious compounds. The ceiling
overhead was thick with hanging bundles of drying herbs and
flowers.

It was a Chinese apothecary shop, Jessie realized, an herbalist's lair. Several huge brass urns smoldered with burning
herbs, giving off the pungent scent of cardamom and cloves.
Jessie also detected a ghosting of some fragrance she could
only have described as burnt roses.

"What do you want?"

The harsh question startled a gasp out of Jessie.

"Nothing," she said, turning to a tiny, tissue-skinned woman
with ink-black hair pulled tight against her skull and the oldest
eyes Jessie had ever seen. She hadn't noticed the woman standing in the shadow of the looming shelves.

"Then why are you in my shop?"

"We just happened in," Jessie said, edging away. "We didn't
mean to intrude." Jessie backed toward the beaded curtain,
only to find that Luc had insinuated himself between her and
the doorway, blocking her escape path.

The woman approached them both, her hand outstretched,
palm down, like a human antenna. The nails on her index
fingers were so long they were beginning to curl under like
claws. "Are you ill?" she asked, gazing at Jessie intently.

"Not at all. I'm fine."

The woman drew back her own hand and turned it over,
consulting something in her lined and flattened palm. "You
are ill," she told Jessie, glancing up. "Your energy is out of
balance, the yin and yang are not complementary." She linked
her fingers together as if to illustrate the ideal relationship of
the two elements. "Your skin is pale, your eyes too bright.
Only cool, moon-dried herbs can help this condition of yours.
I will make you an infusion."

"I don't have a condition." Jessie shook her head, wanting only to leave. "Really, I'm fine." She pushed back against Luc, but he didn't budge.

"She'll take the infusion," Luc said.

The woman had already vanished through a door hidden by the bookshelves, creating the momentary illusion that she had walked through the wall.

Jessie blinked her eyes, wondering if it was her vision or her grip on reality that was faltering. When she turned to Luc, she found herself in his arms. "I don't want an infusion," she said, aware that his closeness felt sheltering and warm and quite pleasant, everything considered. The hand she'd pressed against his chest slipped beneath the soft cape collar of his coat, creating a sharp and undeniable sense of intimacy.

Something shivered and sighed down deep inside her, distracting her from whatever else she'd meant to say. With the despair of a religious backslider, she realized she wanted Luc Warnecke to take her into his arms, all the way in, to hold her. *Why did she persist in wanting such things from him? And why did she want them so badly?*

"Try the infusion," he said reassuringly, tracing his fingers over the vein that throbbed in her temple and studying her as if he could read something terribly personal in her gaze. "I think Madame Sin Quai is right. Your eyes are too bright."

"Madame Sin Quai? You've been here before?"

He nodded. Something about the way he was touching her and smiling made her feel calmer inside, safe almost. He smelled of coffee and icy breath mints, an oasis of normality in this perfumed den of inscrutability. And yet he was purposefully blocking her way. He wouldn't let her out of the place. She didn't understand that, or anything else about their excursion so far.

"What are we doing?" she asked.

"We're getting our energy balanced. It's a yin and yang thing, like Madame Sin Quai said."

"No, I mean what are *we* doing? You and I? Today?"

"You and I? We're spending some time . . . nonviolently. Wasn't that the deal?"

Yes, that was the deal. She gazed at him imploringly, never more aware of her desire to accept the strength and shelter he seemed to possess in such abundance. She longed to let herself trust him. That was all she could remember lately, the longing, and how much she'd wanted to be with him as a girl, to be *his* girl. She had no idea what had happened to the rest of it, the pain he'd caused, the soul-shriveling hatred she'd nurtured for so many years. It had been her shield, and she felt terribly vulnerable without it.

"If I drink this yang stuff," she asked. "Then can we go?"

"The minute it passes your lips," he promised.

Madame Sin Quai returned with a beaker of pale blue liquid that gave off a mist the color of San Francisco fog. It tasted like flowers, Jessie decided as she sipped it, like a honeyed hyacinth tea.

"How do you feel?" Luc asked when she'd finished.

"Cool and mysterious, like moonlight. How am I supposed to feel?"

He laughed and stroked her lips with his thumb. "Strange, warm, as if you wanted me to kiss you."

"That too," she said. But it came as a surprise that she wanted his kiss. Her heart went crazy as he tilted her head up. The powerful scents of cardamom and burning incense swirled around them as he pressed his lips to hers, caressing her face as he did so . . . .

A door slammed somewhere in the house, exploding Jessie out of her reflections of yesterday. She turned, wrenched from the strange pleasure of her daydream but not quite grounded in the real world, as Luc entered the front parlor. He had a shopping bag in his hand and a curious smile on his face. The hesitation in his stride was pronounced as he approached her.

"Were you waiting for me?" he asked.

"No, I—" She heaved a sigh and nodded.

He smiled, drawing an object from the sack.

Jessie took the box of intricately woven wood he offered her and removed the lid. Inside was the ivory statue from the herbalist's shop. The nude Chinese woman peered up at her as if to suggest that maybe the male population wasn't all bad. "You bought it?" she asked Luc.

He nodded, his smile sexy and faintly tender. "In case you ever decide to tell me where it hurts."

Jessie was startled and confused. Her throat stung as she tried to swallow, making it impossible to express what she couldn't have put words to anyway. At that moment it hurt to breathe.

The silence that spun out from her awkwardness was like soft, sad music-shivering violins, heartstrings drawn too tight. Jessie didn't know how to end it. And then she didn't have to. He pulled something else from the sack, a tiny blue-satin drawstring bag. It hung at the end of a loop of silky blue rope and smelled sweetly of the familiar and the exotic.

"It's a talisman," he explained.

"To ward off evil?"

"Some of them do, but this one was specifically mixed to bring health and happiness to the wearer." He opened the satchel up to give her a look at the contents. "There's angelica root to prolong life. It's said to have the fragrance of the angels. The periwinkle flowers are for matters of the heart, and the rose petals bring love and devotion."

"What a lovely idea, it's beautiful." She couldn't bring herself to take the talisman from him.

"There's also valerian root for restoring the peace between two people." He caught hold of her curled fingertips and drew her closer, slipping the satin rope over her wrist. "Wear it for me, will you?" he asked. "If you're going to live a long time, you might as well be happy."

"Might as well." Jessie's laughter was throaty and hoarse.

"Wear it tonight?" he suggested.

"Tonight?" A mist of roses, smoke and something much more potent drifted up from the pouch. Did opium have a scent? she wondered. Was it possible to be drugged by a smell? She breathed in deeply, smiling. The stuff was making her giddy. The flowers would bring her love and devotion. Was that what he'd said? She was thrilled that he was being so generous and sweet, but she didn't understand it.

"We're going to the opera," he told her. "I have tickets for *La Bohème*."

Jessie wore white that evening. Her silk chiffon gypsy dress was a far better complement than black to the talisman's vibrant blue, and anyway, she liked the idea of being as cool and mysterious as moonlight. The gauzy translucence of her tiered off-the-shoulder dress overlaid a silk camisole bodysuit that hung tantalizingly low on the rise of her breasts and was cut high on her hips. Demure and yet breathtakingly sexy, the outfit called for sandaled feet and a gypsy dancer's hair, worn in wild, luxuriant waves.

Luc was standing in the foyer when she came down the stairway, and he was clearly surprised and pleased at her look, and perhaps at her color choice too.

"The butterfly has emerged from her cocoon," he said.

A blush formed as Jessie returned his smile. She hadn't thought of her outfit that way, but it was certainly apt. Everything he did these days was apt. At the restaurant he'd said her abductor would know her better than she knew herself. He seemed to be keeping that promise.

If she was a butterfly, then Luc was a phantom, she decided. He was wearing a black tie and with his equally black hair swept carelessly back from the widow's peak on his forehead, he was a breathtaking sight. The catch in his gait as he walked toward her lent him a faintly tragic Byronic air that added immeasurably to his dark appeal. She'd never seen him look so starkly handsome.

The opera brought tears to Jessie's eyes. In the last act, when the lovers were separated by death and Puccini's music soared with both joy and sorrow, she was reduced to mute wonderment at the beauty, and yet the underlying message seemed to be one of inevitable tragedy, that great love was doomed.

As they drove home afterward, Luc stretched his arm along the back of the bucket seat and rested his hand in the silky curls at Jessie's nape. The scent of his cologne permeated her senses. She closed her eyes briefly, still vulnerable to the romantic mood of the opera. As his long fingers worked gently beneath the fall of her rich russet hair, she was aware of several thrilling sensations at once. His palm was curved into the space between her shoulder blades, and his little finger caressed her bare skin with a steady, tender stroke.

The intimacy of his touch had a gradual but devastating effect on her defenses. At first it soothed her into a blissful state of mind, and then it began to work on her imagination, triggering sensual flashes and at the same time feeding her nerves with a strange, sweet weakness. She grew as warm and flushed as if she were being undressed and fondled by a thorough and expert lover. Luc was seducing her mind with his careless touch, making her imagine the tantalizingly light stroke all over her body.

They stopped at a streetlight, and as the Mercedes idled, he began to play with the lobe of her ear, arousing the sensitive point where the delicate flesh met her jaw. It took all of her control to keep her eyes on the road ahead. As the tension mounted inside her, she let out a sigh that was unmistakable in its urgency. It quavered in her throat, becoming an erotic little moan as he cupped her chin and drew her face around.

"What is it?" he asked.

"I don't know."

"Do you want to make love?"

"Yes." She touched his thigh and felt the recoil of his muscles. They were spring steel, unforgiving. She was trembling, she realized.

He turned into a side street and pulled up to the curb, cutting the engine. With the same slow, ravishing touch, he drew his little finger along the arc of her cheekbone and then dipped down toward her mouth, mesmerizing her. She emitted another throaty moan as he began to play with the fullness of her lower lip. When he penetrated her parted lips a moment later, she couldn't help herself. She responded by biting down gently, by drawing on his finger like a candy stick.

"You want it here?" he asked. "In the car?"

She nodded her head, ready at that point to admit anything, to do anything. She had never been so hot, so sexually hungry, so *wanton*. What was happening to her? The car was steeped in his cologne and the rich, exotic essences that emanated from her talisman—smoke, roses and seemingly powerful opiates. As Jessie drew more and more of it into her lungs with each deepening breath, she wondered again if the scent had the power to drug her.

"Jessie . . . you're sure?"

"*Yes*." She was, urgently.

He continued stroking her, his dark eyes flaring with desire. But something seemed to be holding him back. She'd expected to be dragged into his arms and kissed with frenzied passion. She'd expected to have her clothes nearly torn off.

"Maybe we ought to talk about this?"

"What's wrong?" she asked. "You don't want to?"

"No, it's not that." He shrugged, still playing with her mouth, still mesmerizing her sexually as if savoring the knowledge that he could control her with a careless stroke of his little finger. "I thought maybe we should talk first, Jessie. There's something I want to tell you."

"Talk?" Heat flashed into the place where he was touching her, stinging her lips, and then it swept her face like fire. She felt as if she were exploding in flames. His hesitation was devastating to her. Any hesitation would have been. She'd come to him naked, offering herself, admitting her need despite everything that had happened between them. She'd taken a terrible risk—

Anguished, she drew away from him. "Talk about what?"

He grew quiet, as if realizing what he'd done. "Look, I'm sorry," he said. "This was a stupid idea."

"Talk about *what*, Luc?"

"Later . . . It can wait."

"No, it can't! I want to know what's so important."

"It's not important." He hit a button, opening the sunroof, apparently to let some air in the car. "I had something planned for tomorrow, and I wanted you with me. I've been trying to figure out how to ask you. I thought tonight—"

Her embarrassment increased as she began to realize how profoundly she'd been overreacting since the first moment he'd touched her. He'd put her in a sexual fever with nothing more than a caress. Even if he hadn't been trying to prove that he could make her want him—and make her admit to it— he'd certainly done it. Shame swept her. And then loathing, not for him, for herself. How could she have been so stupid, so gullible? *She was desperate to make love with Luc Warnecke? Groveling? After what he'd done to her?*

She glanced at him, struck by the dark sensuality in his shadowed features. The nuances of cruelty that kept evidencing themselves weren't tricks of the light. They were real. He *was* cruel. Cruel in the way he pulled strings, cruel in how he manipulated her, even emotionally. How many times and in what excruciatingly painful ways did she need to have that proven to her? He was determined to avenge himself on his dead father through her. He'd even blackmailed her into marriage to that end. And he'd warned her himself that she would wish she'd killed him before he was through.

He turned the key and started the car. "Let's go home," he said.

When they were back on the highway, she gave in to another failing, burning curiosity. This wasn't her night for delaying gratification, even when the gratification promised to be self-destructive. "What did you want to talk to me about?" she asked.

It was some time before he answered her. He'd taken a scenic route home along the waterfront to Northpoint Beach, and now they were passing the wharf, with its famous restaurants and landmarks. "Do you remember our conversation the night we were married?"

She remembered an argument. It was the reason she'd come with him to San Francisco. "You announced rather grandly that someone had to bring Warnecke Communications out of the dark ages. That conversation?"

He glanced at her, suddenly cold. "No one *has* to do anything. The company could die of its own inability to adjust, like a beetle flipped over on its back. Like my father, in fact. That would be poetic, don't you think? Simon's company has his fatal flaw—tunnel vision, rigid inflexibility."

She remained silent, unwilling to defend Simon. Someday perhaps Luc would understand how poetic his father's death was, how fatal the flaw.

"Is that what you want?" he asked.

"The company won't fail," Jessie insisted, glad she'd done her homework. "Marketing wizards have been calling newspapers an anachronism since the advent of television and before. Most of those wizards are gone, but newspapers are still around. They're a vital part of the culture, a ritual part of daily life. They provide some continuity and cohesion in this crazy world, or they should. If a newspaper is doing its job, it's like a friend, like family."

"Nice speech," he allowed. "Unfortunately, I could shoot it full of holes with a Daisy Air Rifle and my eyes closed. Do I need to tell you how deeply the electronic media has cut into print media's profits? It's pretty simple arithmetic."

That infuriated her. "Simple enough for even me to understand? Is that what you're saying."

"No, I'm saying wake up, Jessie. I'm meeting with a consortium tomorrow, some of the largest names in cable, telecommunications and computers. They're looking for ways to merge the technology and develop new concepts. They need seed money investors. You've already heard about fiber-optic networks and information highways. Well, now they're going into orbit, literally—space satellites, global constellations. You're going to be left behind, eating dust."

"I'd rather eat dust than crow."

He spiked the button that closed the sunroof, swearing when it didn't move fast enough to suit him. "What are you afraid of?" he asked.

"You," she said sharply. "What is it you want from me? What do you want to do?"

"I want to expand, of course. I want to get out of print and into electronics while the getting's good. I have a task force doing the feasibility studies right now. We're hunting for the right media opportunities—cable, space, maybe even another global news network, only bigger, better, faster."

"So do it! Do all of it, but leave Warnecke Communications out of it."

"I can't do it alone, Jessie. It's going to take more revenue than I've got, more than you and I combined. We need deeper pockets, a fresh influx of capital."

Jessie had already begun to shake her head. She knew what he wanted. "No, I won't do it, Luc. I won't take Warnecke public. Even if it hadn't been your father's last wish that I keep the company private, I don't have your driving need to expand. I have several hundred employees to think about, and a child. I'm interested in security. I don't want to take risks."

"Is that why you married Simon? Security?" He laughed coldly. "And all along I thought it was the great sex."

"You agreed not to ask me about Simon," she reminded him sharply. "My relationship with your father is off limits!"

He glanced at her, an icy flash of cruelty in his eyes. "How was the old man? Any good? Did the two of you get it on in the car?"

His words came at her like flicks of a whip, swift and painful. Jessie could hardly believe he'd said something so hostile. She felt as if she were coming out of a trance, as if in the last thirty-six hours he'd hypnotized her into believing that he could be one of the "nice guys." Matt was right, she realized, heartsick at the thought. Luc Warnecke was obsessed with Simon. He was sick.

She glanced down at the blue satin pouch dangling from her belt and wanted to rip it off. "You've been softening me up the entire weekend, haven't you? The breakfast at the Cliff House, the gifts, the pretense of tenderness when all you wanted was venture capital." Even more than he wanted sex, she thought. God, the ultimate humiliation.

"Don't be ridiculous. I didn't want to take advantage of you. I thought we ought to talk first. Hell, some women might have appreciated that."

"Take advantage?" She nearly gasped with outrage. "Of what? My utter stupidity? My trembling desire for you? You *smug* son of a bitch! Stop this car!" She threw open the car door as he slammed on the brakes.

"Where are you going?" he shouted.

He lunged for her, but she was already out of the door and running, feverishly intent on getting away from him. She spotted the mouth of a narrow one-way alley, knowing he couldn't follow her there in the car. The darkness enveloped her, branching off into bewildering arteries as she plunged into it. There wasn't time for conscious decisions. With her chiffon skirt wadded in her hands, she fled instinctively, darting from one corridor to another.

She kept on going until the alley she'd taken dead-ended on a steep hillside. Panting, she spun around in the thin stream of moonlight that illuminated the street, trying to get her bearings. She didn't recognize the homes or any of the landmarks. A strange little bubble of hysteria took shape inside her, and her lungs ached as she filled them with moist, dank air. What was she doing dashing around Pacific Heights alone in the dark?

The sound of running footsteps made her twist around to look behind her, but there was no one there. The street was empty in every direction. Trolley tracks gleamed like razor blades, reflecting some mysterious light. The moon? She searched the shadows made by the trees and doorways, panic rising inside her. She was sure she'd heard someone behind her. Had Luc parked the car to follow her on foot?

She began to jog up the hill, knowing she couldn't sustain the pace on the steep grade for long. Her thighs burned with fatigue, and the soles of her feet stung from mounting friction. Thank God, she'd worn low heels. She had no idea if she was heading in the right direction or how far she had to go, but the thud of running footsteps spurred her on.

Her muscles screamed with relief as she reached the top and searched the darkness behind her. There was still no sign of anyone, and yet the urgent pounding persisted. Was it the clamor of her own heart? At the next intersection she realized she was at her street. At the same moment that she spotted the Victorian halfway down the hill, she heard the footsteps again. Someone *was* behind her! She glanced over her shoulder, blinded by streetlights, and saw a nightmarish figure surging toward her, his raincoat billowing like a cape.

A scream ripped through her mind, freezing every response but the most primal of fears. She couldn't think or feel or even see clearly. She couldn't do anything but plunge down the hill, her body as rigid as a stick figure's. The thundering footsteps were on top of her! She heard someone shouting her name as she scrambled frantically to outrun the grasping hands of her attacker. In the distance a horn blared and lights flashed as if a car had turned up the street.

A patch of wet pavement spun her feet out from under her. Fighting to catch her balance, she reached the stairway to the house and slammed up against the porch post. The collision might have knocked her cold if she hadn't been insulated by adrenaline. The powerful stimulant was steaming through her veins like fire. She was crazed by it, wild to survive.

A hand gripped her ankle, throwing her forward. She broke the fall with her hands and twisted around on the stairway, lashing out desperately with her foot. She hit her attacker in the chest and knocked him backward, but her heel caught in the cape collar of his coat and nearly ripped it off.

"Bitch!" he snarled. "White trash bitch! I'll kill you!"

She made it to the landing before he was on her again. This time he snagged her by the chiffon material of her skirt, but she wrenched free and flung herself at the umbrella stand near the doorway, whipping out the first one she could get her hands on. She assumed he meant to rape or rob her, but maybe he really meant to kill her, and she wasn't going to make any of it easy for him.

"*Fire!*" she screamed, praying the neighbors would hear her. "*Fire!*" She slashed wildly at him, then thrust the umbrella at him like a sword, hitting the open button at the same time. The frame shot forward and opened like a missile, throwing him off balance. He tumbled backward down the stairs, giving her a clear break for the front door.

She slammed the door and threw the dead bolt the moment she got inside. Crumbling to her knees on the foyer floor, she clutched herself and shook with terrible relief. A dry, aching sob welled in her throat. She'd done it. She'd fought him off.

Despite her exhaustion, a spark of triumph kindled inside her. It was more than a matter of physical survival, this feat. It reaffirmed who she was. Growing up isolated, with a drunken stepfather and no mother, had given her a feral child's instincts. The ordeals she'd endured, the adversity she'd overcome, defined her as nothing else had in her life. They were her badge of individuality, her thumbprint.

Jessie's a fighter.

A poignant memory of her mother flashed into Jessie's mind. Lynette had used those words proudly in her daughter's defense when Jessie was called to the principal's office for bloodying noses and splitting lips in the second grade. Jessie had been taunted into fights by a gang of kids from town who'd ridiculed her family as trash. That same year Jessie's mother had run off, leaving her youngest daughter nothing to ease the emptiness but a scribbled note of regret and the memory of those painful, prideful words.

Jessie's a fighter. My little Jessie's a fighter.

She was still on the floor moments later as someone shouted her name and pounded on the door. She stood up and brushed at the tattered chiffon tiers of her dress, aware that the talisman was gone. It must have been ripped from her belt in the struggle. She'd barely unbolted the door before it swung back with a crack and Luc stormed into the house.

"What happened?" he demanded, looking her over. "Are you all right?"

Jessie nodded, reluctant to go into detail. He was already angry at her. The incident would only convince him she'd acted recklessly. He looked almost as disheveled as she did, she realized. Even his face was smudged with dirt. But there was something else that bothered her. It took her a moment to realize what it was. "Where's your raincoat?" she asked.

"I don't know." He shrugged the question off. "In the car, I suppose. I must have left it there."

Jessie barely heard him. She was remembering the style of his raincoat, the cut, the material—the caped collar. She was remembering that someone had shouted her name and that her attacker had called her "white trash."

Luc's words in the restaurant came to her next—

I'd know what you were going to do before you did it. That's how I'd catch you off guard. By knowing when you were going to blink, and striking then, in that split second while your eyes were closed and you were blind.

Her stomach lurched and the acid taste of fear regurgitated into her throat as she stared at him. She couldn't allow herself to think that he was the one who'd chased her, or that he could have brutally attacked her. No, that was impossible, but she also couldn't forget Matt's warning that Luc was capable of anything. *It could be as simple as an accident,* Matt had said. *Once he marries you, he'll have everything to gain by edging you out.*

Jessie turned away from her husband of less than a week, her decision instantaneous. She couldn't stay here any longer. Even if she hadn't been assaulted and frightened half to death, she wasn't emotionally ready to deal with Luc Warnecke. The episode in the car had proved that.

"I'm leaving," she told him. "Stay here and go to your meeting, or do whatever you must, but I'm going home in the morning."

CHAPTER
·· TWENTY-TWO ··

"LOVE YOUR TRENCH coat," Shelby purred. "The last time I saw one like that, I was being flashed in Central Park."

Matt Sandusky's startled laughter turned husky as he opened his coat, revealing a gray blazer jacket and navy slacks. "Sorry, I didn't *undress* for the occasion."

"Just my luck," she lamented.

Matt happened to be standing at the double doors of the entryway to Echos. Shelby Flood had answered the bell when he rang, and now she was draped in the open doorway, barefoot and playing with the drawstring of her hooded workout jacket. The clingy little pink zip-up number she wore beneath the jacket looked as if it had been designed for a workout in the bedroom rather than the gym. But what did Matt Sandusky know about women's athletic wear?

He knew he liked her whistle.

A shiny police whistle hung on a silver chain around her neck. To ward men off or summon them? he wondered.

"Good to see you again, Matthew," she said, standing aside with an inviting smile. "You don't drop by enough."

He nodded and walked past her. "My pleasure."

"That could be arranged," she murmured.

Matt contained a quick grin before he turned back to her. "I need to get some material that Simon kept in his personal files. It would be in the library, if no one minds."

"Help yourself." she gestured in the general direction of the library, then accompanied him through the vast living room area and into the hallway that led to the east wing. The library was through the first door past the music room.

"Can I get you something?" she asked, hesitating in the

doorway as he entered. "Coffee? Tea or . . ."

His mind automatically supplied the third option. Maybe that was the idea. Their eyes met briefly, and Matt experienced a pleasurable clutch of awareness. Her lashes were so dark and lush, they reminded him of a velvet fringe. She was too beautiful to be selling it, he thought. And if it wasn't for sale, then why was she advertising it so aggressively?

Matt shrugged out of the trench coat she'd admired and draped it over a wingback chair. "Coffee, thanks, if it's not too much trouble."

She nodded and was gone, giving him the opportunity he needed. Matt's key opened all the file drawers but one. That was Simon's confidential file, and as far as Matt knew, the only key to it was in the possession of Simon's attorney. The cabinet was old enough to be an antique, and not easily tampered with, but Matt was reasonably sure he could jimmy it. Simon had often implied that he kept files on the Warnecke directors, including information that could be used against them, if necessary. With Luc Warnecke about to raid the coffers, Matt wanted to be prepared in case any of the directors needed to be "persuaded" not to sell out. Matt didn't think of it as coercion; he thought of it as insurance. And he was sure he would have had Simon's blessings. Jessie was another story, which was why he'd made the trip when she wasn't around . . .

By the time Shelby returned moments later, Matt had already returned the tiny screwdriver to his jacket pocket and was going through the files. He'd found one on each director, just as he'd hoped, as well as one on himself. He was surprised not to have come across something on Luc or Jessie. It was possible Simon kept that sort of information in one of his bedroom safes.

"Coming up," she said brightly, "one black coffee. You do take it straight?"

Matt pulled the files in question, hoping Shelby couldn't see the droll expression on his face. She did know how to set up a punch line. "Straight is exactly how I take it," he said, coming around to face her.

She smiled and set down the tray she was carrying. "I thought it might be," she murmured.

Matt couldn't help but notice that the tray held two bone-china cups and a thermal coffee carafe. Apparently she was planning to join him. He held up the folders. "Found what I was looking for," he said. "I just need a few minutes to go through them. I'll use the desk if that's okay."

The desk he spoke of was a valuable antique, but Shelby glanced at the inlaid leather top as if it had been suddenly transformed into a playpen for randy adults. "Please," she said, handing him a cup she'd just poured. "Take as long as you need. I always do."

The coffee had been laced with brandy, Matt realized, wincing as the fiery liquid seared his throat. Shelby played a dedicated game. He wondered what she wanted, then decided not to concern himself with that. She wasn't going to get it unless it was sex. And she might not even get that. Messing with Jessie's beautiful older sister might seem fabulous in the abstract, but the reality posed some problems. He doubted very much if Shelby could be counted on to keep a secret, and he damn well didn't want the Warnecke-Flood soap opera to get any more complicated than it already was.

Shelby had other ideas, of course. As he sat down and opened one of the files, she took it upon herself to wander around behind him and gaze over his shoulder.

"Anything I can do?" she asked. Even the soft, wet sounds she made sipping her coffee somehow managed to be sensual.

Come to think of it, there is something, he thought. You could set the cup down and give me a blow job, *unless that would be too much trouble.* "I think I can handle it."

"Hmmm . . . I'll bet."

He glanced around at her, taking in the full impact of her baby, baby, oh, *baby* sensuality. Emboldened by her lazy wink, he let his gaze prowl at will, moving from the lush curves of her breasts to the place where her tight pink shorts creased between her legs. He doubted it was possible to offend her. She probably would have been more offended if he hadn't checked her out.

She smiled as if she had him in the bag.

A hot spark of regret burned in his groin as he turned back to the file and began to leaf through it. "I think I've got everything I need here. Thanks, Shelby. Coffee's great."

"You're sure?" She sounded crestfallen, but her fingernail feathered the back of his neck. "Not even a one-minute massage for the busy executive? I give good—"

"Not even," he said quickly. "Lots to do." It was called responsible self-denial, a concept she probably wasn't terribly familiar with. *I must be nuts*, he thought.

"Party poop." She came around his desk on the other side, trailing her hand along the edge and knocking a pencil to the floor. "I'll get that."

"No, no, never mind," he insisted. His dismissive tone told her it was a good try, but he wasn't coming out to play today.

"Okay," she sighed. "Whatever you say." She wagged a finger at him and headed for the door, reminding him with every sweet twitch of her damn near irresistible ass what he was missing.

After quickly glancing through the folders and assuring himself he had the ammunition he needed to deal with the board, he proceeded to have a look at his own file. It was fascinating to see what kind of information his former boss and mentor had compiled on him over the years. There were references to the prostitute who fronted as a masseuse and had been making "home visits" to Matt's Telegraph Hill condo for years. Matt's problems with the IRS some years ago had been documented, as well as some of the more excruciatingly intimate details of his life, including his gallbladder problems and his musophobia, a rather embarrassing fear of rodents. Even his preferences in food had been detailed.

The SOB must have had a detective on full-time retainer, Matt realized, not totally surprised. The old man had grown increasingly paranoid toward the end, succumbing to the same fears he'd always exploited in others to keep them in line. He'd become convinced someone was trying to harm him after the bank robbery attempt, even when the police assured him it was a coincidence that the heist had occurred during his visit to the bank that morning. The robbers were caught the same day, a trio of career hoodlums from the San Jose area, apparently out to pick up some quick drug money.

Simon had his share of professional enemies, but Matt knew of no one with a revenge motive except Luc. Still, the elder

Warnecke had persisted in believing that "a conspiracy of
enemies" was stalking him. Jessie was the only one he'd
seemed to trust as his illness progressed, probably because
during that same bank robbery attempt, she'd put her own
life in jeopardy to save his. Fortunately Matt's only personal
foray outside the law had been instigated years ago by Simon
himself, making Simon as vulnerable to detection as he was.
And now, with the old man gone, the file could be safely
destroyed with no one the wiser.

The grandfather clock in the hall began to chime as he read
on. In the back of his mind, he counted ten strokes, vaguely
aware of another sound in the background—a quick, scuttling
noise that reminded him of scurrying mice. He glanced up and
saw that Shelby had left the library door open, but otherwise,
there didn't seem to be any cause for concern. There were
no signs of the grotesque little things with sharp claws on
the march. God, how he loathed rats, mice and anything else
with beady rodent eyes and twitching whiskers.

A moment later he felt something slither over his shoe
and curl itself around his ankle bone. "*Jesus*," he breathed,
his heart going wild. His first impulse was to do something
unmanly, like scream. Some instinct for self-preservation kept
him mute as another sensation riveted his attention. Whatever
it was, it was crawling up his pants leg! The quick feathery
motion made him utter a sound choked with disbelief.

Would it attack if he moved? Horrified, he imagined his
vital parts being savaged by a tiny, sharp-fanged creature,
determined to chew its way out of the dead-end tunnel his
pants would soon become if the thing didn't stop advancing!
He had to do something, but short of removing his slacks and
risking his manhood in the process, he didn't have the faintest
idea what.

Endless seconds flashed by before he could convince himself to push his chair back and look under the desk. And when
he did, it took several more seconds to comprehend what he
was seeing. Not a weasel, a woman? A woman with glow-in-
the-dark blue eyes, a pencil between her teeth and one hand
up his pants? His orderly, to-every-man-there-is-a-season mind
could barely stretch far enough to grasp the incongruity of it.

"Shelby?" he said, dumbfounded.

Shelby gazed up at him, eyelashes fluttering as she took the pencil from her mouth. It was a classic yellow number two, medium point, soft lead. "Sure you wouldn't like me to sharpen this?" she asked. "The point seems a little dull." She twirled the pencil in her fingers, then stroked the shaft over her cheek, drawing it very near her lips.

Matt's heart was thundering so hard he couldn't appreciate the symbolism. He couldn't even speak at first. "You almost gave me a heart attack," he croaked.

"Don't thank me yet." She tucked the pencil into her sleek pageboy for safekeeping and flashed him a smile hot enough to melt the polar caps. When he'd caught his breath, she hooked her little finger under the silver chain around her neck and drew it up, dangling the police whistle. "Want to see me blow it?"

Her eyes sparkled wickedly as she gazed at him, waiting for his reaction. Her lips were moist and parted, promising a veritable garden of earthly delights. When he didn't respond, she drew the whistle across her pouting mouth in a languid motion, dragging her lower lip down just enough to reveal a flash of white teeth and a glimpse of deep pink.

It was one of the most erotic sights Matt had ever seen. This had to be her "take me, use me, abuse me" routine, he decided, the come-on she saved for reluctant males. God, it was working. The hot spark in his groin had kindled into a roaring blaze.

She blew softly on the whistle, and he responded with all the control of a trained circus animal. His mouth watered copiously, and his cock leapt to attention. *Be careful what you wish for*, he thought, sighing with the crazy thrill of it all. She did have him in the bag.

"Go ahead," he murmured as she reached to unzip his burgeoning fly. "Blow your brains out."

Matt Sandusky's BMW was still parked in the driveway as the airport limo swept up the crescent drive to deposit Jessie at the mansion's front door. As relieved as she was to be home, Jessie couldn't cope with the thought of company just yet, not even Matt. She'd planned to go directly to her room, where she could regroup. After the ordeal in San Francisco, she needed to feel safe and secure. She needed a refuge.

Letting herself into the house, she left her bags at the door, where the driver had deposited them. She would ask Roger to bring them up later. To her relief there didn't seem to be anyone around as she entered the main hall, including Matt.

Wondering if Mel and Gina had gone out, Jessie started up the stairway and stopped on the first landing just long enough to appreciate the beauty of the scene below her. The quiet grandeur of the mansion's thirty-five-foot vaulted ceilings and the magnificence of the great fireplace, with its intricately hand-carved oriental mantel, which soared nearly to the skylights, always had a calming effect on her.

Everywhere she looked fresh-cut flowers graced the occasional tables, thanks to Margie, she imagined. In the anteroom that led to the dining area, a crystal vase of burgundy red roses sat on the grand piano, a 1917 Steinway. With accents of fine Irish lace and an antique wall mirror framed in gold, the scene resembled a Cezanne still life.

Muffled laughter drifted from down the hallway that led to the east wing. Curious, Jessie listened a moment, then descended the steps, thinking that Mel might be playing in the library. As she neared the open doorway, she heard a high-pitched burst that made her think of a traffic cop's whistle. Was there a bird trapped in the house?

She was tempted to call out but thought better of it.

There was someone in the library when she reached it, but to Jessie's surprise, it wasn't Mel. Matt Sandusky was sitting at the desk, busily at work. "Matt, is there something wrong? Aren't you supposed to be in San Francisco?"

Matt's head snapped up in surprise. "Jessie? What are you doing here? Is there something wrong? Aren't you supposed to be in San Francisco?"

Jessie smiled, wondering if there was an echo in the room. "Are you all right?" she asked him, concerned. He looked distinctly odd to her. His face was flushed rosy pink, and his voice sounded hoarse.

"Of course," he assured her effusively. "I'm fine. What about you? Did you and Luc decide to come back early?"

"It's a long story, Matt."

"How long?" he asked, clearing his throat.

Matt definitely needed some R&R, Jessie decided. He'd been working nonstop since Simon's death, and the pressure seemed to be getting to him. She'd never seen him so tense. "Do you think we could talk later?" she asked him. "I'd like to go up and rest a bit. And you do look very busy."

"Oh, God, you have no idea. I . . . uh . . . it's that problem we talked about before you left."

"Oh, is there anything I can help you with?" She started into the room.

"No!" He waved her off. "I just need another minute to finish things up here. You—you go on up. Unpack—or whatever it is you need to do. We'll talk later. *Later*."

"Okay . . ." She turned to leave, then hesitated at the odd noise that came from his general direction—sort of a gurgle or a slurp, she couldn't decide. It sounded like someone trying to suck Jell-O through a straw. "Is there something wrong, Matt?"

"W-wrong?" His voice cracked and he sat forward, laughing nervously. A bullet of perspiration rolled down his forehead, traveling all the way to the end of his nose before it stopped, quivering on the tip. He made no attempt to brush it off.

Jessie studied him with growing concern. "Matt, what is it? Are you ill?"

He struggled to get out of his jacket. "Is it hot in here? Maybe if I took off this coat—"

Now Jessie was worried. Matt never perspired, and she'd rarely seen him looking disheveled. He was normally meticulous, not a hair out of place. "Can I get you something? Ice water? An aspirin?"

He slid back in the chair, a moan burbling in his throat as he reached under the desk for something. A stuporous smile crossed his face, glazing his eyes. "An aspirin," he rasped. "Several of them, in fact. Oh . . . God, thank you Jessie."

Jessie gaped at him. Maybe he really was cracking up under the stress of taking Simon's place. "No problem, Matt," she said soothingly. "Everything's going to be all right. I'll just go get that aspirin, okay?"

"Take your time," he urged.

She shuffled backward toward the door. He kept waving her away, but he so clearly needed help. Perhaps he was embarrassed. Men were like that about illness. They hated being vulnerable. It was a macho thing.

"I'll be all right," he gasped, sweat pouring off him. "Go ahead, *please!*"

"Okay, then," she said. "I'll be right back with the—" She was turning to leave when a flesh-toned object caught her eye. Something was protruding out from under the front of the desk. She blinked, trying to bring her eyes into focus. A second later, she was staring in utter disbelief. It couldn't be! *Feet?*

"Aspirin, Jessie," Matt implored weakly.

Jessie barely heard him. She was still fixated on the feet. They were small and bare, the soles up, a woman's feet without doubt. *A woman on her knees.*

"Jessie, would you, could you—"

"Sure thing, Matt," she said archly. "Aspirin coming right up." She stared at his sweat-drenched countenance for a moment before she let her gaze drop purposefully. "And how about you, Shelby? Can I get you anything?"

A mumbled response came from under the desk.

"Apparently no one taught my sister manners," Jessie said, her voice sharp with sarcasm as she glared at Matt. "I thought she knew better than to talk with her mouth full."

With that Jessie turned and walked out the door in disgust. The way Matt was sweating, made her hope he'd be dead of electrolyte imbalance before Shelby got through with him. Wasn't there a man in the whole goddamned world who could resist her sister?

CHAPTER
·· **TWENTY-THREE** ··

SPRING BURST FORTH in all its fertile glory in the next few days. A cloudburst drenched the estate, soaking down the hills and valleys before giving way to a rainbow of such radiance it brought pain to the naked eye. Raindrops quivered on rose petals, becoming bright, sparkling crystals when the sunlight touched them. Tender green grass sprang up, and wildflowers blossomed everywhere, carpeting the meadows and attracting honeybees and butterflies in great swarms.

But if the world outside Echos seemed to be enveloped in a cocoon of unseasonably warm weather, the climate inside the house was anything but balmy. It had dropped into the frigid zones. Jessie had taken to wearing black again, and she had absented herself from everyone but Mel. Her life had virtually ground to a stop since returning from San Francisco, deadlocked by a stormy mix of confusion, fear and anger. There were imminent decisions to be made about her bewildering marriage, her amoral sister and the imperiled company she'd inherited, but she hadn't been able to focus on any of that. The assault had taken over her thoughts. Her mind scrolled the incident like a video player, winding and rewinding, playing it back at piercingly high speeds, then slowing to stark and harrowing detail, when she was awake, and in her dreams as well. She could only imagine that it was some kind of delayed-stress reaction.

Someone had wanted to hurt her, perhaps to take her life, that much was clear. But who? And why? Luc had a motive, but she couldn't bring herself to believe he was revenge-driven enough to harm her in order to get control of the company. He was many things, but not a cold-blooded killer, despite Matt

Sandusky's doubts. She was certain of that, and yet the entire honeymoon haunted her, including the night she woke up to find someone in her room—

Her nape prickled, seized by a chill so icy it was hot.

She needed to talk, to filter her fears and concerns through someone she trusted, but there was no one she could turn to now. She most assuredly wasn't in the mood to discuss the situation with Matt, although she had admitted to him, in a terse telephone conversation the day before, that she'd been assaulted. His reaction had been explosive. He'd called repeatedly, despite her refusals to talk to him and her assurances through Gina that she hadn't been hurt.

At least Matt had bothered to show some concern, she acknowledged, toying with a piece of the jigsaw puzzle she'd spread out for her and Mel to work on that morning. Luc's silence had become more ominous with each passing day. He hadn't once inquired to see how she was doing since she'd been home, not even a casual call to see if she'd arrived safely.

"Mom? Are you listening to me?"

Jessie was jolted out of her reverie by her daughter's question. Mel was wearing on her nerves this morning. The nine-year-old had been whining and cajoling since breakfast.

"Why *can't* I go swimming?" Mel persisted, ignoring the puzzle Jessie had been trying to distract her with. "The weather is *bella*," she said as she jumped up and skipped over to the playroom's sun-filled window seat. "See, *molta bella!* I kiss my fingers to it."

Jessie tried not to smile as Mel made a smacking noise and burst open her fingers like an exuberant Neopolitan chef. "Your asthma, Mel—"

"I swam almost every night you were in San Francisco, and my asthma hardly acted up at all."

"Hardly? What does that mean?"

"One night I coughed up blood for twenty minutes, that's all."

Jessie sprang up. "*What?*"

"Kidinnnnng." Mel flopped onto her stomach and gazed longingly out the window, her nose pressed to the pane. "Aunt Shelby thinks I could be on the swim team this year. She says I'm a natural swimmer."

Jessie's temper flared, but she held her tongue. Shelby had no right filling Mel's head full of fantasies like that. It was bad enough that her sister had had the child in the pool night after night without bothering to mention it to Jessie. Shelby would have to be made to understand how fragile Mel's health was. Good Lord! Just thinking about the time her daughter had ended up in the emergency room, unable to breathe, left Jessie weak. This wasn't an Andy Hardy movie, it was a child's life.

Of all of the decisions Jessie had hanging, the one about Shelby promised to be the easiest. She was very close to asking her sister to move out. No, make that *telling* her sister to move out. The sooner Shelby packed her bags and blew town the better!

Jessie's heart was beating so fiercely, she had to draw in a breath to calm herself. Every bit of resentment she'd ever felt toward Shelby had resurfaced in the last few days. Like an old shipwreck in a storm, ragged pieces of helpless childhood fury had been dragged to the surface. It was typical of her conniving older sibling to sneak around behind people's backs like an incorrigible child, plotting to get her own way, *stealing things that weren't hers*. It was a wonder Mel didn't have pneumonia.

And as for Matt, he was old enough to know better. If he chose to play the sacrificial insect to Shelby's black widow spider, it was his funeral, but Jessie had no intention of letting her daughter be drawn into her aunt's seductive web.

"Look!" Mel cried as a colorful garland of monarch butterflies swooped by. "You had a butterfly collection when you were a kid, didn't you, Mom?"

"Not a collection," Jessie said, banishing the anger with a faint smile. Her time with Mel was too precious to ruin it with thoughts of Shelby. She went to sit beside her daughter in the window seat and shuddered a little at the bath of warm sunshine that poured over her, not realizing until then how chilled she'd been. The butterflies had descended on a meadow of blue-eyed grass and buttercups. It really was the most glorious weather Jessie could remember in years. She might have felt freer to enjoy it if there hadn't been so much weighing on her mind. "Tell me about the butterflies," Mel pressed.

"It seems silly now," Jessie admitted. "My childhood dream was to harvest them. Every spring I'd search out the fattest, furriest caterpillars I could find, and then I'd feed them on tender leaves and buds until they were ready to burst."

"Burst into butterflies?"

"Well, that was the general idea, but I never actually saw it happen." Jessie settled back against the ruffled chintz curtains that framed the window and gazed out at the miracle that nature recreated every year. "I'd watch them for days on end—all summer long—and then one day they'd all be gone, vanished from the old aquarium I kept them in."

"An unsolved mystery," Mel said softly. "*Excellent*. What happened to them?"

"I don't know, but every year it was the same thing. They disappeared without a trace." Much like Lynette, Jessie thought, remembering the abruptness of her mother's disappearance. One morning Lynette was standing at the kitchen sink snapping green beans for dinner, and that night she was gone.

"How old were you?"

"Around your age, I guess."

Mel sat up, her voice soft and imploring. "Let's try it again, okay? We'll harvest butterflies, you and I. We could start today."

"Not today," Jessie said, a sadness overcoming her. She and Mel hadn't been as close recently, and this would have been the perfect way to bring them back together. Everyone seemed to think Jessie was overprotective, and perhaps she was. But it wasn't her concern for Mel's health that was stopping her now. Even her desire to be close to her daughter couldn't overcome the reluctance she felt to relive that part of her youth. She didn't want those childhood years resurrected, and not just because of the pain. It was the sweetness she couldn't bear. Despite the hardships, or perhaps because of them, there was so much uncompromising hope back then, so much stolen joy.

"Why are you so sad, Mom?" Mel asked. "Is it him? Luc? Shelby said you might be splitting up."

"Shelby should mind her own *business*."

Mel looked stung, and Jessie immediately regretted her sharpness. Mel couldn't be expected to understand the tension between her and Shelby. "Sorry," she said at once. "There are some problems between me and Luc. I just haven't figured out what to do about them yet."

"Do you love him?"

Jessie's breath caught sharply. *Out of the mouths of babes*, she thought. "Once," she said, her voice thickening. "I did once."

"Then it's him making you sad. It's not the butterflies, it's him."

"A little of both, I think." But it was Luc, of course. He had come into her life at a crucial time, filling the void her mother had left, and for that reason he would always be one of the most poignant parts of the lost sweetness she mourned. He was a piece of her heart that could never be recovered. Perhaps that was why she couldn't believe he would hurt her, at least not in the way that Matt meant. But why hadn't he called?

Jessie gazed out at the gardens and beyond, to the windbreak of cypresses that bordered the ravine. Except for that day when the coyote had died, she hadn't been as far as the ravine in years, a lifetime. Sometimes she wondered if by avoiding the memories rather than dealing with them, she had trapped their energy in some way, causing them to take on greater intensity. If she could confront her early relationship with Luc, perhaps she would find that their bond wasn't as close as she remembered, that it had taken on a halo effect over the years, the special luster that attaches itself to the memory of lost loved ones and overlaps any darkness that might have existed.

"I have to go out, Mel," she said after a long space of silence.

Mel studied her intently, looking very much the child wiser than her years. "Are you going to hunt for caterpillars?"

"In a way," Jessie admitted, laughing with bittersweet surprise. "How did you know?" She touched Mel's hand, and a moment later mother and daughter were in each other's arms. Jessie's eyes burned with tears. Her heart ached with a love that was sharpened by sadness. There was so much welling in her heart that she couldn't seem to say. Expressing the depth of her emotion had never been easy for her, even with this child she loved so much.

"I hope you find some," Mel said gravely, breaking the embrace to lend support to her mother's quest. "I don't want you to be sad, Mom. Remember what you told me when I was a kid? It makes your lip droop."

Jessie smiled through her tears and kissed the bright curls on the top of her daughter's head.

"I could come along if you want," Mel suggested consolingly. "You might need some help."

"Next time, *bambina*," Jessie promised. "I have to make this pilgrimage by myself. But tonight, or sometime very soon, you can show me how you're learning to swim, okay? I'd really like to see that."

Mel beamed, and all the glory of the spring morning seemed to be reflected in her blue eyes. Jessie saw sunshine there and wildflowers and the infinite power of renewal. Her heart welled again. And for just a moment she allowed herself to believe that perhaps everything was going to be all right.

The breeze from the ocean felt almost tropical as Jessie walked among the cypress trees. The deep ravine looked as wild and untamed as she remembered. Made rich and rank by the spring rains, emerald green with new growth, it beckoned to her. *Come discover what wonderful mysteries lie within*, it seemed to say. *Come find the secrets of life, the secret you.*

That was what had attracted her as a child—the promise of adventure and discovery, of reaching the same dizzying, soaring heights of freedom as the hawks who glided on air currents, and the sleek, furred creatures who stole through the underbrush. The cathedral-like stillness offered a spiritual solace she'd never known anywhere else. It saddened her that she'd stayed away so long. It was clear to her now that this was where her heart longed to be, where her soul resided.

Memories pierced her when she finally reached the place where she'd found Luc on that icy spring morning years ago. The spindly tree bridge he'd tried to cross was split down the middle as if struck by lightning, half of it tumbling into the ravine. The environment was forever changing, but the recollections were stored in Jessie's mind like sepia photographs. Distance had given them the burnish of twilight dreams.

Her reluctance to reawaken the bittersweet feelings made it a difficult trip to the bottom of the ravine. Like a child tormented with the anticipation of some fearful thing lying ahead, she could see Luc in her mind, sprawled on the ground. But instead of the broken body of a boy, she found a man standing where the boy had been.

At first she thought she was imagining him, that she'd conjured him out of memories. Haggard and hollow-eyed, he looked as if he hadn't eaten or slept in days. His stillness made him seem dreamlike and unreal—a ghost projected by her mind. He could have been a vivid sense painting, a momentary hallucination.

And then he turned to her.

Pain knifed through her heart. "Luc," she whispered. "My God, Luc." The grief in his dark eyes was terrible. "What are you doing here?"

He stared at her wordlessly, her name on his lips, as if he were having the same trouble discerning reality from fantasy that she was. He looked as if he'd been dwelling so deeply in the past, he couldn't find his way back. But to Jessie, he looked exactly like the dark wraith who'd emerged from a white limousine on one magical summer afternoon so many years ago, his eyes shining in that strange, wild way, with the luminous glitter of a madman, the sadness of a priest.

"You didn't tell me—" His voice was husky with regret. "Why?"

"Tell you what?"

"That you were assaulted the night of the opera." He searched her face and her drooping chignon, even surveying her ankle-length skirt and embroidered peasant blouse as if to assure himself that she was all right, that she hadn't been hurt in any way.

She could see his confusion and especially his concern, but she didn't answer either. "How did you find out?"

"Matt. He said someone attacked you, threatened to kill you. He said you thought it was me—"

"I didn't say it that way."

"Jessie, Jessie . . ." He shook his head. "You might not have said it, but you must have thought it. Otherwise, you would have told me what happened." He lifted a hand. "You left San Francisco without even telling me you'd been attacked. *Why?*"

"I was frightened, Luc."

"Of me? God, what have I done to make you think I would want to hurt you that way?"

There was disbelief in his voice, even bitterness. Jessie responded without thinking, tears sparkling in her eyes. "Revenge, Luc. You're consumed by it. I don't think you have any idea how frightening you can be. I thought you'd linked me with Simon in your mind, that you wanted to destroy everything associated with him. I didn't want to believe it was you. I told myself it wasn't, but—"

She broke off, struck by what she was about to say. She *had* thought it was him. She'd tried to convince herself otherwise, but in some hidden corner of her heart, she must have known he was capable of hurting her, of physical violence. Even now she could sense how little it would take to trigger that violence. There was so much fury locked up inside Luc Warnecke, so much black rage.

"But what?" A barb of anguish seemed to cut through every other emotion as he said her name. "Jessie . . . for God's sake, if you don't believe anything else about me, even if you can't accept anything that's happened between us as worthwhile, you must believe this. It *wasn't* me. Whatever you think of me, however much you might despise me, I didn't attack you in San Francisco." His voice was soft, then harsh. "I swear to God, it wasn't me."

He took a step toward her and staggered, trying to catch his balance. Watching him struggle brought Jessie a painful realization. She had been wrong. The man who pursued her had run her to the ground. He'd run like an athlete. How could Luc have chased her and sent her sprawling onto the stairway with his leg damaged since childhood, and recently reinjured?

"I don't despise you, Luc. I only—" Welling tears cut off whatever else she'd wanted to say.

"Jessie, don't, please." Shadows flared as he came toward her. His eyes caught the light, glittering wildly. A madman's eyes.

She flinched back instinctively. "No! Stay away—" Fear had opened up an icy pit in her stomach. She didn't know what had frightened her so, whether it was his potential for violence or her own vulnerability, but she couldn't let him near her. She had no idea what would happen if he touched her, but she could feel herself shrinking away from him, hear herself gasping with fear . . .

"Jesus," he whispered, staring at her. "Maybe I am a monster. Maybe I've become my own nightmare."

He found his footing and turned away, fixing on the ground

again, revulsion etched into his profile. A shudder moved through him, and he crouched down as if to touch something. She had the feeling he was trying to find some evidence of the fourteen-year-old who'd fallen from Devil's Drop, as if somehow he could reconcile what had happened to that frightened, battered boy in the intervening years.

Finally he sagged back on his haunches and shook his head. When he glanced up at her, his eyes were dulled by resignation. He knew it too, she realized. He could have been the one who assaulted her that night in San Francisco. He might even have been capable of murder. He had the violence in him. He was imploding with it. He hadn't done it, but he could have.

"I'm sorry," was all he could say.

The tone of his voice frightened Jessie. There was a lifeless quality to it she'd never heard before. Even that terrible day she'd found him here, in the ravine, he hadn't sounded this way, emptied of everything, even the rage.

If she'd ever wanted to escape him, now was the time, she realized. He wouldn't try to stop her. There would be no physical confrontation. She could simply walk away and never have to see him again. Perhaps for the first time since she met him as a girl, she would be free of him. That possibility tugged at her. He was defeated. He had defeated himself. She could run now, escape him. She could be *free*.

He said nothing as she backed away from him. He didn't even look up when she turned to leave. Spotting a patch of wild spring grass on the hillside, Jessie began to walk toward it, her legs unsteady, her heart careening toward her throat. And then something stopped her as surely as if he'd spoken her name. It was a meadowlark crying sweetly in the distance. The sound was so rich and sad, it made her quake with remembered longing, forcing her to acknowledge the crushing sadness inside her. She couldn't run from Luc Warnecke any more than she could these feelings. They were a part of her. He was a part of her. *She loved him.*

"Keep going, Jessie. Get out of here."

The warning had come from behind her, and Jessie could feel the whispered words as if they were climbing her spine. God, how he frightened her. "I can't, Luc," she said, turning back to him. "There's no place to go."

He stared at her pale face and clenched hands. "Look at you, for Christ's sake. You're trembling. You're quaking like a scared school kid. You don't want to be here, Jessie. You want to run, so do it. *Run.*"

"Yes, I'm frightened!" she admitted. "I'm frightened of you, of what's happening to you. I'm scared to death, Luc, but I'm here. And I'm staying."

"Then you're as crazy as I am . . . and God knows, I'm one sick bastard."

"Not sick! You're angry. You should be angry."

He shook his head, past arguing, past caring.

He *was* giving up, she realized. Some vital part of him, perhaps the part that his hatred had kept alive, had been extinguished. He hadn't beaten Simon. He had become him. Or at least that's what he believed. He had become the thing he hated most. And now he was turning that hatred against himself.

Anger rose inside her. "I'm not the one who's frightened, Luc. You are! Somewhere inside you're trembling, *quaking,* just like that scared school kid. Only you haven't got the guts to admit it."

He didn't respond, except to turn away.

She wanted to walk over and slap him, to make him react! Instead she lowered her voice disdainfully. "Someday you're going to have to deal with him, Luc. That scared-shitless little wimp inside you is going to have to deal with the monster that frightened him the most, his own father! You'll never be any good to anyone, not even yourself, unless you do."

A nerve ticked, pulling at his cheek muscle. "Simon's *dead.*"

"And you're not! What are you so terrified of, Luc? You're a man, aren't you? Act like one dammit! Deal with him. Deal with what your father and Jed Dawson did to you!"

Still on his knees, he whirled in her direction, glaring at her with quick and sudden loathing, as if she were the thing he hated. "What do you know about what they did to me, Jessie? *What do you know about anything?*"

He sounded irrational, and he looked enraged enough to attack her. In a moment of breathing shock, she realized it was too late to escape. She should have done it when she had the chance. Now she wanted to run, desperately, but something

wouldn't let her. Something held her there in the grip of his
wild animal eyes.

"I know they beat you," she said, shaken. "I saw the scars on
your back and legs. Who did it? Dawson, the groundskeeper?"

"What the fuck does it matter now?" His anger was raw,
quick, blistery.

If she pursued this, she would certainly provoke him to some
kind of retaliation, perhaps even to violence. But it was too
late for caution now. She was already committed. She'd been
committed to saving him from himself from the moment they
met, fifteen years ago. With fleeting despair, she wondered
if she were caught in one of destiny's eternal loops, fated to
sacrifice herself for Luc Warnecke in one way or another until
there was nothing left of her but her last sighing breath.

She shook off the haunting thought.

"It *does* matter," she told him. "If you don't let it out, it will
eat you alive. It already has! My God, look at you."

He was quiet for so long she thought he'd slipped into some
kind of trance. Crouched on the ground, his fist clenched, he
stared at nothing, an icy glitter of hatred sheening his eyes.

What had they done to him?

Another realization hit her then, crystallizing her thoughts. If
he was brutal, it was because he'd been brutalized. Cruelty had
made him cruel. He'd been reduced to wild animal instincts,
and when he lashed out, it was as much to defend himself as
to inflict pain. But the thing he truly hated was not Simon
Warnecke or Jessie Flood, it was himself. Though he might
not know it consciously, he was compelled to carry out his
father's wishes and destroy himself.

"Don't give up, Luc," she whispered. "That's what Simon
would have wanted. *Don't let him win.*"

A sound seemed to snag in his throat, low and harsh.

Guardedly aware that she had touched something raw and
unprotected, she waited silently, willing him to give in to
whatever he was feeling at that moment, yet knowing she
didn't dare push him any further. He was too volatile.

His hand jerked back as if he could bring himself under
control through gut strength alone, but instead of blocking
the emotions, it seemed to intensify them. He buckled like a
man who'd been hit in the stomach, and the cords of his neck

knotted against a shock wave of recoiling muscle. And then, just as it seemed as if his struggle might go on forever, as if he would never get control of the emotional storm, he dragged in a deep breath and let out a shaking curse.

"*Bastards,*" he moaned. "Fucking *bastards.*"

To Jessie's utter astonishment, he began a savage and disconnected indictment of his father and Jed Dawson. Haltingly, as if the choked words were being torn out of him against his will, he described the abuse he'd suffered at their hands. It was a journey into the abyss, a trip into his past that was so unbelievably hideous, Jessie wished she had never pushed him to make it.

Staring at the ground, his facial muscles armored against the turmoil inside him, he related memories at random. But not for her benefit, she realized, not even for his own. It was as if he had no choice, as if his soul were purging itself of the poison.

He spoke of Dawson's attempt to gain control over him through militarylike discipline, and when that didn't work, through emotional terrorism and physical torture. He described how, on Simon's orders, the groundskeeper had force-fed him and then devised punishments when he couldn't keep the food down.

But that was only the beginning.

"He ran his life—and mine—like a boot camp. He put me through drills until I dropped, and then, egalitarian that he was, he would give me my choice of 'disciplinary action'—a cane with notches cut into it or a perforated rawhide strop—

"Dawson and my father were philosophical soul mates," he continued, his voice so flattened by pain it was nearly toneless. "They both considered fear a moral failing, even in dumb animals. Dawson brought an attack dog home one day, a beautiful German shepherd that I made the mistake of befriending while he was training it. Dawson found out, and he was enraged. He sicced the dog on me, and when the animal wouldn't attack me, when it cowered and dropped to the ground, Dawson went insane. He destroyed it."

"My God," Jessie breathed.

There was more and Luc told it all.

"He was a monster." Jessie's voice cracked with conviction. "He should have been jailed. *He should have been buried alive*." The compassion for Luc that had been locked inside her flared up, hot and tender. She knew he'd been tortured, but she'd only guessed at what it had involved. Her fear of him vanished. Her only thought at that point was to help him.

"Luc, I'm sorry." She started toward him.

He thrust out a hand to stop her. "No," he said savagely. "You wanted to hear it. There's more."

His whole body was shaking by then, and his voice had dropped to a terrible hush. "Once, when I was ten and I'd disappointed Simon in some stupid, meaningless way, he decided to make a lasting impression on me by telling me how my mother died. He sat me down, all very stern and fatherly, as if he were doing me a great favor, and explained that my mother began to deteriorate emotionally after I was born. 'She couldn't bear the thought of having given birth to a defective child,' he said. And that was exactly how he put it—a defective child. He told me that my mother had taken her own life, that she'd killed herself because of me, and the only way to redeem myself in the eyes of God was to master my childish fears and shortcomings."

"Oh, Luc . . . dear God."

He shuddered, and his jaw muscles clenched so tightly Jessie thought they might burst. It was as if something had broken apart inside him, and he was fighting it, fighting the flood of emotion. But it was a battle he couldn't win. He bowed his head and brought his hand to his forehead, turning his face into it. The tears that slipped through his rigid fingers and rolled down his cheeks were silent and aching, a release of pressure too terrible for any human to bear. His mouth moved as if he were trying to say something, but the words were choked and unintelligible.

Jessie's own eyes blurred with tears. She wanted to go to him, but she didn't know what to say or do. What kind of consolation could she possibly offer when he didn't seem to want her near him? The Simon Warnecke he'd described bore little resemblance to the desperately ill man she'd married, but she could hardly expect Luc to believe that at this point.

He gathered himself together at last, dragging in one deep breath after another. The dampness around his eyes had nearly dried by the time he spoke. "Jesus," he breathed, still crouched on the ground. His voice cracked with disgust as he realized what he'd done. "What kind of a pathetic idiot am I? What the hell am I doing?"

"No!" She was terrified he would turn the rage on himself again. "You don't have anything to apologize for. My God, after what they did to you! It was honest emotion—"

He rose with effort, dragging in another ragged breath, as if he were dazed by the blunt force of so much inner turmoil. "Yeah, what a spectacle, huh? Let's revisit this place every ten years or so, so I can make a total ass of myself."

"Luc, don't, please. Don't ridicule yourself this way." She stepped forward, knowing how desperate she must sound. "I won't let you." Her face was hot, burning with purpose.

He tried unsuccessfully to shake the dark hair out of his eyes and finally had to shove it back with his hand as he looked at her askance. "So tell me, Jessie," he said, his voice raspy, softened. "How are you going to stop me?"

She broke out in a sweat, knowing he could turn against her at any moment. He must be desperate to salvage something, a little pride, a semblance of personal dignity, and she couldn't humiliate him any further. She couldn't do that, and yet she had to stop him from hurting himself.

Better that he hurt me, she thought.

"I don't know how I'll stop you, but I will," she said. "If you're going to self-destruct, it's not going to be in front of me, you bastard! I saved your ass when we were kids, Warnecke. Don't make me have to do it again."

His smile was shaky, hurting. His voice was bitterly sarcastic. "Yeah, right, Wonder Woman, whatever you say."

The breezes had picked up, sifting through the trees above them with a soft soughing sound. Given the horrors this place evoked, the wind's silvery music created a compellingly gentle contrast. Jessie longed to let herself be soothed by it, to release some of the anguish she was feeling. The throaty chuckle of the meadowlark in the near distance reminded her of better days, better times between them.

"Are you going to be all right?" It wasn't the concern she wanted to convey, but it was all she could manage.

"All right?" He sounded as if he weren't sure he'd heard her correctly. His hair fell forward against his profile, a darkly uxuriant mantle that cloaked everything but the hard, sad bite of his mouth.

"I'm so sorry," she admitted. "I would kill Jed Dawson if I could." The sadness she'd been fighting gripped her then, gripped her fiercely. She couldn't control it. The tears began to flow, soaking her face and the hand she raised to brush them away.

The meadowlark spoke again, lonely and sweet.

As the sound faded, Luc dug his hands into the pockets of his chamois jacket. "Jessie, don't cry," he said harshly, as if fighting for control too. "It's bad enough that I'm coming apart, for Christ's sake. Don't you too."

She held out her hand, not sure why she'd done it, except that she wanted to touch him and he seemed so far away.

He began to walk toward her then, and the catch in his gait was obvious, painful. She would have given anything to spare him that, the awkwardness of his movements, the repeated savaging of his male pride. She knew how inadequate he'd been made to feel about his body.

Luc Warnecke, she thought, her heart aching as she watched him make the difficult journey. *Maybe we are caught in some loop of destiny, you and I, fated to hurt each other. But I can't help loving you. I have always loved you.*

She broke then, moving toward him, and suddenly everything around her seemed to lose dimension. She couldn't feel the ground under her feet. She couldn't hear the meadowlarks or sense the breezes. She wasn't walking anymore, she was skimming the ground, floating like a rose in a bowl. It felt as if she were being tugged by some as yet undiscovered force of nature, and that her world had telescoped down to the line of bright space that connected her to him.

"Jesus," Luc breathed as she reached him. He gazed at her for an instant before he took her in his arms. They came together swiftly, clutching at each other, laughing and crying, raging and joyous at the same time. It was insane that she was in Luc Warnecke's arms, as insane as it was inevitable. Her pulse was aroused to hard, stunning beats that felt as if they might drive her heart through her ribcage. She could feel the deep throb in Luc's throat where her face was pressed.

"Jessie, Jessie?" he asked, his voice fierce. "What is this? What's happening?"

"Just hold me," she implored, curling her hands into the soft leather of his chamois jacket and gripping it fiercely. Their coming together seemed so precarious, so fraught with risk, she didn't want to move from the circle of his arms for fear of upsetting some precious balance that might split them apart. She wanted to stave off destiny, to stay in this beautiful curve of the loop for as long as they could, even if it meant that tragedy was inevitable.

His breath was shaking as he kissed her hair.

"We're doing what we have to," she told him. It was true, she realized. They had hurt each other so irreparably that this might be the only way they could heal. Maybe there was some divine law of restitution that required wounds to be healed by the ones who had made them.

When at last she felt safe enough to break their embrace, she looked up at him, and the two images of Luc Warnecke began to merge in her mind, man and boy. Dark hair, sad eyes, tender and cruel, he was gradually becoming one. In everyone's lifetime there would always be that one special person, she realized. The one who, without rhyme or reason, came to mean everything that was precious to you, the whole world. For her, it was him.

Luc took her hands and brought them to his lips, closing his eyes as if he needed a moment to recover, perhaps even to understand. Jessie tried very hard to smile normally when he glanced up at her again, but what happened next was as inevitable as the tides that lapped the shores of Half Moon Bay. He led her to a bed of soft grass and eucalyptus leaves, dappled by sunlight. As they sat together on the fragrant carpet, the meadowlarks began to cry in the trees above them. The sound was so searingly sweet that Jessie couldn't hear anything else. It seemed they were fated for this as well, to make love in the place where they'd met, where memories cut like flashing glass and the wind whispered through the trees like silver music.

His fingers stroked her face, tender and whispering. The first tentative touch of his lips swirled her back in time, and for a moment they were young again, teenagers playing in a moonlit bay, startled by the sight of each other's naked bodies. It was perfect and dreamlike, as if time hadn't touched them.

And then he brought her back to reality with a caress.

He dipped his hands inside the droopy neckline of her peasant blouse and drew it slowly down her arms, trailing kisses over her bare shoulders. Jessie sighed out her excitement, trembled with it. The anticipation of pleasure was sharp, almost more than she could bear. This was the culmination of her adolescent dream, the moment when he began to make love to her in earnest, when he touched her with such tenderness that the intimate reaches of her body shivered and shook with wanting.

She caught the scent of his cologne as he bent his head to her breasts. The essence of sandlewood rose with his body heat, tantalizing her with the promise of exotic pleasures, and the touch of his cool lips against her swollen flesh stirred a thrill that glittered like sunlight on a mirror's surface. He was inflaming her thoughts as well as her body. Shaking inside, she imagined herself being undressed down to the skin, pinned to the ground by his body weight and thoroughly, exquisitely ravished.

Instead, he left her peasant blouse in a soft cloud just beneath her breasts and began to unbutton the length of her skirt, exposing her legs, first to his eyes and then to his hands and mouth. For an instant as he coaxed opened her thighs, she burned to cover herself, to hide from him, which made her surrender to his caresses all the more poignant. And though he hadn't actually removed any of her clothing, she felt naked and beautiful as he stroked her in tender, vulnerable places and whispered searing intimacies against her bare skin.

And finally, when he pressed her legs open even wider and took her gently with his mouth and his tongue, she cried out in surprise and seized up inside with ecstasy. She was crazy with the pleasure of it, paralyzed with the wonder of her fantasies being realized in such a swift, explosive way. But somehow the wild release of energy didn't leave her satisfied. It left her shaking, wanting him more.

"Your body is beautiful," she told him moments later, as he removed his own clothing. She insisted he do it while she watched, and all the while, she admired him with her ardent gaze and with the worshipful touch of her fingers. The warmth of his skin soothed and aroused her, and the webbing of scars on his back stirred her to passionate tears. *How could they have hurt him this way?*

"I would kill them if I could," she said.

"Jessie . . ."

"I love you."

The words slipped out as their bodies came together. Jessie wasn't sure who'd said them. She only knew that she was breaking apart with sweetness. He seemed to be entering her body and her soul at the same time. She had imagined that he would be beautiful, that she would feel him like a glowing light moving inside her. It was all that and more. He *was* her soul. His power shone out from the very center of her, becoming the one bright spot of her existence.

The meadowlarks' cries took on a haunting sound as Jessie buried her hands in the lush weight of his hair and held him to her. High in the trees, flying from limb to limb, the birds seemed to be calling out a warning. But Jessie couldn't listen. She wanted this too much.

The deepening thrusts of his hardened body and the slow, sensual dance of their lovemaking created a radiant flush of excitement. It washed over her like a fever rising languidly toward its breaking point. Passion enveloped her with the heated sounds of mating, with its moist perfumes. Pinned to the fragrant grass by his weight, she gloried in the wild pleasure of their coming together, in the miracle of male and female, indistinguishably hard and soft.

She gloried in the knowledge that it was him.

At last, Luc . . .

Love burned through her heart like fire through tinder. Tears stung her eyes and the sweet fear of loss clutched at her. She'd never recovered from loving him. Or losing him. The memory was still tender and agonizing. She couldn't go through that again. *She couldn't.* And yet it didn't seem possible to love this man without pain.

Anguish mixed explosively with her passion. It tore at her, reducing her to gasps and at the same time, storming her senses with wild, ineffable beauty. As the fever soared toward its breaking point, she clutched at him, crying out his name and begging him not to stop, never to stop! He gathered her up in his arms, kissing her flushed face and cradling her gently until the crisis had passed.

It was such fierce bliss.

It was everything she'd dreamed about . . .

And then suddenly it wasn't a dream. It was a nightmare.

Luc began to shudder uncontrollably over her, pinning her to the ground with a physical force that confused her. She roused herself enough to say his name as his body bucked urgently into hers, but he didn't seem to hear her.

Don't leave me! Don't ever leave me.

Jessie froze inside, wondering if she was going crazy. Was it Luc who'd spoken? Had he really said those words?

No, don't! A cry shrieked through her memory, but it wasn't him screaming now, it was her. *Stop! I'm not—* and then suddenly she knew that it *was* her crying out, and that she had to make him stop! She was desperate, but the words got lost, strangled off in her spasming throat. And when she tried to push him away, he caught hold of her hands and slammed them against the ground, locking her beneath him. In the throes of his release, he dragged her into his arms, embracing her roughly.

"Let go!" she gasped, but he couldn't or wouldn't hear her. She was crushed against the wall of his chest, unable to get free, unable to breathe. And before he was done, she had been ripped backward in time, back to the night Hank Flood died.

"Jessie, what is it?" he asked, releasing her, searching her ashen face. "What's wrong?"

She had gone rigid in his arms, preternaturally still. The shrieking inside her was deafening now. Her heartbeat was so frantic she was afraid she would fly apart if she did anything more than shake her head.

"What is it?" he pressed. "*Jessie—*" He cupped her head and gave her a gentle shake, jarring her out of the memories.

"*It was me,*" she told him. A violent shudder cut off anything else she might have said.

"What do you mean it was you?" He lifted her toward him, his fingers biting into the flesh of her face. "What are you talking about, Jessie? What happened!"

"You didn't know it was me!" She couldn't go on, but by that time it wasn't necessary. Luc had released her and he was up on his haunches, staring down at her, horror in his eyes. He did remember, she realized. *Only he thought it was Shelby he'd brutalized.*

CHAPTER
·· TWENTY-FOUR ··

"OH, PLEASE, GOD," Luc whispered, staring at the pale, brittle woman beneath him. A nerve quivered in her cheek, and the delicate blue veins in her lowered eyelids seemed to be throbbing. "That wasn't you, Jessie? It *couldn't* have been you. That's impossible."

He could never have mistaken the two women. Shelby was nineteen, older than he was by more than a year. She was dark and voluptuous, sexually experienced. Jessie was a kid, sixteen years old, barely able to talk to a boy without blushing. He couldn't have done that to Jessie. Back then she'd never aroused the lustful, hungry feelings in him that Shelby had. He'd been protective toward her, brotherly.

"Answer me, for God's sake. It was you that night?" He reached out to touch her, but she flinched away.

"Who did you think it was?"

He hesitated, not sure what to think "I don't know. I guess I'd convinced myself it was a dream—a wild, drunken dream about Shelby, brought on by too much booze and a head injury. I had a concussion, Jessie. I was out of my head. I didn't know who it was. I didn't know who *I* was—"

"It was me," she said in a small voice. "*Me,* damn you."

"We made love?"

"Not love. That wasn't love."

He was still between her parted legs, still inside her body, as he stared down at her in disbelief. His heart had yanked tight, aching with every beat. What little he could remember of the dream he'd had that night was disturbingly dark. Maybe he'd convinced himself it wasn't real because he didn't want to believe he could have been that rough with a woman. He'd been in pain that night—unthinking, unreasoning, barbaric pain. Shelby had not only jilted him, she'd gutted him and left him for dead with her brutal rejection. And then Hank Flood had made the mistake of picking a fight. The years of abuse, of kindling hatred and bottled rage, had exploded. Luc had wanted to kill someone.

"Let me up," Jessie breathed, trying to push out from under him.

"*No.*" He clamped his forearm across the bridge of her collarbones. It was more reflex than reasoning. Moments ago she'd been clinging to him, whispering and crying beneath him, and now she was as icy and remote as the night she menaced him with the Beretta. He had the horrible feeling she would vanish altogether if he let her up. He was losing her and he still didn't understand why. He didn't understand any of this. They'd just found each other again.

"Then at least—"

She tried to disengage her lower body from his, and he obliged immediately, withdrawing. With quick, deft movements, he freed her blouse, covered her legs with her skirt and then secured his own pants. He felt a violent shudder go through her, but he stayed where he was, holding her in place with his weight. He couldn't let her go, not this way.

"You never told me it was you," he said. "Not even afterward. Why?"

"I hated you."

She turned away, refusing to look at him, but the pain in her profile ripped through him like talons. It couldn't be hidden. Her mouth was compressed and terribly sad. Her face was smudged and tear-streaked.

"Tell me what happened." He eased his hold, anchoring her shoulder. The softness of her breast pillowed against the inside of his forearm, and she flinched, telling him that even that much accidental contact was a violation to her. "What happened, Jessie? I don't remember."

"*You forced me,*" she whispered.

He felt as if he'd been kicked in the stomach. His impulse was to let her go, to free her and let her run away as she so clearly wanted to. Then neither of them would have to deal with this gruesome thing that was unfolding between them. But he couldn't let her vanish. He had feelings for her he'd only begun to acknowledge, deep and tangled feelings that had begun when they were kids and were taking on new dimensions with a speed and intensity that was staggering.

He hadn't begun to sort out his emotions, and if they weren't complicated enough, there was the history between them, the byzantine relationship between their two families, the quagmire of sex and death, secrets and betrayals. He couldn't let her go because she was *there* that night. She remembered. Jessie Flood had all the answers to the mysteries that obsessed him. "I have to know what happened," he told her. "Everything, you've got to tell me."

Her head snapped back, and she stared up at him like a startled animal. "You can't expect me to talk about it?"

"You're damn right I do," he said softly, steeling himself against her trembling shock. It took a savage effort of will, but she'd just accused him of forcing sex on her. If he'd really done that, then he was capable of anything, even of killing Hank. He had no desire to put either one of them through more pain, but he had to know.

"Why did you come to the cottage that night?" he asked her. "You couldn't have known I was there."

Jessie went silent beneath him, drawing into herself and wishing she could retreat to a place where he couldn't find her. There was no longer any point in trying to keep the truth from him. She'd already lashed out with it like a weapon. She'd wanted to hurt him, and she had, but at what cost? His suspicions had been triggered. He wouldn't let up now until he knew the truth. He was going to force her to relive the nightmare.

So tell him, she thought recklessly. *He already knows what happened. Tell him how it happened. Tell him what a heartless bastard he is.*

Finally, bitterly, she began to recount that night. "I showed up at the house right after the fight between you and Hank. Shelby told me you'd been hurt. She said you'd gone into hiding, so I went looking for you."

"What about Hank? Was he dead or alive when you got there?"

"Dead, according to Shelby. I took her word for it."

Luc's indrawn breath gave Jessie grim satisfaction. *He didn't want to hear that. Good. Because that was only the beginning. There was so much more to come.*

"And by the time you found me in the cottage, I'd passed out?" he asked.

"Yes, I thought you were dead too, at first. You were bleeding from the head wound and nearly frozen. I found some blankets, and when I covered you, you woke up and asked—begged—me not to leave you."

"Did I know who you were?"

"I thought you did. I wouldn't have stayed otherwise." *You'd already hurt me enough by betraying me with my own sister.*

"Did I call you by name?" he asked.

No, you bastard, not once! Pain flared into her throat. "You were hurt, blue with cold. If I hadn't stayed, you would have frozen." She went on, refusing to answer his question directly. He'd been delirious, lapsing in and out of consciousness. She'd wanted to go for help, but he wouldn't let her, and finally they'd fallen asleep that way.

"And when I woke up?" he asked, searching her face.

She ducked her head angrily, avoiding the intimacy of meeting his eyes. It was becoming more and more difficult to go on. "That's not the way it happened," she said, her voice dropping off. "I woke up to find you kissing me and telling me how desperately you needed me. It all happened so fast after that. Before I knew what you were doing, it was too late. You were already—"

Inside you? His eyes posed the question. But when he spoke, it was to ask her another question, the only one she couldn't answer with brutal honesty.

"Did you try to stop me?" he asked.

"Yes." She barely got the word out. Heat raced up the back of her neck, stinging her pride far more than her flesh. It was the truth, at least as much of it as he would ever hear. In her raw state, she couldn't possibly endure the humiliation of admitting that she'd wanted him to make love to her at first, that she'd been dreaming about it since the night they kissed in the moonlit bay. When she'd awakened next to him deep in the night, it was to the wondrous heat of his lips on her throat. He'd dragged her close, caressing her hair and moaning with desire. His urgency had touched her own unrequited needs. His passion had melted her . . . until he'd murmured words so monstrous she'd never been able to forget them.

Yes, then she'd asked him to stop! God, she'd implored him, but he'd been caught up in some horrible hallucination. He had thought he was with Shelby, and nothing else mattered. Jessie had to believe he didn't know he'd taken her virginity and shattered her sixteen-year-old life. She had to believe that or else she really should have killed him when she had the chance.

"Jessie . . . ?"

Ice-cold, she met his probing, dark-eyed gaze. She wanted him to know the unbearable pain he'd caused her, even if just a fraction of it. "Yes," she said. "I tried to stop you. I begged you to stop."

"But I didn't stop, is that what you're saying? That I held you down, that I raped you? Because if that's true, why didn't you have me arrested? My recollection of that night may be hazy, but I do remember one thing. The woman in my dream was more than willing to make love with me—she was passionate. She didn't make any attempt to stop me, not until—"

He hesitated, confusion shadowing his features as if he'd suddenly begun to realize what must have happened that night.

"Until you told her that you loved her and wanted the baby?" Jessie cut in, her voice soft, savage. "Until you called her by the wrong name? Her *sister's* name? God, Luc, I screamed at you, I fought you, I did everything I could to make you understand that I wasn't Shelby! But you were enraged. You held me down as if you were trying to prove something, as if you were going to force me—or the person you thought I was—to respond to you. Yes, Luc, *yes*! By my definition that was rape."

"Christ," he breathed. He reared back to look at her, disbelief and guilt and contrition storming his features all at once. His jaw tautened, as if he were under some crushing pressure to express himself. And then, seemingly unable to find the words, he rolled off her and sat up, his shoulders heaving.

Jessie turned away from him. There wasn't anything he could have said that would have blocked out the devastating reverberations of that night. His voice haunted her like the screaming cries of the birds above them. *Don't leave me, Shelby,* he'd pleaded harshly. *I love you. I want this baby . . .*

Jessie hadn't known her sister was pregnant until that moment. She'd tried to push Luc off her, but he'd gone crazy. He'd restrained her as if it were the only way he could keep her from getting away, as if he could make her admit that she loved him. What made it so torturous was that she—Jessie—did love him. Or she had until then.

Now, coiled in silence, she tried to force the incident from her mind. She needed to concentrate on one thing and one thing only—surviving this ordeal. If she could gather herself together, if she could find the strength to get up, she might be able to get away from here, from him. She rocked to a sitting position and felt his hand on her arm.

"Whose child is she?" Luc asked.

Her heart froze. It was the question she'd been dreading. She tried to twist away from him, but he wouldn't let her. With a gasp of realization, he recaptured her wrist and brought her back to look at him. "Mel?" His voice fell off, whisper-harsh. "Is she mine, Jessie? Is she ours?"

She didn't have the strength to fight him, and he was clearly aroused to the point of obsession. "Tell me," he demanded, hurting her with his grip on her wrist.

"No! You promised you'd accept whatever I told you about Mel's parentage. You said you would drop the investigation. That was our agreement!"

"That was before I knew you and I had been together."

She wrenched away from him, springing to her feet with shaking fury. "For God's sake, Luc, we weren't *together*. I was sixteen years old, desperately in love, and you destroyed me! Haven't you done enough to me? You've blackmailed me into marriage, threatened to take over the company. What's left besides Mel? Are you going to destroy what I have with her too?"

He started to get up and then sank back in defeat, crumbling into himself with a horrible sound, as if his heart and lungs, as if all of his interior organs, had collapsed. He didn't even seem to hear her as she turned and left.

Luc left for San Francisco that afternoon, but only after a long and torturous debate with himself. It had been one of the most harrowing mornings of his life. Jessie's admission had left him reeling. The possibility that Mel might be his child, and what he would do about it if she were, had obsessed him all morning. Finally, only one thing had stopped him from pursuing the truth. He'd taken stock of how much damage he'd already done.

It wasn't enough that he'd forced himself on a sixteen-year-old girl. He'd compounded the sin by making Jessie recount every detail of her humiliation. He doubted he would ever forget the raw misery in her eyes when she'd told him what he'd said that night. No, he couldn't be responsible for inflicting any more pain on her. Even if he were Mel's father, no good could possibly come of proving it. He would only bring turmoil to the little girl's life. And ruin another child.

He'd tried to apologize to Jessie before he left, but he felt like a stumbling fool. Words were hopelessly inadequate. His only justification was a head injury and a drunken stupor, which made him seem all the more a bastard. Was she supposed to forgive him because he didn't know what he was doing or who he was doing it with? That he'd mistaken her for her sister didn't excuse anything. It added insult to the injury.

He couldn't change what had happened, but at least by absenting himself from Jessie's and Mel's lives, he could make certain he wasn't the source of any more pain. His need to avenge himself against Simon had been so great, he hadn't given a moment's thought to who might be hurt by forcing Jessie into a marriage against her will. He still loathed his father's memory. That hadn't changed, but he was weary of hurting innocent bystanders, of crushing them under the wheels of his runaway obsessions. He was weary and ashamed.

There were no Historical Society tours being conducted as he pulled the Mercedes into the narrow garage on Franklin Street. In the amber glow of twilight, the quiet, deserted residential hillside triggered a sense of profound loneliness. There was sadness in the deep breath he took, but there was also resignation and even a semblance of peace. He had come to a major decision. He was going to give Jessie what she wanted.

"Knock, knock."

"Nobody's home," Jessie said curtly, concentrating on an article she was writing for the garden section of *The Half Moon Bay Monitor*. She knew by his voice who was standing in her office doorway, and she'd already decided to overlook his transgression, but she didn't want Matt Sandusky to know that just yet. She wasn't in a forgiving mood these days, especially where the opposite sex was concerned.

"Am I still persona non grata around here?" Matt asked, entering the room.

Jessie swung around, an eyebrow arched. "I assume you came by to see Shelby. She's out by the pool like a good barracuda."

Matt winced, then smiled. "I've been worried. You won't take my calls."

"Nothing to worry about. I didn't want to talk to you." Actually Matt's voice on her message machine had seemed like one of the few constants in her life lately. She'd come close to picking up the phone in the two days since her encounter with Luc. That was how desperate she'd been for a sympathetic ear.

Now, watching Matt fuss with the knot in his tie, Jessie decided he'd squirmed long enough. He looked absolutely pristine in a chalk-stripe double-breasted suit, but if he kept tugging and perspiring, he would soon be a mess. Again. "What brings you here?" she asked.

"Gil Stratton called me. Apparently he hasn't been able to get through to you either. He has some pretty amazing news,

Jessie. He says Luc's been in touch with him, and he's willing to give you an uncontested divorce if you want one. No strings, no conditions, you're home free. He's even agreed to let Gil handle things for both of you."

"Divorce?" Jessie felt as if a trapdoor had dropped out from under her. "But I haven't asked Luc for a divorce."

"Now you won't have to." Matt shrugged, almost boyish in his pleasure. "This is what you want, isn't it? From where I stand it's nothing short of a godsend."

A godsend . . . ? Jessie couldn't take it all in. She ought to have been happy, or at the very least relieved. But she wasn't. She felt confused and strangely bereft. It was almost as if something had been taken from her, as if she were losing the things that defined her existence—the past with all its torment and sweetness.

"It doesn't solve the Company's budget problems, but it eliminates any threat from Luc," Matt was saying. "And of course, against your personal fortune, not to mention Mel."

"Yes, of course." Jessie rose and walked to the window, staring out at the pool area, where Mel was proudly demonstrating her swimming skills to Gina and Roger. Shelby was in the water with Mel, acting as the official coach and looking indecently sleek and gorgeous in a blindingly white thong bikini. Maybe she should try the Jane Fonda workout tapes, Jessie thought absently, then mentally shook her head. She could work out for the next millennium, and she would never have Shelby's hard body.

Why was she feeling so stunned about Luc wanting a divorce? It was what she wanted. It had to be. And yet she felt lost, a bottle with a message tossing on the open seas. She wanted to grab for something to anchor her, cling to it . . .

"Jessie? You're okay about this, aren't you?"

"Yes," she said, pulling a breath. "I just didn't expect Luc to be so cooperative."

Matt came over to stand beside her. "Proves there is a god, right?"

Jessie nodded. His buoyant enthusiasm made her feel all the more empty for not being able to share it. She didn't know how to respond to his news or his mood. In an effort to fill the void, she turned her attention to Mel's fierce prowess at swimming underwater. "She's good, isn't she?" Glancing at Matt, Jessie was surprised to see him redden. "Mel, I mean. She's a good little swimmer."

"Oh, yes! Right."

They both watched quietly for a few moments, and Jessie found herself wondering what feelings Matt might have for Shelby beyond the obvious sexual attraction. She hoped, for his sake, it didn't go any deeper. He wasn't either jaded or tough enough for Shelby. Though he was in his forties and divorced, Jessie knew he didn't date, especially not barracudas like her sister. In the last few days she'd even begun to wonder whether he was tough enough to run Warnecke. Perhaps it was her morose mood.

"I've never seen Mel so excited as she is about this idea of being on a swim team," Matt ventured. "It's given her something to strive for, don't you think?"

"Well, yes, but—" Jessie was about to point out all the reasons Mel shouldn't participate, but found she couldn't. She clutched her arms lightly, hugging herself as she watched Mel and Shelby cavort. *It made her so lonely to watch them. She felt like a kid again, a scruffy outsider with no one to play with.* Perhaps she would have been happier about Mel's progress if Shelby hadn't been so instrumental in it. She probably should have been grateful to her sister, but she was worried about the other influences Shelby might have on Mel. She could already see the signs of hero worship in Mel. She was taken with her glamorous aunt, given to watching her with rapt attention and mimicking Shelby's rowdy jokes and husky laughter. Jessie admitted to some jealousy, but she was also concerned.

Jessie gradually became aware that Matt Sandusky was watching her. "What is it?" she asked self-consciously.

"Do you swim?"

It was a conversational question, but Jessie found herself putting another interpretation on it. Was he suggesting that she should take up swimming if she didn't want to lose her daughter altogether? Jessie had already thought of that possibility, and it was too disturbing to contemplate. It made her feel utterly helpless, and she'd never been helpless, except where Luc and her daughter were concerned. Mel was all she had left now. *All the more reason for Shelby to try and steal her daughter's heart away,* Jessie thought.

But Matt's intent gaze said he wasn't thinking about either Mel or Shelby. He was thinking about her, Jessie. "I was just trying to imagine you in a swimsuit," he said.

Startled, Jessie glanced down at her black tunic sweater and jeans. "No surprise what color it would be."

They both laughed.

"You don't like black?" she asked him, pretending to be astonished.

"Black underwear is nice," Matt admitted, flushing slightly.

Jessie felt a stirring of surprise as he reached out and touched her hand. For a moment as his fingers patted hers, she thought about what it might be like with Matt Sandusky—and was aware that it had never occurred to her before. He was a kind, caring man, and she was genuinely fond of him. There weren't any fireworks between them, but then maybe that was a blessing. She could do with a man who didn't twist her vital organs into knots. She could do with a friend.

She glanced up, met Matt's steady blue gaze and smiled.

The laughter and shouting from the pool area was a bitter-sweet counterpoint to their companionable silence.

"What are we going to do about this divorce thing, Jessie?" Matt asked finally, growing serious. "Shall I tell Gil Stratton to go ahead with the paperwork?"

The divorce. Jessie's smile faded.

"Attsa some gooood pizza," Mel said, kissing her fingers to a dripping wedge of mozzarella, mushrooms, onions, and spicy pepperoni rounds.

"You gotta that right," Shelby agreed, holding a loaded section over her head and angling it so that an impossibly long string of cheese dangled into her open mouth.

Everyone laughed as a wad of cheese, pepperoni and sauce plopped onto Shelby's face. "Shit," she muttered, breaking into laughter as she wiped the glop out of her eye.

"How do you say 'shit' in Italian?" Mel wondered aloud.

"Mel," Jessie warned.

"I've got it!" Roger Metcalf said. The caretaker pulled a pen from his denim jacket, scribbled something on a napkin and held it up for everyone to see. "Deep shitaroni?"

Gina gasped in despair. "*Ti sei bevuto il cervello?*" she asked him. "Have you swallowed your brain?"

Shelby choked on the cheese and Mel laughed uproariously, giving Roger's attempt at the language about a five on a scale of ten.

"Don't encourage the imp," Jessie said, tweaking the napkin from Roger's fingers and tucking the evidence into her sweater pocket.

"Shitaroni's not bad," Mel opined. "But I think I prefer shittola. Or maybe some variation on ca-ca?"

"*Mellll*," Jessie pleaded. "Not at dinner."

"Such a mouth, this child." Gina sighed helplessly, then cast a look Shelby's way. "Now I see where she gets it."

"Speaking of dinner—" Roger indicated the last piece of pizza on the tray. "Anyone going to eat that?"

A chorus of "no's" went up as the rest of the group moaned and groaned about their inability to eat another bite. Jessie moaned right along with them, quite certain she would never be able to do battle with another piece of pepperoni pizza. The dinner had been Matt's idea. He'd rounded up everyone at Echos, including Gina and Roger, and driven them all into town to a tiny Italian restaurant on Main Street.

Jessie suspected Matt was celebrating her decision to go ahead with the divorce, although he hadn't said so. When she'd finally made the choice, she'd done so decisively, mindful of the immediate protection it would provide the company and her daughter. Although the underlying problems remained. She might have done things differently if it had been only her involved, but it *wasn't* only her.

Now she was grateful Matt had suggested the pizza party. It had been reasonably congenial so far, except that Shelby didn't seem one bit pleased at the attention Matt was showing Jessie. In fact, she'd been drinking steadily all evening and glaring at them as if she were spoiling for a fight.

"More wine?" Matt asked Jessie. He refilled both his glass and Jessie's, then held up the carafe of Chianti to see if there were any other takers at the table.

"Pass the jug this way," Shelby said.

"How about some vino for me, *per favóre*?" Mel suggested as the carafe was passed around. She tapped her empty soft-drink glass with her knife.

"Sure, you little Italian lush." Laughing, Shelby poured herself a generous glassful, then turned to give Mel some. "*Cin cin!*" she said.

"I don't think so, Shelby." Jessie's voice was low but emphatic, drawing the attention of nearly everyone at the table. "Mel doesn't need any wine."

"You're kidding, of course." Without the slightest hesitation, Shelby sloshed some Chianti into Mel's glass.

"Not at all," Jessie assured her, fighting a powerful urge to pluck the carafe out of Shelby's hand and pour it over her sister's head.

"Mommmm," Mel groaned. "Kids in Italy drink *vino* all the time. It's a family custom."

"This isn't Italy, Mel. And you have allergies."

"What Mel has," Shelby cut back, "is a pain in the ass for a mother. Loosen up, Jess, a little wine won't hurt her any more than the swimming did. You're not growing an exotic orchid here. You're raising a kid."

"And you're the expert?"

Shelby flushed and picked up her wineglass. "You'd be surprised how much I know. I'll bet everybody at this table has something juicy to hide. You most of all, right, Sis?"

The tension shot up by a magnitude of ten. Jessie went silent. She was aware of the implied threat in Shelby's statement, but that wasn't what had stopped her. Jessie had no appetite for public spectacles. She would not fight with her sister in front of everyone, though Shelby might have welcomed that. But there would be a confrontation when they got home. *Shelby could count on it.*

Jessie rapped sharply on her sister's door, waiting a moment before she twisted the latch. Shelby's clothes were thrown over a chair, and the anguished sounds of some new pop balladeer were emanating from the CD player. She came upon Shelby in the bathroom, peering intently into the medicine-cabinet mirror and flossing her dazzlingly white, cosmetically bonded teeth.

"They look sharp enough to me," Jessie observed.

Sighing deeply, Shelby stopped what she was doing and glanced around at Jessie with the expression she'd elevated to an art form: supreme boredom. "I suppose this is about the wine, right? God, Jess, you're *so* provincial. Is it any wonder the kid prefers me?"

There was only one other person in the world who could trigger her to unthinking violence the way Luc Warnecke did, and that was Shelby. It didn't matter that at five seven, her sister was three inches taller than she was. It didn't matter that Shelby worked out religiously and was in better physical condition. Her older sister's careless cruelty was unforgivable. It stung like a whip, triggering all the other humiliations Jessie had suffered at Shelby's hands.

"What Matt sees in you I'll never know," Shelby mumbled, having returned her attention to the flossing. "Besides the money."

"I wonder what he saw in you? Besides the mouth."

Shelby glanced around at Jessie with an expression that mingled boredom with disdain. "Are we having a fight? Is that what this is? Because I really haven't got time right now, *okay*? I'm very busy."

She flicked a piece of used floss at Jessie, and the damp strand hit her in the face, clinging to her cheek.

Jessie grimaced, her temper flaring as she peeled the disgustingly sticky thing from her skin. She'd endured Shelby's abuse as a kid because she'd had to. Shelby had been bigger and stronger, and she'd had Hank as a backup. But they weren't kids anymore, and Hank wasn't here in all his belligerent glory. Every bully needed a taste of schoolyard justice, Jessie decided. And Shelby was long overdue. One more cute move like that and her big sister would be picking dental floss out of her tonsils!

"No, this isn't a fight," Jessie said evenly. "This is a dis*cuss*ion, Shelby. If we were having a fight, you'd be on your butt by now."

"Little punk," Shelby muttered.

"Don't ever go against me again where Mel is concerned," Jessie warned, turning serious. "I won't stand for it, Shelby. Do you understand?"

Shelby glanced up, petulant. "I do have some claim, Jessie."

"You have no claim! None!"

"The hell I don't! Mel's my blood too."

"Legally she's your niece, Shelby. Your *niece*, dammit!"

The two women glared at each other, both seething with things that couldn't be said, neither willing to take the confrontation any further. They were bound together by their mutual enmity and their desperate lies.

A suffocating veil of Red perfume permeated the air. It was Shelby's favorite fragrance, but at least the pop singer had stopped agonizing about his love life in the other room.

"It doesn't matter anyway," Shelby said finally, coldly. "I'm leaving in the morning."

"Leaving?" This was the first Jessie had heard of it.

Shelby returned to the mirror and her dental floss. "Yes, I'm going to San Francisco, as a matter of fact." She smiled suddenly as if pleased to be having the last word. "I have some things to take care of, and while I'm there, I'm meeting Luc for dinner."

"Luc?" Jessie's head snapped around as she stared up at Shelby in disbelief. "*Why?*"

"He's agreed to discuss my business venture with me. I certainly can't get an image consulting service going in this one-horse burg. I'll have to find a place up there, of course. I'll need a San Francisco address in order to solidify my contacts and get things rolling on this coast. It's going to be a bitch without the seed money I need, but you know me, ever resourceful."

Jessie felt as if she'd been struck by a blunt object. Was this some new form of blackmail to get her to come across with the money? *If you don't give it to me, Luc will.*

Jessie was too dazed to try and reason through Shelby's motives. And she would never stoop to buying her off. All she knew was that she wanted to put her foot down as she just had concerning Mel. She wanted to give her sister an ultimatum. Stay away from my husband, dammit! I won't stand for it! But Luc wasn't her husband. He was the man who had come between her and Shelby before. He was the unattainable object. No, she couldn't fight her sister over him. It was impossible, unthinkable. There were a thousand reasons, including savaged pride and self-respect. But even if it weren't a matter of personal honor, Jessie couldn't fight this battle, not with Shelby. *She would lose.*

Shelby turned on the faucet and began to splash her face. "Is there a problem, Jessie?" she asked, her voice as cool as the running water. "Surely you don't object to Luc's helping me. This is business, after all."

"Nothing with you is just business, Shelby."

Shelby took a hand towel from its brass ring holder and began to pat her face dry. "Well, what if it isn't? You've relinquished all claim."

"I never thought of it in those terms," she said bitterly.

"I did, exactly those terms. Let's cut the crap, shall we, Jessie? You know what I mean. You had your chance with Luc and you blew it. Now I want mine."

Jessie felt as if she were withering inside, dying. She wanted to get up and stalk out of the room, but she didn't have the strength, and she refused to let Shelby see how shaken she was. After a moment she pushed to her feet, wincing at the searing pain in her hip—and covering it with cold indifference. "Do anything you want as long as you don't interfere in my relationship with Mel," she said, turning to leave the room. "And stay away from this house. I don't want you here."

"You're making a mistake, Jessie," Shelby called after her. "Mel will resent you for this."

"I'll chance it," Jessie muttered.

CHAPTER
·· TWENTY-FIVE ··

LUC WASN'T QUITE blind drunk yet, but he had a good start on it. Things were looking very blurry as he stopped at a quiet intersection in Pacific Heights, trying to decide whether he lived uphill or down. He spotted the proud gray Victorian two houses down and nodded, pleased with himself. Yup, he'd had a hunch it was that way. He'd spent the entire afternoon at Reilly's, a neighborhood pub, and he would have still been there, well on his way to needing a Seeing Eye dog, if the bartender hadn't clapped him on the back and told him to take a walk and get some air.

Get some air? A sobering thought. Shuddering at the possibility of having his life come back into focus, he'd headed for home, where the booze was free and the friendly advice was nil. Now, as he climbed the Victorian's creaky wooden stairs, a flash of white caught his eye. He hesitated, squinting at the piece of crumpled notepaper with the awareness that it would probably take more coordination than he had at that moment to bend down and pick it up. If he hadn't spotted the butterfly, he might have kept on climbing.

Curiosity prompted him to have a closer look. The booze prompted him to sit down first. He did so, heavily.

The paper was from a kitchen notepad. He'd seen it on the countertop by the wall phone at Echos. The rainbow-splashed butterfly in the upper corner made it instantly recognizable. It was Jessie's trademark. Luc wondered when she'd written it, and why. It was the address of this house, the Victorian, though some of the numbers were so blurred he could hardly read them.

She must have jotted it down while they were on their

honeymoon, he decided. Sometime between the slow dancing and the apothecary shop, maybe? He stuffed the note in his jacket pocket as a wave of despair rolled over him. If there was a reason he was sitting on these steps, bleary-eyed, it was her. He might have done the noble thing by her, leaving town to spare her any more pain, but what the hell was he supposed to do with the shitload of misery he was carrying around?

Be a man, Luc, he thought. *Eat your Wheaties.*

Work, his anesthesia of choice, wasn't doing the trick these days. It couldn't quite plug the gaping holes in his life, and it didn't fill the silence when he sat down to eat alone, when he went to bed and woke up alone. Work wasn't working . . . so he'd turned to booze.

"Luc? What are you doing down there?"

Luc's vision might have been fuzzy, but his hearing was fine. He knew exactly who the owner of that sexy contralto was. His ex-wife's sister was the other reason he'd been hiding out in bars. He had no idea what to do with Shelby Flood, though he was sure she would have been happy to give him a hint.

"Sobering up," he said, pushing to his feet. He shambled around on the narrow tread to a smile so bright it made him feel as if he were something really special, like maybe the last intact man on the planet. Shelby could turn it on, he admitted. And she was looking gorgeous with her hair all dark and shiny and playing peekaboo with one eye. Or was he seeing single?

"Are you coming in?" she asked. "I've got some wine on ice, and I'll even rub your feet if you ask nice."

"You got me with the wine."

By the time he reached the landing where she was waiting for him, he remembered a minor detail. "Correct me if I misunderstood, Shelby, but weren't you going to find yourself an apartment today?"

She shrugged, and the furry cowl neck of her powder-blue sweater slid even farther down her bare shoulder. *God, but she looked soft and warm and comforting.* Shelby? Comforting? Yes, he *was* drunk.

"The manager reneged," she explained. "But I'm still looking. In the meantime, I really appreciate your letting me stay here, Luc. I mean, you're hardly ever around, and you've got so much room, and I just love this place, and—"

"Easy," he said, flagging her down with his hand. "You can stay as long as you need to. I'll be leaving again tomorrow anyway." He had a business trip scheduled. It was a lousy reason to sober up, but he had to stop in at his corporate offices in Denver and give Mary Greenblatt, his noble lieutenant, proof he was still alive before he took off for the east coast to check out a potential investment his task force had recommended.

"Tomorrow?" She looked sincerely concerned. "I hope you'll be back in time for my launch party. I've got the Northpoint Yacht Club reserved for this Friday night."

"Launch party? What did you do? Buy a boat?"

"Not exactly." She crooked a finger at him and backed seductively into the foyer. "Come on in, darlin'. That's what I've been wanting to talk to you about."

Luc had known he was in trouble last week when she'd called and asked him to have dinner with her. Somehow the casual date had escalated into a permanent houseguest situation. She'd talked vaguely about a business deal that day, but hadn't given him any specifics, and he'd been ducking her ever since. Apparently now he was going to get the serious pitch. She'd picked a good day. He was too mellow to put up a fight.

"Right in here," she said, leading him to the family parlor, where a silver ice bucket stood next to the big chair by the fireplace. "It's a little warm for a fire, but you just relax and get comfy, okay? I'll pour you some chardonnay."

Luc had the feeling all this attention was going to prove expensive, but at least Shelby was turning out to be an interesting distraction. She never failed to be that. In fact, she was being so solicitous, he had little choice but to sprawl in the chair and submit to her aid and succor. Here's the lamb, he thought, kicking up his feet on a petit-point footstool. Bring on the slaughter.

As he took off his jacket and draped it over the back of the chair, Jessie's note fell out of the pocket and floated to the floor, giving the illusion for a moment that the butterfly was in flight. He picked it up, thinking to toss it into the fireplace. He wasn't into depressing keepsakes, thanks just the same. Instead he studied it for a moment. Was his vision still playing tricks or was there something odd about her handwriting? He'd never noticed before, but she dotted her *i*s with a little check mark.

On impulse he dug his wallet from the back pocket of his jeans and took out the threatening note he'd received weeks ago. "STAY AWAY FROM HALF MOON BAY," it warned. "HANK FLOOD'S DEATH WAS MURDER AND I HAVE NEW EVIDENCE LINKING YOU TO THE CRIME." The words were written in a childish scrawl to disguise the handwriting, and all the *i*s were dotted, except the last one, which had something resembling a check mark above it. Nervousness had caused her to slip up, he suspected. It seemed sad to him now that she'd been so desperate. Sad, but not surprising. She'd been dealing with a madman. Him.

"What's that?" Shelby asked, returning with the wine.

He looked up at her blankly until she indicated the tattered papers he was holding. With one last glance at the touchstones—one a reminder of the nightmare that started it all, the other a reminder of his own disastrous marriage—he wadded the notes and tossed them at the fireplace.

"Nothing important," he said.

Shelby smiled.

"Just the person I wanted to talk to," said a voice as soft as rustling silk.

Jessie immediately regretted picking up the telephone. It was Shelby on the other end, and Jessie would have preferred walking barefoot on blazing coals to a conversation with her sister. Mel had been in a sulk ever since Shelby left, and the child was down now with a relapse of asthma. On the other hand, Jessie was insane to know what was going on in San Francisco.

"Shelby, I'm very busy," she said, none too politely. She was, in fact. She'd been working on her input for a presentation to Warnecke's board on the new business and editorial direction for the company. She and Matt had been laboring over it all week, knowing the board would need more than a show of esprit de corps, they would need a solid plan for putting the newspaper arm of the company back on its feet.

"Surely you can take a minute," Shelby said. "I thought you might like some good news."

"I'd love some good news. Are you dying of something?"

"Jessie! Could you be any more of a bitch?"

"Then I guess we're talking about good news for you?"

The line went silent for a moment before Shelby resumed. "I'm throwing a party," she said, recovering nicely. "You're invited, of course."

"A party?" Jessie tried to sound nonchalant, but her breath went thready. "Does that mean there's something to celebrate?"

"Oh, yes!"

Jessie could hear the catch of emotion in Shelby's voice. Her sister was bubbling over with excitement, and for an instant Jessie felt a flicker of regret that she couldn't share Shelby's good news the way sisters who cared about each other might.

"I'm throwing a launch party for my consulting service," Shelby explained. "I've got the start-up money I need, and this is my way of saying thank you to the investors."

"Really? How did you manage that so quickly?"

"Luc," she said breathlessly. "He's putting up most of the money. He's even going to give me a personal endorsement by wearing the clothes I've chosen for him at the party. I'm still trying to persuade him to be part of my publicity campaign. Don't you think Luc would make a marvelous model? The dark hair and eyes? I love that funny little hesitation in his walk, don't you? It's so *sexy*."

Jessie's throat had drawn so tight she couldn't speak. In her mind she saw the way Luc had walked toward to her in the ravine, tears in his eyes, laboring awkwardly. Somehow Shelby managed to desecrate even her private, sacred memories. She swallowed furiously. She'd been hoping—praying—that Luc would tell Shelby to get lost in a fog bank. She certainly hadn't expected to hear that he was financing her business and she was picking out his clothes! *What a cozy little arrangement.*

"He's just been a darling," Shelby went on. "Letting me stay here at the townhouse. I don't know what I would have done without him."

"Letting you . . . stay?"

"Oh, yes! I'm living here now, didn't I mention that?"

Jessie nearly dropped the phone. Her whole body had begun to tremble, and she was afraid to breathe for fear Shelby would hear it. She'd blocked out the horrifying flashbacks, refusing to torture herself with images of Luc and Shelby, or even to imagine what might happen between them now that Shelby had decided he was fair game. Perhaps she'd convinced herself it was impossible, that Luc would never let himself be seduced by her sister twice. But she couldn't have been more wrong. The thought of them living together, sleeping together, sickened her! God, she couldn't bear it. Her hand clenched around the receiver.

"Jessie, are you there?"

"Congratulations," Jessie said faintly.

"Jessie, I hope you—"

But Jessie never heard what Shelby intended to say. The phone had slipped from her fingers and dropped into its cradle, breaking the connection. It was some time before the trembling subsided and she was able to get up from her desk. She walked to the window on shaky legs and stared out at the gazebo where she and Luc had been married.

The climbing roses were blooming in wild profusion, and a misty sun shower bathed the gardens, creating a glory of prism light and rainbow hues. The play of soft rain and bright sunshine made Jessie emit a tight, aching breath. She didn't understand how the gazebo could look so beautiful, so magical, when such bitterness and heartbreak had come of what happened there.

There were tears in her eyes, angry, stinging, acid-hot tears, but she wouldn't let herself cry them. He wasn't worth her pain. She would never shed another tear over Luc Warnecke, she vowed. Not one. She had allowed herself to be the victim of his, and Shelby's, whims long enough. There were other ways to deal with misery and loss, with the treachery of your own flesh and blood. There were better ways.

Draped in sheer black chiffon and marabou feathers, a mystery guest arrived at the Northpoint Yacht Club by limo, alone and conspicuously unescorted. Fear and excitement raced in the young woman's blood as the chauffeur came around to help her out. He couldn't take his eyes off her as she threw off her chiffon wrap, swung her legs out of the car and rose to her feet, a champagne glass in her hand.

And she knew why he was staring.

Her outfit was flirting with the point of no return. The curve-hugging black satin slip dress with rhinestone straps had crept up her sleek thighs, leaving no doubt as to what she'd chosen in the way of underwear—nothing. She was as pink and touchable underneath as the day she was born, and the clingy, deeply cut bodice caressed her naked breasts like a lover's hands.

Nylons were her only concession to feminine modesty. Smoky black silk, they made her legs look endless. And the dance-hall-girl seams up the back did more to shape and sensualize her calves than bare skin could ever have accomplished. A scarlet rosebud, tucked into her wild auburn curls, completed the look, promising adventurous males everywhere the exotic, the erotic.

"More champagne, Mrs. Warnecke?" the driver asked, whisking the magnum from its icy silver reservoir in the limo.

"Why not?" Jessie said, holding up the crystal flute. She'd almost corrected him. She didn't feel at all like Mrs. Warnecke tonight. She felt like a twenty-seven-year-old woman who had finally decided to step out of the shadow of her older sister's dazzling allure and discover her own sensuality. Jessie Flood felt absolutely wicked tonight. She hadn't realized how much fun Shelby must have been having with those V words—vamp and vixen. She hadn't known what it was like to have men stop and stare at you as if they couldn't quite focus their eyes or complete the breath they'd just taken.

She liked it. Mmmm, yes, she decided, aware of the flute's coolness against her fingers as her driver filled it with frothy Dom Perignon. *She did.*

The party was already underway as she entered the yacht club's glassed-in dancing pavilion. A small army of upscale guests were milling about with drinks in their hands, and a dusky-skinned chanteuse was crooning softly to the accompaniment of a live jazz band ensemble. Banners hung from the walls and ceiling, proclaiming Portfolio, Shelby's executive image-consulting service, as a blue-chip career investment.

At the four corners of the room, revolving platforms show-cased models wearing images à la Shelby Flood, with looks ranging from the Sophisticated Male to the Uncomplicated Male and everything in between. There were even images presented for the Domesticated Male, featuring coordinated father-and-son looks.

Jessie admitted to being secretly impressed. It was all very hip and sophisticated, and yet a touch too conservative for Shelby's taste. Her sister must be serious about making a good impression.

The czarina of image herself was holding court near a window wall that overlooked the glittering lights of the bay. Not surprisingly Shelby was surrounded by a group of male admirers, who all looked as if they'd love to ditch their dates and whisk her away to the nearest yacht for a private consultation.

Shelby, however, was clearly on her best behavior. Her outfit, a delicately beaded white sheath was sexy, yet surprisingly tasteful. And her manner was subtly flirtatious. How ironic that Shelby had chosen to clean up her act on the very night that Jessie was determined to do just the opposite. It must be some kind of cosmic balancing act, she decided. The planet could only handle one femme fatale in the Flood family at a time or it would light up like a pinball machine.

Champagne bubbles tickled Jessie's lips as she took a sip from her glass. But her insouciance vanished as Luc appeared from out of nowhere. Moving into Shelby's orbit, he looked as dark and broodingly romantic as she did radiant. They were a stunning couple, Jessie admitted, despairing at the mere sight of them. She'd never seen Luc in formal wear, and his black velvet smoking jacket, worn over a herringbone woven-silk vest, was a magnificent contrast to his disreputably long, wavy hair. The widow's peak and his restless gaze added to the aura of decadence, bringing to mind an eighteenth-century highwayman—an aristocratic scoundrel caught out of time. Shelby had chosen well for him, Jessie had to admit, but not without an emerald-green pang of jealousy.

Jessie's heart caught as Luc pulled Shelby aside and whispered lingeringly in her ear. It was an undeniably intimate gesture, and Shelby's breathy laughter confirmed Jessie's worst fears. He was sleeping with her. "Bastard," Jessie breathed, unable to stop herself. A nerve caught fire in her cheek.

His betrayal outraged her far more than Shelby's, she realized. She was getting used to her sister's sexual treachery. Glaring at Luc, she willed him to look her way, to be drawn to her by the sheer force of her feminine wrath. But he didn't even glance up.

Spinning around, she swept the room with her winter-blue gaze. So be it, she thought, smoldering with renewed purpose. There were other ways to get a man's attention, especially when you were . . . *the mystery guest.* A tallish, rather handsome chestnut-haired man caught Jessie's eye first. He seemed to be alone, and as he helped himself to a glass of champagne from a waiter's tray, Jessie realized her own glass was empty. Time for more bubbly.

She strolled over and deposited her empty flute on the tray, casually bumping the man's arm just as he was about to take a drink. He nearly spilled his champagne, but by the time Jessie was through with her effusive apology, conveyed with a fairly breathless willingness to pat him dry if he so desired, they were both laughing. And he was clearly taken with her.

"Would you like to dance?" he asked.

"Maybe later?" she said, affecting what she hoped were languid lashes and a matching smile. "I'm partial to slow dancing . . . aren't you?"

"I'm partial to anything you're partial to," he assured her huskily.

"Why, aren't you nice." She waggled her fingers as she turned and strolled away from him, aware that his eyes were glued to the saucy swing and sway of her backside. "Later?" she reminded him, winking.

He blew her a kiss, and Jessie turned away with a gurgle of disbelief. Her very first conquest. Lord, it was so easy! The sweet boy had done everything but paw the ground. And the masses thought making money was a power trip.

Temptation was a highly underrated pastime, Jessie soon discovered. All she had to do was curl her shoulders, lower her lashes flirtatiously and moisten her lips. The accidental bump had worked so well, she tried it again on her next conquest, a graying-at-the-temples stockbroker type. Unfortunately, she put a little too much oomph into it this time, and the champagne exploded out of the man's glass, drenching his tuxedo jacket.

Jessie didn't even bother with an apology. She simply whisked some drink napkins off a passing tray and began to blot the snowy white ruffles of his formal shirt. "Has anyone ever told you you look fabulous wet?" she inquired, lowering her voice to a rustling whisper. "I just knew you would."

He seemed totally flummoxed. "You bumped into me on purpose?"

"I couldn't help myself," she admitted, laughing softly, blushing naughtily. "You're not going to be angry with me, now are you?"

He blushed, too, nearly as deeply as she had, and then he caught her darting hand and brought it to his lips.

She had him, wet ruffles and all. *The sweet boy was hers.*

He was making moist, passionate love to her fingertips when she noticed that Luc was watching them. She'd almost forgotten about her ex-husband, inconceivable as that seemed. It concerned her a little that Luc appeared to be glowering darkly, but she was having far too much fun to let a scowl deter her. Still, she did try to draw her hand away.

"You're a *dangerous* woman," the stockbroker murmured tremulously, capturing her fingers as they slid through his grasp.

"You have no idea," Jessie advised him.

"And I like living dangerously."

"Oh, really?" She flashed him a beguiling smile and glanced over at Luc. "Then you won't mind that my husband is insanely jealous?"

The magic words, apparently. The stockbroker excused himself and hustled off, presumably to blow-dry his soggy evening apparel in the men's room. And Jessie, her fingers freed, pursued the jungle for bigger game. Who would have believed she'd be so good at this? She'd had a lifelong role model in her sister, but Jessie had no intention of mimicking Shelby. She wanted this evening's adventure to bear her own unique thumbprint. Shelby might be gorgeous, but she didn't have a headful of red-gold lioness hair or a sexy little scar on her upper lip. And she *wasn't* the mystery guest.

The band was playing an appropriate blues oldie, "Lover Man, Oh Where Can You Be?", when Jessie spotted a veritable golden god of a man, resplendent in a midnight blue tux and a white satin shawl scarf. Unfortunately he was standing right next to Shelby, who was flanked on her other side by Luc. Wasn't it just like Shelby to monopolize the most attractive men? This was a call to action, Jessie decided. She'd always thought of herself as an egalitarian, ready to further the causes of fair play and equal opportunity. Besides, Shelby needed to learn how to share.

Hello, handsome, she thought as she strolled into the blond god's field of vision. When she was sure she had his attention, she crooked her finger and smiled mysteriously.

Who, me? his surprised expression inquired.

The band suddenly picked up volume and the singer belted out a husky rendition of "Baby, Won't You Please Come Home."

High on a double shot of fear and excitement, Jessie began to walk toward her next conquest, concentrating every breathless ounce of energy she had on her mission. Armed with attitude and a breezy smile, she introduced a little sass into her stride for good measure. This *was* fun. She could only imagine what Shelby and Luc were thinking, but she never once glanced their way.

"Do I know you?" the golden one asked as she approached, drenching her with eyes so ocean blue she realized he must be wearing contact lenses. No matter, she told herself. Compared to Luc's dark menace, he had the countenance of an angel.

"Would you like to?" she asked him. Aware that Luc must be watching her every move, listening to her every word, Jessie couldn't quite control the tremble in her voice. It didn't occur to her in her preoccupation with being the object of irresistible allure, that adding vulnerability to the explosive mix of sensuality and simmering outrage would be just that. *Irresistible.* To every man within eyeshot, including her ex-husband. Especially her ex-husband.

The band's buxom singer was begging her sweet baby to come home, and the golden one's dreamy blue eyes were traveling Jessie's form with the thoroughness of a police flashlight. It was all the encouragement Jessie needed.

"Hear that, sugar?" She laughed softly, sidling up to him and giving him a friendly little nudge with her hip. "They're playin' our song."

Her insouciance was back. To spare.

His laughter had a rich, throaty sound to it. "In that case, take me home, baby," he said.

With a toss of her head, Jessie caught Shelby's expression and knew her sister must be about to ignite like a surface-to-air missile. Happy landing, Jessie thought, unrepentant. Her sister had mortified her more than once. This was payback. But it was Luc's dark gaze that made Jessie's heart stumble.

Time for the mystery guest to show her stuff, Jessie decided impetuously. With a demure little wink, she caught hold of one end of her dance partner's tassled scarf and swung around, slowly reeling him in. She drew the scarf over her shoulder until he was flush up against her backside, and then she gave it a wicked little shimmy, shaking everything, including her fanny, to the beat of the torchy song. Her undulating hips made it abundantly clear what kind of dancing she had in mind. Lowdown and dirty.

By this time a crowd had gathered, waiting to see what Jessie was going to do next, and she was loving every crazy, cracked minute of it! No wonder Shelby had made a career out of being outrageous. There was incredible power in flaunting convention. Among other things, there was the element of surprise. Jessie felt as if she were in that gray area where you made up the rules as you went along—outside the boundaries of social etiquette, but inside the law, strictly speaking.

As she was blithely towing her stolen cargo toward the gleaming parquet dance floor, and doing a mean merengue on the way, his scarf came loose in her hand. Realizing she'd been abandoned, she turned to him.

His raffish grin surprised and delighted her.

"I've got an idea," he said, contact lenses twinkling. "I think you should dance for me."

"For you? As opposed to *with* you?"

"Absolutely, baby. You're hot tonight. I'd only cramp your style."

Aware of a sudden hush in the room, Jessie had a moment of clutching, what-am-I-doing-here doubt. Her dance partner had just issued a challenge, and she couldn't very well back out in front of the entire assembly. But in truth, there was only one person on her mind at that moment, only one person who made it impossible to even consider backing down. Summoning a deep breath, she fought off that old devil insecurity.

She answered the golden one's grin with a wickedly arched brow and the coolest of smiles. And then, as she swung around, strolling onward, ever so sultry, she trailed the scarf behind her like a cape.

The bearded bandleader grinned flirtatiously as she approached the bandstand. "I'd like to make a request," she announced in a voice sexy enough to set off the smoke alarms.

"I'll bet you would, Beautiful."

Jessie was charmed to her painted toenails by the man's wide smile and bedroom eyes. "And I'll just bet you know 'A Good Man Is Hard to Find,' don't you," she coaxed.

"You win the pot." He picked up his tenor sax, brought the reed to his lips, and in the space of a few opening bars, he began to ravish the torch song, baptizing it with such sensual fire that Jessie thought he might melt the instrument. Every riff was slow and bluesy, every note aching with angst and urgency, saturated with sex. His utter abandon and his half-lidded glances at Jessie challenged her to get down and work it out with him, to lose herself in the blues.

As the band's vocalist picked up the microphone to sing, Jessie swung around to face her expectant audience, favoring them with a toss of her coppery hair and a wink that promised *you ain't seen nothing yet folks*. Draping the scarf around her bare shoulders like an exotic dancer's boa, she began to draw it back and forth, working her shoulders in time to the torrid music, her hips swaying in sinuous counterpoint. She'd never felt so deliberately, uncompromisingly sexy in her life. This was madness! She could hardly believe what she was doing, but there was no stopping now. She wasn't Jessie Flood. She was every woman who had ever wanted to strut her stuff to a blues beat and the amazed admiration of a speechless party crowd.

Most of the guests watched with wide-eyed wonder, but some had already begun to clap to the beat, and Jessie's soggy stockbroker was calling out his approval. Shelby was nowhere to be seen, but Luc was still very much in evidence, and his displeasure seemed to be rising like a thermometer's mercury on a scorcher of a summer day.

Behind Jessie the singer began to lament about a good man being hard to find.

Jessie flashed Luc a dark glance, putting him on notice. She was dedicating this song to him, Luc Warnecke. He shot back an equally dark look, putting her on warning. *If she didn't stop this nonsense, he would.* But if Jessie's heart hesitated, her body didn't miss a beat. Giving in to an irresistible impulse, she began to mouth the lyric along with the vocalist.

Jessie put such sweltering emphasis on the words that heads turned toward Luc, curious about the new object of the mystery guest's attention. Had he done her wrong? their eyes asked. Emboldened, Jessie gave in to an even more dangerous impulse. Still singing along with the words, she began to saunter toward Luc, emphasizing the words about seeing him laying in his grave.

She came to a stop not ten feet from him, her hip cocked like a pistol, the scarf fluttering over her forearms. His narrowing gaze sent a painful thrill down her spine. Heat was arcing off him like an overcharge of electricity. But Jessie couldn't be backed down. It was high noon and she had a hot date with destiny. She drew a gun from her hip holster, cocked her thumb and aimed the barrel dead-center between Luc's eyes. "Bang," she said softly, squeezing the trigger.

As she brought the barrel to her mouth and blew imaginary smoke away, Shelby's launch party erupted in hoots and cat-calls, stomping feet, clapping hands and, finally, a roar of approval. Jessie was bringing down the house.

Excitement spilled through her like uncorked champagne. She was stone-cold sober, but she'd never been so high! Ignoring Luc's black stare, she acknowledged her noisy admirers one and all with the trembling flash of her smile. To the blond god's delight, she blew him a breathy kiss. And then, knowing she had them all in the palm of her hand, she began to draw on the short end of the scarf, snaking the long end across her shoulders and down her arm as if she were a stripper removing a glove.

She played it for all it was worth, rotating one hip in time to the music and pouting her persimmon lips, vamping for every red-blooded male in the place. She was every bit as shameless as the hometown gossips had whispered. But when it came time to toss the scarf into the crowd, she turned her attention back to Luc. With a flick of her wrist, she sent her "glove" sailing high over everyone's head. A drumroll sounded, and as Luc reached up and snatched the scarf out of the air, the band burst to life, cymbals crashing, saxes wailing.

The singer crooned on about loving him every morning and night.

The noise level in the room soared, and the excitement was contagious, intoxicating. Jessie was drunk on it. Abandoning herself to the music, she threw back her head and gave out a sexy, breathy wail of a moan. A moment later she was arching her back and shimmying toward the ground like one of Tina Turner's Ikettes. She was giddy with a power she barely understood, delirious with it, ready for anything. She felt as if she'd broken through some personal boundary and was spinning free.

To rising cries of "Shake it, baby," she rose and spun around, exultant, her back to the crowd, her shoulders thrown foreward and her hips shaking it out with all the brazen finesse of a bartop go-go dancer.

Even if she couldn't fully comprehend the crazy triumph of the moment, she could feel Luc's eyes on her and knew she'd been waiting a lifetime to give this performance. In days to come, when she thought about this night and rolled her eyes, wondering what could have possessed her, she would remember this feeling of being transfigured by a crazy torch song.

The music had taken on a bump-and-grind quality, and Jessie caught her cue. She slipped a finger under the rhinestone strap of her dress and coaxed it off her shoulder. Her breasts swayed within the satin caresses of the clingy bodice, and it was a startling, delicious sensation.

"Take it all off!" someone shouted.

Could she? Would she?

She answered the question with a soft gasp of laughter and a flick of her fingertips. The other rhinestone strap fell, glittering against her bare arm like a slave bracelet. But just as she was about to kick off one of her high heels, a hand clamped her arm and spun her around toward the door. The room swirled dizzily as she came face to face with her ex-husband, *the very man who had done her wrong*. The only thing darker than his black velvet jacket was his malevolent expression.

"Let's cool it off," Luc growled under his breath.

Jessie made the mistake of giggling. "Are you asking me to dance, sir?" she inquired, resisting him as he tugged her toward him.

Apparently not! Caught off balance, she was swept along with his stride as he hustled her bodily off the dance floor. He held her so firmly in his powerful grip that her feet barely touched the ground. He didn't seem to care in the slightest that this was her hour of liberation or that she was rewriting her personal history on this night of nights.

As Jessie's head cleared, she dug in her heels. "Wait a minute!" She swung around and swallowed her words at the sight of Luc's eyes. They were balefires. She had no doubt whatsoever that they would glow in the dark. "I'm not ready to leave," she said, somewhat less forcefully.

Luc took the scarf she'd tossed him and looped it around her wrists, making a slipknot out of it. "*Get ready, Jessie,*" he said, his voice dangerously low. "You can either walk out of here under your own power, or we can do the simpering little sex-kitten-on-a-leash routine. It's your choice."

"I'm a damn good sex kitten!" she informed him indignantly.

"So be it." He pulled the slipknot tight.

CHAPTER
·· TWENTY-SIX ··

LUC'S BLOOD WAS ablaze. Anger, desire, and explosive jealousy had all fused. In his unreasoning state, he hadn't given much thought to what he was going to do with Jessie once he got her out of the Yacht Club.

"You're making a scene," Jessie chided, infuriating him all the more. With her wrists tied, her hair wildly astray and her skirt creeping up her thighs, she looked like a Barbie Doll gone nympho.

"*I'm* making a scene?" He'd intended to find an exit, drive her to the nearest motel and have it out with her. But he couldn't wait that long. His heart was pumping fire, and his guts were twisting inside out. He'd give her a scene!

"That way." He pointed toward a door at the back of the room, alongside the bandstand. It opened onto a T-shaped hallway with no exit in sight. The next door they came to was the Commodore's office. Not a motel, but close enough, Luc decided. He strong-armed Jessie inside and slammed the door behind them.

Animal passions exploded the moment she spun around and glared at him. "Stop *manhandling* me!" she bit out. "Nobody pushes me around like that, especially you!"

He threw up a hand in frustration. "What the hell was that out there? A bad Shelby imitation?"

"No!" Her hair flew, red-gold curls exploding everywhere, and her eyes flared. "That was *me*, you son of a bitch. Jessie Flood can break hearts with the best of them, Warnecke. So get used to it!"

"Breaking hearts? You were breaking balls, Jessie. At least Shelby knows the difference."

"Stop comparing me to Shelby!"

"Stop acting like her!"

"Stop fucking her!"

Luc blinked in surprise, and Jessie's face went violently red. A bomb might as well have exploded in the room. She stepped back, then averted her eyes, hotly refusing to look at him as he stared at her with great and wondrous curiosity.

"Is that what this is all about?" he asked, unable to smother the laughter that gusted out of him. "Me and Shelby? You're *jealous*?!"

Jessie's head flashed up, and the next thing Luc knew she'd worked her wrists free of the bonds and cracked his jaw with the flat of her hand.

"In your dreams," she hissed furiously. "I could have had any one of those men. I would *rather* have had any one of them!"

Her palm print stung, but her words were body blows. They caught him in the stomach, inciting a shudder of violent passion that nearly burned through his control. As it was, he was shaking. "You want to know what you could have had?" he asked her. "Watch this."

He spun her around and pinned her to the closest wall, kissing her with bruising passion before she could get another word out of that deadly mouth of hers. Her startled gasp gave him the most satisfaction he'd had in days. It was breathless with outrage, trembling with fury. Desire shook through him like a storm. He'd never been so hungry for a woman in his life.

She tried to twist away from him, but her struggles only aroused him more. He couldn't tell if her startled moans were anger or passion, and he had no intention of letting her get away until he found out. His thoughts were still burning with lurid images of a dance-hall hussy, a flame-haired temptress with bouncing breasts and a swaying fanny. Watching her perform for other men had made him writhe with possessive lust. She was his, goddammit! She was *his*. That thought had driven itself through his animal brain stem like a stake.

He released her wrists and felt her shudder as if she didn't know quite what to do. Her erotic confusion made him hesitate, creating a fever of expectation at the same time. She *was* aroused. He could hear it in her breathy panting. But was she hot for him or for those ten other guys out there? Blood rushed from his extremities, pounding into the center of his body with the force of a pile driver. In search of relief, he brought her up against the erection that was already raging between his legs. As the yielding softness of her belly cradled him, he released the sound that had been building up inside him all night, a throaty growl of pleasure and pain. A mating call. God, he had to have her or go *insane*.

Jessie swallowed back an outraged protest as Luc locked her to the wall with his body, rotating his hips and grinding them into hers in a slow, wanton simulation of sex. His mouth searched hers restlessly. His hands had begun to prowl her body, hot and violating, fondling her breasts and dragging up her skirt. She wanted to shout at him to stop, to shove him away, but the blunt force of his invasion had left her breathless and spinning.

"Bastard" was all she could get out as he wedged his knee between her clenched thighs and coaxed them apart. "You *bastard*." To her reeling shock, she found herself clinging to him, clawing at him as he began to arouse her with his leg. Her stomach fluttered and clenched as he touched the hardened muscles of his thigh to her intimate parts. His strokes created a friction that flared irresistibly, licking like fire. And then he found her secret place and sent a lightning bolt arcing through her. It flooded her loins with melting pleasure.

The sensations were so intense, so startlingly vibrant, Jessie felt as if she were going to slither to the floor and dissolve in a puddle of hot female juices. A moan shuddered in her throat as he slid his hands into the depths of her panty hose to palm her naked buttocks. The illicit touch was drugging her senses. And the sight of her own exposed legs startled and aroused her even further. Somehow he had bunched her miniskirt up around her waist!

Why did that excite her? Why did this whole insane encounter excite her? She'd meant to stop him the moment he'd pinned her to the wall, to scream for help or shove him away. But instead she'd found herself clutching at his hips, digging her fingernails into the flesh of his buttocks. His rough kisses had thrilled her. His touch was like a branding iron on bare flesh. How had that happened? When had it suddenly become thrilling?

She wanted him. She wanted him now. Urgently! As that realization struck her, she tried to get away from him, tried to fight her way out of his hold.

"No way," he breathed, thrusting her back against the wall. He caught hold of her panty hose, but instead of pulling them down, he ripped a gaping hole in the front seam, all the way to her crotch.

"Luc, you can't!"

But he could. And he did. He pressed her to the wall and kissed her passionately, curving his hand to the fiery mound between her legs. She choked on a fierce cry of shock and pleasure as he opened the delicate furls and petals to his touch. Nothing else existed but the maddening, silky swirl of his fingers. The sensations were so terrible, so sublime, that she convulsed as he penetrated her with his finger, plunging deeply.

"You're wet," he whispered. "You want it, don't you?"

She couldn't speak. She could barely breathe. She was shaking her head no, but she was saying yes. "*Yes.*"

"But who do you want it from, Jessie? Me? Or one of those other assholes out there?"

"From you, Luc. Only from you."

She could feel his sex against her leg. It dug into her soft flesh, bitingly hard. It made her weak imagining that same rigid muscle moving inside her.

"Touch me," he said. "Take it out of my pants."

She reached down and pressed her fingers to the throbbing heat that filled his slacks. She had never felt such tensile power. It hardly seemed possible it was human flesh. Her fingers were trembling, and she couldn't grasp the tab of his zipper until he steadied her hand. Even then it was no easy task drawing the tab down. He was huge. He bulged against her fingers, arousing her terribly. His moan of frustration told her she was arousing him too, driving him wild.

"Take it out, for Christ's sake. Touch me," he urged.

The material of his cotton briefs was stretched tight, giving her very little working room, but she curled her fingers around the base of his penis, gasping as it sprang free.

"Ah, Jessie," he breathed, shuddering.

Everything seemed to pause for an instant, even her heart, before the energy surged again. There was a table behind her, and she fell against it as he hooked his hands under her legs to draw them up. She was wanton in the way that she opened herself to him, wanting him instantly, knowing she would die if he wasn't inside her *instantly*. But he took her mouth first, his lips hot against hers, his tongue stroking. As he bent her head back deeply, he dipped a hand between her legs and aroused her, sending a writhing jolt of electricity through her. He slipped one finger inside her, then two. But it wasn't enough.

"Do it," she told him, frantic in her need. "Do it now! Yes, now, please—ohhhh, *please!*" she cried as he obliged, entering her body with a force that pressed her up against the wall.

The pointed edge of the table cut into her buttocks, but Jessie could hardly feel the sharpness. It blended indistinguishably with the riotous pleasure tumbling through her. It was dark and primal, this longing she had for Luc Warnecke. She was afraid of it, thrilled by it. And yet whatever power it was that he had over her, she held that same power over him. A touch of her fingertips reduced him to shudders and aroused him to near savagery. They fed each other, enticed and incited each other. Each thrust he took seemed to go higher, deeper, bringing both of them mindless, groaning rapture.

She was carried along on a shock wave of stark beauty, a tremor that was building to something indescribable, when his voice came to her, husky and male.

"Jessie—We're not alone."

She didn't understand him at first. She was too dazed by confusion. But then he cupped her face and brought her head around, gently forcing her to shake off her erotic trance long enough to see that Shelby had entered the room. Her sister was gaping at them in disbelief.

Jessie's muscles clutched wildly as Luc began to withdraw.

"No," she whispered. "*Don't stop.*"

Some violent, primitive instinct had taken over Jessie's will. Had it been anyone else, she would have panicked or tried desperately to cover herself. But it wasn't someone else, it was Shelby, the woman who'd casually crooked a finger and stolen Luc away when they were young. Perhaps Jessie wanted her sister to see the raw passion between her and Luc now, to witness firsthand Luc's unbridled desire for her. Perhaps she was trying to extinguish the terrible memories of seeing Luc and Shelby together, to burn them to ashes. Whatever the impulse, she couldn't let anything interrupt this sweet, violent union until it was complete, especially not Shelby.

"Don't stop—"

Jessie's trembling gasp filled the room as Luc kissed her.

She cried out wildly as he lifted and plunged into her. It was as much an act of commitment as it was of defiance, and her body shook helplessly with the deep thrusts. Clinging to him with her arms, her mouth, she caught her legs around his hips and hung on tightly, possessively, as he pinned her to the wall and buried himself inside her, driving again and again.

Shelby seemed paralyzed by what was happening, but Jessie glimpsed a flash of icy hatred in her sister's eyes. Finally, with a muffled howl of anguish, Shelby ran from the room.

The door slammed shut, and Jessie buckled with a deep, primal upheaval. Her head curled forward and her knees jerked up. She didn't cry out. The pleasure was locked inside her, imploding into ecstasy. She was coming. It was over as suddenly and violently as it had begun.

"No, Jessie, not yet!" Luc gripped her face in the shock of his own undoing.

She began to sob as he came inside her. His fluids erupted hotly, like a spurt of fire from a rifle barrel. They impaled her secret heart, wounding her. A searing wetness flooded her senses. It was semen and tears and something even more precious—joy. They were all mingling in the place where he was joined to her, flowing through her like life. She felt as if a flash of fire from a gleaming sword had run her through.

When it was over, they both slumped to the floor, shaking.

Luc covered her tears with kisses, and Jessie accepted his mute tribute silently, her heart squeezing, bursting. But her triumph was tainted with guilt. She could not cause pain without feeling pain, even to Shelby. The look on her sister's face would haunt her, she knew. And yet for now, for this moment, the emotion flooding through her felt poignant and purifying. Hatred had been her shield against the love and longing she couldn't express. Now the shield was gone, and she was naked in every possible way. Naked but not alone.

The San Francisco Victorian became their lover's hideaway that weekend. Luc and Jessie were insatiable as the minutes and hours merged into days. Jessie felt as if some hidden identity had taken hold of her—a passionate, hungry, soul-starved woman she barely knew. She didn't want to be out of Luc's reach for a moment, never farther away than the curve of his palm, the kiss of his fingertips, or the scrape of his curled knuckles. She wanted to be held and petted and fondled. If he wasn't touching her, then she was playing with the dark curls at his neckline or dipping with her fingertips into the intimacy of his waistband. She knew the bumpy terrain of his cinnamon brown nipples by heart.

They were naked most of the time. It was easier than removing their clothes whenever they wanted to make love, which they did constantly and with unbearable sweetness. Jessie had never thought of herself as a sensual woman, but she indulged herself with Luc in ways that made her blush. She admitted to him that there had never been anyone else but him, though neither of them spoke of the other time they'd been together. The past wasn't allowed to intrude as long as their passion could keep it at bay.

Luc had never reveled in a woman's body the way he did in Jessie's. He explored every nook and cranny, every tender orifice, and took pleasure in finding new ways to fill them. He fingered her deep pink ruffles and folds. He plumbed her mouth with his tongue. His cock became a divining rod, gliding over her planes and surfaces, stiffening eagerly as it caught the moist scent of desire, of woman.

He took her lustfully in the Victorian bathroom, bending her forward over the claw-footed tub and curving his palms to her buttocks. He made love to her with fevered passion in front of the parlor fireplace, and then he cherished her tenderly in the master bedroom's four-poster, never more aware of her vulnerability and his own mounting male need to protect her, whatever the cost. He was awed by the pale fire of her beauty, humbled by her fierce spirit. He loved her so often and in so many different ways, the well finally ran dry. And when there was nothing left in him but the need to be closer to her, still closer in ways he couldn't articulate, he grew quiet.

Jessie sensed his need to talk, but she was reluctant to brave the forest of their past. There were too many deadfalls in those woods, too many hidden traps and silent, waiting phantoms. There were things she wanted to know, questions she wanted to ask him, but if she did, and if he answered her, wouldn't she be obliged to answer *his* questions?

Now, as they sat in front of a crackling fire in the family parlor, drinking Courvoisier, the curtains closed against a chilly, fogbound night, she knew it was time to face the phantoms. Otherwise the distance between them would soon be a chasm too wide to reach across.

She was curious about his relationship with her sister. Shelby had been living with him as far as she knew. "Shelby told me she was staying here," she said, trying for a conversational tone. "Do you think she'll come back?"

He was holding his snifter in both hands, and the reflection of the firelight in the brandy was mesmerizing. "It's possible," he said. "She still has some things here."

"Do you want her to come back?"

Without any hesitation he shook his head. "There was nothing between Shelby and me, despite what she may have told you. She needed a place to stay, and the business deal she proposed intrigued me."

"That's all there was to it?"

He shrugged. "I don't know . . . Maybe I needed to prove to myself that I could deal with her, that the thrill was gone."

Jessie breathed a sigh of relief. She had prepared herself for the worst. But she was pleased—no, jubilant!—to hear that Luc no longer considered himself susceptible. She was also certain that Shelby wouldn't show up at the town house while Jessie was there. Her sister was too proud to endure any further humiliation.

Luc stretched out on his side on the Mahal carpet, staring into the fire. Jessie began to rub his back, absently aware through the soft material of his cotton T-shirt of the web work of scars he bore. Curious, she drew up his shirt and began to trace the marks, disbelief in her voice as she spoke. "Jed Dawson must have been a fiend to do this."

Luc sat up, gazing down at his legs, which he crossed Indian style. "We both know who the fiend was, Jessie. It was Simon. Why did you do it? What made you marry him?"

Her throat tightened painfully. How could she ever make him understand? If she drew one card, revealed one secret, wouldn't the house come tumbling down? "There were reasons. I wish I could tell you what they were, but I can't. It's not just me involved, Luc. Maybe someday I'll be free to talk about it."

"Someday?" He heaved a sigh. "Funny how that particular day never seems to come around."

"Your father had changed when I married him," she said, her voice rising defensively. "He was a frightened man, a sick man. He thought people were trying to harm him, and I was the only one he trusted. If you could have seen him, Luc. It was pathetic. The chemotherapy had affected his mind. He was afraid of his own shadow, totally paranoid. And you know how he despised fear and weakness. To be destroyed by the very thing he loathed, it was horrible to watch."

"Horrible? Or poetic?"

Luc hadn't looked at her, but at least she knew he was listening. "Yes, then, poetic," she admitted. "That too. Remember that day in the ravine when you told me you were forced to choose your punishment? Well, Simon's father did the same thing to him. He confessed some things to me while he was dying, and that was one of them."

"How fatherly of him to pass on the legacy," Luc bit out. "And how ironic that he ended up with a son like me. He probably saw me as some kind of punishment from God."

"Or as the embodiment of his own weaknesses and defects. That's why he was so cruel. You represented everything he most feared about himself. It wasn't you, Luc. It was him. Your disability was only physical. Simon's was spiritual, and it destroyed him."

He swung around, his eyes blazing, yet cold. "What are you trying to do, Jessie? Move me to tears? Am I supposed to break down and admit my father was a victim? That he was abused and that's why he abused me? I don't care if he was flayed naked. That doesn't excuse him, for Christ's sake!"

She realized then that she'd been acting as Simon's defender, and she didn't want that. She didn't want to be on the opposite side from Luc. "Simon is dead," she told him, imploring him to do more than listen, to hear what she was saying. "Let him go, Luc. Your hatred is the only thing keeping him alive, don't you see that? He can't hurt you anymore. Only you can do that."

She couldn't bring herself to say the rest. *You need to forgive him. And to forgive yourself for not being the son he wanted.*

His expression was unchanged and yet sad in a way she couldn't describe, as if something were pushing through the anger, a hurt he'd never allowed. "I tried my damnedest to please him," he said at last. "That time you saw me fall from the tree lying across the ravine wasn't my first attempt to cross it. When I was much younger, I made the mistake of thinking an act of bravery would impress my father. The tree had been uprooted in a storm the day before, so I tried to cross it. Naturally, I didn't make it, and Simon was furious. I thought it was because I'd failed, but he sat me down and lectured me on how to commit suicide like a man. 'If you're trying to kill yourself,' he said, 'at least have the dignity not to disgrace the family. Take a gun from my study and blow your head off.' "

Luc hesitated, shuddered. "I was six years old."

Jessie couldn't find words. There were no arguments she could make in the face of such emotional butchery. "No wonder you hate him," she said simply.

Luc rose and walked to the window seat, where he drew open the curtains. The fog loomed, dank and forbidding, suffocating the normal sounds of the night, blotting out all light. It made Jessie feel cold and very much alone. To Luc it must still have seemed as if she'd aligned herself with Simon against him. That wasn't the case, but she didn't know how to make him understand.

She forced herself to get up and go to him. But as she stood behind him, silenced by the barrier of his shoulders, she was afraid to make a sound, for fear he would know she was there. She was afraid to breathe. Did he hate her now? Had this conversation brought back all his animosity?

Finally, though it cost her more than he would ever know, perhaps more than she could afford, given her lifetime's emotional debt, she touched his arm and whispered the words "I love you, Luc."

Somewhere in the distance, the clang of a streetcar's bell broke the silence. Luc turned to her slowly, the boyish lock of dark hair falling into his eyes. "I keep forgetting who you are," he said.

"Who am I?" In the seconds it took him to form the words, Jessie's heart froze with fear.

"You're the only friend I've ever had," he told her. "You're the tough little redhead who rescued me, the sixteen-year-old who hated me, and now my wife—" He hesitated, his voice catching, roughening. "The woman who loves me.

"Jessie," he said, emitting hoarse laughter. "My Jessie."

He touched her face, and she flew into his arms, glorying in his warmth, his gentleness. And when he told her that he loved her too, that somewhere in his wounded soul, he had always loved her, Jessie, who had sworn she would never again cry over Luc Warnecke, wept.

Jessie didn't want to leave the town house. She'd awakened earlier that morning and left Luc upstairs in bed, not wanting him to sense her fears. She missed Mel terribly and had called several times to make sure her asthma hadn't worsened, but even her daughter's presence at Echos wasn't enough to override her uneasiness about returning. The fog outside was still heavy and probably wouldn't burn off for some time, if at all, but Jessie was grateful for its banking effect. She felt protected by it, walled off from the world. She wanted to be fogged in here with Luc forever.

"There you are," Luc said, throaty-voiced from sleep.

He came up behind her and drew her against him, wrapping his arms around her. "I hope you're not going to make a habit of this," he said, nuzzling her hair. "I want you in my bed when I wake up, woman. I can't handle it when you're not there. I go crazy and start hugging pillows."

"Wonderful idea," she said, turning in his arms. "Let's go back to bed, pull the covers over our heads and hug each other for days. Let's never get out of bed. Let's never leave this house."

"Hey . . . what is it? You're frightened."

"Not frightened," she lied. "Just happy. So happy I don't want anything to ruin it." Her concerns were probably too silly and groundless to share. She'd been wondering if the magic would be lost when they left this house, if they could sustain the closeness when they returned to Echos. They always seemed to hurt each other there.

He snuggled her closer, pretending to shiver. "The only way we could ruin it is by freezing to death. It's cold in here."

"How about a fire?" she suggested. "It will take the chill off."

"Okay, but do I have to let go of you?"

"Just for a second."

He released her and checked his wrist as if he were consulting his watch. "Time's up."

She laughed and evaded his quick reach, turning to the wood bin. "Come and help me," she said, bending down to pick out a fat, pitchy log for their fire. As she rummaged through the tinder, she noticed the crumpled pieces of paper that had fallen behind the bin.

"What's this?" she asked, picking up one of the notes. She smoothed the paper and read silently. It was the warning Luc had received telling him not to return to Half Moon Bay. She opened the second note and was startled by the butterfly in the upper corner. It was her paper. As she read the address of the Victorian, Luc knelt beside her.

"I figured it was you who sent the threat, Jessie. It's okay," he assured her. "I know you must have been frightened at the thought of my coming back."

She glanced at the warning note again, confused. "You thought I wrote this?"

He nodded. "You did, didn't you? I assumed you wrote them both. The handwriting is similar."

She scrutinized the notes, her eye for details coming in handy as she quickly spotted several similarities, including a tiny slash mark over the letter i. "I didn't write these notes," she told him, "either one of them. This isn't my handwriting, but—"

"But what?" he asked. "Jessie, what is it? What's wrong?"

In her nervousness, Jessie had crumpled the papers. She stood so suddenly the room began to spin. Her rather useless talent for spotting patterns and motifs had come in handy. And now she was remembering something, another note, another tiny slash mark . . . *Oh, God*!

"We have to go back to Echos, Luc. Now!"

CHAPTER
·· TWENTY-SEVEN ··

"JESSIE, ARE YOU going to tell me what the hell's going on?" Luc hadn't even cut the engine of the Mercedes before Jessie was out the door and bolting up the walk toward Echos. Drawn back in a loosely knotted coil, her copper hair blew free of its restraints as she ran. Luc let himself out of the car and followed her, wondering what was so crucial that she had felt it necessary to risk traffic tickets and high-speed collisions on the drive back. And why she couldn't tell him about it.

"Where are you going?" he shouted after her.

"To my bedroom," she called back.

She was already in her room, going through a laundry hamper, by the time he got there. "Here it is!" she muttered to herself, yanking out a black cardigan sweater by its sleeve. She dug through the sweater's pockets, pulled out what looked like a paper napkin and skimmed whatever was written on it. "I thought so," she panted, still trying to catch her breath. "It *is* the same."

Luc walked over to see what had provoked all the excitement. The napkin was stained with red splotches that could have been blood, and there were some scribbled words he could barely make out. He propped a fist on his hip, both amused and confused. " 'Deep shitaroni'? What's that supposed to mean?"

"Not the words," she said impatiently. "It's the handwriting." She pointed at the tiny slashes above both *i*s.

Luc got the connection instantly. "Who wrote this?"

"Roger Metcalf, the caretaker. Matt took us all out for pizza one night, and Mel wanted to know how to swear in Italian."

"And this was Roger's contribution to Mel's cultural education?"

Jessie didn't respond. She was lost in thought and worrying the edges of the napkin with her fingers. "Roger sent you that threatening note, didn't he, Luc? But why?" She glanced at him, clearly distressed.

He nodded slowly, aware of the carriage clock's steady ticking in the background as he thought through the ramifications of her questions. He had a hunch about what the caretaker's motive might have been, but it was almost as improbable as it was disturbing. "That may not be all Roger did," he said after a moment.

She stared at him, confused.

"I found the second note—the one with the address—on the front-porch steps in Pacific Heights. And by the look of it, it had been there awhile. The paper was tattered, and some of the numbers were so blurred I could hardly read them. It could have been the fog, but I'm guessing the note got wet in the rainstorm that night we went to the opera."

"I still don't understand."

Luc wasn't sure he did either, but he was determined to make some kind of sense of the bizarre scenario that was unfolding in his mind. "The night you were attacked, Jessie, you fought him off?"

"I kicked at him," she said, "trying to get free, and then I pulled an umbrella from the stand and hit the button. It opened in his face and threw him off balance."

"Somewhere in that scuffle, could he have lost the note? Could it have fallen out of his pocket or wherever he had put it?" Luc asked. "We'd have to assume it wasn't a random attack, that the man was looking specifically for that house, or he wouldn't have written the address down. The point is, Jessie, whoever dropped the note used paper from right here in the kitchen at Echos."

Jessie looked as if she didn't want to believe the puzzle her mind was piecing together. "You think it was Roger that night, don't you? But why would he do something like that? Why would Roger want to hurt me?"

"I don't know." Luc tucked the napkin into an inner pocket of his chamois jacket, along with the other two notes. "Let's go over to the caretaker's cottage and find out."

Jessie was clearly hanging back as Luc started for the doorway. "Is something wrong?" He was learning to read her body language, and she'd been acting oddly since she discovered the notes in the fireplace, as if she were torn between wanting to know the writer's identity and fearing it. He wasn't surprised that she might be uneasy about dealing with Roger, especially if she believed he was the one who'd attacked her. But he suspected this was something else. There was so damn much he didn't know about her, he realized.

"I haven't been inside the caretaker's cottage in over ten years," she admitted. "Not since the night I found you there."

He felt both surprise and regret. The past seemed to rule her life too, even more than their present concerns. It explained her reluctance, and yet he still wondered if that was all there was to it. "You don't have to go," he said, feeling a stirring of protectiveness toward her. "I can deal with Roger by myself."

She studied the napkin, continuing to work the edges between her thumb and forefinger as if she were making one of the more momentous decisions of her life. The long, misty-blue voile dress she had on today made her look vulnerable, very vulnerable.

"Jessie, let me handle it," he said.

"No!" Her reaction was so instantaneous she seemed to startle even herself. "No, Luc, I'm going," she said, heaving a pressured sigh. "I was the one who was assaulted. If it was Roger who did it, I want to confront him. I want to know his reasons, and I want to hear them from him."

Moments later, as they were leaving the house, Gina rushed into the foyer, calling out Jessie's name. Her urgent tone ricocheted off the deep walls, taking on a frantic quality as it echoed upward. "*Aspetti un momento!*" she cried. "Wait!"

"What is it?" Jessie asked as Gina came to a halt in front of them. "It is Mel? Is she worse?"

"No, Mel is the same," the au pair assured her. "It's the police—" She touched her chest as if to cross herself. "They were here this morning, two of them, detectives, I think. They wouldn't say what it was about, but they were asking questions about you and Mr. Warnecke. They wanted to know where you were and when you'd be back."

Gina looked about to expire. "It's all right," Luc assured her. "It was probably something routine. Maybe someone called them with a complaint about the tree that blew down during the last storm."

"No, I don't think so—"

"Gina, calm down," Luc insisted, a hint of impatience in his tone. "It'll be fine. Whatever it is, I'll take care of it." He signaled to Jessie, anxious to get to the cottage and question Roger. It had just occurred to Luc that there might be a more ominous reason for the police having shown up, but he didn't want to mention it in front of Gina. He had a note in his pocket warning him to stay away from Half Moon Bay. If Roger, or whoever sent the note, weren't bluffing, he might have decided to make good his threat and involve the police.

"No, Mr. Warnecke," Gina said hurriedly. "You don't understand! The police didn't come about a tree. They wanted to talk to Jessie. They came for Jessie!"

"Me?" Jessie went pale. Her hand fluttered in the air, and then she brought her fingers to her mouth. "What do you mean, Gina? What did they want?"

"I don't know." The au pair glanced from Jessie to Luc as if she were waiting for him to reassure her again. This time she did cross herself.

But Luc was barely aware of Gina's frightened scrutiny. He was studying his beautiful wife's expression. She had kept a great deal from him, he realized. She harbored secrets that couldn't be shared with anyone, not even him. Were they finally catching up with her?

The door to the caretaker's cottage hung open. Either Roger had been in a hurry or he was very careless, Jessie decided as she and Luc approached the small stone house.

Luc held up his hand, cautioning her to stay where she was on the gravel walkway as he went ahead. Rusty hinges creaked as Luc eased the door open, then hesitated on the stoop, scanning the interior. No one appeared to be home.

A moment later he and Jessie were standing in the cottage's combination kitchen and living room. The area smelled faintly of incense, and Roger had added some of his own touches to the spare furnishings—rock music posters, a set of barbells and an impressive collection of comic books, among other things.

The cluttered, college dorm surroundings didn't trigger the memories Jessie had anticipated. Oddly it seemed as if her encounter with Luc had happened somewhere else. "Where do you suppose Roger—"

The flush of a toilet interrupted Jessie's question. She turned in the direction of the noise, and the bathroom door swung open. In the process of zipping up his jeans, Roger Metcalf glanced up like a kid caught shoplifting. His eyes darted from Jessie to Luc. "What are you doing here?"

"We need to talk, Roger." Luc indicated the living room's cluttered couch. "Maybe you ought to sit down."

Roger didn't look like he wanted to sit down. He looked like he wanted to make a run for it. Could this boyish college student have been the one who attacked her? Jessie wondered as he nervously tucked his T-shirt into his jeans. He didn't seem nearly big or menacing enough. In her memory her pursuer had been gigantic and terrifying.

"What's the problem?" Roger asked, eyeing them warily.

Luc pulled the threatening note from his jacket pocket and held it up as he walked toward the caretaker.

"What the hell's that?" Suddenly Roger exploded out of the bathroom door. He slammed into Luc's shoulder as if to knock him down. Luc grabbed a fistful of the kid's T-shirt. He spun around as Roger broke for the door, nearly ripping the shirt off the caretaker's body.

Roger bucked and thrashed wildly as Luc dragged him back, muscled him into an arm lock and jammed him up against the nearest wall. Jessie looked around for a weapon, pulling open drawers and cabinets, but by the time she'd picked up a table lamp, Luc was already forcing the caretaker toward the bathroom door. Roger was more agile, but Luc was bigger and stronger.

"I've always wanted to drown someone in a toilet bowl," Luc growled. He pressed the caretaker to his knees in front of the commode and flipped up the lid. "It's a perverse fantasy of mine, Roger. Want to get baptized?"

"No!" Roger snarled.

"You're in some deep shitaroni, Roger," he said, hauling the college student to his feet. "Why don't you make this easier on everyone concerned and tell me why you sent me the note? And while you're at it, explain why you attacked Jessie pretending to be me, you sick little creep."

Roger, clearly no hero, blurted out the startling truth in two choked sentences. "Sandusky told me to do it, all of it. He paid me to follow Mrs. Warnecke, to frighten her."

Luc glanced at Jessie. "Matt Sandusky?"

Jessie shook her head. Her mind had created nightmarish adversaries. It couldn't be Matt behind all this. He was her friend, her confidant, a touchstone through Simon's illness, throughout all her ordeals.

"Do you work for Sandusky?"

"He asked me to keep an eye on things at Echos," Roger admitted, mopping his face and his drenched hair.

"Matt recommended Roger for the job," Jessie interjected. She was still unwilling to accept the connection, a conspiracy between Roger and Matt. There had to be another explanation.

"I guess it's clear who I talk to next," Luc said.

"I want to go along." Jessie had no choice but to go. Matt was a friend, and until she had some reason to believe he'd done what Roger accused him of, he would remain one.

"No way," Luc countered. "This could get dicey. You're not getting anywhere near Matt Sandusky until I've had a chance to find out what he's up to."

Abruptly Roger flung the wet towel at Luc and lurched for the bathroom door. Luc had him on his face before he'd covered three feet of ground. "You crazy punk!" he said, dragging the caretaker's hands behind his back. "I've got enough on you to have you locked up for two decades! One more stupid move like that and I'll turn you over to the cops. Do you understand?"

Roger nodded eagerly. "Yeah, sure—no problem. I just wanted to get a clean shirt."

"Get used to the one you're wearing," Luc advised. "You're going to be spending some time in it." He ripped the belt from his own slacks and used it to secure the caretaker's hands. "This is to make sure you don't go anywhere, don't talk to anybody—and don't warn Sandusky."

As if to assure himself that Roger would indeed not be going anywhere or talking to anyone, Luc placed a fifty-pound dumbbell over each of the caretaker's ankles. Then he yanked the telephone cord out of the wall.

As Jessie and Luc were leaving, a ribbon of blue caught her attention. "Wait a minute," she told Luc, stopping to investigate the satin cord that dangled from one of the kitchen drawers she'd opened. At the back of the drawer, stuffed behind dish towels and potholders, she found the vibrant blue talisman Luc had given her as a good luck charm. The scent of roses, herbs and exotic incense was powerful as she picked the small pouch up. There was no longer any doubt in her mind that Roger Metcalf was the man who'd attacked her.

She felt Luc's hand on her arm. "Let's go," he said.

Jessie made it outside the cottage, but it wasn't until Luc steadied her that she realized how shaken she was. She accepted his support, yet knew she had to find the strength within herself to deal with this situation. The police were looking for her, and it was beginning to seem possible that her good friend Matt Sandusky had ordered a college kid to spy on her, to attack her. Those things were frightening enough on their face. But Jessie knew the deeper implications, and they terrified her.

Matt Sandusky's BMW 750iL was idling in the garage of his San Francisco town house as Luc pulled up across the street. The garage door was open, and Luc could see Matt inside the car, talking on the cellular phone. Had somebody called to warn him? Luc wondered. Surely not Jessie.

Luc made certain he wasn't seen as he approached the car from behind. Matt had just returned the phone to its cradle when Luc tapped on the driver's side window.

Matt looked up, startled. "What the hell are you doing here, Warnecke?" The CEO's voice carried through the glass, and then the pane shot down. "Is something wrong?" he demanded, searching Luc's face. "Is it Jessie? Where is she?"

Either he was a damn good actor or he hadn't talked to Jessie, Luc decided. "Get out of the car, Matt."

"What the fuck's going on, Warnecke?"

"Get the *fuck* out of the car and I'll tell you."

Matt shut off the engine and slammed out of the car, clearly irate. He was nearly as tall as Luc, but he was several pounds lighter and not particularly fit. Luc imagined he could hold his own with the man if the confrontation turned physical, but he didn't expect that to happen. It had taken muscle to subdue Roger. With Matt it would take cunning.

"Nice wheels," Luc said, indicating the silvery four-door sedan, which Matt clearly prized. If a car could be groomed, this one was, immaculately. It gleamed of pristine iridescence all the way down to its chrome cross-spoke wheels. Digging his car keys from the pocket of his jacket, Luc drew his thumb across the notched blade of one key and pretended to wince.

"Damn, these are sharp," he said. "I just hate it when teenage vandals key a sixty-thousand-dollar car, don't you?" He tapped the BMW's door, the keys loosely held in his hand. "Smart of you to keep this baby parked in the garage."

Matt went as pale as his white dress shirt. "Jesus, Warnecke! Get those things away from my car!"

"Oh, damn." Luc drew his hand away. "I didn't scratch it, did I?"

The silver surface gleamed, unmarked. Matt breathed an audible sigh of relief, calming himself. "What are you up to, Warnecke? What the hell do you want?"

"Just curious, Matt. Roger Metcalf tells me you had him send me a threatening note. He also claims you were behind the attack on Jessie. Now, why would you want to go and do something like that?"

Matt's eyes were suddenly piercingly blue. "Roger who?"

Luc pressed the key to the luminous expanse of car door and raked it across the surface. The noise was excruciating, like nails on a chalkboard.

"Christ!" Matt shrieked, horrified.

"This car is the least of your worries, Matt," Luc warned him evenly. He let a beat or two pass, then lifted his hand to show that he'd used his thumbnail. The paint job was still pristine. "If I wanted to do some real damage, I'd call the cops and tell them what I know. Roger would be more than happy to testify against you for immunity, I'm sure."

Matt staggered as if he'd been struck, and Luc felt the swift satisfaction of knowing he had the man. He was virtually certain that Matt had been behind the threatening note he'd received. He was also sure Matt had been bluffing. If he knew of any evidence that could link Luc to Hank Flood's death, he would have used it by now, as a bargaining chip. "Why did you have Jessie assaulted, Matt? I think you're going to want to explain that to me and explain it very carefully."

"I was trying to protect her," Matt said, steadying himself against his treasured car.

"Protect her? From what?"

"From you." He flared then, his face heating. "You're a dangerous son of a bitch, Warnecke. I told her you were capable of anything. I warned her she was at risk, that *everything* was at risk, but she didn't believe me. She was making a disastrous mistake. Someone had to make her see that."

"So you had Roger assault her?"

"*Frighten* her. I told him to frighten her, that's all."

"And she was supposed to think he was me? Enterprising of you, Matt. Too bad it didn't work."

"Oh, but it did," Matt pointed out acidly. "She left you, didn't she? If Roger hadn't screwed up, we wouldn't be having this conversation."

Luc glanced at the keys in his hand and felt a moment of fleeting sympathy for Simon's protégé. He had been the king's vassal, loyal to the end, only to have the faithless son swoop down and steal the "keys" to the kingdom. If Luc had been in Matt's situation, he would have done some Machiavellian plotting too. He hoped he would have done it better. If Matt had a fatal flaw, it was his lack of depravity. He wasn't good at being bad.

"What now?" Matt asked. "You're holding all the cards. I assume you want my ass in a sling, right? I'm supposed to hand over my badge and get the hell out of town?"

An interesting mix of metaphors. "I'm sure we can come to some understanding," Luc assured him. "At the moment what I want is information."

Matt actually looked relieved.

Luc briefly told him about the transcript of the coroner's inquest he'd read in the library at Half Moon Bay. "It said you were questioned by the police, but never called to testify. I got curious about that, Matt, so I hired a private detective. He told me you'd been seen at Hank Flood's place several times in the year before his death. He said you used to go there on a regular basis, every couple of months or so, and you always showed up early in the morning before Hank left for work."

Matt bent over the car as if ill, his head bowed into the cradle of his hand. He looked utterly defeated.

"You killed him, didn't you?" Luc's voice was hushed, taut.

"No! Jesus—It was nothing like that."

"What was it like then?"

"I was making deliveries."

"Deliveries? Like *pizza*? Flowers?"

Matt glanced up, haggard, aging at about a decade a minute. "Like hush money from Simon. I was his bagman."

Suddenly Luc knew what a heart attack must be like. He couldn't catch his breath.

"Hank did some handiwork for your dad when you were a kid," Matt hurried to explain. "Remodeling or something, I don't know the details, except that it was the wing where your parents had their bedroom and he overheard them having a fight. Your mother wanted a divorce, but Simon wouldn't give her one. He told her she was an unfit mother because of all the medication she took, that he'd never let her have you. When she threatened to kill herself, he began to taunt her about not having the courage and challenging her to do it. He actually went to her medicine cabinet, pulled out the drugs and dumped them in her lap."

Luc found himself leaning against the car too. His legs felt weak. His jaw burned with the need to say something, yet his lips were unmanageable. He couldn't have spoken if he'd wanted to. *She killed herself because of him, not me,* he thought. *It wasn't me.* On some emotional level, he had accepted Simon's version of Frances Warnecke's death. Despite trying to convince himself otherwise, he'd really believed all these years that he was the reason his mother had taken her life at a tragically young age.

"Hank discovered your mother dead that same afternoon," Matt was saying. "Technically it was an overdose, but Simon enlisted Hank's aid to make it look like an accident, as if she'd mixed contraindicated medications. I don't know exactly when it was that Hank started blackmailing Simon. I was in my twenties and working as Simon's personal assistant at *The Globe* when he asked me to drop off a package at the Flood place in Half Moon Bay. It became a regular thing after that. Simon never told me what I was delivering, but Hank was drunk one morning when I showed up, and he blurted out more than he should have, bragging about his hold over the great Simon Warnecke. I warned Simon . . ."

Luc didn't need to hear the rest. Now he understood why Matt had been anointed the surrogate son and heir. Simon wasn't just paying Matt back for his loyalty, he was insuring his discretion. *Now Luc knew who had killed Hank Flood.*

"He did it, didn't he?" Luc whispered, more to himself than to Matt. "Simon killed Hank—or had him killed—and let me take the rap."

"What?" Matt looked up, confused. "No, I don't think—"

But Luc was already imagining—relishing—the savage triumph of publicly exposing Simon Warnecke. He was a *murderer*. He was responsible for two deaths and willing to let his own son take the rap for both of them. It was insane, unbelievable!

The impulse that swept through Luc was hot with vindication, wild with the desire for vengeance. Before he could stop himself, before he was even aware of what he was doing, he had Matt Sandusky smashed up against the garage wall, his hands at Matt's throat. "Simon did it, didn't he? Tell me the truth or I'll destroy more than your car, I'll destroy you, you fucking bastard. He let me take the rap and you knew all along, didn't you? You were in on it!"

"No. Christ!" Matt gasped. "I didn't know anything! I admit Simon had a motive for killing Hank. But if he did it, he never told me, I swear!"

Luc released him, his hands shaking so violently he could barely control them. He stooped to pick up the keys he'd dropped when he'd gone after Matt, and as he strode out of the garage, he dragged the blade along the BMW's mirrored surface, leaving a jagged, brutal scratch.

Matt's scream was still echoing in Luc's ears as he swung into the Mercedes and started it up.

CHAPTER
·· TWENTY-EIGHT ··

"IS SOMETHING WRONG, Mom? Your hands are so cold."

Jessie released her daughter with a sharp sigh, aware that she'd revealed too much of her inner turmoil in the emotional embrace. "No, baby, everything's fine," she said, smoothing Mel's brightly braided hair. "I missed you, that's all."

Mel didn't seem to be relieved by her reassurances. "Is it because the police were here?" she asked, her turquoise eyes dense with curiosity and alarm. Her breathing was raspy from an ongoing bout with asthma that even a course of new medication hadn't alleviated.

"No, that was nothing—a big mistake." Jessie had been hoping that Mel hadn't heard Gina's outburst, but she should have known better. The child missed nothing. "Now tell me, what have you been up to while I was gone?"

Jessie had found Mel in the glass-enclosed sunroom, having lunch and reading a book of myths about the phases of the moon. Her immediate relief at seeing the child had mixed explosively with the stress of her encounter with Roger, and she'd overreacted.

"Well . . ." Mel dragged the suspense out, then grinned quickly. "Gina's learning to swim—only the shallow end, like you said, but it was great! I've been coaching her from the sidelines, but she's got a long way to go. She gets water up her nose, and she splashes a lot."

Mel's sigh of forbearance made Jessie laugh and hug her daughter again. "Be patient with her, Mel. Good au pairs are hard to find."

Mel took a bite of her tuna fish sandwich, swallowing it

emingly without chewing. "How was San Francisco?" she
sked thickly. "Did you see Shelby? Gina told me she went
lere to start her career."

"Shelby?" Caught off guard, Jessie searched for a response
that would answer Mel's curiosity quickly and safely. Her
laughter no longer seemed to resent her for Shelby's leav-
ig, and Jessie was grateful for that, but she didn't want to
ncourage Mel to idolize Shelby any more than she already
id. "Shelby's involved with the fashion industry," she said.
Clothing, image, that sort of thing."

"I guess she'll be good at that."

"Shelby will be good at whatever she puts her mind to. I
ink we can count on that."

Mel's dejected sigh made Jessie's heart sink. "Do you miss
er that much?" she asked.

Mel set her sandwich down and nodded. "I miss the swim-
ing, but it's not just that. Shelby never talked to me like I
as a kid. She swore and everything. And she told me stuff,
ecrets."

"Secrets? Like what?" The wicker chair creaked loudly as
ssie sat forward. Her heart rate had shot off the scale, but
le didn't want Mel to see her trepidation.

"Nothing bad. Just stuff like where she used to hang out as
kid. She had a hiding place, did you know that?"

"No, I didn't." Jessie had thought Shelby's hangout was
le Main Street Grill. She was surprised that her sister, who
emed to crave constant attention, had felt the need for a
ecret place . . . unless it was to hide from Hank.

An explosive crack brought Jessie to her feet. The man-
on's front door had opened and slammed shut with enough
rce to shake the walls.

"Jessie!" Luc shouted. "Where are you?! *Jessie!*"

What could have happened to make him sound that way?
ssie's imagination ran wild as she glanced at Mel, trying to
ink how to reassure her daughter. She saw apprehension in
e child's eyes, but there was no time.

"Let me go see what that is, okay, honey?" She grasped
lel's hand to squeeze it, but when she tried to pull away,
e little girl wouldn't let go.

"What's wrong?" Mel asked. Her voice had begun to rasp,

as if she were having trouble breathing, but she hung on tightl
to Jessie's hand.

"It's Luc." Jessie pried Mel's fingers loose and bent to brus
a kiss on her daughter's cheek, tears springing uncontrollabl
to her eyes. "Just let me see what he wants. I'll call Gina
come stay with you, okay, *bambina*? Everything's going to b
fine, Mel, really. Don't worry, now. Let me go, darling."

Jessie's heart nearly broke as she rushed from the room an
left the frightened child sitting at the table staring after he
She felt torn apart. Even through her battles with asthma, Me
was amazingly unflappable for a nine-year-old. She hadn
wavered through the ordeal of Simon's death or her mother
remarriage. But now, when Mel clearly needed reassuranc
Jessie couldn't be there to give it.

Luc was coming through the kitchen toward her as Jessi
left the sunroom. He looked as turbulent as he sounded, h
hair in dark disarray, his gait made almost stable by the she
force of his stride. "What's wrong?" she asked.

"It was Simon—" His breath was coming hard, his shou
ders heaving. "Simon killed Hank Flood."

Simon? Jessie stared at him, bewildered. "*Wait*," she whi
pered, thinking to get him out of earshot of the sunroom. Aft
she'd called Gina on the intercom, she beckoned for Luc
follow her, both of them moving with silent haste through th
mansion's darkened, cathedral-like ground floor. When the
reached the filtered sunlight of the terrace, she turned to hin
"What are you saying?"

"Matt confessed everything," he told her. "He was behin
the note and the attack. He claims he was acting out of som
protective impulse—trying to save you from me. But there'
more. Years ago, he was Simon's bagman. Hank Flood wa
blackmailing Simon and Matt was the one who delivered th
money."

Luc briefly described the circumstances of his mother'
suicide and Hank's involvement. In the midst of Luc's savag
excitement and her own rising dread, Jessie was aware of
pressure in her chest that made it nearly impossible to breath

"He used to bring the money to your place," Luc was say
ing. "Maybe you saw him?"

Jessie hesitated. "I may have. It was a long time ago. Han

d lots of male friends, and they were always hanging around r place."

"But Sandusky would have stood out—as fastidious as he —a young newspaper executive on his way to the top, well essed. You would have noticed."

"I don't know, Luc." There was despair in her voice. She dn't know which was worse anymore, the lies or the truth.

He was staring at her searchingly, his dark eyes boring to hers. "I have to reopen the investigation, Jessie. I won't volve the police if I can help it, but I have to pursue this ing on my own. I'm sure I can prove Simon did it. I'll have talk to everyone involved, even Shelby—"

Jessie shook her head, backing away from him. The breezes afting from the garden brought with them the suffocatingly veet smell of roses and honeysuckle. "No," she breathed. ou promised, Luc. That was our deal. You told me you'd op the investigation and accept whatever I said."

"Jessie, for God's sake, be reasonable. Simon killed my other. He killed your stepfather. I have to do this."

"Why? The man is dead. They're all dead and have been r years, even your mother. Let it stay that way! Stop trying resurrect them."

Luc shook his head as if saddened and bewildered that she dn't understand. "Simon killed two people, one of whom cared about deeply. He allowed me to believe that I was sponsible for both their deaths, Jessie—"

But Jessie was as desperate as he was, and couldn't be mpassionate or understanding. "If you can't crucify Simon, ou'll crucify his memory, is that it? Luc, please, that's sick. ou have to give it up. If you won't, I don't want you re."

He was stunned, disbelieving. "What are you saying?"

"I'm saying if you break your promise to me, it will destroy r relationship. I'll go through with the divorce that's already progress."

"Jessie, you can't—"

She began to shake then, to come apart right in front of m. "Yes, I can—I *will*! Please, Luc, don't do this. There's ore at stake than you could possibly know."

"Then *tell* me what's at stake," he demanded. "For God's

sake, take me into your confidence. I'm your husband." In
low, urgent rasp, he added, "I love you."

He moved as if to touch her, but she stepped back, out c
his reach.

"I can't" was all she would say.

"And I can't back away from this," he said, his voice goin
equally cold.

The silence that fell between them was louder than an
shout or cry could possibly have been. Finally he ended i
"I'll send someone for my things."

Jessie was unable to respond as she watched him turn an
leave. She had cut herself off, severed the connection wit
her feelings so totally she could have been a victim of shock
Her breath was shaking, burning, and she was aware of th
repercussions jolting through her, trembling in her icy col
extremities, but she couldn't feel them as pain.

The front door shut with a resounding thud, but Jessie didn'
move. As she stood there, protected by her own frozen immo
bility, yet cut off from everything she knew, a remark Luc ha
made flashed into her mind, galvanizing her. *I'll have to tal
to everyone involved, including Shelby.*

She had to get to her sister before he did.

Jessie found a listing for Portfolio, Shelby's image consul
ing agency, through an information operator in San Francisc
They couldn't provide her with a street address, so she left
message on Shelby's voice mail and then tried several busi
ness bureaus in an effort to track down the address. Th
county clerk's office issued occupational licenses, but the
curtly refused to give out the information, which left Jessi
with nowhere else to turn. She knew almost nothing abou
Shelby's personal or professional life.

The minutes crept by as she paced her office floor, waitin
for the phone to ring and hoping to hear her sister's voic
something of an irony, considering her reaction the last tim
Shelby had called. Her own reflection bounced back at her a
she glanced out the window at the terrace where she and Lu
had virtually ended their relationship earlier that morning.

Her face was drawn with what must have been pain, an
yet she still felt numb. A ticking sensation moved within he

ips, pulling at the tiny, whitened scar, and her eyes were as
aunted as an apparition's. *Be grateful*, she told herself. *Be
grateful you feel nothing. It will allow you to do what you
ave to do.*

The talisman hung by its drawstring cord from her desk
amp. She lifted it off, breathing in the beguiling scents of
araway places and trying to remember what protection the
various ingredients afforded—angelica root to prolong life,
ose petals and periwinkle flowers for matters of the heart,
nd valerian root. Odd that she couldn't remember what the
valerian root was for . . .

She was fingering the blue satin ribbons when the phone
ang. She snatched up the receiver, breathless. "Hello!"

"Jessie? Are you all right?"

Jessie was sharply disappointed at the sound of Matt
Sandusky's voice, though she knew why he must have
called. "I'm fine," she assured him, hoping to avoid any
attempt on his part to explain or apologize. She didn't have
ime! "Actually, I'm trying to track down Shelby," she told
im. "She's staying somewhere in San Francisco. Have you
eard from her, Matt? It's urgent."

"Shelby? No, but there was a reference to her launch party
n *The Globe's* gossip column yesterday. Apparently some
mystery woman crashed the yacht club and upstaged our host-
ess in a major way. Shelby's probably got a swat team hunting
lown the poor unfortunate right now."

More likely the entire FBI, Jessie thought. "I have to go,
Matt."

"Wait! Jessie, please. Luc was here this morning—"

"It's all right. I know. He's already been here and gone. He
old me what happened."

"I never meant you any harm, Jessie, quite the opposite—"

"We'll talk about it," she assured him. "We'll talk about
everything, but right now I have to find my sister."

She hung up the phone, certain that Matt Sandusky was
elling the truth. She didn't believe he'd meant her harm. But
he was equally certain that he was on the ragged edges and
probably no longer capable of running the company.

Warnecke Communications was a ship without a captain or
rudder, she realized, a ship heading for the shoals. That

prospect should have filled her with fear and trepidation, but Jessie had the dubious good fortune of being able to predict the future in this case. She knew what lay ahead, and the shoals were the least of her problems. None of it would matter, not even the shipwreck of a multimillion-dollar communications empire, if she didn't find Shelby.

As she continued to walk the floor and stroke the talisman, a fragment of her conversation with Mel came to mind. Her daughter had said something about Shelby having a hiding place. The remark had surprised Jessie at the time, but as she thought about it now, she realized there was a place where Shelby had stashed prized objects, cosmetics she'd swiped from Burrell's Drugstore and the money she was saving for her eventual escape from Half Moon Bay. Jessie stopped short, arrested by a frisson of shock and a dawning realization. Suddenly she knew exactly where Shelby's hiding place was!

Jessie ran along the edge of the ravine toward her childhood home, her tennis shoes digging into the moist earth and flinging clods of dirt out behind her. The hawks soaring overhead reminded her of a young girl's dreams of freedom. They made her feel as if she were running backward in time, as if she might be twelve years old again by the time she reached the Flood property. Her destination was the crumbling garage that Hank had once attempted to convert to a rental apartment. That was the secret location where her sister had stashed all her ill-gotten gain, including Luc Warnecke on one hot summer night.

The door to the garage was hanging open as Jessie approached. She remembered vividly what she'd seen the last time she stood in that doorway, but that didn't in any way prepare her for what awaited her this time. The room was wreathed with cobwebs and littered with broken tools left over from Hank's handyman days. Nothing had changed physically except that the dust had thickened by several inches and the woman inside was no longer a teenager.

Shelby sat crosslegged amid the dirt and clutter, staring at a corroded metal strongbox that lay open at her sandaled feet. Her linen slacks and vest were filthy, and her normally sleek hair was tangled. Behind her, rusty springs popped out of the

ld mattress like vital organs from a moldering corpse. And
cross the room where the cracked slab of cement ended, a
mall trapdoor stood open, revealing what had once been a
oot cellar.

Jessie stood on the threshold, wondering what had pos-
essed her sister to come here, but at the same time preternaturally afraid that she knew the reason.

Shelby looked up, her face streaked with dirt, her eyes dull.
It's too late," she said. "They've already been here. They
ound it."

"What are you talking about?"

"They found the shovel. I told them where it was."

Jessie staggered backward. "You did what?"

Shelby's head was bowed and shaking as if she couldn't
elieve it herself. "I made an anonymous phone call. Jessie,
told them what really happened."

"Who did you call?"

"The police—they know, they know everything."

"What do you mean, everything?"

"I told them about Hank, all of it, how he really died. Where
he weapon was hidden."

Jessie could hardly feel the ground beneath her. The force
f gravity seemed to have been ripped away. "What about *who*
lid it, Shelby? Did you tell them that too?"

The latch of the strongbox creaked sadly as Shelby opened
nd closed it, forcing its rusty hinges.

"Did you tell them who did it?"

"Yes," she admitted.

Jessie's numbness had vanished with the earth's gravity.
he was shaking with shock, with sudden cold fury. "Do you
ave any idea what you've done? Do you?" Her voice rose
o a keening, piercing pitch. *"Do you, Shelby?"*

Shelby continued to work the groaning latch until Jessie
ouldn't stand it anymore. She lunged toward her, then swung
ack as if to slap her, but Shelby sprang up and caught Jessie's
and, throwing her off in a fit of raw, blistering pain.

"Yes, I know what I did!" she gasped. "I blew it wide open.
screwed things up good!"

Jessie had to lean against the door frame to keep from
alling. Nausea blurred her vision and left a hot, vile taste

in her throat. "Why? You couldn't possibly hate me that much."

Shelby's eyes glittered with a brightness that might have been tears if there hadn't been so much anger and jealousy mixed in. "Don't kid yourself. You're easy to hate."

"Shelby, if this is about your launch party—"

"Yes!" she hissed. "It is about the party! That was my shot at something real, at something legitimate, and you turned it into a circus. *Yes*, I hate you for that!"

A hawk swept low over the garage, dropping its shadow in the doorway where Jessie stood. The fleeting darkness chilled her through and through. It made her aware of the door frame pressing sharply against the bone of her shoulder and, oddly, it made her think of the horrible noises she'd heard that other night—the thrust of wet flesh, the moans . . .

"You really don't get it, do you?" Shelby's voice rose angrily as she tried to reclaim her sister's attention. "You have everything I've ever dreamed of, Jessie. You have it all, you took trash I threw away and turned it to gold, and you never even *wanted* it!"

"So now you're going to take it away from me? Is that it Shelby? That won't get you what you want."

"Maybe not, but you won't have it either! At least I'll know that much."

"And that's why you did this? That's why you're destroying my life?"

Shelby's chin trembled uncontrollably. Her mouth curled into a grimace that was as contorted with pain as it was anger. "No," she said brokenly. "I did it because you're so frigging homely you're beautiful, Jessie. Beautiful in a way that I'll never be . . . and because Luc Warnecke loves you. No man—no one!—has ever loved me."

"Shelby, that isn't true."

"Who loved me, Jessie? *Who?*" she shrieked. "Lynette our runaway mother? She didn't give a damn about me and you know it. It was you she loved. It was you she regretted having to leave. Never me. And Hank, our stepfather? He loved having his own personal piece of teenage tail. That's what Hank Flood loved. I don't know why I didn't kill him the filthy bastard!"

As if realizing what she'd said, she gave out a shocked moan and kicked the strongbox away.

Jessie dropped to her knees and picked up the heavy box in a burst of fury, heaving it against the far wall of the garage. 'But you *didn't* kill him, did you, Shelby? You didn't kill him because you're a coward!"

"No!" Shelby flared. "I could have done it. It was me he abused. I'm the one who had the reason to kill him. *It should have been me!*" She sank down suddenly, stricken, as if realizing that she couldn't have done it, that along with all the other ways in which she believed herself inferior to Jessie, she also lacked her little sister's courage.

She let out a furious, choking sob, swallowing back tears as if to cry would destroy her.

Jessie closed her eyes, trying to shut out the sound, yet absorbing her sister's misery nonetheless.

Finally Shelby gathered herself together enough to speak. 'It doesn't matter why I did it," she said, without looking up at her sister. "It's done. I told them the truth. I told them you killed Hank."

Jessie sat down on the garage's stoop, one hand resting on the pulse at her throat, the other propped against the door frame.

They both fell quiet then, Jessie remembering that night. Hank Flood had turned violent when Shelby told him she was not only sleeping with Luc, she was pregnant by him. He'd picked a fight with Luc and been knocked cold. When he'd come to in a rage, Luc was gone, and Hank had taken his wrath out on Shelby. Jessie had shown up in the middle of it. Unable to stop Hank, she'd picked up the coal shovel and hit him. One blow had done it, perhaps because of his injuries in the fight with Luc. Afterward she and Shelby had tried to make it look like an accident, as if Hank had struck his head on the Ben Franklin stove. Shelby had hidden the shovel in the strongbox and buried it in the root cellar, and Jessie had gone to find Luc.

All these years the Flood sisters had shared that secret, never speaking of it to anyone, not even to each other, until this moment. Now the truth had come out, but at terrible cost. Several lives would undoubtedly be devastated, but none more

than Jessie's own. The truth was expensive, she thought. An
yet holding it back was costly too. She'd paid a price over th
years, living in fear.

Shelby broke the silence at last. "What now?" she asked.

Jessie sighed heavily, a strange kind of resignation comin
over her. "Now there won't be any more lies, Shelby. No
it's over. Finally . . . it's really over."

"Over?" Shelby was surprised, confused. "What are yo
talking about? There'll be an investigation, charges. You migl
even have to stand trial."

There was a desperation in Shelby's voice that told Jessi
her sister was starting to realize what she'd done. Sadly, n
amount of desperation could change anything now. "I'll ge
a good attorney, I suppose. That's what people accused c
murder usually do."

"But what about Mel? What will happen to her if you g
to jail?"

The pain that flared through Jessie made her lash out angri
ly, though she barely had the heart for it. "Maybe you shoul
have thought about that before you called the cops," she saic
"You get to do the honors, Shelby. You get to raise her, dea
with her asthma, put her through school! You are her natura
mother, after all. Mel is *yours* . . . and Hank Flood's."

Shelby went pale. She tried to stand and staggered. "Yo
knew she was Hank's? You've always known?"

Jessie rose from the stoop and walked out into the over
grown yard, kicking at a piece of broken glass, which wa
probably the remains of one of Hank's whiskey bottles. Sur
light glared blindingly against the windows of the old clap
board house, hurting her eyes as she turned back to Shelby
"No," she said. "I believed you when you told me she wa
Luc's, at first anyway. It wasn't until after I married Simo
that I realized if Mel had really been Luc's child, you woul
have gone after the Warnecke money yourself."

The old bitterness crept into Shelby's voice. "Apparentl
you didn't have any problem going after the Warnecke money
or the whole damn empire for that matter."

"It didn't happen that way," Jessie said. "Simon approache
me. He'd had me investigated after I saved his life, an
the detective told him that Mel was his grandchild. Simo

vanted to raise her with all the advantages his money could
give her, and he offered to settle a great deal of money
on me as well, *if* I would give her up. He was already
ill by then, already starting to realize and to regret what
he'd done to Luc. When I refused to give Mel up, he
threatened to take her away from me. It was only because
I knew Hank had blackmailed Simon that I was able to
bargain with him, to set my own terms."

"And your terms were marriage?"

"That was one of my conditions. I wanted the kind of
legitimacy for Mel that being a Flood could never bring her.
I thought if she had the Warnecke name, the doors that had
always been closed to me would be open to her."

"You always do the 'right' thing, don't you, Jess?" Shelby
observed acidly. "Even when you blackmail someone, even
when you *kill* someone, it's for the right reasons. God, don't
you ever get sick of being noble?"

"Would you rather I hadn't stopped Hank?"

Shelby let out an explosive sigh, as if loathing the very
thought that she might be obligated to Jessie in any way. "If
you hadn't, he would probably have killed me," she admitted,
though without any hint of gratefulness. It was a simple statement of fact, as if she were still trying to come to terms with
what had happened. "Mel too, for that matter. I was only two
months pregnant. She probably wouldn't have survived if I'd
died or been severely injured."

Yes, Mel too, Jessie thought. Though she hadn't known
Shelby was pregnant at the time, the later awareness that she'd
saved the baby helped her to rationalize what she'd done that
night. Her instinct for self-preservation and for protecting others had driven her to taking responsibility for the defenseless
Mel. And even though she had never regretted any of her
desperate measures, she didn't believe in taking lives, even a
life as worthless as Hank's.

The sound of sirens in the distance made Shelby spring to
her feet. Her turquoise eyes were brilliant with fear.

"Jessie, they're coming! What are we going to do?"

The police arrived before Jessie could answer, roaring up in
half dozen cars, their sirens blaring unnecessarily. A moment
later Jessie and Shelby were surrounded by officers.

"Which one of you is Mrs. Warnecke?" one of them asked.
Jessie stepped forward.

"Jessie Flood-Warnecke?" As she nodded, he began tonelessly to read her her rights. "I have a warrant for your arrest for the murder of Hank Flood. You have the right to remain silent. Anything you say can and will be used against you in court . . ."

Jessie didn't hear the rest. She was thinking about Luc, the man who wasn't really her husband, and about Mel, the child who wasn't really her daughter. She was losing them both. Luc would surely hate her when he realized what she'd done. She'd testified against him, then let him think he'd killed Hank all these years. And Mel . . . God, she could hardly stand the thought of Shelby raising her daughter.

A tear welled, hanging on her lower lashes. Some time later she reached up to wipe it away and realized she couldn't. Her hands were cuffed behind her.

CHAPTER
·· TWENTY-NINE ··

A CELLBLOCK DOOR clanged thunderously, echoing through the San Mateo County lockup like an explosion in an underground tunnel. It set Jessie's heart on edge and jerked her roughly to her feet. The rasp of scuffling shoes and jangling keys alerted her that someone was coming.

"Warnecke, you've got a visitor," a matron said through the bars of the holding cell where Jessie was being detained.

"Who is it?" Jessie moved stiffly toward the woman, rubbing the circulation back into her aching arms. She'd hardly budged from the concrete cot since they'd locked her up earlier that afternoon, and her body felt permanently bruised from its collisions with the cold, brutal bed.

"No idea. I'm here to take you to the interview room. That's all I know."

Keys jangled again. Iron clanked against iron as the cell door caromed open and crashed into its casings. The deafening force of it made Jessie's stomach swim with nausea. She hadn't eaten since the night before, nearly twenty-four hours ago. But even if they'd offered her food, the pervasive stench of urine and mold would have robbed her of an appetite.

The matron, a sturdy, silent woman in her fifties, escorted Jessie from the cell and walked her down a series of short hallways to the cubicle she'd euphemistically referred to as the interview room. The four-by-five area was bare of furniture except for two chairs and a countertop that was divided by a glass wall with a hole in it.

Luc sat on the other side of the glass, his gaze fixed restlessly on Jessie as she entered the room. His scrutiny made her aware of her appearance. She wore no makeup, not even lipstick and there was dirt beneath her fingernails, she realized, as she glanced at her hands.

It was impossible to meet Luc's eyes. She didn't even attempt it until she was sitting in the chair opposite him and the matron had stationed herself outside the door. When Jessie did look up, she could barely take in the guardedness she saw in his expression, the hidden hurt, the questions. She was culpable, a criminal even in his eyes. She'd not only betrayed him, she'd done it knowingly. She didn't have the excuse of a head injury or a blackout.

"Are you all right?" he asked.

She nodded as if the question were a formality. She couldn't have spoken anyway. Her throat ached with dryness.

"You'll be arraigned in the morning," he told her. "Gil Stratton will be here on your behalf. He's going to try to get the amount of your bail reduced and the preliminary hearing scheduled as quickly as possible."

"How much is it . . . the bail?"

"It's high, a million dollars."

Jessie entwined her hands on the counter in front of her, prayerlike. A million dollars. They must consider her very dangerous, indeed. Either that or they expected her to run. Like her white trash mother.

Luc broke into her thoughts. "I have one question, Jessie. And please, the truth. Did you kill Hank?"

She nodded again, without looking up.

His chair scraped jarringly across the floor as he sat forward. "You implicated me at the inquest and then you let me wonder all those years if I'd killed a man? If they had tried me and found me guilty, would you have let me spend the last ten years in jail?"

"I don't know," she told him with despairing honesty. "I was devastated by what happened that night. Yes, I probably would have let them put you in jail. I'm sorry, Luc. You wanted the truth."

His chair rocked backward, nearly tumbling over as he shot up and walked away from the table. The room was clearly too small to give him the distance he needed.

"Luc—"

"What's the point, Jessie? The police gave me your account of how it happened. They said you were trying to stop Hank from beating Shelby. Apparently you did what you had to do, and I was the fall guy. I'll tell you the truth though—" He turned to her, his mouth white with anger. "I liked it a whole lot better when I thought Simon murdered Hank. That was poetry. This is . . . hopeless."

She sprang up, pressing her palm to the window to steady herself. "Luc, I need your help. There's no one else—"

"My help? Are you crazy?"

"Luc, please. I'm not asking for myself."

He let out a heavy, tortured sigh. After a moment he strode back and jerked the chair into place as if he couldn't decide whether to fling it across the room or sit down. "You're tearing me apart, Jessie. Do you know that?" He stared at her hand, at her bloodless fingers, and then slowly, achingly, as if it were the last thing in the world he wanted to do, he pressed his palm to the glass, splaying his hand against hers.

Jessie bowed her head, shuddering. She could feel the heat of him through the barrier.

"I didn't know it was possible to love someone and hate her this way," he said brokenly. "With both feelings bombarding you at the same time, equally intense. *Jessie—*"

Tears filled her eyes as she looked up at him.

"Goddamn you," he whispered.

Jessie shook her head, barely able to focus through the mist of her wet lashes. Still, with his angry, soul-dark eyes and clenched features, he was the most beautiful sight she'd ever seen. She caught his scent through the opening in the glass, a male perfume so intoxicating to her hungry senses that she drank it in, forgetting for a moment that she was in a dank, mildewy jail. It was a woodsy fragrance that held hints of dark green grottos and mossy streams. It made her think of the ravine, of soaring hawks . . . and freedom.

"Can you ever forgive me?" she asked him.

He didn't respond, but his stormy expression said that he probably wouldn't have any choice in the matter.

"I'm so sorry, Luc. Telling the police was a crazy, destructive thing to do. But once I'd done it, I couldn't back out. Afterward, I convinced myself that your father would get you out of it with a top attorney, and when he did I was actually relieved. As much as I thought I hated you, I didn't want to see you end up like this."

"Like this?" His jaw flexed as if saying the words was torture. "In jail? What are you doing behind bars, Jessie? I don't know how to deal with this. It's insane."

"*We have to deal with it.*"

Somewhere in the facility a cellblock door slammed shut and people were shouting. An alarm jangled as the noises of a jailyard scuffle carried to the interview room.

Luc stared at Jessie hard. "You said there was something you wanted from me. What is it?"

"Two things. Promise you'll do them both if anything happens to me."

"Nothing's going to happen. Stratton will find you the best criminal defense mind in the business."

"I know, but just in case." She couldn't tell him how deep her fears ran. She was the object of both curiosity and envy in this town, the sort of woman a lynch mob mentality would love to see pilloried in public. Shelby would probably be granted immunity for her testimony, and her sister had everything to gain by keeping her locked up. It wouldn't have surprised Jessie if at her arraignment tomorrow the prosecutor convinced the judge to deny her bail altogether. They would call her a flight risk. Her mother had run off, hadn't she. Shelby had disappeared too, when she was in trouble. In her darkest moments since being arrested, Jessie had imagined never getting out of this jail.

"I want you to run Warnecke for me," she told Luc, hurrying on as she saw the questions in his eyes. "Matt isn't capable, and even if he were, the trust isn't there anymore."

"Matt's already resigned. Gil Stratton had a copy of Matt's letter of resignation to the board when I called."

Jessie was more relieved than surprised. In all of this insanity, at least Matt was making one thing easier for her. "Will you do it, Luc? Will you take over?"

"How can I, Jessie? We have different visions for the company. I want to go public, to expand."

Jessie's fingers curled inward, her nails scraping the glass. "I'll go along with whatever you want to do. I just don't want the newspapers disbanded. Promise me you won't sell them off."

He nodded slowly. "Don't worry. I'll talk to Stratton tomorrow. There are ways to go public and still maintain family control. Nonvoting shares can be traded on the stock exchange. That way you and Warnecke's directors will hold the only voting shares, and thus, the power."

Jessie sank back in the chair, unaware of how tense she'd been until that moment. It was a major concession on his part, she realized. He'd wanted to wipe out Warnecke, not preserve it. "Thank you," she whispered.

He pressed his fisted hand against the glass with a force that moved the barrier. "God, I can't decide whether to run from the room or to come through this glass and—"

"What?" she asked him. "Beat me?"

"Hold you," he said, his voice aching.

Jessie had to brace herself against the table edge. The physical sensation of longing was as powerful as anything she'd ever known. It spilled through her like flood water through a rupture. "I wish you could," she said. "Hold me."

There was nothing else to say, no words either one of them could summon. For a moment it was enough just to be in the same room and to meet each other's eyes through the window wall that separated them. It had to be enough.

The pain of wanting him rose in Jessie until finally she had to end it. "There's something else," she told him. "I have to know that Mel is going to be okay, that you'll take care of her. Shelby isn't capable of it, and I don't want to see my daughter put under the guardianship of Simon's lawyers and shipped off to boarding schools."

He fell away, dropping back against the chair. "I can't raise a child, Jessie. What do I know about nine-year-old girls?"

"Mel isn't like other nine-year-olds. She's an old soul, more adult than either one of us in some ways."

"It has nothing to do with Mel," he argued. "It has to do with me. There's an instinct to parenting. I don't have it. I don't even like kids."

"I don't believe that. The day you found her in the ravine, you didn't want to give her up! I thought I was going to have to fight you for her."

"That was a protective impulse, a momentary thing. Mel needs to be raised by someone who can care for her emotional needs as well as her physical ones. I'm not sure I'm capable of either."

"Then who is capable, Luc? Who else is there? Shelby?"

He grew quiet, as if he were beginning to see how insurmountable the problem was. "Is she mine, Jessie?"

"Does that make a difference?"

"No, but I'd like to know. I have a right to know."

She wanted to lie. She had never had more reason. But lies had brought her to this place, and she couldn't resort to anything so self-defeating now. So she told him the truth, searching his face for the proof that it really didn't make any difference. "She isn't yours, Luc. And she isn't mine, either. She's Shelby's child . . . by Hank Flood."

He seemed to flinch beneath the mask of his thoughts. She couldn't tell if it was from surprise or disappointment, but he said nothing.

"When I made the decision to take Mel," she explained, "I promised myself she would never be abandoned, that I'd never leave her the way Lynette left me. Or the way Shelby left her. I was going to be the one Flood female who didn't run away."

"None of this is necessary," he said, rising from the chair. His voice was harsh. "You're going to get out. I'll talk to the governor. He was an old friend of Simon's. I'll talk to the attorney general—"

"Stop it, Luc! If you're trying to ease my mind, there's only one way to do it."

"For God's sake, Jessie. Mel is ill. What if something happened to her?"

Jessie could see the conflict rising in him. He seemed truly frightened at the prospect of raising a child with special needs. Suddenly she was angry. "Don't you realize what you're doing? You're treating Mel the way Simon treated you, as if she were defective!"

"Yes, exactly! That's why I can't do what you're asking. I was raised thinking I was subhuman and repulsive. What if that's so ingrained in me that I begin to treat her the way Simon treated me? What if I were abusive? *What if I hurt her?*"

"You wouldn't."

"There are other kinds of abuse than physical. I don't have to tell you that. There's neglect. I travel constantly. I'd be gone more than I'd be there. Do you want her raised by nurses?"

Jessie turned away from him in despair. He seemed nearly as desperate not to assume responsibility for Mel as she was to have him take it. And she didn't understand why.

"You're grasping at straws," he said. "If you searched your heart, you'd know this wasn't the best solution for Mel."

"Then what is?"

"I don't know. Give me a chance and I'll find one."

He didn't understand. She wanted Mel with him. Why couldn't he see how terribly important that was to her? It was the only thought that brought her any comfort in this hellhole. If she couldn't be with the two people she loved, then at least she would know they were together. *But she wasn't going to change his mind.* She had already searched her heart enough to understand that.

The bony ridge of her spine came up against a metal rung as she dropped back in the folding chair. The impact was sudden and excruciatingly sharp, but instead of moving away, instead of ending the torment, she increased it, thrusting back with a twist of her body. It hurt so badly she looked away, knowing the pain would show in her eyes. Her world was crumbling.

A rap of knuckles and the scrape of an opening door announced the matron. "Warnecke," the woman said brusquely. "Time's up."

The room fell silent, except for the sad creak of door hinges and the slow shuffle of the matron's movements as she entered the room and positioned herself, waiting for Jessie.

Help me, Jessie thought, imploring Luc silently as she rose and walked away from the table. If anything that's happened between us has ever meant anything to you, *help me.*

All it would have taken was one word. But he said nothing.

Shelby Flood was the last person Luc expected to see when he returned to Echos that afternoon. She was in the living room, leaning indolently against the lustrous black walnut bar of the antique pub that Luc's mother had discovered in an English train station on her honeymoon with Simon.

"What are you doing here?" Luc peeled off his chamois jacket and dropped it across the arm of an overstuffed couch, making no attempt to be polite.

"Getting drunk," Shelby announced, waving a bottle of 1928 Mouton Rothchild. She had the fifth clutched in one hand and a Baccarat wineglass in the other.

"Drowning our guilt?" He was about to rescue the pricey booze by suggesting that she drown herself instead, when a shaft of sunlight filtered through the vaulted ceiling's skylight and struck her dark hair, creating a nimbus that was disturbingly halolike. Some kind of a sign? he wondered sardonically. If Shelby Flood was supposed to be an angel of mercy, hell must have sent her.

"How is our little jailbird?" she asked, splashing more wine into her glass. "Have you seen her?"

Luc smothered a savage urge to knock the bottle out of Shelby's hand and toss her butt out the front door. "Jessie's doing all right, no thanks to you."

He sank into the depths of the couch's pillows, eyeing his unwanted visitor. "What are you going to do while your sister rots in jail, Shelby? Charge ahead with your plans to storm the fashion world?"

"Sure, why not? Do you have a better suggestion?"

He rose from the couch, giving way to the fury that burned in his blood. "Is this how you repay her for saving your life? You drink her booze and stink up her house with your presence? If it weren't for Jessie, you'd be dead, Shelby. Dead and rotting in the ground. And if I had my choice that's exactly how it would have happened."

She whirled around. "Jesus, Luc—"

"She saved your life, for Christ's sake. She raised your child! You weren't the one who quit school at sixteen and gave up any chance of college. You didn't give up your career. I'd say you owe her."

The color left Shelby's face, except for two hot, woundlike slashes beneath her perfect cheekbones. After draining her glass, she held it up, stiff-fingered, and dropped it into the Japanese bronze vase at her feet. The sound of shattering crystal brought a wince of both pain and satisfaction to her face. "I don't need to be reminded of the sacrifices my sister's made for me," she informed him acidly. "I've been thinking about nothing else."

"I'm pleased to hear that." He jerked his thumb toward the foyer. "Think about it somewhere else, would you?"

"I came over here to help, dammit! But if you're going to be an ass about it—"

"Yes, I'm going to be an ass about it! *Get out of here.*"

She scooped up her purse in a huff and swept past him on her way out. Luc watched her go, her gold sandals flashing in the reflected light, her jeans-clad legs whipping. He waited until she was about to disappear into the foyer before he stopped her.

"*Shelby.* If you testify against Jessie, I'll come after you for every cent of the seed money I invested. Trust me, there won't be anything left of you when I'm done."

"Testify against her?" She jerked around, seemingly startled at the suggestion. "Why would I do that? I want her out of there as badly as you do."

"You're the one who *put* her there!"

She turned and stalked from the room. Frustrated, he wheeled around and saw Gina hurrying down the stairway, her youthful features pinched with worry.

"Was that her?" Gina asked. "Did she leave?"

"If you mean Shelby, yes, she left." Luc went to the bar to pour himself a glass of the first-growth Bordeaux she'd defiled, then thought better of it.

Gina followed him, clearly distraught. "Shelby was acting, how do you say it? *Pazzo.* Crazy."

"What do you mean?"

"She was threatening to tell Mel who her real mother was. She said the child needed to know the truth, that it would reassure her she wasn't all alone now. And then, in the next breath, she swore she was going to get her sister out of jail."

The au pair pressed her fingers to her mouth in confusion, her chin trembling with the threat of tears. "I don't understand. I thought Jessie was Mel's mother."

"It's okay, Gina," Luc said, reaching out to calm her. He touched her arm, steadying her. "Does Mel know that Jessie's been arrested?"

"No, I couldn't tell her. But she knows something's wrong. She could hardly breathe when I found her this morning. She thought Jessie had gone to the ravine, and she was on her way there. Poor thing got no farther than the rose garden. She was hunched over, wheezing and struggling for every breath. God in heaven, I was so frightened."

"Gina, someone has to tell Mel what's happened."

The au pair stepped back and came up against a Victorian armchair. "It will kill her," she said, sagging onto the petit-point cushion. In a hushed, rapid voice she began to recite something in Latin that sounded like a rosary.

Gina's mumbled prayers confirmed Luc's fears. She couldn't be of any help to Mel. She was too distraught. He glanced up the stairway, wondering if he, himself, was capable of doing what had to be done. He was a virtual stranger, and yet someone had to let her know that her mother had been arrested for murder before she heard it through the media. Harder still, he would have to find some way to make a sick and frightened child believe that everything was going to be all right.

His guts churned with an emotion that must have been dread as he climbed the stairs to the second floor and turned down the hallway. But it wasn't just the prospect of reassuring Mel that had him disturbed. The children's wing was the stuff of nightmares for Luc. The area had looked very different when he'd lived here—more like a barracks—but his old room still loomed at the end of the hall and the things that had been done to him were still etched on his soul in blood.

Sweat chilled his temples as he took hold of the doorknob. Cold brass twisted in his grip and sleeping demons stirred in their dark corners. He opened the door slowly, letting his eyes adjust to the fading light from the windows. He'd expected to see the internment camp of his childhood, but everything had been altered. This room looked like a traditional child's bedroom with pillows and curtains on the window seat, a four-poster bed.

He felt a moment's relief until the sounds of labored breathing sent a shaft of cold steel through his gut. A small form was huddled under the covers, fighting to breathe. Luc felt as if he were standing on the threshold of the past, staring at himself. Mel's roupy gasps sounded like his own urgent attempts to suck air into his lungs, his own reflexive need to cling to life when what he'd really wanted was to let go.

Now all he wanted was to leave, to shut the door and block this new nightmare out of his mind—the room, the past, and especially this child. She was a living reminder of what it was to be sick and vulnerable, he realized. She represented everything he was trying to escape.

He was about to shut the door when she roused.

"Who's there?" she croaked, blue eyes peeking out from under the fortress of her blankets.

"It's just me, Luc," he told her reassuringly. "I thought you were sleeping."

"Huh! Not likely." Seized by a sneezing fit, she pushed the covers down and rolled her head toward him, exhausted. "You ever try to sl-sleep through an asthma attack? Feels like dragons are tag-team wrestling in your chest."

She began struggling then to prop herself up with pillows. Luc had no choice but to help her.

Once he had her settled, he forced himself to stay put. Guilt even drove him so far as to sit uncomfortably on the edge of her bed. "You okay?" he asked, indicating her bluish lips and sucked-in cheeks. "You don't look so good."

"I must look like holy *letame*," she agreed gamely. "That's Italian for—"

"Don't tell me. Fertilizer, right?"

She laughed with obvious difficulty, but the sight of her wan smile made Luc feel as if he'd accomplished something remarkable.

"Your mother's in some trouble," he said.

Mel nodded. "I was afr-afraid of that."

"You know who Hank Flood is, don't you? Your mom's stepfather? He died before you were born." To Luc's relief, she nodded. Now all he had to do was explain what had happened in the last twenty-four hours. "The police have reopened the investigation," he told her, "and they're saying it wasn't an accident, Mel. Well, actually . . . they're saying your mother was involved and they arrested her."

"Involved? How?"

Luc hesitated, watching for any adverse reactions. But her curiosity seemed to be winning out over her asthma as she gazed up at him. Her breathing was actually easing a bit.

"Do they think she did it?" Mel pressed.

"Well, in a way, yes, but—"

"No kidding?" The child's eyes widened with both fear and excitement. "My *mom*? I guess it must have been self-defense, huh?"

"Not exactly, she was protecting someone else."

To Luc's surprise, she sat up eagerly, wheezing with the effort. "Yeah? Well, then why'd they arrest her? If she was protecting someone, that would make her a h-hero, wouldn't it? She oughta get a reward or something."

Now *he* was smiling, Luc realized. Wasn't he supposed to be making *her* feel better? How was it that this strange little creature had found a way to ease his sense of impending doom with a few hopeful words? "You've got a point," he admitted. "I'll pass that on to her attorney."

Mel settled back as Luc explained that Jessie was spending the night in jail and would be arraigned in the morning.

"I'll bet the food's lousy," she said, wrinkling her nose as she glanced up at him. "When you see her, would you tell her the caterpillars haven't changed yet, but I'm keeping an eye on them? And could you tell her this for me too . . . could you tell her that I miss her?"

Luc felt a moment of utter helplessness. For the first time she'd sounded almost wistful, and the sight of her forlorn little smile left him nearly wild with the need to ease her mind. He hesitated, feeling clumsy and inept, then took her hand and squeezed it. "She's going to be all right, Mel. Your mom's tough."

Mel nodded, her lips compressed. Resting her head against the pillow, she studied the very large hand that had gently cradled hers. "Can I ask you a question?"

"Sure, but make it a good one."

As she looked up at him, helplessness struck him again. The way her eyes searched his features, he had the feeling she was going to ask him something wrenching and deeply personal. But she drew in a quick, raspy breath as if she'd changed her mind.

"A long time ago when you and my mom were kids," she said, "you told her a legend about the half moon. She started to tell it to me once, but she couldn't finish because it made her cry. She never wanted me to talk about it after that, and—"

"And you want to know how it ended?"

"Mostly I want to know how the kid scooped the moon out of the water. There's gotta be some trick to that, right?"

Luc smiled, trying to remember how the legend went. It had to do with an Indian boy who was afraid of the dawn and had never gone outside to play. When first light crept into his parent's teepee, he would huddle beneath the blankets and refuse to budge until sunset. As Luc recalled it, the boy saw the full moon reflected in a pond one night, and he was so dazzled by its beauty, he tried to scoop it out. But he only got half of it, and when he looked up, the other half was shining in the sky.

"He used a deerskin pouch," Luc explained. "It had been given to his father by the tribe's medicine man, and it was said to have magical qualities."

Mel sighed. "No wonder I've been getting nowhere. It's really tough on us kids nowadays. I mean where do you find magical deerskin pouches anymore?"

"Not at the Price Club," he sympathized. "But don't forget that harnessing the power of magic can be dangerous."

"Why? Did something happen to the kid?"

"Lots of things happened to him. First, he tried to keep the moonlight hidden, but it was so bright it glowed through the pouch, and his father discovered it. His father warned him to return it to the pond immediately, but the boy didn't do it."

"Uh-oh . . . why not?"

"Because for the first time in his life he wasn't frightened. He felt whole and happy. You see he'd always believed he was born with something missing, some essential part that would have made him just like everyone else. And he thought the half moon must be that missing part."

"So he wouldn't give it up?"

"No, not even when the storms blew in and the floods rained down. The Indian boy had lost his fear, but everyone else was terrified. His own father was so frightened, he took the half moon from the pouch and tried to fling it back into the sky."

"I'll bet he couldn't do it, right? That's the way these legends always go."

Luc answered her with a wry smile. "You're half right. The

father couldn't release the moon, and he flew into the sky with it. But the boy's fear had come back, and he cried out for the father to let go."

"Yeah? What happened?"

"Well, according to the *legend*, when the father let go, he fell toward earth and became the first falling star. But the moonlight scattered in all directions, vanishing, so the moon was never full again, except once a month. The rest of the time it searched for its missing light and found it bit by bit."

"Not bad," she allowed. "But what about the boy? Was he frightened of the dawn after that?"

"No, but I think he was probably sad about his father."

"So I guess there's a moral to this story, right? Something like don't mess with Mother Nature?"

"That could work," he conceded. He wanted to laugh she was so point-blank serious. He had actually made up the legend himself, pasting together bits and pieces of the secret reading he'd done in the mansion's library. But he hadn't really thought much about what it meant until right now.

"I suppose it could mean a lot of things," he mused aloud, as much for his own edification as hers. "Such as not to be afraid of fear. And never to believe that you need anything but exactly what you are to make you whole. Even when you feel like shit—excuse me, *fertilizer*—and you have dragons wrestling in your chest."

She laughed and fell forward, beginning to cough so violently that Luc had to search frantically for her atomizer, which was hidden in the bedcovers.

As he settled her back into the pillows, she gazed up at him, her heart seeming to have taken up residence in her bright blue eyes. "Are you my father? My real father?"

He drew in deeply. "What made you ask that?"

"Well, my mom always told me my real dad was dead, but she never wanted to talk about him, you know? And I guess maybe I didn't really believe her. Anyway, when she came back from her honeymoon with you, she was sad and everything, so I asked her if she loved you. And there was something about the way she answered that made me think maybe . . ." She broke off with a small shrug.

Luc's heart had gone wild. "How did she answer you?"

"She said she'd loved you once. But it was the way she said , that word, *once*." She continued to gaze at him, unblinking. Are you my father?"

Luc found himself wanting very much to look away—at the aisy-strewn bedspread that covered Mel's frail body and her eemingly unconquerable spirit, at the wallpaper—anything to reak the connection with her. It astonished him how badly he vanted to lie to her, to tell her that yes, he was her father. And es, he loved her with all his heart. But that was impossible. would have complicated things unbelievably. And yet what vas he supposed to tell her instead? The truth? There would e plenty of time for the truth, he reasoned. He couldn't do now, not with her mother gone.

He caught hold of her hand again, feeling the warmth and he slight weight of it in his palm as he brushed his thumb over er wrist bone. "How would you feel if I were your father?" e asked.

She pursed her lips and blinked her eyes, ever thoughtful. I think I'd like it. I've never had a dad to do things with. imon wasn't that way, you know, like a father."

Luc nodded, his throat tightening.

"Yeah, I guess it would be cool if you were," she concluded, azing up at him.

Her trusting expression was enough to move mountains and ake angels weep. It was more than enough to crack open a nely man's heart. "Then I'll try, Mel," he heard himself aying. "I'll try to be your dad."

Somehow he ended up with the child in his arms, though e couldn't have said how it happened. He didn't trust himself talk, so he just held her and tried to swallow back the trange, aching lump in his throat. Her small hands patted is back as if she sensed that he needed some kind of com- ort too.

"I could call you *papa*," she whispered. "That's Italian or *dad*."

"*Papa*," he repeated softly. He closed his eyes as emotion elled up. "Yeah . . . that would be cool."

Luc felt as if all the scars on his heart were tearing open at nce. He'd never known such pain, but there was a sweetness ouring into the wounds too. So much sweetness he almost

didn't want the fiery flood to end. Was this love? he won
dered. Was this joy?

Finally, it was Mel who ended his torment.

"What about Mom?" she asked, hope stirring in her voice
as she settled her cheek against his chest and whispered the
words into the folds of his shirt sleeve. She smelled of dai
sies and fresh-washed hair, of asthma medicine and mentho
eucalyptus. She smelled just like a little girl, he supposed . . .
wonderful.

When Luc could manage it, he moved back to look at her
this strange, too-thin child with dazzling turquoise eyes and
tiny red corkscrews for hair. God, how he pitied the boy who
fell in love with her. She was a funny looking little thing who
seemed to belong nowhere, just as he, himself, had belonged
nowhere. An orphan. But the guy who fell for her—that poor
unsuspecting fool—he would never know what had dropped
from the heavens and hit him.

"Your mom's coming back," he promised her. He had
thought he would never have a child, that his upbringing
had somehow left him unfit. But rocking Mel in his arm
felt as natural to him as breathing, as warm and vital as hi
own heartbeat. If his deepest fear had been that he might hur
her, it was also this, that he might love her.

"She has to come back, Mel," he said. "Because you and
are going to wait for her right here."

CHAPTER
·· THIRTY ··

"NOT AGAIN? YOU'RE insatiable!"

A hand clamped over Jessie's questing fingers, discouraging her from further exploration of the male body sprawled next to hers in the bed. The magnificent and very naked male body, if she was into intimate details. Which she most certainly was in this case.

"Spoilsport," she mumbled, contenting herself to snuggle into the crook of Luc's shoulder. Her noisy sigh let him know he had an unsatisfied woman on his hands.

"*Jessie.*" He said her name with a sexy little groan, very much in the tone of a man whose patience was being as sorely tested as his magnificent body. "We haven't let up since you were released on bail, baby. At this rate there'll be nothing left of me by the time you go to trial!"

"Nothing but fabulous memories," she assured him, tracing the letter *J* in the dark hair that swept down his belly. "That's the point, Luc. I'm out on a million-dollar bond, and that makes every day of freedom worth a fortune. I don't want to waste a penny of it!"

With no more warning than a naughty wink, she ducked her head under the bedcovers and penetrated the primordial jungle in search of hidden treasure troves and magic elixirs. Burrowing into the cool dark cave of their black satin sheets, he made the mistake of flipping onto all fours, which uncovered the part of her that was now pointed toward his head.

"Hey, cut that out!" she cried, wincing at the smart little smack he gave her bottom. If the impact stung a bit, it also brought her a startling flush of pleasure that streaked from the spot he'd targeted to other much more sensitive nerve ending in the vicinity.

"Oh!" she cried as feathery fingers purled up her inner thighs. Apparently he wasn't finished! And then, what he did next brought an astonished gasp to her lips and a blushing smile to her face. Wait a minute! *Who was seducing whom here?*

By the time she'd squirreled around and got herself out of his range, she realized she'd stumbled onto exactly what she was looking for, his treasure trove. She entertained herself for a moment or two, pretending that he was a creamsicle. Yum, rootbeer, her favorite flavor. But the instant he began to respond—the dirty old man!—she stopped and shimmied upward, popping her head out from underneath the covers. Her smile said he was a fool to try and resist her. Ever.

Apparently he didn't intend to. He caught her by the arm before she could scramble away and held her fast, his grasp gentle but firm. Desire crackled in the black depths of his eyes. And his voice had the burred quality of a man whose darker instincts had been awakened.

"You're bad, Jessie . . ."

"Oh, *good*. Do I get points for bad behavior?"

A growl rumbled in his throat as he rolled her onto her back and loomed over her, holding her prisoner as he straddled her with his legs.

"What are you doing?" she gasped as he locked her hands above her head and bent toward her breasts.

"Rewarding your bad behavior."

She was as naked as he was, and therefore, exquisitely vulnerable. The heat of his breath against her skin made her spine arch with anticipation. The moist tug of his lips elicited a throaty moan. And then, with one quick flick of his tongue, he sent a sweet riot of excitement tumbling through her bowed and trembling body. With the next flick, he made her rise up off the bed. "Ahhhh . . . Luc, Luc, *Luc*."

A thunderous crash from on high was the only thing that kept Jessie from actually levitating. But it wasn't a storm on the horizon, or lightning in the night sky, it was thunder on the stairway. Someone was in a big hurry to get downstairs.

"Mom! Papa!" Mel's shouts carried from somewhere down
e hallway to their bedroom. "Come quick! Aunt Shelby's
n television."

Grateful she'd locked the bedroom door, Jessie twisted her
ead around, struggling to get a look at the bedside clock
rough the barrier of Luc's arm. "What time is it? Eleven
M.? Didn't we put that child to bed over an hour ago?"

"She needs to work on her timing," Luc agreed dryly. Sighing,
e relinquished his hold on Jessie, freeing her to slip into her
be. Mel had very nearly broken in the bedroom door by the
me Jessie got it unlocked and opened.

"Mom! Luc!" The child fairly jumped up and down.
helby's on the tube!"

Jessie glanced over her shoulder at Luc, who was tying his
rry robe. "Television? What do you think it could be?" she
ked him. "A commercial for Portfolio?"

A newscast was playing on the large-screen television as
e three of them entered the mansion's gameroom moments
ter. The comfortably furnished room was the only spot in the
ouse with a TV set, and this wasn't the first time Mel had
en known to sneak in here after bedtime to watch late-night
ograms.

"See!" Mel pointed to what looked like a press conference
the screen as she dove into the buttery depths of a well-
orn leather couch and curled up. "It's the eleven o'clock
ws. That's Shelby talking to the reporters. And see those
en in suits? They're her attorneys."

Jessie and Luc joined Mel on the couch, their eyes riveted to
e set as Shelby, flanked by three somber men in dark suits,
elded a barrage of questions that seemed to have nothing
natsoever to do with Portfolio.

"When did the abuse start, Ms. Flood? How old were you?"

"Abuse?" Jessie murmured, touching Luc's hand. What was
r sister doing? Shelby looked slightly dazed, even frightened
all the commotion, but her hair was carefully combed, her
ce made up as if she'd prepared herself for the appearance.
"I can't remember exactly," Shelby admitted, her voice
usually soft and grainy. "I'm sure I've blocked a lot of
but I was very young, perhaps nine or ten."

"Did he abuse your sister too?"

"No, just me."

Jessie listened with growing alarm as her sister went o[n]
answering questions about the nature of the abusive relatio[n]
ship with her stepfather. Where was she headed with thi[s]
Jessie wondered. Surely she wasn't going to go public wi[th]
her account of the night Hank died? That kind of admissi[on]
could be disastrous. It could seal Jessie's fate. But it cou[ld]
also backfire and compromise the defense's case, making [it]
almost impossible to convene a jury.

"What's she up to?" Luc sat forward. "She swore to Gi[na]
last week that she was going to get you out."

"Oh, my God," Jessie breathed.

"Ms. Flood!" a reporter called out from the throng. "Yo[ur]
sister's been accused of killing your stepfather. Was she tryi[ng]
to protect you?"

"Yes, but not the way you think." Shelby cleared her thro[at]
as if trying to get control of her emotions, and then s[he]
touched one of the myriad of microphones in front of h[er]
and spoke into it. "My sister didn't kill Hank Flood," s[he]
told the waiting crowd. "I was there. I saw what happene[d]
and whoever called in that anonymous tip was lying. Jess[ie]
was trying to protect me from the very thing that's happeni[ng]
here today, from exactly this kind of public spectacle."

"But *you* called this press conference," the man point[ed]
out.

"Why are you here?" someone else shouted.

"Who *did* kill Hank Flood?" another yelled.

Shelby's eyes sparkled with sudden, angry tears as s[he]
gripped the microphone, taking it out of its stand.

Jessie watched with growing disbelief, unable to imagi[ne]
what her sister was going to say next. If she was acting, th[is]
was the performance of her life.

Shelby raised her voice urgently as the buzz of electron[ic]
feedback and the noise of the crowd threatened to drown h[er]
out. "I'm here because I can't let this go on any longer," s[he]
cried. "I can't let my sister go to jail for me! She didn't k[ill]
Hank Flood. *I did.*"

Jessie swayed forward and would have tumbled off t[he]
couch if Luc hadn't caught her.

"My God," Luc breathed. "She meant it."

"It's just like you said," Mel chimed in, staring at the screen. "Mom's been protecting her."

The crowd went crazy, shouting out indistinguishable questions. One of the reporters plunged to the front, making himself heard above the din. "Why did you wait this long to come forward?" he demanded to know.

Shelby flushed with anger as she defended herself, but Jessie was too stunned to focus on what she was saying. Clearly Shelby had had something much more dramatic in mind than having the murder case thrown out of court. She was going for a full-blown public confession!

"I can't let her do this," Jessie whispered to Luc.

"Don't be so quick to come to her rescue again," he suggested softly. "Maybe she doesn't need saving this time."

"What do you mean?"

"Look at her. This may be the first decent thing Shelby's ever done in her life. How can you take that away from her? And besides, *she* was Hank's victim, Jessie, not you. The public will enshrine her. The networks will be climbing all over each other to make movies of her life. And, believe me, nobody's going to convict her. They'll get lynched if they do."

Jessie stared at the screen, still in shock. Was Luc right? She had very little doubt about the movie angle. The media loved a good phoenix-rising-out-of-the-ashes story. And so did Hollywood. It was unfortunate that something so sordid had turned out to be Shelby's chance for recognition, but it wasn't too farfetched to think that her sister might have had it in mind to capitalize on the publicity when she arranged the press conference. Otherwise why hadn't she simply turned herself in to the police? Am I misjudging her again? Jessie wondered. Was the emotion in her sister's voice real this time?

Jessie heard a snuffling noise behind her and glanced around. Gina was standing at the end of the couch, her nose red, her eyes watering as she listened to Shelby's story. And her emotion was very real.

"Come sit down," Jessie urged the au pair, patting the couch cushions.

Gina nodded, but couldn't seem to wrest herself from the televised drama as she wiped at her eyes.

"Ms. Flood! Shelby!" A reporter's shout brought Jessie's attention back to the screen. "Is it true that you're already entertaining offers from all three networks for your story?"

An attorney stepped forward as if to stop that line of questioning, but Shelby held up her hand. "Of course, I am," she said emphatically. "After twenty years of living a lie I'm finally coming out of the closet. I want people to know what happened to me. I want them to know it can happen to anyone, in any family, rich or poor. And most of all I want them to know you can survive it and move on. You can even be better!"

The stirring in the crowd was audible. Jessie thought they might actually break out in a cheer. She glanced around at Mel and Gina and saw that they were completely enraptured with Shelby's passionate message. Only Luc was less reverent.

"I never thought I'd live to hear our Shelby inspiring the masses," he remarked under his breath.

"Go figure," Jessie agreed.

"This may be her finest hour, Jess," Luc pointed out. He scooped her hand into his and met her eyes, gazing so deeply that Jessie felt slightly disoriented. "Shelby's getting her chance to play Joan of Arc. You can't take that away from her."

Jessie understood his urgency in trying to convince her to go along with Shelby's wild scheme. There was more than her own freedom at stake, there was her new and very precious relationship with him, and, of course, there was Mel's future. Shelby was giving Jessie a chance to salvage all that, to have the life she'd always dreamed of with the people she loved. And no matter what happened, she would always be grateful to her sister for that gesture. Still, Jessie didn't know what to do. She was weary of lies and intrigue, and this confession of Shelby's was another secret they would all have to keep for the rest of their lives. And yet, in some strange and irrefutable way, Shelby's story didn't seem so much a lie as it did her own personal way of rewriting history. She was telling it the way it ought to have happened. If it was Hank Flood's destiny to breathe his last on that horrible night in November, it should have been Shelby wielding the shovel.

"Ms. Flood! Who would you like to star in your story?"

Shelby brightened noticeably at the question. "I don't know. Who do you think would be good? Demi Moore, maybe? She would have to lose a few pounds, but her hair's the right color. And Jack Nicholson as Hank, of course."

Jessie met Luc's droll smile with one of her own. Shelby was Shelby, after all. Jessie waved for Gina to come join them on the couch, and then she sank rapturously into the curve of Luc's arm, realizing as she sighed that her own daughter was curled every bit as dreamily in the crook of his other shoulder.

Mel had been following Luc around adoringly all week, referring to him as her *bella papa*. She'd also conned Gina into teaching her how to cook Italian so she could make him his favorite pasta—linguini with clams in a garlic-butter sauce. Luc had reciprocated valiantly by eating every bite, though it wasn't just the clams that were chewy to the point of toughness. "*Duro come una suola di scarpa,*" Gina had warned him in whispers. "Tough as old boots."

Even more gallantly, Luc had reassured Mel when she'd confided her breast anxieties. "Breasts are fine," he'd told her. "But I guarantee you, there isn't a nine-year-old boy on the planet who wouldn't prefer a nine-year-old girl like you just the way you are now—willowy and gorgeous."

The next day, as if to prove his point, he'd driven into town, searched out a red-headed imp he met in the library and brought him back for Mel to play with. The boy's name had turned out to be Mario Andretti O'Sullivan, he was one-quarter Sicilian on his mother's side, and Mel was ecstatic.

When Jessie looked up at the screen again, Shelby's lawyers were assuring the media that they were confident of a speedy acquittal for their "courageous client," and Shelby was looking very much the staunch heroine of her own true-life story, perhaps for the first time in her entire life.

But Jessie was still uncertain. Could she really let her sister do this? And even if she'd wanted to, would she be able to stop the juggernaut Shelby had already put into place with her press conference and her attorneys and her imminent movie deal?

Jessie glanced out the window at the moon, secret and wise, suspended like a crystal ball in the sky. Remembering its power to turn tides and change seasons, she thought of the night she and Luc had bathed in moonlight. They had wished for good luck that night, and if the luck had been late in coming, it was all the more wonderful for the delay. She felt so blessed by the abundance in her life. Like the moon with its glowing aura, she was surrounded by joy and beauty and bright promise.

The luminous ring that surrounded the moon tonight seemed to promise a glimpse of the future for all those who came seeking guidance. Jessie closed her eyes with a silent request that her sister would be the next to be blessed, that one day Shelby's life would be as fulfilled as her own. *And let her always be as free as the hawks soaring over the ravine,* Jessie thought. When she opened her eyes again, the moon was winking at her, and its aura was shimmering like something alive.

Blessed be, it seemed to say.

Smiling, she acknowledged the spring night's radiance one last time, offering up her own silent prayer of thanks. *I couldn't possibly love them more—Luc, Mel, Gina, even Shelby. So this is my destiny, let me be worthy. Let me always believe in the heart's capacity to heal, in the power of redemption and in the magic of legends.*